GUARDIAN

GUARDIAN

DAN GLEED

Matador
9 Priory Business Park
Kibworth Beauchamp
Leicestershire LE8 0RX, UK
Tel: (+44) 116 279 2299
Email: books@troubador.co.uk
Web: www.troubador.co.uk/matador

ISBN 978 1784623 081

British Library Cataloguing in Publication Data.
A catalogue record for this book is available from the British Library.

Printed and bound by CPI Group (UK) Ltd, Croydon, CR0 4YY
Typeset in Bembo by Troubador Publishing Ltd

Matador is an imprint of Troubador Publishing Ltd

Dedicated to my wife, Vicki, our son, Antony,
and our daughter, Marie.

I would also like to thank those who gave me invaluable
advice and guidance in refining the text, particularly our
good friends Neil and Daphne Carlier.

CHAPTER 1

The hot sun beat down on my naked back, browned from years of living on the high Kenyan veldt. Below me and as far out as the eye could see, dust devils stirred the dry plain. Their erratic wanderings only emphasised the oppressive heat that mirrored the air and sucked the moisture from what was then a lean, adolescent body. Around me, the parched, rock-strewn world seemed to hold its breath, glaring back in sullen silence at the brassy sky. Even the irritating buzz of fat, indolent blowflies no longer intruded as I tensed in single-minded concentration, all thought and emotion focused down into my squinting eyes and finger curled around the trigger. A moment of almost sexual intensity, of life and death being played out, as it had so often over the end of this particular rifle during my admittedly brief life of fewer than twenty years.

Mutuku, the universally respected and dignified old Kamba tracker, had taught me his art well and it remained a source of quiet pride that when this apprentice was stalking prey, they almost never knew I was there. The first most of them sensed of danger was the very last thing they knew, because I seldom missed. Slowly and quietly that day I had settled the oiled and carefully tended Lee Enfield .303 into my left shoulder, extended the rear sight to its full height and drawn a bead on the slow-moving stag still grazing nervously on the short dry grass of the Eldoret plain, about a hundred yards ahead and some fifty feet below. Beside me, my close friend Matt Cryer shifted uncomfortably on the hot granite as he waited for the hunt to be played out. Both our families would eat well in the coming days. You could count on it.

It would take only an imperceptible tightening of my forefinger on the carefully balanced hair trigger, That, and the act of bringing my breathing to a standstill, to make what I knew was going to be a difficult, falling shot. But I was good. And confident. So, breathing slowly and steadying the foresight, I zeroed in a little above and ahead of the point I wanted the bullet to strike. For me in such moments time always stood still, but I can clearly remember the unexpected shiver of remorse that day. Perhaps it was pity. At any rate, emotion stopped me for a full second, just long enough for my restless thoughts to fly back down the trail we had negotiated as we shadowed the wary animals.

Riding quietly, heads up and looking for the nervous creatures, which blended so easily into the background of thorny scrub, we had first spotted a small group of eland well ahead of our track, drifting between the scattered fever trees. Following at a distance, we had watched the elegant does, herded by a magnificent stag in the prime of life, as the group moved with unhurried grace, some feeding, some with heads up, always alert as they wandered towards one of the many rocky outcrops that disfigured the rolling grasslands. Eventually, just as we had hoped, a jagged tor introduced itself between us and them. Un-spooked, the herd had moved out of sight and, just as importantly, out of earshot. We had dismounted and left the horses tethered in a secluded donga[(1)], its steep dry sides carved clean by the flash floods that occasionally plagued the land during the rainy seasons. Moving cautiously forward, we had begun the short scramble towards an ascent known universally as 'Cat Hill', an abrupt, sixty-foot pile of jumbled rock and grass, beloved by hyraxes and snakes alike. Cat Hill had been named for the local lion pride, which, since anyone could remember, had staked out the summit as a favoured platform for lazily surveying the passing banquet, often completely unnoticed by their intended prey. Lying within the protective screen of rocks, sheltered for much of the day from the worst of the oppressive sun, the pride could often be seen dropping down the steep sides to set out on a hunt shortly before dusk.

Now, however, lions were scarce and not just around Eldoret, the only town of note within a hundred miles. Their numbers had been decimated by the prolonged drought and a scarcity of suitable prey. Even in the nearby hills bordering the Great Rift Valley, the mass migration of animals towards more certain water sources had slowed to a trickle. So scarce had game become that lions hadn't been seen in the area for over a year. But, wary as ever, we automatically checked for signs as we approached the hill. Seeing nothing, we had made swift but careful progress up the rocky outcrop, screened from the eland.

Matt and I worked well together. Years of riding, shooting, comparing girlfriends, lampooning authority and generally creating mayhem meant we had grown as close as it was possible for any two hot-headed young men to get. He was the taller, already a shade over six feet and, given his father's towering and rangy physique, set to grow a few inches yet. Being by far the better-looking (*"yes, I admit it"*), he was also viewed with lustful eyes by the local virgins, but at nineteen and constrained under the social mores of post-war Kenyan society, anything more than a quick kiss and a clumsy grope behind a convenient bush had so far proved 'mission impossible'. Except, I must confess, I was beginning to wonder. For once in his life Matt had been less than forthcoming and whereas the two of us had previously sniggered over any and every juvenile venture with girls, all seemed to have changed over the last few weeks. Ever since the stunningly beautiful Rosalind had stepped suddenly into our lives. Just five short weeks earlier – I had found myself counting the days – she had swung down onto the station platform and from that moment on, as far as any and every boy in town was concerned, she quite simply dominated Eldoret's skyline.

Once a day, as regular as clockwork, the old passenger train that had brought her could be heard from miles out on the plain.

Its distinctive, lonely whistle heralding a distant presence on the long, laborious route from the East African coast, all the way to the northern end of the line at Kitale, nestled at the foot of Mount Elgon, a settlement hardly bigger than our home town of Eldoret. And every evening a motley band of weary travellers disgorged themselves almost reluctantly from the old world charm of the Victorian carriages onto Eldoret's one and only platform. Yet it was purely by chance we had been there that early December evening, just in time to catch the arrival of Ted and Vera Lescal, complete with their young son and the object of our immediate interest: Rosalind. Willowy, flaxen-haired and in the full bloom of young womanhood, she had lit up our immediate horizons in the way only a pretty girl can. Even as we stood staring with open admiration and rapt attention, I realised I was jealous; jealous of Matt's easy charm and more obvious attractions. Not that the girl had given either of us more than a passing glance, but the hormones that had been affecting us both lately needed little excuse to start jumping. All I knew was even then I couldn't look at Rosalind without my heart racing and my body responding with embarrassing tautness under, dare I mention, a pair of fashionably brief khaki shorts. And her simple presence had been the problem. Although I can't say I had been particularly aware of it until then, I had found myself in real male competition for the first time in my life because, from that moment on, Rosalind had, all unknowingly, stepped firmly between us.

CHAPTER 2

Suddenly alive to a lack of concentration, I shook my head slightly, intent on clearing my thoughts. I noticed Matt was looking at me oddly too, leaning slightly away, surprised at the delay as hesitation allowed the eland to drift ever further. It was hot enough to cook on the surrounding rocks and the sweat was already making my hands slippery, so once again I settled and, narrowing my eyes against the glare, sighted down the rifle and began to track the target in earnest.

The low, lingering snarl was almost conversational in its delivery. Barely rising above the call of birds wheeling high above, the sound hit us both with all the explosive force of an ice-cold bucket of water taken full in the face. I remember I froze, blood seeming to congeal in every limb. Then with my mind exploding in panic, I felt the bitter taste of bile ripping through my unnaturally dry mouth, felt the fear paralysing me. I couldn't help it. I simply couldn't move. It wasn't common sense that held every muscle still. Just pure, unadulterated terror. I knew the lion could not be more than a few feet behind and off to my right – that much I had worked out even as both mind and reason flipped, then went into overdrive. And then there was the sun. Despite the hour, it had suddenly grown preternaturally cold as I waited, every muscle in spasm, wanting to scream but unable to make my mouth work. Beside me, the silken sound of pure malice had reached Matt in the same instance, but twisted to the side and half up on one elbow, Matt was already facing the rock from beneath which the malevolent sound had emanated and it only needed his eyes to refocus on the pool of shadow at its bottom right-hand side for the full horror of our exposure to make itself clear.

He would have seen two narrowed yellow eyes, pools of merciless concentration staring straight back at him above a wrinkled, heavily scarred old muzzle. I hadn't needed the view. I just knew the fearsome upper canines would have been exposed, tied with dripping strands of saliva to the lower jaw now wide open in anticipation of business. But it was the stillness and evident preparation in the cat's announcement that was so terrifying. Matt would have known, even as he looked, that there would be no stopping the predator. He would have been in no doubt that it had already made its decision. The evidence would have been traced in every exposed sinew, every taut muscle of the emaciated body and above all in the flexing paws gathered almost delicately underneath the deep barrel chest. And with that realisation had come my friend's involuntary jerk backwards, away from me, a last desperate attempt to put distance between himself and the oncoming danger. And that was his undoing. The big cat's paws would have shifted slightly, re-gauging the distance, raising the height of the pounce. The tail no doubt flicking once as it always did before a charge. And then, almost silently, the animal had exploded forward, flowing effortlessly across the short strip of ground that separated us, straight over my prone body, its head thrown forward, ears flat, jaws wide and lips drawn tightly back, driving for the exposed throat.

Matt's flapping hands and arms tried desperately to protect his face and neck. To stop the unstoppable. But the lunge struck true and a hopeless scream tore through his lips, only to be choked off to a gurgle before it could gather any strength. Three hundred and seventy-five pounds of emaciated and starving lion pounded down onto its victim, dust exploding around them as the two, locked together in an obscene embrace, crashed backwards, Matt no match for the unbridled ferocity he faced. Skidding to a halt, the lion had scrabbled for purchase against my still inert torso, rolling me abruptly, almost casually away from the thrashing climax of the kill. And even as I rolled, I knew I should do something. Anything. Use my gun. Shoot. Club. Just anything. Matt's agonised eyes, bulging in torment, glared wildly around the lion's slavering jaws, pleading for me, his so-called friend, to save him, darting desperately from my face to the gun dragging uselessly in my left hand as I scrabbled frantically backwards, anything to get away from those already blood-stained jaws. As though in a slow-motion dream, I squinted through dust-bleared eyes at the macabre scene, both players now deathly still. I don't think I even felt it, but eventually my back had thudded into the rock from where the charge had come. Every instinct was screaming at me to get out, to get away, to get off the hill and make for the horses, but even as my mind skittered through the possibilities of flight, I knew I should be fighting back, helping Matt, mastering the blind panic by then boiling through every fibre of my being. I knew Matt still wasn't dead and yet I couldn't get myself under control, couldn't gather my courage, couldn't stop the urge to flee. Even the shame rising like hot waves wasn't strong enough to stop that flight. Desperately, I forced myself to my knees, my helpless, paralysed limbs rebelling at every demand and my outstretched hand fumbling behind me for a way round the solid granite block standing between me and freedom.

A sudden burst of frantic kicking from Matt brought a deep, pitiless growl rumbling up through those locked jaws. It was enough. Galvanised into despairing action, I burst around the rock, running as though all the hounds of Hell were after me, the sight of Matt's despairing eyes burning into my back, my mind, my psyche. And though Hell might freeze over, I will never be able to erase those moments. Unable and unwilling to stop, I half fell, half slid down the jutting rocks we had so recently climbed, my now discarded rifle clattering down beside me, the skin stripping from my shins, hands and elbows as every part of me banged and bounced against the unyielding granite throughout that uncontrolled descent. All too soon, the ground rushed up to meet me, catching me unprepared and the last thing I remember was the sound and fury of pain as my leg broke between two protruding boulders and my head struck the dry earth with enough force to render me instantly and comprehensively unconscious.

CHAPTER 3

Rosalind was bewildered, her comfortable world disturbed. Her father, Ted, the man she had idolised since earliest memory, who always seemed so certain of everything, so powerful and dependable, now sat hunched forward in his favourite chair, hands gesticulating in futility, shoulders drooped and a look of despair etched across his rugged face. On the other side of the room Vera stood crying quietly, the soft sound carried away by the whirring of the ceiling fan, their only means of keeping cool in the baking heat that gripped the thirteenth-century coastal port of Malindi year in and year out. The Lescals' sprawling, single-storey, ranch-like home with its wrap-around veranda stood apart from the languid Arab settlement, surrounded on all sides by luxurious hibiscus, frangipani and bougainvillea. Rustling groves of tall coconut palms completed their seclusion. Each tree with a line of footholds chopped into the length of its trunk, mute evidence to its owner's chosen means of harvesting the prized green fruits from their lofty perch.

Just north of the house, clustered around the port that was already ancient when Vasco da Gama came visiting in 1498, the town's close-packed, dreaming houses provided austere reminders of the Arabic influence that had left its centuries-old mark all along the East African coast. Barely into their thirties and desperate to get away from war-torn Europe, the young Lescals had gone to ground in this forgotten, exotic corner of the world, content simply to wrest a bare living from the teeming azure blue waters of the Indian Ocean. Vivid, sparkling, it surged and murmured not twenty yards from their front door. Neither Ted norVera had ever needed anyone else to populate their idyll. From the moment they met they had fallen passionately in love, each knowing that not only would their very existence be barren without the other, but together they could face anything fate might throw at them. It was a deep, soul love and it had become like a precious jewel held firmly yet lightly between them. Mutually supportive, the years had been kind to the couple and, as they matured, their little family had grown. First, with flaxen-haired Rosalind, then her younger brother, Ben. And together Ted and Vera had revelled in life, content to raise both children alongside their African friends, the Giriama[1], a tribe which divided its time between subsistence farming and fishing.

Immersed in their unassuming way of life, the two adults had been almost unable to grasp the enormity of their loss with the news that their recently acquired sixty-foot fishing launch had gone swiftly to the bottom, just outside the entrance to Mombasa's Kilindini harbour, far to the south. Her bow ripped wide open on an uncharted head of brain coral, the uninsured 'Marlin' had taken all their charter business hopes down with her. But not only those. Far from being able to simply forget their ill-starred venture into the commercial world and return to the undemanding existence of daily fishing trips, the proceeds of which had, until then, kept them financially afloat, they now faced what was almost certainly an insurmountable barrier of debt.

Just three months earlier – was it only that long? – Rosalind's world had appeared complete. Her father had finally found buyers for his two old fishing smacks and, together with the help of a loan grudgingly arranged through the Bank of East Africa, had acquired the newest and most powerful sport fishing launch on the coast. Rich Americans were already hunting the fierce barracuda, wahoo, sail fish and abundant shark life, and the lure of a more secure future had taken Ted, quite literally, into uncharted waters. For which the family was now about to pay an unintended but enormous price. His trusted captain, Jumah, had barely escaped with his life. But with no hope of salvage and the bank now threatening to foreclose on the loan, Rosalind had listened in mounting distress as her dejected parents debated their only recourse. Rent out the house, pack their meagre belongings and head up country to the other side of the Rift Valley, beyond the Mau Hills and out to Moiben, a small settlement twenty miles north of Eldoret.

Here a distant cousin was farming tilapia in a large natural lake and, faced with a rapidly increasing demand for this popular fish, Uncle Joe was in need of a manager. If nothing else, Ted knew fish and, as he was saying, he was lucky to have any job to go to. Anything that would help repay the loan. But Rosalind barely heard him. From the moment she could walk, the stunning blue of the deep ocean, shading to translucent aquamarine over the sandy shallows, had been the loadstar around which she had built her whole life. Even when she had been sent up country to a boarding school in distant Limuru, not far from the capital Nairobi, her focus of attention had seldom strayed far from home. Now the thought of leaving, possibly for good – and not just her childhood friends, but all that she lived for – was threatening to choke her with a sense of loss beyond anything she had ever experienced. At eighteen, on the threshold of life in late fifties Kenya, untouched by failure, full of the confidence only a loving family can generate, Rosalind was totally unprepared for the cold winds of reality.

CHAPTER 4

Peter Cryer was checking through the tack room when two of his horses came thundering side by side into the paddock. Glancing up in surprise, one look told him trouble was afoot. Tangled reins hanging limply from their lowered heads, Blue and Star stumbled to a trembling halt, their sweat-stained flanks heaving, white foam flecking bits and curbs. Alarmed, Peter strode towards them, trying not to spook them further.

"Steady now, steady," he crooned, his voice controlled to what he hoped was a reassuring cadence, while he reached out to pat their necks and grab the dangling reins.

With the horses secured, he turned to yell for Peta, who came running from the house, her face reflecting the alarm she had heard in her husband's voice.

"Peta, the horses are back without the boys. There must have been an accident."

Peta shivered despite the heat. She was strong, a seasoned 'frontier' woman, not given to nerves, but lately she had become uneasy as her only son and I roamed further and further afield, revelling in our newfound release from the old disciplines of school life and the more recent pressure of exams. True, we were young men now, with all of life in front of us, and she knew she had to let Matt go. But it wasn't easy, although she trusted us both and knew we were as safe as anyone could be on the surrounding plains. Even the unlikely threat once posed by far-ranging gangs of marauding Mau Mau was long since over. But this was the first time such a thing had happened and her imagination was swift to run riot.

"Syce[1]!" Peter's command rang out loudly and two young Africans came running to take the restless horses. "John, saddle Prince for me, take Hawk yourself. Get Mzee[2] Mutuku and tell him to ride Talon. Nia, saddle two more horses for Matt and Paul and when we've gone, I want you to rub these two down and make sure they're OK. We're going to have to search for the boys."

The slow, almost lazy, yet strangely mellifluous tones of Kiswahili, the Afro-Arabic dialect, floated back as John ran off, calling over his shoulder, "Ndiyo, bwana[3]."

"Peta, call Lynn and let her know what's going on. If Bob's sober, tell him we may need his help."

Peta nodded and ran back into the house to ring the Monctons on the party line shared by most of the Moiben families. It wouldn't be long before everyone knew the score.

★ ★ ★

Twenty miles to the south, Lynn Moncton was having one of her routinely awful days. Wary, on edge, she spent most of her waking hours waiting nervously for her unpredictable husband to suddenly decide she was once again getting on his nerves. Which usually led to physical violence. Not enough to bring her to the doctor's attention. Just enough to make life hell. Bob's fierce and unpredictable temper was legendary and very few would willingly cross him. Certainly none of his family. Short, built like a tank with broad shoulders and a neck as thick as most men's thighs; about the only thing Bob could be relied upon to do with any certainty was hit the bottle at regular intervals. The outcome of which was inevitable. A cursing, swearing rant backed up by two ham-sized fists that lashed out at anyone who got in the way. His few friends were the dregs of Eldoret society, but amongst them he was something of a legend. He could drink like a fish, but, long before he had taken a bellyful, the alcohol would have

13

released every last shred of inhibition. Allowing his talent for fighting to come to the fore. The local chief of police, the District Commissioner, regarded him as a walking disaster zone; his distaste for the usually out-of-work engineer bordering on downright loathing.

Lynn, however, had rather more cause to dread his moods. She lived on shredded nerves, jumping like a scalded cat at any unexpected noise. Terrified not only for herself, but much more for me. The son to whom Bob had never taken, never liked and now, with this same scion poised on the edge of manhood, simply regarded as one more male threat, treading where he had no right to be. A target to be destroyed whenever the mood took him. Bob had long regarded me as a wimp, too close to my mother by half, a boy who needed whipping into shape. So, along with the ever-present physical threat, my dad took a perverse pleasure in telling me exactly what he thought of me, regularly and at colourful length. And now the phone was sounding. Two 'short' rings, followed by a 'long', telling Lynn the call was for her; – something she always dreaded. The intrusive jangling that inevitably cut straight through any reverie, destroyed any temporarily good mood and jerked her back to reality with all the finesse of a striking cobra.

★ ★ ★

I remember hearing myself groan. It was the first sound that penetrated my world as I surfaced. For a moment I couldn't place where I was, but then, suddenly, and with terrifying clarity, the whole nightmare scythed through the fog of my awakening mind. And with the sound came the searing pain of that broken leg. Trapped. And far above me I could hear a perverted snuffling, accompanied by the sound of something wet being torn. I just couldn't help it, my stomach heaved and vomit forced its way out between my clenched teeth like a projectile, spurting all down my chest. Fear, overwhelming dread, filled me once again as I realised the smell of vomit would quickly drift upwards to where I could hear the nature of the lion's restless movements beginning to change. The sun was well down to the west, so it was hardly surprising to discover I had started to shiver. It wasn't just the approaching night cold though. It was the stark reality of death's proximity, coupled with the knowledge that if I escaped the lion's attentions, it would only be to face an exposed night in agony. And I was under no illusion about surviving that, either. With my right leg caught fast at an unnatural angle, preventing anything much more than a gingerly shove upwards to relieve the pressure, I would be easy prey to whatever might pass, unless I could reach my rifle, lying tantalisingly out of reach.

I was just trying to stretch for it without detonating a new wave of pain, when the muffled sounds of a heavy but lithe body descending the slope above caused me to freeze, not even daring to look up, lest any movement attract the fast-descending lion. A heavier thump off to my right was followed by silence. Ominous silence. Unable to bear the suspense, there was nothing for it but to risk a glance and, when I did so, my blood ran cold, as I found myself staring straight into a pair of golden yellow eyes not fifteen feet away. The lion that had so recently killed and, no doubt, eaten all the good bits of my friend stood there, staring at me, its bloody jowls shut for once, its gaze focused, as only that of a big cat can be. However, this time the intensity was gone and the unblinking inspection was laced with indifference. It had fed. It didn't need me. I was to be spared. Slowly, almost haughtily, it had turned and paced out of my line of sight. And as it did so, for the first time I could see one of its back legs dragging slightly. The departure left me no option. With other predators now free to approach, I had to make the one supreme effort left to my broken, pain-racked body. I had to get hold of the only means of defence and survival available. Gritting my teeth, I recall listening to my ragged breath as it whistled between now nerveless lips. It was harsh and unnaturally loud in my ears and it told me I was nearing the end of my tether. But I snagged the rifle.

CHAPTER 5

It didn't take old man Mutuku long because, as he was fond of saying, even a child could backtrack the trail of two maddened horses. Peter, for whom Mzee had worked for over twenty years, believed him, even though at times he was hard pushed to pick out what the old Nandi could apparently see so clearly. Within an hour, the grizzled, white-haired old man was pointing to a large, broken branch dangling over the edge of a donga, mute evidence of the fight to tear free that would have been the wild prelude to the stallions' bolt for home. And it was quickly evident why. Fresh lion tracks showed what had spooked them, although they must have sensed the cat coming and pulled away from the picket long before it got there, or at least one of them would have been killed and eaten.

"Matt and Paul walked from here, bwana, and the lion followed. It's a large male and it's lame in a back paw."

A vein had begun to thump in Peter's temple as a terrible premonition took hold of his mind. Jacking a round up the spout of his hunting rifle, he had urged the restless Prince forward, but the horse had caught the taint of lion on the wind and wasn't happy. Nevertheless, in response to the rake of spurs he had surged forward behind Talon as Mzee quietly followed up on the boys' trail. An injured lion was the last thing they needed to encounter. Silence had descended as all three peered around, tense and alert, knowing that danger could be very close.

"Huko, bwana, huko[1]." The old man had pointed off to the left, not far from the western end of a granite outcrop rearing up several hundred yards ahead. Just in time the other two had caught a fleeting glimpse of a large male lion, its tawny flank disappearing rapidly into the scrub behind a stand of flame trees.

"That's Cat Hill." The others had nodded.

"But there've been no lions around here for months."

Although the boys' trail curved to the right, it was obvious where it was headed and the men had pressed forward as rapidly as they could, Peter ever more afraid of what he was going to find. The bundu[(2)] itself seemed to hold its breath, as if anticipating a reaction to the shameful secret it was about to reveal. Then a sharp exclamation, followed by a swift rattle of sound from up ahead, told Peter that Mzee had spotted something and it wasn't like him to make unnecessary noise. Cresting the slight rise, Peter's gaze had followed the direction of Mzee's pointing finger and his heart had leapt. Despite the lengthening shadows of evening, there was still enough light to recognise me, although he couldn't see his own son, Matt.

Apparently, I had seemed strangely still and awkward to him, almost as though I was ignoring the presence of help, although I distinctly remember hearing their approach. And to a certain extent his supposition was true. Shame had kept my head firmly turned away, rifle gripped rigidly across my chest.

"Paul!" Peter's sharp call had cracked out like a rifle shot and, to his evident astonishment, I had jerked guiltily, but refused to look round. Confused, Peter had dismounted swiftly and run forward, taking in the awkward angle of my leg and realising I was hurt. I remember he reached down to touch me reassuringly on the shoulder, aware of the tears streaming down my face.

"Paul, what is it? Where's Matt?" The question hung in the air like a lance waiting to pin me back to the earth from which I was struggling to rise. "Paul, where's Matt?" he repeated.

I remember how Peter's voice rose, grinding out the words as fears like poisonous snakes had begun to slither around his mind, but my choking sobs almost drowned his efforts at communication.

"He's – he's dead."

Like beads of poison my words had dropped, one by one, into Peter's ears. I just couldn't help it. Everything conspired to overwhelm me and, as my despair surfaced, I began to shriek again and again, "He's dead. Dead! We were attacked and I couldn't do anything. There was a lion."

"Where? Where's Matt?"

"I did everything I could." The lie dropped easily off my tongue as I pointed stiffly upwards, finger waving somewhere above my head, indicating the hill behind me before dropping back exhausted to clutch the rifle to my chest again, like a talisman. Then I had begun to shake uncontrollably as the hopelessness, the plunging cold and the pain all conspired to hit me at the same time, and I remember lapsing into an almost comatose silence.

"Quick, Mzee, see if you can get him free. Splint his leg. John, you come with me. I've got to see."

With the expertise of years, and the fitness for which he was famed, Peter had launched himself straight up the granite slope, not bothering to pick a route, just taking the shortest way to the top. Sheer speed had carried him over the brow and into the boulder-strewn killing zone. The churned, dark-streaked and sticky earth had instantly clung to his shoes where only light dust should have been, and the rocks framed a tableau that would be fixed forever in his fevered mind. He had stopped, stunned. Unable to comprehend what lay before him as he stared at the torn earth and shattered, bloody remains of his only son. A sight no parent should have to endure brought Peter to his knees as though poleaxed. A thin moan dribbled through his lips just as John came bolting up behind his boss, arriving barely in time to hear the words of pure anguish pouring from Peter's mouth. "My son, my son, what has it done to you? Oh, what has it done to you?"

Almost unable to maintain his sanity, Peter had begun to rock gently from side to side, hands pressed to his temples as he stared, practically unseeing, at the scarcely recognisable ruin of what had once been a vibrant young man. And as he did so, murderous, implacable intent blossomed full-formed in his heart. If it was the last thing he ever did, he would put a bullet through that lion and make sure it didn't die quickly. For Peter the world had narrowed to a single dreadful spectacle, his whole existence distilled into a dream-like quality. Staggering to his feet he had steadied himself against John, whose distress and grief were all too quickly catching up with his own. Then, with a supreme effort, moving as if on autopilot, Peter had forced himself to step forward, to stoop and gather his son's bloody remains together and to whisper to John, "Get one of the horse blankets and bring it here to me."

His night would be spent in vigil. Alone. No one and nothing would come near his son now. Of that he was grimly certain. And from a short distance, John would watch over his boss, his own pain little less. Mzee had been dispatched with me and together we would take the dread news to Peta. It was enough for now. The morning would bring action. And with it, seething revenge.

CHAPTER 6

It took weeks for my leg to mend, but that was the easy part. What wouldn't heal was the deep wound I felt in my spirit, the festering knowledge that I had failed. Failed my friend, failed myself, and been found utterly wanting the first time I'd ever needed to show any real courage. And boy, did that hurt. I can remember how the pain dug deep into my psyche, how it got into everything I did or thought, shredding my ego and whispering its insidious charge day in, day out. Slowly but surely, the memory of disaster and its associated pain ate into my soul, destroying me piece by piece more comprehensively than any physical wound could ever achieve. I had survived the leg break, but what I was singularly failing to do was learning to live with myself. True, the neighbours had all shown sympathy, treated me with kid gloves but, even so, I was in such a state of mental turmoil that it only took what, usually mistakenly, I assumed to be a thinly veiled reproach and I was off again.

Except where my father was concerned. He just came right out with it. Expected, of course, but no less destructive for all that. Every reserve I'd ever had was used up, finished. And my guard was down. I remember I became totally vulnerable. Eaten up by the unrelenting blackness of the despair I felt over Matt's loss. Drowning in a remorseless and relentless self-criticism which can be the most insidious poison of all. Through it all I had tried desperately to come to terms with my cowardice, while picking at the wound almost every minute of every day. I neither knew nor really cared that, actually, I was no less a human than anyone else. I suppose I was too young and my idealism had not yet been tempered in the fires of life. I was completely unable to see that the only difference between me and the people who surrounded me was that I had been forced to meet my supreme test too young. Too untried. And all in the glaring light of the inevitable publicity; not only that of my own community, but that of the furthest reaches of East Africa. Kenya's one national newspaper had splashed a biased report and an awful photograph of me right across its front page, and then kept the story running for days. There was no escape. No way out of the private Hell in which I was forced to live. I guess my mother had an inkling of the time bomb ticking away in me. So did Rosalind. And apparently they both ached for me. Together, they loved me but, stupidly, I could neither understand nor tap into the support on offer.

Mzee had brought me back as quickly as he could that night. I was barely conscious from the harrowing journey, with the bones of my broken leg grinding to the rhythm of the horse's lurching, awkward gait. Nevertheless, the old man had pressed on, anxious to reach medical care. And I can remember thinking it would be a close run thing. Either he slowed up, or I wouldn't make it anyway. At first, our approach had caused a collective sigh of relief amongst the assembled group because they had been waiting for news, any news, with growing apprehension. Several families had gathered swiftly, intuition and a well-developed and practiced sense of community drawing them to the Cryer homestead.

My mother had driven over from Eldoret in a hurry, her sudden high-speed appearance in the old Peugeot van covering everyone in a thin coating of red dust. Old Joe Payne was there, patriarch to the sprawling Moiben community and appreciated for his fund of knowledge on all things African. Flanked by the new arrivals to the community, Ted Lescal and his daughter Rosalind, they made an attractive group. Within minutes the Weavers joined them, driving in from the next farm over to the west. Apparently Mother had barely recognised the Lescals, but she had heard they were pleasant enough, fitting in quickly with the often insular, sometimes taciturn farming community. Together with the Salters and a number of farmhands, they already made a sizeable support party. Everyone had been trying to keep Peta's spirits up, but the conversation had grown desultory amidst the mounting anxiety, heightened by the swift onset of tropical darkness.

Then had come the uneven beat of hooves and a general rush to the corral. Hastily seized paraffin pressure lamps cast warm pools of yellow light at their feet as they ran, compensating for the huge, malevolent shadows dancing counterpoint in the velvet blackness of the African night. As light and shadow mirrored the jerky swing of the hissing lanterns on their hooped metal handles, shouted enquiries brought no response from the two of us riding low in our saddles. Peta, running shoulder to shoulder with Lynn, bit back the sobs she could feel rising in her gullet as she saw who was and, more importantly, who was not there and how we sat our horses. Mzee with his normally ramrod straight back bowed and shoulders slumped. Me, barely holding on as I swayed drunkenly from side to side, throwing the horse's natural rhythm.

Peta had felt the rising panic and knew she was close to losing control, knew she had to hold on, if only for the sake of her friends. They had lifted me tenderly enough, responding to my sudden howl of pain with swift and efficient consideration, rushing me into the house to fill me with one of the morphine ampoules kept by every isolated homestead. And all the while Mzee had waited outside, waited quietly to unburden himself of every detail of his macabre story, yet in no hurry to condemn Peta to the living nightmare he knew would forever blight her sensitive mother's soul. Even the men, for all their outward show of strength, would remember this night as perhaps no other. And so, with me temporarily knocked cold, they crowded round the old hunter, a protective ring supporting Peta, and listened to the detail that only a tracker of Mzee's consummate skill could relate.

Every facet vivid and clear to the astute old mind and keen eye that saw everything, missed nothing. And as the story unfolded, their eyes had drifted from Mzee to Peta to my unused rifle now casually propped against the front door jamb. But Peta saw only the shadows flickering across Mzee's earnest, expressive face, heard only the words of death that numbed her mind as her heart died little by little, and her body ached for the comfort of her husband's arms. Shuddering, she lived again and again the light, phantom touch of Matt's hand on her shoulder; his familiar, intimate gesture to the mother he loved. Her pain all the more intense from the so recent yet now forever final parting. Mercifully, when that pain reached full throttle, it had numbed her senses and, later, Peta would remember little of that lonely, empty and unending night.

CHAPTER 7

Rosalind, or 'Roz' as she preferred, leaned towards me, her brow creased with concern. Those who had carried me to the bed had left me lying on my side, upper arm extended across the bare mattress on which they had hastily positioned me. For now I was out cold, with my broken leg held immobile in a temporary splint formed from boards snatched from the very bed on which I lay. Mercifully, the pain would be dulled over the next few hours, but Roz could see there was more troubling me than a mangled leg, bad as that was. They told me later that despite the morphine-fuelled sleep, my head, which in those days was framed in short, dark, almost Romanesque curls, kept rocking left and right while low, feverish mutterings escaped my slack lips.

Even in my obvious vulnerability, Roz later told me she couldn't help but notice how lean and fit I seemed. How strikingly young I looked, despite the ravages of pain and morphine. Well, young women can be relied upon to respond to those in trouble. So it was hardly surprising that her heart beat a little faster as she stared down at me. It was the first time she had been able to linger beside me and no doubt her eyes had wandered down the length of my body, half naked as I recall, because the rough blanket had slipped from my bare torso. Later she told me her cheeks had flushed a sudden pink as her thoughts caught her unaware and she hastily withdrew the hand that had wandered out to caress my bare forearm, trailed carelessly towards her. Catching herself, she had shaken her head, bringing to an abrupt end the disconcerting thoughts which had so surprised her.

Raised voices transported her back to reality and a renewed awareness that she couldn't actually hear what was going on out on the veranda. But she could sense the mood had changed. There was a new tone to their distant voices as they plied Mzee with sharp questions. What was going on? For a moment she was torn between staying with me as I lay helpless in front of her and joining her father outside, but she had promised to stand watch. Moreover, she found she couldn't actually bring herself to leave, despite developments. Particularly as I had begun to jerk roughly from side to side, making her afraid I would damage myself even more. Even so, impatience gripped her as she strained to listen, only to discover it was hopeless. She would just have to wait. And when finally she did hear, she wished she hadn't.

★ ★ ★

The funeral had been harrowing for everyone. Matt, or what little there was left of him, had been buried in the community graveyard beside the tiny church that was so much a part of 'expat' life, redolent in every line and fixture of its English country counterpart. The design, even down to the grey stone from which it had been built, spoke of a never quite extinguished longing for the 'old' country. Standing foursquare, it sat on the side of a hill overlooking the large dam that provided not only a natural social centre for the community with its forever open bar, but also a sleepy sailing club, its members free to make desultory use of one of the area's few dependable water sources. A precious asset when all but the deepest boreholes had dried to a trickle. However, despite the sombre nature of the day, it had not been all bad for Roz. She was beginning to appreciate her new neighbours, to savour time with them, enchanted by their open-handed hospitality, impressed by the protective way in which they had drawn around the Cryers. Just as naturally as they had encompassed my 'outsider' mother within their community family, so it had proved with Roz, who was beginning to feel accepted and who, despite recent events, had started to quite like the place. And daily cycling visits to my home weren't exactly detracting from the process.

"Morning, Mrs Moncton." Roz's cheerful call preceded her as she rounded the open door into the cool but austere sitting room that reflected my father more than it did my mother. Roz was certain he was out, or she would never have come so early. She had already learned to give him a wide berth and couldn't understand how a woman as nice as my mother could love such an unpleasant man; *always assuming she does*", she had thought on occasion. She knew her own mother and father couldn't get enough of each other, and the strength of their affection meant her home was almost always cheerful and welcoming. The ever-tense atmosphere of the Moncton home was the very opposite.

Nevertheless, I had apparently become an irresistible lure to Roz, who by now (I later realised) was falling ever more deeply in love and was determined to see me whenever she could. It certainly hadn't been like that from the start but, during the long weeks of my recovery, when the only excuse she'd needed had been caring friendliness, we had cemented a bond that had begun to blossom into something rather more. For Roz, at least. What she couldn't understand was why my moods fluctuated so much. One moment I tried hard to be attentive and charming, the next I found myself growing cold and indifferent to the point of rudeness. I couldn't help it, even though I was aware I was hurting her. But Roz had always been encouraged to be open about her emotions and she was determined to get to the bottom of the conundrum, to confront me head on if necessary.

I suppose that day had begun as well as any. I was sitting on the step at the back of the house, enjoying the morning sun before the advancing hours drew it to its zenith and direct sunlight became too hot to endure. My mind was where it always was these days, on Cat Hill whilst, almost unseeing, I had been watching a trail of soldier ants hurry past in a long, snaking line on their way to some unguessed destination, no doubt drawn by the scent of scurrying prey. The thought of yet another victim was making me wince, but just then Roz's cheery call to my mother cut through my reverie. Heaving a sigh of resignation, I turned to greet her.

"Hi, Roz. How's it going?" She looked utterly beautiful in her wide white skirt, the light cotton puffed out over layers of crisp netting edged with narrow rainbow ribbons, the whole set off by a blouse the colour of her light blue eyes. So stunning was the effect that, momentarily, the breath caught in my throat and my heart somersaulted. For a moment she even made me forget the pain twisting in my gut. But only for a moment, until the brutal accusations came flooding back into my still aching mind. I remember wondering, *"How could I let this beautiful young girl waste her love over such a coward, such a pariah?"* Reluctantly, I killed the smile and, by sheer force of will, eradicated the tenderness she had no doubt already caught dancing in my eyes. All I could offer anyone attached to me was a life of rejection and so, almost subconsciously, I had put on my best impersonation of impassivity in an effort to blot out all hope for either of us. Watching as she filled up with tears, I almost felt the shadow of despondency draw its cold embrace around the morning. It was time to talk.

"Paul, why? Why do you cut me out? I hate it when you do that. What's wrong? Don't you want to see me? Are you trying to hurt me? Do you want me to go? I will if that's what you want."

I could hear the ache in her voice as the words tumbled out and it twisted the knife even further, but I felt helpless to do anything about it. Blind instinct would have had me struggle to my feet there and then, reaching out to her, holding her tight and whispering the nascent love I knew was struggling to get out into the light. Love that, even then, was becoming ever more desperate to declare itself. Yet I simply could not prevail against the desolation that configured the grey plains of my mental horizon.

I might as well have bayed for the moon. Anguish bit deep, giving birth to a morbid determination to see this rejection through. True, I could still feel for others, but only just. And yet, in spite of everything, I still cared enough to want to save this girl from any further pain, pain I knew would follow as surely as night follows day; pain that would get worse the longer I dragged it out. It was starkly clear. I had done enough damage already, allowed her to get too close, too soon. She was starting to rely on me, just like Matt had done. Matt! His very name was able to induce a violent reaction within me. The breath hissed out between my teeth as the demon of guilt dug its filthy talons into my crumbling, almost surrendered will and I turned to face the wall before she saw too much of this new and alien hardness. I had no option but to sever the link between head and heart. Permanently. To this day, I believe that at the time I had no choice. I had to distance myself from everyone – family, friends and particularly Roz. And I had to start immediately.

"Roz, I –." How to say this? I shook my head distractedly and began again. "Roz, I'm sorry. I just can't go on with this. It's too much. You've been really kind, a good friend and believe me, I've appreciated your company, but I'm no good for you. No good. And I know I don't feel, can't feel, the same way you do."

My voice had grown almost inaudible, so I set off once more.

"Please, you have to understand. I'm not in love with you and I doubt I ever will be. In fact, I'm not even sure I want to see you again. I'm sorry, Roz. Really I am, but you must understand this can't go anywhere. There'd be no future in it. Please try to understand. Please, Roz."

I had said it and the harsh polemic finally faltered and died. But all I had achieved was to draw a mantle of depression firmly over my own heart as well as hers. So, to mask the feeling still reflecting in my eyes, I remember turning abruptly and staring out over the veranda at the familiar but now strangely blurred skyline. Tears pricked my eyelids and behind me I heard Roz stepping back as though she had been slapped. Given the unexpected sting of the confrontation, she might as well have been. Too numb to reply, she stared at the only bit of me she could see. My stiffened back, which was trying desperately to shut her out, daring her to cross the divide. Biting back the tears, however, she refused to leave immediately, refused to believe she had just been summarily dismissed.

"How could you say that? You know we're good together. And who do you think you are, anyway?" A sudden need to strike back loosened her tongue. "You were happy enough to have me here when you really needed company. You were pleased enough to see me then. And what about yesterday? Are you going to tell me that meant nothing to you?"

Accompanying her declaration, a picture of that event floated into my mind. The two of us together at the end of the track that led from home, revelling in the solitude, the silence, holding hands, watching a pair of buzzards wheel and dip in the turquoise sky as they rode the long thermals, feathers glinting in unison as soaring, synchronised flight took them through lazy arcs past the flaring sun. I had managed the short walk with just a stick, crutches firmly put aside and, with the exercise my spirits had lifted and she had no doubt sensed the black cloud shredding away in the warmth of our mutual attraction. Animated conversation and slow, affectionate laughter had punctuated each precious minute, but now all that had been changed by my sudden outburst, which still clutched her in bewildered disbelief. The abyss of rejection yawned wide and cruel, so coldly insensitive in the strength of its finality. Yet she had stood her ground for what seemed an age, hearing only the slow ticking of the old grandfather clock in the passageway behind her. Dazed.

A sudden draught flirted with the edge of her skirt, emphasising the space that separated us. A space so easily crossed with a single stride, one lovingly extended hand, yet as far as I was concerned, an impossible divide. I could no longer acknowledge that such things had passed between us. Roz's cheeks flamed and her shoulders slumped as dismissal whispered its callous message of indifference in an ear made suddenly vulnerable to every treacherous insinuation. And pride, that old snake, followed up with its familiar, devastating reaction to attack, a desire to hurt right back, to strike at the one who is the object of love, to have the last word. And even as she achieved that aim, she had despised herself but couldn't stop. And she certainly had every right. Tears of deep distress streaming down her pretty face, Roz spat out words of hate she didn't feel, a language of reprisal she didn't mean. And with the full recognition of what was happening came the great wracking sobs that tore her so recently restored world into the painful shreds of a broken heart. The last thing I heard was the sound of her racing footsteps and every one reverberated like a hammer nailing down my coffin lid.

CHAPTER 8

Mother knew but said nothing. Anxious as ever, she had been standing not far from where my last conversation had taken place and her heart had gone out to the vulnerable young girl racing blindly past her shadowed niche, fists clenched and eyes screwed half shut in the pain of her hasty, bewildered retreat. For several long minutes Mum had waited, heart in mouth, half expecting an outburst of anguish from me, but one that never came. Eventually, she had seen me straighten and, with weariness brought on by yet another betrayal, reach for my crutches before stumping off to the back of the house, heading for the only retreat I could call my own. My bedroom. Our paths hadn't crossed for the rest of the day, both of us preferring to let things lie and both afraid that anything said would only spark more distress.

I confess that since the night Matt died, I had effectively withdrawn from her, my lone advocate. For the first time in my life, I had ducked every question, avoided every gesture of intimacy and manoeuvred to ensure we were seldom alone together. And my father wasn't helping either. She dreaded his homecoming even more in those days. Especially Fridays. Friday nights were bad because, whether he had work or not, Friday for Dad was the day to hit town, to chug down innumerable draughts of beer and get paralysed with his mates. Men like himself who could never quite face up to life's demands, who found it easier to avoid the spectre of disappointment by obliterating everything in cheap local booze. The only difference between most of them being the presence or absence of a cowed woman at home, someone to terrorise in their drunken inadequacy. Which, in

Dad's case, meant a raucous, shambling arrival long after we had eaten and an angry demand to produce something more than "the bloody useless pap you usually serve up." Always demanding, never satisfied, he would insist on simple fare, the sort "I can get my teeth into." Washed down with a never-ending flow of the local Tusker beer. And some time before he passed out would come the inevitable *pièce de résistance*; a comprehensive and destructive assault on me and my fledgling intellectual achievements, my sporting prowess (or lack of it) and even the looks inherited directly from my mother. Everything I counted success and everything the failure that was my father so bitterly resented. Majoring on every mistake I had ever made, real or imagined, selecting evidence in the way only someone with an intimate knowledge of the subject could ever achieve, my father would condemn me with ruthless efficiency. A barbed demolition as comprehensive as it was unwarranted, but the injustice of the attacks never occurred to him, drunk or sober. And Mum, whose courage ebbed and flowed with the moment, was always waiting for his fury and resentment towards me to finally spill over onto her.

The danger signals had been there for days and the sound of the old van rattling up the drive and sliding to a halt just outside drained any resistance she might have contemplated. Mesmerised, she had watched through the open kitchen door, her sense of foreboding sharpened to a razor's edge as Father slammed his way across the veranda shouting for me, before marching unsteadily towards my firmly shut and carefully locked bedroom door.

"Get out here, you gutless wonder. What are you hiding from, you little yellow bastard? So help me, if I have to come in there, I'll take my belt to you so you'll never bloody well forget."

A stream of crude invective underscored the threat and with her hands over her ears, Mother had frantically tried to shut out the sound, totally unable to defend me in the face of such concentrated, alcohol-fuelled venom. But in his inebriated state, even my father couldn't keep hammering incessantly and eventually, with a final, petulant kick, he had stepped back, momentarily nonplussed. And in that moment, with a click that only emphasised the sudden quiet, I had turned the key and stepped white-faced into the bedroom doorway. Why, I don't know, but wracked with guilt and with a very real fear of my physically powerful father, I confronted him in much the same way as a rabbit prepares for the imminent arrival of a stoat.

Supremely confident in his alcoholic judgement, he needed no one to tell me I was gutless. It was the one thing of which he was totally sure. The problem was, I now knew he was right and, deeply afraid, uncertain of what to do, fearful of how to act towards this man whom I despised, I remained half in and half out of my refuge. A well-developed instinct told me to keep quiet, to remain still. But it made no difference. With heartless and chilling precision, the old man had proceeded to tell me exactly what he and thus the world thought of me. Sparing no detail that would wound, no speculation that might tighten the destructive screw of self-loathing, he had ridiculed me, his only son, describing in graphic detail the sheer force of his contempt. So, once again, piece by piece, he had dismantled me until the job was complete. Colourfully. Comprehensively. Conclusively. Before turning away without a thought for the consequences. Simply pleased, as only a bully can be, to have scored so heavily. Shambling towards his chair and already bellowing for his wife, I doubt he even heard the quiet click of the closing door. And wouldn't have cared less.

Slowly and carefully, hands numbed into exaggerated precision by physical shock, I had picked up the pen lying discarded on top of my cluttered desk and begun to write a last note. I could feel nothing, not even towards Mum, the beneficiary of this last letter. I was beyond that. My movements had reduced to the automatic, my mind finally made up, and my body ready to accept what only the truly desperate or uncaring ever contemplate. Those last few minutes had drained me to the point where I simply wanted to get things over. As quickly and cleanly as possible. My heart was devastated and battered and now it was telling me what my head had been saying for weeks. I was useless; no good to anyone, least of all myself. The blackness of the night matched the blackness in my soul and my activities were reduced to little more than the mechanical as I moved about the room. There was little to do, little to prepare. Only the method produced any uncertainty. Not the fact of my decision. With an ego so battered, so appalled at itself, little was needed to tip the balance. Just a word or a gesture. No more. And certainly not the monstrous tirade still ringing in my ears from a father who, despite everything, I had still loved, deep down, as only a child could. Until now. Now hate and despair hovered at my shoulder, goading me on, whispering to me of revulsion and self-loathing, misery and heartache. Articulating the malicious lie so easy to believe – that it would serve my father right to know he had been the cause of his own son's death. How much had changed in so short a time. Just one ill-fated, chance encounter and my whole future, whatever it might have been, was over. Gone forever. I was the wrong person in the wrong place at the wrong time.

"Mum," the terse note began, penned in what was to her a familiar, barely mature hand that was nevertheless beginning to display the strong curls and loops of a natural extrovert. "By the time you read this it will all be over. Don't come looking for me. Dad's right. I've let you both down. There's no excuse for what I've done or what I've become, so it's better for everyone that I end it. I've nothing to live for. Please don't blame yourself. Please tell Roz I'm sorry, but to forget me. I can't get away from Matt, so I've decided to join him. Forgive me. I love you, Paul."

CHAPTER 9

And so began the real story. The soft blackness of the African night cocooned me in its comforting embrace as the last engine note stuttered off the surrounding trees and died swiftly away. A subdued wind sighed out of the east, stirring just the tops of the yellow-barked fever trees in the grove ahead. There was no menace for me in the dark shadows, no fear in the open spaces, and no dread of the wild. I was a young man who had grown to love its solitude, learned to respect its unforgiving yet strangely predictable nature. The incessant croaking of bullfrogs in the nearby pools stopped momentarily as they sensed my presence. Woodenly, and feeling as if I was moving in a deep sleep, I stepped away from the shelter of the old van my father had so recently raced into the driveway and to which, with the passing of midnight, I had slipped out, knowing the keys would still be in the ignition.

The house had been quiet. I knew Mother would be lying rigid beside her snoring husband, careful even in sleep not to arouse or antagonise him. Too terrified even to defend her son. So I had let the van roll quietly down the hill away from the house before firing the ignition.

"Oh, Mum, why do you have to be so afraid of him?" I had tilted my head back as so often before, letting my eyes drink in the incredible beauty of the Milky Way, spread out in its familiar swathe across the star-lit tropical sky. The pale silky light of a million stars almost, but not quite, sufficient to read the sighting calibrations on my rifle. I had always loved the night, navigating so often by the Southern Cross, familiar with the starry clusters

from Orion's Belt to Sagittarius A and now, at the end, I wanted to hold them in mind as a last conscious picture. A part of my world that never accused me. For several minutes I stood staring, oblivious to the tears streaming down my upturned face. Then with a last shake of my head, I turned once more towards the dark grove. This was where I wanted to die. A favourite place. One to which Matt and I had come so often. A place where together, in silent admiration, we had learned so much about the hidden world of nature that surrounded us. A world of freewheeling birds and wild, graceful animals. The place to which we had often slipped away since first being allowed to wander alone, revelling in the heady absence of parental discipline. A secret place. Off the beaten track, shunned by everything except the restless animals warily looking for water in the shallow pools and scrapes of the thorny copse. I had known perfectly well there could be an ambush waiting. Most likely a shy leopard, one of several I knew roamed their immense ranges between here and the Nandi Hills, far to the south. Possibly even then two pin-sharp and alert eyes were watching me from the branches of a nearby tree, body utterly still. Only the head ducking left and right in quick, intense movements and the tip of a tail consenting to the smallest twitch as the cat followed my every step, anxious not to miss a single nuance of the intruder's progress. "*How fitting,*" I thought, "*if I'm right.*"

"I'm coming, Matt, I'm coming." The sound of my voice startled not only me, but something large up ahead in the dense bush, which fled in a sudden cascade of sound as it crashed towards open ground and safety, away from the deadly trap inherent in every waterhole. Only the sway of the low-lying foliage marked where it had passed. But by now my nerves were too numbed to react with any speed and I stumbled on, oblivious to the thorns that reached out to rake my bare arms and legs. And the thunder in my head was growing too intense for any other input to gain attention. Waves of guilt and anguish swept over me, threatening to drown me in their intensity. My breath came in great gasping sobs and my pounding heart raced as I staggered against the thorns, their lance-like spikes stabbing cruelly through the thin cotton of my shirt, great drops of blood smearing swiftly across the khaki material, each one simply an exchange for a drop of the throbbing poison waiting on each sharp tip. What little strength I had left ebbed swiftly as I dropped to my knees in the small clearing that opened up in front of me, the rifle butt punching cruelly upwards into my belly as the muzzle caught in the loamy soil.

Tears blurred my sight, but long familiarity helped. Jerking the bolt back, I managed to lever a round into the chamber, forcing the bolt forward and down until it snapped sharply into the locked position, leaving the mechanism cocked and ready. Feverishly, I groped around in the blackness for a stick long enough to strike the trigger because, with the muzzle in my mouth, I knew that reaching past the trigger guard would prove awkward. But awkward or not, it was time. I would have to shoot myself now, or what little courage I had left would desert me.

Of their own accord, my fingers danced frantically as they looked for and closed upon a stick that felt as though it should be strong enough, leaving me to swing the rifle round. Quickly now, every movement a desperate race to get the unspeakable act over. The butt grounded in the angle between the rough earth and the base of a small tree and with one last despairing look above me, I opened my mouth, forced the business end of the rifle against my chattering teeth and closed my lips over the cold metal. It tasted foul. The harsh, urine-sprayed earth smeared over the muzzle, the product of so many watering animals, splattered across my tongue. My left hand, jabbing for the trigger with the end of the stick, was momentarily blocked as it caught against the guard and I remember scrabbling frantically to get past it and end my life.

But there was something else going on in the clearing.

Something I would never have guessed at or given any credence to, even if I had been told. An unseen world which, had I been able to sense it, might have brought the vile flavour of putrefaction and the stench of utter decay to my nostrils. But invisible, unknown, a shadow darker than the blackest night flickered suddenly backwards, away from me, the better to observe this final act of destruction. Now it watched in drooling expectation, revelling in the only genuine satisfaction left to it – the violent annihilation of a human being. Any human.

For weeks, the demonic outcast from its own spiritual realm had ridden me, preternatural claws hooked into the flesh of my back, their pulsing grip goading me, an unsuspecting victim, whilst the slavering mouth whispered despair, self-loathing and selfish revenge directly into my fevered mind, well below the conscious level. Repulsive in its ugliness, rejected even by its own kind, the repellent, almost rat-like creature had been looking for a host in the right frame of mind. Preferably depressed or, better still, already despairing. And it had found me, helpless and hurting at the base of Cat Hill, a perfect target upon which to begin feeding like some loathsome parasite. Yet its eerie concentration, leaning forward in bloody expectation of the final downward plunge onto the trigger and the upward smashing of the bullet, caused it to miss the only warning of looming destruction it would ever get from its own universe.

Even as the stick slid clear of the trigger guard, a shaft of pure, brilliant white light struck downwards, unseen by the natural world but spread in a great cone around me, and the tip of a dazzling sword arrested the stick's forward thrust. And at the very edge of this lightning bolt, the solid blackness exploded in a ball of screaming fire, leathery limbs juddering suddenly outwards in writhing agony for a fraction of time, before dissolving to a rapidly thinning smear of oily smoke that drifted into nothingness.

With a grim sense of satisfaction, the majestic angel who had simultaneously materialised at my side sheathed his long, glittering sword in a single, smooth movement. Totally unconcerned as to whether or not he was observed. For as with humanity, even more so in this spiritual world, inhabited by angels and prying demons, there was always a witness. And so it was, not far away, hidden deep in one of the shallow pools, something else watched intently. A low-ranking excrescence with the unlikely name of Altoid was trembling with the very real fear that close proximity to any angel tended to induce. But not so much fear that it prevented him from calculating how he might present this information so as to curry favour with his superiors. And it might have saved the underworld a deal of trouble if they had bothered to consider a word of his report.

"Stop!" As though from a great distance, I remember the clear command ringing in my head, but I sensed nothing, saw nothing. Dazed, I let the stick fall from near-lifeless fingers. And in that very act, with an awful clarity, the full force of what I was doing hit home. Death was looking me straight in the face and for a moment I stared right back before cringing away, the instance forever stamped into my soul. And with that confrontation, the driving, headlong rush to destruction leached away as swiftly as it had begun, no longer fed by my now obliterated and unseen adversary. And hard on the heels of reprieve came a mixture of utter, heartfelt relief, mixed with a heady dose of fright over what had so nearly been done. And in the moment of discovering I didn't really want to die, I was overwhelmed by a great sorrow. Scalding grief over my actions, and deep remorse over the hurt that Roz, my Mother, my friends would undoubtedly have felt. And with the recognition came a deep craving to get away, to put distance between myself and my world. To lick my wounds in the calm of anonymity.

Parking at the back of the station, I made my way furtively through the early morning shadows towards the far end of the long freight train. If I was going to make it all the way to Mombasa, I needed cover as well as transport and was looking for a wagon with an unlocked door. I was just beginning to think such things didn't exist, when right at the end of the train I found what I was looking for and when I stopped to listen, the desultory sounds still reaching me from the distant platform were reassuring. Clearly, I hadn't been seen. So, keeping out of sight as best I could, I pulled at the protesting door until it was wide enough to toss my rifle through and wriggle in after it. Once inside, although I could barely see, I rushed to stand up and get the door shut, with the result that my shoulder cracked against one of a pile of long wooden boxes stacked around the interior. It went over with a crash that reverberated loud enough to wake the dead, let alone summon the nearby night watchmen. Aghast, I swung round to see what I had done and found myself looking at the blurred image of a matched pair of glimmering white elephant tusks sticking out of the splintered box. The problem was, I was looking at them over the business end of a very much in focus pistol, the silencer held directly and firmly between my eyes.

CHAPTER 10

Dawn. Roz stirred and let the pale light of early morning draw her slowly into consciousness. The house was still and not even Ben would be awake at this hour, but it was a magic time, cool, quiet, beckoning. Quickly, she slipped out from under the covers, the sudden cold stiffening her nipples and causing an involuntary shudder as the morning air pressed in through the open window, flowing over her slim, naked body. Drawing on an old towelling robe, she swung long, sun-browned legs out over the windowsill onto the veranda and on bare feet pattered across the coarse marram grass[1] surrounding the farmhouse, heading for the paddock rail corralling her surprise birthday present.

The stocky palomino mare, a contrition offering from her dad, looked up briefly before returning to the rather more pressing matter of tearing at the long dry grass; gloomy disapproval registered in every heavy snort. Roz didn't mind. It was early days and they hadn't bonded yet. Outside the paddock, the veldt stretched away in undulating waves to the far horizon speckled with distant herds of deer and the occasional clutch of zebra. Close in to the settlement no sound rode the gentle morning breeze and to the east the new day glowed with fresh tints of pink and gold, shading slowly to indigo above her head, awaiting only the promised sun to turn it all to deepest blue. But for now that star lay well below the sharp division of earth and sky, the very contrast heralding the approach of another perfect day. Except no day could be perfect now. Not the way she was feeling, her heart aching over her harsh dismissal.

Shivering, Roz drew her robe tighter, ignoring the tantalising fragrance of frangipani blossom spicing the air, all mixed with an indefinable but unmistakeable aroma of wood smoke and native village life. She was still perplexed. *"Why, Paul, why are you being like this?"* The question formed in her mind and her cheeks flamed suddenly with remembered guilt at the way she had struck back. *"Oh, Paul."* Her throat ached as she bit back the tears. She didn't, couldn't, believe we were finished. Mere days before, I had clearly been only too happy to stand next to her, hands linked, hearts dancing to the delicious thrill of a shared but undeclared love, while we gazed with rapt attention at the buzzards wheeling and soaring overhead.

Watching, she had suddenly understood with mysterious and inexplicable intensity, deep in the secret recesses of her soul, that a powerful bond was being forged. As though something or someone was revealing the future, briefly drawing aside a curtain veiling the womb of time. For better or worse, she had apparently felt bound to me from that moment. In her eyes I had become a strangely exciting young man whose presence, unexpectedly, had generated neither fear nor surprise, only elation that rose in smooth, fulfilling waves to anchor her heart in a certainty she could not deny. So intense had been the experience, she had been sure I must have sensed it too. But of course, I'd said nothing and the mystifying encounter with Love (she could only describe the experience with a capital 'L') had burned itself indelibly into her mind. Though she had failed to appreciate it at the time, that moment had forged a lifeline into her soul, a certainty to which she would return again and again in the dark days ahead.

★ ★ ★

Her father's voice calling from the veranda cut through her musing.

"Roz, it's the phone; Paul's Mum for you." She could tell by the puzzlement in his voice he was as perplexed as she was by this early-morning call. What on earth could be so pressing?

"Roz, it's me, Lynn Moncton. I'm sorry to bother you, but have you seen Paul? He's not here and I'm worried about him." It hardly seemed worth pointing out that it was barely sun-up and, in any case, Roz had caught the suppressed edge of panic in Lynn's voice.

"Haven't seen him since I left you yesterday, Mrs Moncton."

"Well, he's gone and oh, Roz, he's left a note saying we mustn't try to look for him." Lynn couldn't quite bring herself to spell out the details, but even she realised the rising note in her voice was betraying any hope of keeping a lid on the real truth.

"Why wouldn't Paul want you to find him?"

The question hung in the air and the silence drew out until it was impossible for Lynn to deny her fears. It came out with a rush. "Paul left a note saying he was going to end it all and join Matt and the van's gone and I – ". Her voice dropped to a sobbing whisper as Roz stood utterly still, the phone slipping from her suddenly lifeless fingers and her mind screaming dissent. "*No! No! No!*" – over and over again.

Ted, curious, had not gone far and, hearing the thud as the phone hit the table, stepped around the door, just in time to see his daughter crumple forwards to the floor, hands clasped on either side of her head, body rocking backwards and forwards on her knees as she retreated into some overwhelming private grief.

"Roz, what is it? Tell me;" he demanded in alarm. Reaching out quickly, he wrapped his arms around her but let her weep, holding her while the storm of tears slowly abated.

"Dad," she eventually whispered. "Dad, Lynn says Paul's gone, that he left a suicide note and oh, Dad –." Her voice broke and the tears began to flow as Ted scooped up the phone and held it to his ear.

"Lynn, are you there? Is this true, is Paul, er, dead?" He listened as Lynn haltingly told him what she knew, before slowly placing the phone back in its cradle. Still holding Roz, his mind racing, Ted brooded over how to get her through the agony tearing at her heart, knowing she had already experienced so much disappointment over the past few months. He knew Roz was a fighter, but this could well be a step too far. He had already guessed something of her true feelings towards Paul. And now this. Carefully, he picked her up, letting her cling to him while he carried her through to the bedroom, where Vera was just beginning to wish she hadn't woken up.

CHAPTER 11

But I was very much alive, or at least, up to that precise moment I was. Whether that was going to last I wasn't sure. The world had contracted down to a thudding pain between my eyes, where cold metal dug into the thin flesh of my forehead and a dark, hard face loomed menacingly at the other end of a long arm. A simple question hung in the air, but the quiet, disinterested menace with which it had been asked left me in no doubt the speaker meant what he said. Which, I have to confess, at any other time would have plunged me into total bewilderment but, right now and for some unfathomable reason, failed to make even the slightest impression.

"Is there any reason I shouldn't kill you?"

I remember I really couldn't think of a suitable answer. The trauma of the last few hours had taxed the very depths of reason and, like all nightmares, the situation seemed almost surreal. All I could do was stare at the pistol and the face, knowing that it wouldn't take much to tip me over the edge. Which led to a calculating, if nascent resentment beginning to build somewhere deep inside. A capability I never knew I had and one that made me realise, for the first time, not everything might be lost. Recovery was possible. Somehow, I might get past this. I could, after all, hope somehow to repair my bruised and battered self-esteem. At which point, the menace intensified.

"You've got five seconds to convince me, or you're dead."
"One". "Two − ." I felt rather than heard the shadowy figure take up the first pressure on the trigger and suddenly I knew it needed only the lightest touch to blow me away. "Three". "Four."

From somewhere out of sight I heard a faint stirring.

"Boss. Hold up. I know who this kid is. I saw his picture in the paper. He's the one who left his friend to die. You remember, the one who got eaten by a lion?" There was a heavy silence. Then the pressure from the silencer eased slightly. I could see the gunman, whoever he was, was interested, despite himself.

"So. We have ourselves a real, live coward."

I watched the gunman's eyes travel slowly down to my feet and then back up. And by the time they returned to meet my gaze, there was speculation in them. "Now, that might be quite handy. Tie him and gag him while I have a think about it."

Rough hands pulled me abruptly to the side and a knee sent me flat on my face, the tip of a tusk digging painfully into my exposed throat. There was swift efficiency in the hands that bound me and tightly fastened I stayed, with bodge tape slapped carelessly across my mouth to keep me quiet. Then with little regard for the niceties, I was dragged face down across the freight car floor to the far corner. Silence. Uncomfortable to say the least, I remember trying to ease the various aches induced by the restraints whilst, at the same time, straining to listen to the terse whispering passing back and forth between my captors. With a total lack of success. In the dark I couldn't even work out how many there were. Thoroughly disorientated and with my hands hauled painfully tight behind my back, I was reduced to little more than turning my head and looking towards the wagon's entrance, where a thin line of light forced its way around the edge of the sliding door and provided the one and only point of reference.

To be honest, by that juncture the sheer shock of what was happening had once again leached away any genuine willingness to fight back. But lying there, abandoned, anger slowly began to overtake the debilitating sense of futility I'd been living with since the encounter with my father the previous evening. Physically, I was completely helpless and knew it, but hidden within me something akin to resolve finally began to take a certain shape.

Because my ear was pressed against the floorboards, I was the first to catch the sound of footsteps crunching through the ballast stones scattered alongside the track. A tuneless whistle, magnified by the wooden floor, floated out of the silence. The sound of a man at ease with his world. Around me I sensed more than saw that the poachers, as I thought of them (for want of a better description), had reacted swiftly to the sound. It stopped right outside the cab and now there was some sort of long-distance, shouted exchange going on. Silently, I willed the man to check the flatbed, trying to alert him by the power of thought alone, but even I knew it was a pretty forlorn hope. Until I heard the guard shouting to someone in the language as familiar to me as my own.

"Haraka, haraka. Watu mpega kifungua."[1] It only took a few seconds before I heard the sound of running feet and, with a screeching shudder, the door was dragged abruptly open, allowing the early morning light to flood into the crowded wagon.

Two disembodied faces, each topped off by the traditional and instantly recognisable tasselled red fez, appeared at floor level, the operational ends of their casually shouldered guns sticking uselessly skywards behind them. The look of consternation and surprise at the sight of two large ivory tusks lying across the entrance with several armed men standing behind them would have been comical in any other circumstances, but I already knew there was nothing funny about this lot. Probably the last thing the taller of the two Askaris[2] remembered was the sharp detonation of a rifle being fired straight at him. To his left, the shorter one watched in horror as his companion acquired a third eye in the centre of his forehead before collapsing gracefully backwards like a swimmer pushing gently away from the pool wall. With a startled grunt and acutely aware of the wind generated by the incoming round, the remaining policeman stumbled frantically backwards, snatching wildly at the too tight rifle sling, trying to extricate himself in time to swing the long

48

rifle into action. With one smooth movement, the man I already recognised as the boss stepped forward, crouched and casually sighted along my rifle at the retreating guard. And still hopelessly pinned to the floor, my ears were battered by the pressure of a second shot let loose in the confined area. So I almost, but not quite, missed the final thud of a falling body as it skidded to its end.

"You, Stephano, Mick, get them in here, quick. See if there's anyone else around." Two athletic, tanned young men swung quickly out through the door and disappeared. Seconds later, a body landed on the flatbed with a sodden thump and two others stepped forward from the shadows to drag the dead man by his khaki webbing strap to where I lay forgotten in the melee. The sound of hurried footsteps crunching through the ballast preceded the airborne arrival of a second body and shortly thereafter, I found myself almost buried beneath two heavy, reeking corpses, blood slowly leaking over me and staining the floor beneath us. Within seconds Stephano and Mick had vaulted back over the sill, sliding the door closed behind them with a solid thump. For long moments there was no movement in the cab until the continuing silence assured them all that no one had reacted to the rifle shots.

CHAPTER 12

Unusually, the long freight train pulled out more or less on time and with its gathering momentum, the wagons began to snub and sway to a familiar and oddly soothing pattern. Around me, the men relaxed visibly. There wouldn't be another halt until the driver needed to take on water – probably at the depot just before the long haul up from the floor of the Rift Valley – a part of the journey that would take us at least six hours. However, with a growing brightness now streaming through the many holes in the wooden walls, I was beginning to see more clearly and what I saw gave little cause for comfort. There were eight of them in all, dressed more or less the same in stained khaki bush shirts and shorts. Several had wide-brimmed leather hats hanging from long, sweat-blackened cords, a style favoured by cattle ranchers the world over. Every one of them sported a deep tan from long periods in the African sun and wind, but their almost mahogany colouring and swarthy skin probably had more to do with their ethnic background. I recall thinking they probably originated from the Mediterranean and occasional lapses into a half-recognisable language convinced me they were Italian.

Whenever anyone did glance in my direction, it was to regard my half-buried body with complete indifference. And now that the fierce sun was starting to warm the early morning air, all attention seemed to focus on settling into the rough and ready 'shake-downs' already rolled out between the surrounding boxes. Only the incessant movement of jaws around the ubiquitous chewing gum betrayed any hint of vigilance as, one by one, they settled down for the duration. The impassive coldness etching the harsh planes of their closed faces left me completely unable to work out the gang's hierarchy, who was who, or how they would respond to any appeal I might make. Eventually I gave up trying, concentrating instead on struggling, as surreptitiously as possible, to squirm out from under the heavy press of Askari bodies.

Vaguely, I became aware of an urgent discussion going on in a far corner between the boss and another of the men. Every so often, glances were thrown in my direction and after a while it became obvious that some agreement had been reached. Standing up and stretching himself, the boss picked his way over to me, body swaying easily to the roll of the slow-moving train, before bending to check my bonds. Satisfied, he wiped his fingerprints thoroughly and carefully from my rifle with the edge of the shorter Askari's dark blue uniform pullover. When it was cleaned to his satisfaction, he cradled the gun carefully in his shirt before pressing it against my bound hands, wrapping them around the butt and right along the barrel, making sure my fingers came in contact with all the working parts. A small, cynical smile playing on his lips, he turned and called two of the men over to him.

Quickly, they lifted the first of the Askaris, dragged him to the door and pitched him out. The second followed with as little ceremony. Watching carefully, I saw the boss step over to the still open door and drawing back his arm, pitch my precious rifle out, to fall somewhere clear of the track. Once again the doors closed and an edgy calm reasserted itself. I already knew full well I was in deep trouble, but strangely, the pantomime with the rifle gave me some hope, even though I bitterly resented its casual loss. It was hardly rocket science to deduce why the gun had been wiped clean before ensuring my fingerprints were once again all over it. Nevertheless, I preferred to assume – for the time being at least – that there was little point in playing out such a charade if they didn't intend to hang on to me as some sort of bargaining chip. It was a pretty thin straw, but any straw was welcome. Being used as a scapegoat cum insurance seemed feasible and it was just as well I still had no inkling of the real purpose behind their actions.

So, for the first time in a traumatic twenty-four hours, I began to think in terms somewhat longer than my immediate future, or lack of it. Somewhere between my introduction to the wrong end of a short-barrelled, silenced weapon and being part buried under two log-heavy bodies, I had managed to get a grip on my natural nausea and, though I didn't know it, had begun to mature. Not much, but enough for the time being. Life had suddenly become worth living again and with that realisation had come hope. And with hope came determination that this time I was not going to disgrace myself, whatever the cost. Thus for many hours I lay on the swaying, shuddering floor, with sweat occasionally dripping onto the stain-darkened planks only to dilute the thick, rapidly congealing pool of blood beneath me, as it turned from vibrant red to ugly black. I will never forget the cloying smell of that blood penetrating my protesting nostrils, or the malignant buzz of the ubiquitous bush flies, which not only offended my ears but made my skin crawl as I watched them bloating themselves on the unexpected feast. The scene haunts me to this day.

★ ★ ★

Back in Moiben, it seemed to Roz as if the very fabric of her life had ruptured. Even time stood still, although the days would soon start to meld into one another with relentless precision. Together with Lynn, she agonised through the hours following my disappearance, desperate to know whether I was alive or dead by my own hand. By midday, Bob Moncton's van had been identified down at the station, which at least proved I had got that far. But where was I now? Down line? Up line? I could only have caught one of two trains – always assuming I had caught anything; either the early morning freight run to Mombasa or, less likely, the local 'up country' train, inevitably crowded with native families, chickens, goats and almost anything else that moved on two or more legs. In such a crowd my white skin would have stood out like a sore thumb and someone would have remembered. But then had come news of a suspicious disappearance. The station's two night-duty Askaris had failed to sign off and when their families finally plucked up enough courage to question the authorities, it turned out no one had seen either of them since they had checked in for duty the previous evening. Which only added to the confusion. Until early the next day, when the spiralling vultures led the now fully aroused police authorities to two bodies dumped by the rail track, several miles southeast of Eldoret. At which point the search had turned into a full-scale murder enquiry. Following which, a cursory exploration of the immediate area duly produced my abandoned rifle. And with me still unaccounted for and suicide less and less likely, the police quickly awarded themselves a suspect for pole position at a one-way interview – requiring only my presence to complete the happy picture. It was unfortunate, therefore, that the Mombasa train from which I might have been triumphantly released had reached its final destination an hour or so before this line of reasoning led to an inevitable conclusion. Allowing the requisite wagon to be emptied of evidence, with the exception of some dried blood, which merely served to confirm what they'd already blithely assumed anyway.

CHAPTER 13

For once, the Moiben farmers had something else to chatter about beyond the usual problems – animal sickness and drought – faced by tropical farmers the world over. And the talk wasn't just about me. Alongside the scandalised assumption that I had gone from bad to worse, first, abandoning Matt to his fate and then killing two policemen, rumours abounded about my relationship with the new girl Roz. And with every telling, the assumptions got worse, rapidly outstripping any possible fact, despite the total lack of supporting evidence.

Not that Roz would have cared even if she had known what was going on. She was following the breaking story with every bit as much attention as the rest of them but, unlike the gossipmongers, she felt only relief that I might be alive, together with a complete certainty that I wasn't the killer I was alleged to be. Moreover, she refused to listen to anyone who thought otherwise. Even her family, who hovered uncertainly between wanting to support her in the implacable determination she had begun to display and their desire to prepare her for the worst, found they could not break through the defensive shield she had erected around her mind. Behind it, despite occasional raging doubts in the face of the conviction everyone else seemed to feel, her feelings for me had apparently strengthened with each passing day, until they blossomed into the kernel of an idea – find me before the police did. To warn me and prove to us both that she not only loved me but that somehow love could transcend the accusations waiting to pin me to the wall. She would prove I was not a killer – to herself, who did not need such proof – and to the world, which clearly did. How, she had not the faintest idea, but that she might not succeed was something she could not allow herself to contemplate. Even the following day, when the police released my photograph, a man now wanted for the murder of two Askaris, capped with news of a substantial sum for information leading to my arrest. And the first Roz knew of this development was when her father was refuelling the car and she saw a poster on the forecourt of the only garage for miles around, Hughes petrol station, which linked the top of Eldoret's two main streets, one set aside exclusively for whites, the other used by the local inhabitants.

Momentarily, the shock had drained her resolve, but not for long. Silent, she had sat next to her father on the drive home, oblivious to his efforts to draw her out, to engage her in conversation, any conversation, as she desperately tried to plan the next move, a move that might hold the seeds of success. She was certain the family would not willingly let her go, but she was equally sure that only by going it alone would she stand any chance of finding me, without risking a trail that even the police could follow.

"Roz, talk to me. You've not said a word since we left town."

Turning slowly but determined not to let him see her uncertainty, she still couldn't stop a tear rolling down her cheek. Instinctively, Ted put out a hand to brush it away, his heart aching for her.

"Roz, you can't go on like this. I know you think he's innocent, but you've got to let the courts prove it." She looked at him, loving him and knowing he wanted only the best for her, but afraid to show weakness, afraid to take him into her confidence until she was more sure of herself. Until the doubt and determination whirling in equal measures within her head were sorted out, she knew she had to keep things to herself and even then, she doubted if she could tell anyone what she really wanted to do.

"Dad, stop here, please. I want to walk a bit." He glanced at her quizzically but allowed the car to roll to a gentle stop. It wasn't far to Moiben, but he was still hesitant to leave her and, for all that she was trying to cover it, he could see the shadows of turmoil chasing across her face, the pain darting in her eyes.

"Are you sure I can't help? You know I'm always here for you."

"I know, Dad, I know. But I've got to sort this out for myself."

He had nodded reluctantly as she stepped out onto the rich red murram[1] of Moiben's only road. A road slashed straight from the bush that wound steadily towards the little settlement she now called home. With the car on its way, the warm silence of the African veldt had closed around her and with it, despite herself, her spirit had lifted a little as it responded to the vibrant life surrounding her. She could never stay low for long and was so attuned to the wilderness that she could hardly help her mind and emotions responding positively to the great blue canopy stretching overhead with its tufts of fluffy white stratus idling down the wind, and the rolling brown and yellow grass hiding the chaffinches as they called in serial competition all around her.

Strangely encouraged, she picked up the pace and began to stride purposefully towards the spot where the car had so recently vanished, soft sandals stirring puffs of fine dust, which quickly covered her feet and legs in a dense red layer. An hour saw her topping a rise to look down on the inland lake and she stopped to absorb the scene with its distant sails making the most of the light winds, and the dazzling reflections from one or two cars parked by the clubhouse twinkling back their random Morse. As her gaze wandered, she noticed again the small, grey church folded into the hill, almost as though it had sprung fully formed from the ground upon which it sat. Watching it, her thoughts fled back to Matt's funeral, the only time she had set foot in the place. The events of that awful day had been firmly thrust to the back of her mind, but now the details leapt forward again and, almost unbidden, her footsteps turned towards the tiny haven.

Hurrying now, she made her way round to the stone arch that sheltered the main entrance and, pushing on the dark wooden doors, discovered they were unlocked. A cool stillness welcomed her as she closed the door and stepped forward to sink into one of the short wooden pews. Dust motes danced in the coloured shafts of light striking through the stained-glass window behind her and an almost palpable silence settled over her. Hardly daring to breathe for fear of breaking the friendly calm, Roz leaned back and looked towards the altar with its austere brass cross flanked by tall, matching candelabra. Silently, she began to contemplate the jumbled events of the last week – was it only seven days since last she'd seen her love? – and found herself subconsciously running through her fears and intentions as though someone was actually there, able to read her mind. To empathise.

Startled by a great peace that flooded through her, almost like a living entity, Roz found her eyes drawn once again to the cross, only to discover that nothing had moved; nothing, seemingly, had changed. No voice responded to her intensely curious gaze, a fact she found momentarily disappointing. Nonetheless, her limbs felt wrapped in a warm embrace that anchored her to the spot and slowly but surely drained the hurt from her aching heart. For perhaps an hour she sat there, unmoving, reluctant to break the spell. And in waiting, she became submerged in a tranquil calm that engulfed her innermost being, impelling a determination to retain every nuance of the event. She knew beyond doubt the occasion was important and, after a while, with thoughts resolved, she understood with complete confidence that I could and would be found. How or why, she was unable to resolve but, in the hushed serenity, her diminishing fears were replaced, almost miraculously, by a full measure of assurance. She could no more explain this than put her finger on it, but her heart didn't need an explanation. It was just certain.

Eventually, she stood and withdrew quietly, latching the door softly behind her. Outside, as she set out on the last mile of her walk, the sun was beginning its steep slide to the western rim of her horizon and by the time she drew near to home, the rapidly lengthening shadows were calling time on the day shift. In the distance she could hear an experimental bullfrog tuning up for the nightly chorus. Just one at first, but gradually tens then hundreds joining in the fierce competition for females, the chaotic mix of calls blending swiftly into one harmonious whole that seemed to saturate the very universe. Until, right on cue, a hyena coughed out its hysterical laughter and the nervousness of night gripped both ends of the food chain.

CHAPTER 14

"Mum, Dad, I'm home." The companionable sounds of a family at ease with itself and the rich smell of an almost-ready meal greeted Roz as she stepped through the hissing light of a storm lantern suspended on the veranda just outside the front door. The light was a ritual, a familiar gesture that was as much a part of any frontier family as breathing. Wherever they were, as soon as the shadows lengthened, the welcome went up to beckon anyone still not home and to summon passing neighbours or strangers in need of a friendly face. And just as routinely, an army of mosquitoes, moths and sausage flies zinged, fluttered and thudded to their incandescent deaths, the fiery carnage only slightly diminished by the patrolling of random bats.

Vera appeared from the kitchen, arms spattered with flour and the cheerful sounds of the kitchen workers rolling about her like a comfortable mantle.

"Hi, darling, welcome home." She rounded the plain oak dining table and gestured towards the heavy old sofa where most of the family business took place. "Dad told me you were walking home. Did it help?"

Roz looked at her Mum and, with courage gained from the still-fresh memory of what she had already come to regard as a profound and significant spiritual experience, decided she had to confide her decision and risk a possible confrontation. After all, without her parents' consent, she couldn't even raid her bank account and unless she could buy a train ticket, there was precious little she could do.

"Mum, I can't stop thinking about Paul. Why hasn't he

contacted anyone – his family or even me? Suppose he's hurt and can't get to a phone? Suppose – suppose he really is dead?" With the dam broken, the words continued to pour out of her. "I've been so worried and Bob Moncton obviously won't do anything, and Paul's mum is too afraid. Someone has to try something – find him, or at least discover what happened. The police obviously think he killed those two Askaris and that's awful. I just know he'd never do anything like that. So it seems to me that if I don't do something, no one else will. I've got to find him, warn him, before the police get to him. What if he doesn't realise quite how serious they are and tries to run if they find him? The way they're advertising this crime, they might well shoot him. If that happened and I was just sitting here doing nothing, I couldn't live with myself."

Vera looked carefully at her eldest child and saw in the set of her jaw and the force of her gaze something of herself at the same age and her heart went out to the grieving young woman, who at just nineteen was barely old enough to leave home, let alone antagonise the police. But it was clear she was already maturing beyond her years. Even so, she would have said something, but, with barely a pause, Roz rushed on.

"When I was walking home I stopped in the church for a bit. I needed to get things sorted out in my mind and it just seemed the right place to be. Mum, while I was sitting there I had the strangest feeling. I was sure someone good was there with me, watching and listening, even though I didn't speak out loud. I didn't feel afraid or anything, I just knew that whoever it was understood me. It felt so right. Anyway, I've made up my mind. Paul could be anywhere between here and Mombasa, but the chances are he's gone right down to the coast and so that's where I'm going to start. He told me once it's where he'd go if he ever needed to get away from everything and if I don't find him there, I'll work my way back up country to Nairobi. Somewhere, someone will know something about him. He can't just vanish into thin air. But, Mum, I need your help. I need you and Dad to let me go. I've got some money saved up, so I can pay for my ticket and it won't cost you anything. Please say yes."

Vera sighed and reached her arm around Roz, knowing it was pointless to try to stop her. "OK. Your father won't be any happier than I am, but I'll fix that. We'll get you to the station in time for tomorrow morning's train. Now get on and pack while I talk to your father."

CHAPTER 15

The long drawn-out squeal of brakes and erratic banging of wagons as they caught up with each other brought me abruptly round from yet another exhausted catnap. Right through that long night beyond Nairobi I had drifted in and out of consciousness. Hungry, thirsty, I remained unable to find any relief from the increasing pain of my tightly bound limbs as they chaffed against the ropes restraining all but the slightest movement. Only twice was I allowed to stand and move my arms around in that entire nightmare journey. And then only to relieve myself over the edge of the open door. Any illusion I might have had regarding sympathy went rapidly out of sight, pretty much in the same direction as my arching urine; they just didn't want the reek of me on top of the foul, cloying odour that already permeated every recess, no doubt from the none-too-sterile ivory, never mind the mixture of dried Askari blood smeared all over me. So, along with the rest of the train, my mobile prison had suddenly jolted and barged its way to a juddering halt, leaving only a merciful silence, over which voices from the outside world alerted me once again to the near presence of strangers. And all I could hope was there wouldn't be a repeat of the senseless violence that had shattered the previous morning.

It didn't take long to clear the wagon and I was the last consignment to go, dragged across the wooden floor until my feet swung out over the door sill and I braced myself for a fall. The glitter of a knife blade swinging up towards my stomach didn't exactly help with the sphincter muscles, but, mercifully, it was aimed at my bindings, not my body. So, with feet liberated, I was shoved from behind and fell the last few feet to the ground, only to stagger in a wide circle before collapsing to the platform as my legs reacted badly to their newfound freedom. They were none too careful about how they picked me up either, before propelling me towards the leading pickup truck, one of several backed up around my erstwhile prison.

I remember trying to get my bearings and, by craning my neck, attempting to see where I was exactly, but there was nothing in sight that I recognised. That said, it was easy enough to guess we were at or near the coast, because of the many tall, green-fringed coconut palms swaying and rustling in the light morning breeze, accompanied by a slight waft of hydrogen sulphide from what I took to be rotting seaweed. The sprawling mass of buildings, what little I could see around the terminal, clinched it. It had to be Mombasa, the biggest station in the country, the beginning of the line. But we were well away from any passenger area, the only part I was even vaguely going to recognise.

What I could see up ahead were several armed men, all dressed in the loose, flowing robes effected by just about every man living in the stultifying coastal heat. Most of them surrounded the trucks, but two stood at a distance, alongside an Askari who fidgeted nervously whilst looking studiously in the opposite direction. Even had the gag not been firmly taped across my mouth, I instinctively knew that trying to attract his attention would do me little good and probably even earn both of us a beating. So, for the time being I gave up and let myself be forced into the cab alongside a skinny old African, his face covered with tribal tattoos. A guard, for that is what I took the only other occupant to be, was already squatting behind the driver and almost immediately after I was shoved unceremoniously into the front passenger seat, an order was passed down the line and the vehicles sprang to life. By straining my head around, I could just make out the rest of the men running to spread themselves around the four open-topped vehicles, guns now dropping down out of sight, but quite clearly not out of reach, as they took up their positions riding shotgun and we began to bump and grind our way out of the yard, heading for a dusty track leading into town.

Pretty soon the ochre murram gave way to tarmac and the vans picked up speed as they entered the almost deserted town, first, turning along the one thoroughfare I was sure I recognised, Princess Elizabeth Avenue. Thereafter, beginning to weave their way southeast towards the narrow streets and alleys surrounding the old harbour. Which was when I understood why they were using such small trucks. The walls of the overhanging houses closed in on either side and soon we were reduced to a crawl, passing between a colourful assortment of mud-spattered walls set with massive old mahogany doors, age darkened and often carved in intricate detail. Each one testifying to the owner's intention to keep a hostile world at bay. High above us, firmly shuttered windows completed the picture as each man assiduously guarded his wives and daughters against any hint of impropriety.

A whitewashed courtyard, just big enough to take the four pickups, signalled the apparent end of our journey, for now at least. Here the few shuttered windows were arranged high up on the mostly blank walls, their only major relief a straight staircase rising steeply to the top and an obvious walkway encircling the wall. That and a wood-framed entrance just wide enough to let the trucks pass carefully through completed its somewhat limited attractions. A houseboy with jet-black face and dressed in a long white kanzu[1] , cinched at the waist with a broad red cummerbund, had latched back the heat-stiffened gates as we arrived and, just as swiftly, had drawn them shut again the moment the last truck was through. A few curt words were exchanged and Giuseppe, as I had since heard the men refer to their boss, hurried after the houseboy, disappearing swiftly through a low door I'd failed to notice as we turned in. I was incredibly tense, but could only sit, agonising about what might be going on. I had already exhausted any hope of gleaning something useful from the driver. The man was either dumb or defiant, because beyond a rather too obvious tightening of his jaw in response to my arrival, there had been absolutely no acknowledgement of the opportunity presented by the momentary departure of our guard to join his mates. Even the minder's single sharp command to keep the speed up had met with little more than an angry, almost dismissive wave of the driver's hand.

Behind us, all the guards had now brought their rifles into sight and were either leaning impassively on them, or picking their teeth with studied indifference. But, for all that, there was a palpable air of tension. I wasn't the only one with something to worry about. Some fifteen minutes went by and I could see the wariness translating into half-raised rifles and abruptly narrowed eyes scanning the tops of the sunlit walls. It occurred to me that down here in what was, effectively, a cockpit, we were totally vulnerable, painfully exposed to anyone who might wish to shoot down from behind the safety of the high white parapets. We couldn't even drive to safety. If things got out of hand, it would likely be carnage and I had a fair idea of who would be doing the bleeding. And it was clear the same thoughts were occupying a number of other minds as they waited with mounting unease for the boss to return. Whatever it was this lot were up to, it wasn't just about ivory, because poaching wasn't a particularly heinous crime by anyone's measure. It had to be something else to warrant this level of security and tense anticipation.

Time dragged, but just as we passed the twenty-minute mark, the houseboy returned and, in the mannered custom of African tribes, beckoned my now returned guard with a time-honoured palm-down motion. Immediately, this stalwart climbed off the truck and disappeared into the cool darkness of the open door, only to return within a few seconds preceded by a shout with which he clearly intended to galvanise the rest into some sort of action. Quickly, I turned to the driver, trying desperately to sign with my eyes and to mumble through the tape still firmly glued to my skin. But the driver merely stared back at me with almost pitying eyes before slowly opening his mouth. To my horror, I saw that behind the betel-blackened stumps[2] that passed for teeth, the man's mouth was empty. A stub, all that was left of his tongue, moved jerkily as he formed a guttural noise somewhere at the back of his throat and shrugged helpless shoulders. His eyes slid towards the men streaming backwards and forwards behind us and I caught the look of pure hatred lancing outwards, momentarily darkening even that ravaged old face, before the mask of indifference dropped firmly back into place.

Stunned and impotent, I remember staring at the man, trying desperately to signal acknowledgement of a senseless crime with just my eyes, before turning slowly and heavily, in time to see the last box of ivory hauled down and carried out of sight. But it was what followed that really caught my attention. For the first time I spotted some tightly wrapped hessian parcels being dragged from beneath where the ivory had been. They were heavy, because the men were having difficulty as, two by two, they laboured across the courtyard into the inky blackness beyond the low door. Surprised at having missed what must have been obvious in the freight wagon, I counted some thirty of the large packages in transit before my guard returned to jerk me roughly out of the vehicle by the hank of rope trailing from my bound arms.

CHAPTER 16

The darkness was something of a relief after the harsh white light and dusty heat of the courtyard and it took me some while to adjust as I was prodded up a flight of stairs and along a corridor to be confronted by a closed door at its very end. Beyond it, I could hear the murmur of voices with an occasional burst of sound as one or other of the occupants raised the tempo. I had barely stopped before the sticky gag was stripped from my mouth, taking with it a couple of days' worth of nascent beard, the guard turning swiftly back towards the door. At the sound of his deferential knock the talking stopped and the old wooden latch sprang up with a sharp click, allowing the door to be pushed outwards by someone waiting on the other side.

By this time I was getting used to being shoved around, but I wasn't ready for the painful blow between the shoulder blades that caused me to measure my length on the cool marble floor. I tried to get up, but a merciless foot in the small of my back meant I simply sprawled forward again, this time connecting my head painfully with the hard floor. "Be still, boy." The words brooked absolutely no argument and recognising the voice of my tormentor, I contented myself with moving just my eyes as I tried to assess the surroundings (this was becoming something of a habit). What I saw did little to reassure me. Ranged around the room on lush Turkish carpets, five swarthy, bearded men in flowing jalabiyas[1] sat cross-legged, drinking the ubiquitous thick black Turkish coffee laced with ginger from small, brightly patterned coffee bowls, the handle-free cups so beloved by coastal Arabs. One of them drew slowly on a hookah and except for the fat one in the middle, whose puffy, calculating eyes were fixed steadily on Giuseppe, the rest were staring straight at me. But it was the arrogant disdain and the speculation I could see quite clearly forming in the row of hooded, almost unblinking eyes that, despite the very palpable menace directed at me, finally triggered a response in me other than abject surrender. Thoroughly riled and probably rendered stupid through exhaustion, I mustered all the venom I could and, looking straight at the fat Arab, advised the lot of them to go roast in Hell. Which probably wasn't the brightest thing I could have done in the circumstances.

* * *

By the time the overnight train drew into Mombasa, Roz had been up and about for some time, watching the flat open grasslands and scattered game give way to the gentle slopes and swaying palms of the coastal region. The tiny, old-fashioned basin in the corner of her sleeping compartment with its dark mahogany cover, latched with a silvery hook, had served well enough. Morning tea had appeared promptly and efficiently at six, delivered by the hand of a shy young African waiter who neatly arranged her newly gleaming shoes at the foot of the bunk. Green blankets with a central grey stripe bearing the legend 'East African Railways' stitched down their entire length lay piled in the corner and her meagre belongings were tightly strapped into the old rucksack now propped upright against the pillows. For most of the night Roz had lain awake, rocking to the rhythm of the bustling train. Every so often a whistle announced yet another stop on the long journey to the coast and in the darkness she had heard the sound of children as they ran up and down beside the hissing, steam-swathed coaches, shouting their wares in high-pitched, laughing voices. She could have bought anything from a bottle of coke to a pineapple, from flip-flops cut straight out of old tyres to packs of Camel cigarettes, universally assumed to be rather too closely acquainted with their namesake's regular by-products. But her mind was elsewhere, endlessly speculating on what might have happened, thoughts running pointlessly down blind alleys, recreating a thousand different scenarios as the night hours dragged her along through well-rehearsed fears. Where to begin her search? How to find me, a needle in the proverbial haystack? What to do when she did find me? However, lulled by the train's hypnotic cadence, she had finally slept, but not before revisiting the strange moment in the Moiben church. A bizarre encounter – and 'encounter' was the only way in which she could think to describe it – the experience being beyond the realms of anything she had faced previously. An event she could neither deny nor forget. There had been something curiously reassuring about the overwhelming sense of a very real presence and, as she mulled it over in the dark, swaying cab, the feeling of well-being that had so captivated her at the time stole quietly back and the balm of reassurance drained away the last barriers to peaceful sleep. Drifting, still just conscious, her mind teasing the final vestiges of thought, she knew there was something there of momentous importance, if only she could put her finger on it. Something or someone. And then had come the deep shadows of sleep.

Well, now it was morning, the night and its fears were behind her and it was time to get going, to start the hard part. Thinking aloud, the words "Copper Kettle" jumped unbidden to her lips. She could do far worse than visit its cool, coffee-laden atmosphere, its uplifting hustle and bustle. Hefting the rucksack, she stepped lightly down from the carriage and started looking for a taxi. There would at least be a satisfying breakfast to be had at the Copper Kettle and, being such a well-known watering hole, it would probably be full of settlers on their way to work. Maybe even someone she knew.

The flurry of hard-pressed waiters and the luxurious smell of freshly ground coffee, the world's finest, transported all the way from the sprawling farms of Kiambu far to the north, dispelled the last vestiges of drowsiness, and Roz revelled in the familiar clamour and heat of the dusty, coastal capital. Ordering from the restaurant's comprehensive array of fruit and well-stuffed omelettes, she leaned back and studied the faces around her. So far she recognised no one and there had been no cheery greeting from any of the many men and women scattered around the room. The staff's constant chatter as they threaded their way between the closely packed tables brought memories of her beloved Malindi flooding back, and she felt content to simply relax and wait. She was certain she would recognise someone sooner or later. After all, there weren't that many whites living along the coast and it tended to be a somewhat introvert, reserved society, adept at recognising its own. She needed a base from which to operate and by time-honoured custom, hospitality would be open and generous.

Half an hour passed and she was just finishing her third cup of sugar-laced black coffee, when a shadow fell across the table and a loud voice, thick with Dutch overtones, announced itself as belonging to one Malcolm. "Roz, it's good to see you. Thought I might find you here. Your Dad called me yesterday and asked me to look out for you. The old man's a bit worried, but I said we'd see you alright and Jill's getting the spare room ready. You remember me? Always a sucker for a gorgeous lady and they don't come much more gorgeous than you."

Roz studied the tall, red-necked settler standing relaxed beside her in his all-purpose khaki shorts and sweat-patched bush jacket. Piercing eyes enlivened by a glint of kindness stared out at her from below a broad forehead, dispelling her sudden suspicion of mockery. A heavily unshaven jaw cluttered with the chewed stub of a half-smoked cigar and hands the size of meat plates completed the picture. There was no mistaking him and no way could she have forgotten. Ever since she could walk Malcolm and Jill Joubert had been part of her parents' close circle of friends, and his booming voice an integral part of childhood memory. His heavy, at times impenetrable Afrikaans accent and ready wit were always the centre of female attention, whenever there was a get-together and the chance of an ale or three. Roz smiled her relief and welcome, standing to receive a bear hug, which she returned with interest: the smoky, slightly stale smell of him transporting her instantly back to her youth.

"Oh, Malcolm, am I pleased to see you. Join me for a coffee, won't you?" She signalled the waiter who came hurrying over with fresh coffee and a cup that almost vanished in the big man's paw, about the only description that could do justice to such a huge hand. Settling himself, Malcolm had soon relit the foul-smelling stub and sniffed in appreciation at the thick black liquid swirling around his cup.

"So tell me. What's going on and who's the lucky lad?" For twenty minutes he listened in silence while Roz started right back at the moment the family had left Malindi to head for Moiben and a new life. She described her first meeting with me and all that had transpired since: our growing friendship; my sudden disappearance; her fears for my safety; her utter certainty that I was innocent of the accusations levelled against me; and her unswerving ambition to find me before the police did. Finally, in halting tones, she let him see into her soul, into the real reason, the one he had already guessed at – the passionate, tender first love that was driving this crusade and, with that confirmation, he understood perfectly.

"Come on, young lady, let's get you back home first, then we can have a think about where we start searching." Malcolm hefted the rucksack and Roz followed him meekly to the battered, open-topped Jeep standing just outside, a much treasured 'leftover' from the big Afrikaner's wartime exploits, the ones no one cared to ask about, not if they valued his friendship.

"Jill's looking forward to seeing you again and she won't thank me for keeping you here." With the warm air riffling her hair and the comforting sound of Malcolm's voice rising above the engine roar, Roz was momentarily almost able to forget her quest, letting herself succumb to the coast's mystical delights. But even so her eyes never stopped their automatic roving, always on the lookout for an 'out-of-place' white face and one face in particular, a face whose features were indelibly etched on her mind and heart. Mine.

CHAPTER 17

And that face was in the process of being judiciously rearranged. I suppose I should have guessed, but I didn't really appreciate I was about to journey into a pit of emotional and spiritual darkness far beyond anything I could have imagined. Descent into the very Hell I had invited Giuseppe and his friends to visit really began with that simple act of defiance. True, forty-eight hours of torment had already left me in considerable shock, alone, disorientated, and with my world turned upside down. But I should have known that retribution for my defiance would be as swift as it was merciless. With barely a glance and only a single, guttural word to the guard standing in the shadows behind me, the fat Arab had set in train my utter humiliation, and the short leather sjambok[1] in the hand of a fully paid-up psychopath had begun its work quickly and efficiently. If you can equate efficiency with ruthless, bloody mayhem. There was nothing I could do except curl up and try to protect at least my head, but even that was futile. By the time the ordeal was over, fresh blood smeared everything. My face was swelling fast, my arms felt as though they were broken and the searing pain around my groin was beyond description. An uncompromising message had been delivered, loud and clear. Even I couldn't miss it.

"Now get up." I tried to keep things simple. But even breathing was hard between my pulverised lips and the bloody gaps left by a couple of missing teeth. I can just about remember staggering to a vaguely upright position to stand swaying against the pull of the leash still held in my guard's hand. There was little I could do about my body but, to my surprise and moderate satisfaction, I discovered that my spirit remained unbowed, ready to fight back, albeit in its own particular way, and any onlookers could have been forgiven for missing the signs. But something of the gritty, determined attitude that had marked out the early years, before my father had all but broken me, was clawing its way out of hibernation. The earlier moment of defiance had itself surprised me. But it gave me a modicum of comfort to know I'd given faint notice of my presence, even if only to myself. For one fleeting second I'd taken the initiative. For all the searing agony, that was at least something to cling to. I wasn't always going to be the dumb animal they could simply ignore. But I must admit I was growing more apprehensive by the minute. Why had the beating been ordered by the Arab and not Giuseppe? The dynamics of what I had seen in those brief moments were enough to tell me this had been a meeting of equals. Well, Giuseppe obviously thought so and, equally clearly, he was providing the Arabs with something important and – judging by the number in the room – he was providing something they all wanted. Which wasn't likely to be just ivory. Ivory simply wasn't that valuable.

And then cutting through the fog of the beating, an image of hessian-covered parcels came into focus. Together with something I had seen in the *East African Standard*. Pictures of police crouching over similar packages, several torn open, with gouts of some white substance spilling out. The melodramatic headlines screaming 'drugs haul' in a bold and outsized font right across the front page. And, in rather smaller print, speculation that the drug runners were not averse to a little slavery on the side. As for the drugs, who knew what they were or where they were destined? Far more chilling in the circumstances was my recollection of the line about slavery. And this was a thought that was beginning to make rather more sense. True, my captors had brought drugs right through the country, just as the newspaper articles had suggested. Equally true, narcotics were nothing new by way of trade from West Africa, where Congolese rebels were growing vast quantities of hashish and opium in the fertile lands they had occupied since well before confronting their Belgian colonisers. Even I had heard about the hard-to-find, lonely farms hacked out of the raw forests of the Congo where, it was generally believed, the bulk of the narcotics were being grown. First shipped across country to the East African coast, then by sea to Ceylon, then out across the world.

The problem agitating the papers and the one on which they seemed to focus was the Kenyan police who had, so far, failed to get anywhere near the real power behind the criminal throne. Contenting themselves purely with chance discoveries on those infrequent occasions when they stumbled on a shipment more by luck than judgement. Even with their monumental mismanagement, they had still occasionally succeeded in rounding up low-level minders shipping insignificant loads in clapped-out vans. But when it came to the big boys, their on-the-spot intelligence was virtually non-existent, and it showed. They desperately needed someone on the inside, someone with the guts and background to fit in, but they simply didn't have the resources, so they never got that close. The sordid drugs and slavery empire, headed up by a megalomaniac known to have shot and terrorised his way through every confrontation he'd ever faced, had only drawn encouragement from the many police failures. By all accounts this capo now considered himself untouchable. And it was all coming back to me; the newspaper's insistent demands for the death penalty and the withering contempt the neighbours held for the scum who killed so indiscriminately, crushing anyone foolish enough to get in their way as dispassionately as they would an annoying insect.

Hence, with shocking clarity, I knew exactly who was holding me. But unlike the police, I was also beginning to understand where the true horror lay. And it wasn't in drugs. Yet even as I reached this stomach-churning conclusion, I was already out of date in the fast-moving world that had wrapped its insidious tentacles around me. Giuseppe grunted, nodded brusquely at the men opposite him, stood, signed to my guard to hand my tether to the psychopath and promptly left. With a leer, that bald-headed maniac, who had worked me over so comprehensively, jerked on the rope and led me out, back down the stairs, but this time further on down, below the ground floor into the coolness of an underground passageway.

I was sure I was going to throw up. With my mind numbed by shock and in growing despair, I stumbled along behind him, fully aware that any opposition to my bull-necked, bald-headed guard would bring instant retribution and this time, with no one else around, who knew what the outcome might be? Right now, I knew I could take no more physical abuse. All I wanted was to stay alive and if that meant doing exactly as I was told and keeping quiet, so be it for now. Barely able to see by the feeble light of a lone bulb, we turned into what appeared to be little more than a black hole in the wall, but one that proved to be the entrance to some sort of low tunnel and after several steps my shoulder struck against something solid as I was spun round. At the same time I heard the sound and felt the pull of a razor-sharp knife slicing through the bindings that held my wrists. And then, with the rope still dropping around me and a sharp shove accompanied by the sound of a door slamming shut, I found myself in pitch darkness, with only the muffled padding of swiftly retreating sandals to disturb the stillness.

In seconds I discovered that I was not only alone, but incarcerated in almost total silence. So quiet and still was the cell that I could even hear the weird susurration of blood pulsing through my ears. "*What little might be left*," I thought sourly. Flexing slowly, trying to moderate the worst of the pain, I rubbed my wrists and arms in an effort to get the muscles to relax back to normal, but was rewarded only with a prickling numbness, which soon gave way to the excruciating pain of a fully restored blood flow. And, one by one, the contusions left by the expertly wielded sjambok sprang back to life until throbbing waves of agony lacerated me to the very core. Sick with nameless fears, caught in an anguish of grief over the full extent of my predicament and rocking to the detonations of pain in my tortured body, my desperate circumstances threatened to overwhelm me. And at that moment, for two pins I could once again have contemplated taking my own life. Except it seemed, on brief and more sober reflection, that I wasn't quite that far down and out yet. Not quite. Not if I could get a grip on my trembling self. It took a deeply physical effort, but I finally steeled myself to explore this limited world.

Moving felt like wading through treacle and my mind constantly threatened to slip away, to spill over into the terror of madness, almost as though it was being pulled by someone or something else. It was weird, but gradually I summoned the strength to overcome the appeal of surrender and instead, slowly and carefully, elevated my arms. With all sight and sound removed, my senses were reduced to touch and smell and I have to say I wasn't too impressed with either. The moment my hands went up, I discovered I had barely an arm's length to left or right. The depth of the cell was little better. It took only a single step before some sixth sense warned me to stop. An exploratory foot discovered a rock wall little more than a couple of inches in front of my face. Clearly, I wasn't even going to be able to lie down and it took no more than a couple of seconds to determine there was nothing but the rough floor to sit on either. But it was the nauseating smell that really got to me. The coarse mixture of decay, urine and faeces that rose in waves every time my feet moved was getting close to unbearable and I had to fight down several involuntary spasms to stop myself adding to the sum of putrefaction plastering the floor. Standing there in abject misery, head hanging in almost hopeless surrender, a raft of conflicting thoughts burst in upon me and for a moment I again lost all rationality.

How could I expect to survive? Even assuming I lasted long

enough to find a way out, surely, it wouldn't be long before some fatal disease contaminated the lacerations peppering my body? And what hope of escape anyway? Who could possibly mount a rescue? No one who mattered knew I was alive, never mind where I was. Even my gaoler appeared to have abandoned me without food or water. Moreover, for the first time in my life, I consciously gave way to the horror of claustrophobia, feeling my senses reel and rebel in the coffin-sized area. For the space of several minutes I couldn't stop jerking and twitching convulsively as I fought to contain an irrational fear of being buried alive. For one long and ghastly moment reason itself teetered on the edge of insanity and only the sound of a long drawn-out howl bursting from my lips anchored me back into reality. The feral sound echoed around the underground cellar, slowly dying away as it bounced from wall to wall, leaving me trembling from the strength of raw emotion torn loose in that profound anguish.

But the reality check was precisely what was needed, because now I knew the odds. It was fight or capitulate then and there. Which really marked the beginning of my resistance as, breath by laboured breath, beginning with the effort of bringing my hyperventilating lungs under control, I embarked on a struggle without end. At the same time and with a profound effort, I managed to wrap my throbbing arms around myself to gain some measure of control over the intense shaking that wracked my body. And from elsewhere deep within me, I found a power whose authority amazed me, but which seemed to assist in the conscious subjugation of the remnants of seething panic still waltzing around, just on the edge of perception. Gritting my teeth until my jaw ached and digging my fingernails deep into my palms, I gradually fought back to a semblance of sanity. And slowly, to my intense satisfaction, I felt the hysterical dread give way to logic as, unseen in the all-pervading darkness, the hot tears slowed and yielded to this newfound determination. And as they did, I told myself firmly that I would survive, promised myself I would never again let go. Thus ever so slowly, I reached a plateau of calm from where I truly began to believe I could make it through, whatever might be thrown at me. It made little rational sense, but it beat anything else I could think of.

CHAPTER 18

And in the surrounding darkness that meant nothing to them, a praetorian guard of recently arrived angels took up a defensive box formation around me and then faced outwards. With only occasional glances towards each other for mutual encouragement, they reserved their taunting smiles for the slavering pack of red-eyed, repulsive demons swarming not far above their heads. A pack compelled to retreat and now holding at a distance sufficient to allow themselves the feeling that really, if only they could summon the courage and discipline to attack en masse, they could take the angels down.

Inhabitants of another world, they were ignoring what I could not – passing backwards and forwards around and through my prison walls with impunity, as though they didn't exist, which as far as they were concerned was as good as fact. Always just out of sword range, they slavered over the thought of me, their intended victim, from whom they had so recently been forced to flee, hissing and snarling at each other in their efforts to stay clear of the angels, lashing out with spiny fingers and sharp stiletto blades whenever one of their own kind got in the way. Brave enough amongst themselves, they were never quite able to defy the immense and dazzling immortals who now stood sentry just outside the four corners of my cell. Guardians of the insignificant lump of flesh and blood slumped against the cell wall, they waited quietly, hands resting lightly on the pommels of their flame-like swords, the razor-sharp tips of which seemed to pierce even the rock upon which their owners stood.

Light glittered along the folds of their fine-woven, thigh-length togas stirring gently in fluid movements that had little to do with any recognisable gravity. Breastplates of pure gold matched by dazzling gold greaves defended them to the front. Across their backs were slung wide silvery white shields embossed with what looked like liquid red lacquer in the shape of a vertical cross, the whole glowing with all the appearance of a living light, so swiftly did a myriad of vivid hues coruscate across their broad surfaces. Completing their protective armour, magnificent red-crested helmets, gold with beautifully worked silver inlays, covered their heads and lent an air of quiet, intimidating authority. Swarming and muttering angrily, the cloud of satanic spirits undulated back and forth as though some ethereal wind blew them, while they threatened and darted in the hope of getting back to me, their unwitting victim. One more moment with me was all they asked, one more moment to finish what they had begun, to savour the forbidden invasion of my body and send me spiralling down through unbearable pain into sudden, grisly suicide. Death, their ultimate spectator sport, their definitive thrill, the final obscenity each longed to inflict on every mortal before their due time.

For long moments the angels stood still, relaxed, almost indifferent to the gruesome creatures flitting round above them. But then a dozen or so, gaining courage in numbers, surged too close. For a second it looked as though, between them, they might even succeed in achieving a co-ordinated attack and actually break through to me but, in the blink of an eye, the two nearest angels launched themselves into action. As one, they stepped swiftly forward and upward, whipping their long, laser-like swords with the expert precision of prolonged practice to cover the six-dimensional hemisphere they were constrained to defend. Behind them, the guard commander spoke quietly and with utter assurance. "To God be the victory."

Perhaps he failed to understand the import, but the nearest demon, bolder than the rest and wearing the insignia of a captain, launched himself straight at Israfel, one of the guards. Instinctively, the latter's sword arced down flat onto the creature's head, as though disdaining the inconvenience of a kill, and the snarling beast was flung backwards to bounce against his nearest subordinate, setting off a chain reaction deep into the rushing horde. Quick as lightning, the second angel thrust forward, impaling another adversary on the end of his weapon before cutting swiftly down then up to split him end to end. But the marauders were quick too, and for a moment there was a melee of cutting, thrusting swords as they tried to take advantage of greater numbers. For several seconds no words were spoken, but the disorganised and hellish rabble was no match for the angels' co-ordinated speed and precision. Nor did their shrunken, withered limbs oozing with undressed sores and rank with the odour of sulphur permit them to deploy any meaningful opposition. They were comprehensively and immediately out-fought and they knew it. Leaving several dead and a dozen or so nursing gaping wounds as they dragged themselves weakly out of sword range, the rest backed off far enough for the four guardians to once again stand easy.

Simultaneously, Tamar, their field commander, acknowledged a voice coming directly to his ear alone, then, nodding, he turned to the others. "The captain of the Lord's Host has ordered that all those involved in this insurrection, dead, wounded or living, are to be dispatched to the pit of Hell. Apollyon[(1)], the keeper of the Deep Pit, can have them. They have wantonly overstepped the mark and done too much harm and there is to be no appeal allowed and no quarter given. This time they went too far."

His voice was deliberately loud, designed to carry to the belligerent mob hovering far enough from the guardians so as not to provoke them, but not so far that they couldn't take advantage of any perceived weakness. But Tamar's words, ringing out with serene authority in a voice that sounded somewhat like a river thundering over a precipice, changed everything. As the significance of the verdict dawned on them, a wave of sound like the wailing of souls already in torment rolled out of their midst, growing in sobbing volume with every passing second. "Not there, not there, it isn't time yet, it isn't 'Judgement Day' yet. It isn't fair, it isn't fair."

Yelping despair mixed with frightened, pointless defiance poured out of them as they flew in an ever tighter, swirling pattern, each lost in the torture of their own depravity, sunk into the total isolation of corruption. Eternally lost and completely beyond rescue through their own free choice. And as the howling lament rose in pitch, those on the edges of the spinning mass got their final look at retribution in the form of a squadron of immense, dazzling angels who appeared as if from nowhere, dividing with military precision to surround and drive the demons. Every one of whom had once been a contemporary of their appointed executioners until they had cast in their lot with Satan, rebelled against God and been thrown out of Heaven.

Whirling a vast net of silver cords, the avenging angels closed relentlessly until, with pinpoint accuracy, they launched an inescapable trap, like fishermen throwing a weighted net ahead of their boat, and promptly drew it tight. No sooner was that done than the newly arrived Squadron Commander, an incredible being of ethereal perfection and masculine splendour, strode forward to swing his blade in a wide arc below the writhing ball of doomed evil. And – as though the very space–time continuum had been rent – a great fissure opened in the living rock. Far, far below, outlined in the awful glow of what looked like red-hot lava, the colossal, fire-blackened demon named Apollyon glowered upwards in enraged anticipation. And in the same instance, the depraved globule of netted misery was swallowed forever as the earth's maw snapped shut above them, once again impenetrable, leaving them lost to Heaven and Earth as if they'd never been. In their wake, only disciplined ranks of the invincible host stood at ease in mid-space, knowledge of a job well done brightening the moment.

And in my cell, totally oblivious to all this, it yet seemed for a moment as though the gloom had lifted slightly, almost as if some profound darkness had been momentarily pierced. For the second time since my arrival. Or was it simply imagination?

CHAPTER 19

Jill's heart went out to the vulnerable young girl sitting beside her and she put an arm out to hug the slim shoulders still shaking from the storm of receding tears. They were sitting together on one of the comfortable, faded old sofas. This one nestled into the far corner of the veranda, tucked away from the glare of the sun that was painting everything around them with an almost silvery sheen of heat. In the distance, through the light green tops of the palms marching down to the wide sandy beach, they could just glimpse the brilliant blue of deep water beyond the reef. Far out at sea, the vivid colours were complemented by an occasional dhow on slow passage north, white triangular sail stretched to the southern monsoon winds that riffled the long rollers arriving all the way from Australia. A tranquil, idyllic scene, in complete contrast to the frenzied distress that, for an hour or so, had been in danger of gaining the upper hand in the Joubert household.

Secretly, Jill harboured very little hope that Paul could be found, but she was impressed by the courage and tenacity Roz had shown over the past few days of tedious, non-stop searching and she wasn't about to dent the girl's hopes any further. "Come on, Roz, I know it's tough, but I'm sure you'll find him. He can't have vanished completely. He has to be somewhere and anyway, Malcolm won't let you down. He'll give you all the help he can. I'm sure Paul will be OK and you said yourself you're convinced he's still alive."

Turning her head, Roz managed to raise a watery smile, grateful for the real friend Jill was rapidly becoming and indebted to her wholehearted support.

"I know you're right, but it's just so hard. We've walked miles and drawn a complete blank with everyone we've talked to. Nobody's seen him, or even had the slightest idea where he might be."

For the eighth straight day in a row, Roz had been up since before dawn and out with Malcolm, tramping the early morning back streets of downtown Mombasa, braving the often gut-wrenching smells slithering out from the open drains, stepping delicately round the less recognisable deposits smearing the cobbled passageways, and stopping to talk to every trader, every early rambler and every late street walker who chanced across their path. They had begun at the railway station and worked their way outwards, following the only road into town, sometimes driving, sometimes walking and always stopping to question anyone they passed, asking the same questions over and over again: "Have you seen or heard about a young white man with thick ginger hair and covered in brown freckles – probably very sunburned?"

The fact that he was almost certainly on his own, without money and in need of help, should have helped concentrate minds, they felt, but few seemed to have any interest. Stubbornly they had pressed on, however, covered from head to toe in the ubiquitous white coral dust and sweating profusely under the stinging heat. But no matter how often they asked, every enquiry drew a complete blank, occasionally accompanied by a sympathetic stare and, rather less often, an offer to contact them if the 'red bwana' turned up. Each day their search had gone on until the setting sun called a necessary halt to progress and a welcome retirement to a cold shower and an even colder Tembo beer. To Malcolm, the only really sensible end to any day, never mind the sort they were currently experiencing.

Slowly at first, but with aching feet and a hoarsening voice, Roz had begun to wallow in the gathering pangs of discouragement. The search that had seen her begin with such high hopes now seemed almost futile. Except for one tenuous possibility that had surfaced right at the very beginning, but which had failed to actually register with them, there had been nothing. A single jarring note amidst a myriad of facts filed away at the back of their collective memory. Filed and forgotten, destined to eventually drop forever from the mental map they were building. They had a tentative lead, but they didn't know it.

One of the first people they had questioned, a station porter, had been too hasty in reply, too shifty-eyed in response, too quick to press on with work and it was this that had registered, albeit subconsciously, and neither of them had realised it.

Now today, the eighth successive day of searching, they were back home early, having finally acknowledged to each other the hopelessness of continuing as they were. They needed to sift through what little they had gleaned, gather their thoughts and perhaps re-plan their strategy. Something different, an alternative approach, a new discernment was needed, if they were to break the cycle of endless failure and move into the realms of progress. And whatever they came up with would have to major on luck, because the way things were progressing, they were unlikely to achieve anything more than premature exhaustion. Certainly no obvious lead from a rapidly cooling, if not entirely imaginary, trail.

Eventually, sensing the storm was over, Malcolm gingerly put his head round the corner. Like so many men before him, the moment feminine emotion had come to the fore he had made himself conspicuous by absence. "Hi, how're you doing?"

A sniff greeted him, followed quickly by a proffered hand. "I'm sorry, Malcolm. You've been so good, but I just couldn't help it. I don't know, it all seems too much at the moment. But it won't happen again, I promise."

He grinned at her. "Don't you worry, Roz, I understand. Anyway, while I was outside I was doing some thinking. Going over everything. We've been at it non-stop for over a week now and nobody admits to knowing anything, nobody's seen anything.

But do you remember the porter we talked to at the station? Almost the first person we saw? The more I think about him, the more I'm convinced something wasn't quite 'kosher' about his reaction. We've talked to all sorts of people since, but as I think back, his attitude now seems all wrong to me. He was definitely different. I may be mistaken, but I have a feeling he knew something he wasn't telling. I've racked my brains, but it's all I can come up with and, if you recall, he's one of the few who wouldn't look us in the eye. Does that ring any sort of bell? At the time I didn't think too much of it, but mulling it over just now, it seemed to me that of all the people we've stopped, his response was the least convincing. OK, lots of them didn't want to know, but at least they said so up front. In fact, the more I considered it, the more I wonder why we didn't spot it at the time. But then, hindsight is a wonderful thing. Of course, there's no guarantee this will lead anywhere, but I think we should at least go and see him again. It's a long shot, but I can't think of anything else we could usefully do."

CHAPTER 20

It was nearly evening by the time Malcolm and Roz arrived at the railway station and little was happening. Certainly, all the porters were gone and only the occasional cleaner could be seen doing anything at all in the waning heat that still struck fiercely from the flagged surfaces of the platforms. Quickly they found and followed a sign which indicated the way to the Station Master's office, but even he seemed to have called it a day. However, they could hear someone in the adjoining office, boasting the name 'Mr Hasim' on the door, so, without hesitation, Malcolm knocked and walked in. Mr Hasim was sitting at his desk with the air of one who knows he is indispensable but, to his later regret, Malcolm simply did what he always did – strode over to the front of the dilapidated piece of furniture that passed as a desk and looked the man squarely in the eye.

"Evening, I'm Bwana Joubert," he said, trying to sound positive.

Hasim looked up, startled by the unexpected intrusion, the unmistakeable air of command. However, unusually for a local Government official, he didn't rise, simply motioned to the only chair. And even more ominously, he appeared totally unmoved by their sudden and somewhat late appearance. "I'll try to overlook the fact that you've barged in here uninvited. So what do you want?"

Nonplussed, Malcolm nevertheless responded hurriedly: "We're looking for a porter we met here about a week ago. He was loading mailbags into a train over in the freight area and we'd like to speak to him quite urgently. I don't know his name, but presumably we can find out from your work roster? I'd be grateful if we could have a look at it, find his details and discover when he's next due in to work." With their earlier mistake very much in mind, Malcolm was watching particularly closely and his early suspicions seemed instantly confirmed by the response. The moment he'd talked about a meeting with one of the staff, the secretary's frown had frozen and his features darkened. Almost as though a switch had been thrown.

When the reply came, it was peremptory and defiant: "So, who are you and why exactly do you want to speak to one of my men?"

Taken aback by the man's hostile attitude, Malcolm instinctively reached for his wallet and, in expectation of the usual reason for making things difficult, swiftly extracted a sheaf of twenty-shilling notes, sliding them across the table towards the secretary. Who ostentatiously left them where they were, before looking straight past Malcolm.

"Obviously you aren't from the police." The cold delivery of this masterpiece of deduction was accompanied by a dismissive flick of the finger, scattering the notes back across the desk towards Malcolm. "You should be more careful with your money. I might think you're trying to bribe me and the police would take a very dim view of that."

Realising he'd made a fundamental error, Malcolm began to back-pedal as fast as he could. "No, we aren't the police, that's true, and I'm not here to cause you any trouble, but I would like to talk to your man, because he might be able to help us." Things seemed to have gone from bad to worse and Malcolm wasn't quite sure why. Clearly, he'd got off on the wrong foot and in doing so, had managed to lose the initiative. Moreover, he wasn't particularly happy with the openly lascivious way in which the man was beginning to eye Roz. Making an instant decision he determined not to tell Hasim what he clearly wanted to know – the date, time and place when they'd talked to his man. Sufficient information from which to work out who it was for himself. Malcolm might get it wrong from time to time, but long experience with people had made him something of a connoisseur of character and it had, above all, taught him to deal with individuals on the basis of what he saw and heard. Now his instincts were clamouring for attention, telling him in no uncertain terms that Hasim was bad news. Why, he didn't know, but something clearly wasn't right and it was time to retreat.

"So I'll ask you again and failing an answer, I may have to ring the police. Who are you and who's this?" he said, indicating Roz with his chin. The tone had hardened and the voice taken on a barbed edge, but by now Malcolm had no intention of responding and with the question still ringing in their ears, he beckoned to Roz and strode out of the room. Not until they reached the Jeep did he speak and then only to urge Roz to get in as fast as possible. Quickly he drove away, trying to get out of sight before Hasim thought to record the number plate.

A mile down the road and safely out of sight, he drew into the side and cut the engine. "I don't know what it is, Roz, but there's a lot about that man that really worries me. Did you notice how quickly the whole atmosphere changed as soon as I mentioned interviewing one of his staff? He's definitely hiding something and I'm pretty sure he knows why we want to see his man."

Roz looked at him, one delicately arched eyebrow raised in uncertainty. "So what do you think we should do?"

"I think we should try again, but this time wait until Hasim's gone and then have a look at the noticeboards – we can try the staff rooms. I'll bet there's a list of duties somewhere and if we can glean the name, we stand a better chance of finding our man, even if someone tries to keep him out of sight. Hopefully, they won't work out who we're interested in and he'll be back at work sometime tomorrow. But we'd better be sure. So first, we need to get off this road, or Hasim might spot us and then the proverbial could really hit the fan."

The station was long dark and almost silent when they slunk back in, only the occasional pale security light providing visual cues, whilst somehow accentuating the inky blackness that gripped the bulk of the sprawling yards. As they had expected, the night watchmen were nowhere to be seen, probably already hunkered down, well out of sight, for the night's 'work'. It didn't take them long to find what was obviously a staff room, cluttered with battered old chairs and strewn with dirty cups. Pinned to the wall were several well-thumbed pieces of paper, but in pride of place was exactly what they were looking for. The only problem was there were quite a few names listed under the previous Saturday morning's porter roster, but it was clear that the same crew were in most mornings and the coming dawn should be no exception. That was all Malcolm needed to know. With the names of the porters hastily scribbled down, the pair of them left as swiftly and silently as they had come, glad to be out of it and on their way home. But by four o'clock next morning, Malcolm was back, loitering alone, screened behind an enormous bougainvillea that had draped itself along the ticket department wall, almost custom-made for anyone needing camouflage. From there he could watch for his man and keep a weather-eye out for any unwelcome sign of Hasim.

Sure enough, it wasn't long before the men began to drift in to work and that was when he got his first lucky break. The man he was looking for was one of the first and Malcolm recognised him the moment he ambled into view. He let him saunter past and followed quietly round the back, towards the workers' entrance. It was darker here and less obvious. Malcolm didn't want to startle him unduly, but he didn't want anyone else around while he was asking questions either, because he had a pretty shrewd idea the porter would be less than forthcoming. Precisely the sort of situation where his superior height and weight could be used to intimidate the opposition. And he was right. The moment the porter saw Malcolm he bolted, but in two enormous strides

Malcolm had him by the arm and nailed him against a wall.

"Quiet, or I'll break your neck! I just want answers to a few questions. Answer and you'll be OK." He might as well have told the man to fly. His eyes rolled wildly, desperately searching for help, but there was none to be had. "Don't even think to call out or I'll break your neck and the sooner you answer me, the sooner I'll let you go. Now, you obviously remember me and I'm willing to bet you remember me asking you about a ginger-haired white man. I'll ask you again and this time, I want the truth. Did you see my friend?"

There was no mistaking the reaction and Malcolm wondered what it was that was scaring the porter enough to clam up, despite being faced with immediate violence. Surely it couldn't just be Hasim? Anyway, this was obviously going to take longer than he had anticipated and gripping the man hard, Malcolm pushed him further into the shadows and away from the entrance where he could hear the sound of others approaching. There was no time for the niceties now, so he twisted the man's arm hard behind his back and forced his chin up with an arm round his throat.

"Start talking, or I really will break your neck."

He could feel the man's Adam's apple bobbing wildly and released the pressure slightly, letting him take in a great gasping breath, but keeping sufficient pressure to emphasise the threat. It was patently clear the man believed Malcolm meant what he said, because as soon as the pressure eased, the words poured out of him.

"Bwana, it's nothing to do with me. I just do what I'm paid to do and keep my mouth shut. If I don't, they'll kill me. I have no choice." The agonised voice trailed off in a whisper.

"Right, well now you do. Five seconds from now you'll be dead anyway if you don't tell me who you are, what you know and who you're afraid of." Fortunately for Malcolm, his man had no idea he was bluffing and had no intention of doing him any serious harm.

"I saw your friend, bwana. He was with the slaver who controls the drug trade. He comes here often, but I don't know his name. Hasim tells us when they're coming and your friend was with them last time. He was tied up and they took him away in a gharry[(1)], but I don't know where." Almost as if pleading for his life, he continued. "One of the drivers is a friend of mine and he drove the gharry your friend was in. It was about a week ago. That's all I know."

"So tell me your name and the name of your friend and where he lives."

"Jelani, bwana, I'm Jelani," he groaned. "But please, you'll get us both killed if I tell you my friend's name." The sudden crack of stretching ligaments settled the argument. "Jomo, bwana. Jomo. He lives down by the creek behind the Muslim Institute. But he can't speak to you. His tongue was cut out for talking too much."

Satisfied he was at last getting something of the truth, Malcolm relaxed his grip again. "This had better be right or I'll be back for you. In the meantime, if you say anything about me, Hasim will get to hear that you implicated him in drug running. And I have friends in the police."

Released, Jelani stumbled away, shoulders hunched, fear evident in the whites of his startled eyes as he backed rapidly towards the platforms and the rest of his crew.

CHAPTER 21

Quickly, Malcolm found the row of dilapidated huts perched in front of the mangrove swamps at the head of the northern creek. Reeking of poverty, they stood forlorn, a little above high-water mark and almost ephemeral in their fragility. Around them the deep holes of massive red coconut crabs peppered the ground, homes to crustaceans that could crack the bones of an unwary foot as easily as they penetrated the bounty of windfall coconuts.

Jelani's directions, although meagre, had been surprisingly exact and in fluent Kiswahili Malcolm questioned the first child he came across, slipping him a summuni[(1)] as he played in the early morning light outside the entrance to his home. Such unexpected riches for a five year old quickly unlocked the little fount of knowledge and it was the work of but a moment to escort the tall white man to the right hut.

A spiral of smoke rose lazily through the woven banana leaf thatch of the selected shelter and the smell of cooking vied unsuccessfully with the overriding stench of nearby open drains. Malcolm rapped the mud and wattle wall and waited in front of the dingy length of cloth serving as a makeshift door. He registered the sudden halt to domestic sounds and sensed the occupant's puzzlement over such an early morning caller, the silence growing rapidly into a loaded question. Finally, renewed shuffling indicated that apprehension had succumbed to curiosity and Malcolm got ready to prevent a repeat of his encounter with Jelani. "Jambo, Jomo. Abari yako?[(2)]" The lilting cadence of the ritual Swahili greeting hung in the air unanswered, vocal reaction being the one response beyond the capability of an aphonic man.

Lifting a corner of the hanging cloth, Jomo came to an abrupt halt, suspicion hijacking the moment. In his eagerness to get started, Malcolm had forgotten Jomo was maimed, unable to speak, until the silence had stretched out to embarrassment. Mortified, his words tumbling over themselves, he began to explain how he had found the place without dropping Jelani in it and barely pausing before going on to outline, as succinctly as he could, the reason for his visit. His reluctant host merely stood stock still until Malcolm drew to an uncertain close. The lines on Jomo's face spoke not just of the vagaries of being poor, which were obviously many, but of special hardship. The suffering and particular horror that accompanies mutilation. On the other hand, the eyes gave little away, but as another awkward silence began to loop its coils around the two men, Jomo finally relented, stood aside and beckoned. Stooping to pass through the low opening, Malcolm stepped into the smoke-charged atmosphere and was grateful when Jomo signed him to sit by the open fire.

No sooner was he seated, mercifully below the thick fog of pollution hanging suspended in slowly moving tendrils down to almost waist height, than Jomo hitched up the kikoi[3] draping him from waist to heel and left. Minutes later he reappeared, leading a young man with the finely chiselled features of the Giriama tribe. It was clear the youth was to be Jomo's spokesman and, relieved, Malcolm began again by renewing his greeting, a salutation returned this time, as the two Africans conversed, using a form of rapid finger, hand and arm touching. Gradually, line by line, Malcolm stitched together the full story behind his search. He explained Roz's part in it and her love for me, their fears for my life, his own wariness over Hasim and his conviction that time was running out. Why, he didn't know, but there was something about the wizened old man sitting mute in front of him that compelled honesty and openness. Jomo listened in stillness, nodding his head occasionally and stirring the fire until Malcolm got to the part where he had allegedly driven me from the station.

At that point Jomo grew suddenly animated, vocal, if that was the word, his hands flying over the interpreter's as he spelt out his reply. Fascinated, Malcolm watched the young Giriama carefully assimilating what was being expressed before turning it into the Swahili language.

"Yes, I saw the red-haired white man of whom you speak, but I know nothing of his fate. Even if I did, why should I tell you? Simply by being here you put me in danger of my life. Am I the first to whom you have spoken? Will I be the last? One word to the right person is all it takes and a hornets' nest will be stirred up and when hornets are angry they look for trouble, attacking anything that moves. You know what has already been done to me, so you will understand when I tell you that if I give anything away, it is to invite trouble. Yet it is true, I hate the men who have ruined my life and care nothing for what they have done. No one leaves their service and lives but, given one chance, I would mutilate them myself or flatten them as carelessly as a cow swats a fly. They are ruthless and have their spies everywhere. If you cross them you must be prepared to kill, or they will surely kill you. Are you the man to do this? I don't think so. You are not like them. You have the appearance, but your eyes tell me you are not a violent man. Men like you do not kill quickly or easily. And that will be your downfall. What if they discover you have been here? They will always find me, no matter how long it takes, because I know too much. Suppose, then, they torture and kill me, what is that to you?" Jomo paused and looked at Malcolm through the thickening haze, waiting for a response. Testing him.

Struck by his candour, Malcolm hesitated, wondering what would convince the old man that he was sincere and trustworthy.

"Mzee, I perceive you are Giriama and you come from a time when loyalty was the measure by which men were judged. When men lived or died by their word to their friends, to their fellow warriors, to their tribe, no matter what the cost. Thus I know you will remember Mtoro. He is of an age with you, a Giriama to his fingertips, much hated by the Government because he was not afraid to demand from them the land he believed they had stolen. Only one other trusted friend has heard this from my lips.

I knew Mtoro well and knew him to be a man of his word, who never made any secret of his commitment to the old ways, or his contempt for the little men to whom a bribe was the only way and who, day by day, inch by inch, stole the reins and trappings of power from their rightful owners. For years he was like a thorn on the path to their bare feet, ridiculing and exposing them wherever and whenever he could. Always, they tried to trap him, to catch him with some falsehood, but they never succeeded. One day during the war, when there was unrest amongst the tribes over conscription, the Governor called a grand conference of all the tribal elders, assuring them their safety would be guaranteed for the course of the meeting. Mtoro went, only to be arrested and detained in gaol the moment the gathering ended. Later he was tried secretly for crimes he did not commit and found guilty, the punishment being death. Word was brought to me and although I stood to lose everything if discovered, I bluffed my way into his cell the night before his execution. With the help of a sympathetic guard, I arranged a suitable distraction and gave Mtoro the opportunity to break out. He fled into exile and had it not been for the war to which I was soon called away, my part in all of this would have been exposed, with inevitable consequences. As it is, the authorities seem to have forgotten and I have not seen Mtoro in many years. However, I believe he is still in contact with the tribal elders in Malindi. Send to them and ask. They will testify that I am to be trusted."

Back home and slaking his thirst with lime juice fresh from the garden, it didn't take Malcolm long to recount all that had passed that morning. What did take the time was explaining to Roz why he had thought it necessary to go without her. Still, Roz could hardly be anything but placated when it was pointed out that since Jomo was taking the trouble to check with the Giriama elders in Malindi, he obviously did have information for which it was worth waiting. The problem would be biding their souls in patient acceptance of the rather slower beat that defined the Giriamas' uniquely African sense of time. So, for three days Roz sat kicking her heels while Malcolm went back to work, catching up on lost hours.

CHAPTER 22

The call, when it came, was precise and to the point. Malcolm was to be told that Jomo could be found at the northwest corner of Fort Jesus that evening. The problem was, Malcolm was unreachable, having gone up country that very afternoon to arrange some business. Roz fumed, but not knowing when he would be back and being absolutely certain Jill would try to prevent a solo foray, she could do nothing except beg a bicycle from a houseboy and swear him to secrecy.

Duly equipped, she set off to cover the three miles into town, relying on Malcolm's description to recognise the man she was due to meet. She found him easily enough, but it took all her charm and some swift talking in fluent Giriama to convince Jomo not to depart in something of a huff over the perceived slight that he, an elder, had been left to deal with a mere girl. Eventually, somewhat mollified by a young white woman who could not only converse in Giriama, but who was clearly acquainted with the social mores so beloved of his generation, Jomo relented.

Together with his young interpreter, they threaded their way through the close-packed streets and alleys, plunging deeper and deeper into the warren of narrow streets that long before the advent of gunpowder had allowed the locals to defend their homes and their ultimate escape hatch – the old harbour. Roz had little difficulty in keeping pace, but in the brooding, unlit alleys she realised it wouldn't take much for her imagination to get the better of her. The absence of normal city sounds didn't help either. So it was unnerving to move in near silence, with nothing said until they eventually stopped in deep shadow outside a tall, whitewashed wall, its ramparts proof against anything but the most determined effort to force entry.

"This is the place where Jomo came with the red-haired man you seek." The interpreter's whispered remark barely carried to Roz as she stood facing the featureless wall. "Jomo was here about two weeks ago and when he left, the white man stayed. Jomo does not know what happened to him, but he knows it was not good. He was being held by the man called Giuseppe, a white slaver, ruthless in all things and one who respects no one. He is one you do not anger. Jomo believes there must have been Arab traders here too, but he did not see them and cannot be certain who or how many. If you want to return, you must remember this place for yourself. Jomo will not come again as it is too dangerous for him. He has nothing more to tell you. Come, we go now."

They turned to leave, but as they did so, an unnatural noise, the suddenly suppressed sound of metal on metal, clanged briefly out from the other side of the gates and for a second they froze where they stood, before retreating further into the shadows. Roz pressed her back as hard as she could against the rough coral blocks behind her, abruptly and keenly aware that she was out of her depth and, as a girl, never mind a white girl, very vulnerable, despite the reassuring presence of the two black men. Anxiously she watched the heavy gates as they were drawn back, surprised by how quietly they swung for such substantial barriers, until she realised they must have been kept well-oiled for just such an occasion of secrecy. No sooner were they fully open than the sound of a car whirring into life and moving off in one swift motion shattered the stillness of the narrow alleyway. Headlights flicked on as the car nosed through the opening and as Roz shrank back the bright lights raked her briefly before the driver turned left down the alley, apparently heading towards the old harbour just a couple of streets away. Temporarily blinded by the unexpected light, they were unable to see who or what was in the car, but the driver obviously had no intention of hanging around long enough to be identified by anyone. Frustrated, Roz listened to the dying sound, satisfied that whoever was involved had not only missed them, but was bound for the tiny space known as Government Square in front of the old harbour, close to the tight-packed warehouses huddled around the docks. Tall and dark, they stood sentinel to the short slipway that, for centuries, had played host to wandering dhows, some of which even now creaked lazily to themselves in the languid rhythms of the inner harbour, their battered hulls spewing water with every rise and fall.

★★★

"Well, what now? Do you think we can find a way in?" Malcolm sank into a chair opposite Roz as she finished speaking. He was far from happy at what she'd done alone, but he watched with sympathy as the tell-tale jump of tightly clenched jaw muscles and the pull of unaccustomed anxiety etched ever more worry lines around her mouth, giving the lie to her almost casual report. It was impossible not to care for this vulnerable young girl who so effortlessly wore her heart on her sleeve but who, for all that, grew in determination with every passing hour. "You say this place is like a fortress and Jomo doesn't know how many there might be inside? One thing we can be certain of is they'll be armed, whoever they are, so, whatever we do, it will have to be done without alerting them. Jomo may well be adamant he left Paul there two weeks ago, but I suspect Paul has been moved on long since. Still, we'll take a look, although I'm convinced it's highly unlikely he's still there. At least we know he was alive then and this is the only lead we're likely to get, so you're absolutely right, we can't ignore it. Which means we really don't have much option, do we? As soon as it's dark tonight, I'll go and take a closer look. See if I can get over the wall while you keep watch." Malcolm raised a hand to stifle the inevitable protest. "I know it could be dangerous, but if you don't want to involve the police, it's the only option we have. I'll give you a promise, though. If I think it's too dangerous, I'll come out, but if I do and we haven't got the information we need, then we have to go to the police. It's that or risk not seeing Paul again."

Malcolm didn't add what he was really thinking, that there was a good chance I was already dead or, at the very least, out of the country and beyond their reach. In which case, as a slave, it could be assumed that I was as good as dead anyway. Perhaps it was fortunate he didn't see the way Roz's jaw stiffened, or notice the look she gave him. If he had, he would have realised there was little hope of breaking and entering without her and so would have been immediately tempted to call the whole thing off.

CHAPTER 23

Footsteps. Throughout my incarceration, it had amazed me how such mundane sounds, any sounds, even caught at the very edge of aural perception, could assume such immense importance. Footsteps had been my last link to humanity, the final event in a sequence that at least had had the merit of anchoring me to a reality of sorts. Now these tiny, teasing sounds filtering from somewhere beyond my prison cell had become the first harbingers of a world that was surprisingly difficult to recall. Darkness, silence, cold and hunger had all seen to that. In my tightly circumscribed world reality had become what I dreamed between waking and the restless drowsing that passed for sleep, or simply became a myriad of jumbled thoughts teased out into emptiness.

But not quite. Deprived of external stimuli, condemned simply to sit because I was unable to lie down with any comfort, I had discovered something that I had previously missed in the hustle and bustle of everyday life. There was more to life than mere physicality. And this had given me the kernel of an idea, a concept, a possibility I couldn't quite grasp, couldn't quite evaluate, as it remained tantalisingly out of reach, in the far recesses of my mind. Familiar, yet somehow alien. Something to do with the soul. Perhaps even something supernatural. An understanding that I felt, if grasped, could somehow unlock the secret of life. But more mundanely, time had long since ceased to have any true meaning and for what might have been a few days or maybe even a few weeks, my body had begun the slow and fitful process of shutting itself down, piece by piece, organ by organ. For one thing, I was convinced my tormentors had long forgotten me and even the sound of my own voice trying to tear down the wall of silence in a vain bid to attract some response had finally petered into silence. Water I had in abundance, licked from the damp wall as it slid silently down from somewhere above me. Food no longer held the imperative it had once demanded. Now I craved human contact above all else. Another face, another voice, some acknowledgement that I was not alone in the universe. Even if that person had to be my very own sjambok-wielding psychopath.

I remember, with utter clarity, the sudden clang of a bolt being withdrawn, because it startled me from an endless reverie. It hurt my ears and, to that injury, was added the insult of a torch's stabbing beam probing through the bars of my cell door, temporarily blinding my light-starved eyes. What did I do, this monument to youthful virtue? I instinctively curled into a foetal ball. My body clearly hadn't forgotten my local psychopath, even if my mind had long since floated off with the fairies. But the expected blows failed to materialise. Instead, my gaoler, for that was whom I supposed this apparition to be, merely grunted and levered me further into the cell with the toe of his foot, before stooping to place something beside me that resonated with a metallic clang. Then, with no further ceremony and without a word spoken, the door was pulled shut and the bolt shoved firmly back home.

Stunned by this sudden intrusion into my lonely world, it took me a while before I could even summon sufficient courage to reach out and touch whatever had been left. Tentatively, I let my fingers do the walking, finding the edge of something cold and uneven, which didn't take more than a couple of seconds to trace out in the form of a battered metal plate. But even before I could begin to explore the contents, my nose told me something else had changed. The first and only clean smell I had known since being ignominiously dumped struggled up from the floor, to bring a modicum of life to the turgid atmosphere that permeated not only the cell but every last pore of my filthy body. I can remember the flood of relief I felt at the presence of this bread. It meant they wanted me alive, that I wasn't forgotten, wasn't discarded to rot and die in the accumulated obscenity of their stinking hellhole. And with that understanding came a surge of pure encouragement flooding through my soul, lifting my morale almost into the stratosphere for a few precious seconds. Clasping my arms tightly about me, I nevertheless sat motionless, consciousness firmly fixed on its own familiar inward gaze, struggling to risk the first savouring of emotions as they creaked to the surface, released from the lonely fear of abandonment. It wasn't much in the great scheme of things, but an intruder, a real live person, had finally broken the drear stillness that characterised the long, lonely hours that had taught me their priceless lesson: how to transcend an unbearable present by harnessing one's mind to a rigorous review of the past and a somewhat cryptic examination of the future. But although now armed with a new-found assurance that life might at last hold some prospect of improvement, I remained helplessly sealed within my fairy world. It was the only real protection that I understood anymore.

Slipping past the bonds that held my body, my free-ranging mind had allowed me to experiment with thoughts of home, to relive life in all its vivid glory, to recall the sounds and colours of Africa, circumscribed only by the limits of imagination. Scrolling across the screen of my mind, I had taken the liberty to examine the vaulting, achingly beautiful prospect of my home skies, studded with slow-moving, fluffy white clouds that slid their light shadows over the long, rolling plains of dry grass and rivers of dark green trees that stained the ancient valley curves. I had heard again the echoing calls of wood pigeons around the house, sensed the high and lonely cry of circling eagles and listened to the alarm cough of restive baboons. Drawn inexorably by beauty, I had faced into the light breeze that always seemed to blow between dawn and dusk, riffling my hair and bringing much needed relief from the heat of the day. My roving eye had fallen on the familiar lines of the only home I had ever known and, as I had watched, those lines had seemed to dissolve before my swooping dream-flight. Dissolve into the startling sight of my ever-anxious mother, her tormented marriage exposed as never before to my spellbound gaze, as she cringed before the thought of her husband's homecoming. For perhaps the first time I had felt some understanding of the deep lines that had always seemed to define her face. Etched, I now saw, by years of humiliation, mute but indelible pointers to a man who derived such sick pleasure from dominating her every mood. Across the miles she had grown more real to me than had ever been the case when I'd been at home. I seemed almost able to touch the dark pall my bullying father had thrown across the fabric of her life and, in doing so, to understand what had been done to her, as well as to him. I had even watched my own craven retreat whenever life threatened to become too difficult and touched in horror upon the dark stain that was all that remained of Matt within my mind. Above all, dominating the landscape of dreams and striding un-opposed across the fabric of my being, the stunning, enigmatic figure of the most beautiful girl I'd ever known held me in her thrall. Roz.

In my surreal dreaming, I yearned to tell her, as now I understood with complete clarity, that I loved her. Now, when it was already too late. Too late to undo the harm I had so recklessly imposed in my desire to withdraw, to run away from the hand of cards that life had dealt me. All at once I had seen my actions for what they were and a desperate anguish had begun again to wrap its hungry tentacles around my hallucinating heart. Even so, despite the proffered nourishment, I would have preferred to stay a while, to revel in every exquisite detail of the girl my mind refused to erase. Reluctantly, slowly, I remember gliding back to the present, permitting my hand to begin again its arrested movement. To slip back down, seeking the dry, flat chunk of coarse bread so carelessly thrown at my feet. But the time for hunger had passed, despite an all-pervading faintness made ever-more immediate by that heavenly scent. With what little sense I still retained, I decided the only possible course of action was to eat but a portion of it and to do that slowly. Most importantly, I would hoard the bulk of the offering, just in case I was once again made to wait awhile before fate, in the form of my nemesis, stepped back into my world. But even the small chunks I broke off were hard to chew in my severely debilitated state and I ended up soaking each small offering one by one against the wall.

CHAPTER 24

"Very well, Ahmed, but you drive a hard bargain. I will make you one last offer. The white boy in exchange for a breeding slave and her female child. The one I have in mind has a good body and if you're careful with her, she will provide you with many more slaves yet. She's also a useful worker. But against this, you must guarantee the white boy is healthy. I don't want another like the last one you traded. We both know why he died before we rounded the Horn of Homuz. That eunuch of yours left little trace of what he'd done, but it was enough. He's cunning, that one."

As expected Ahmed, the consummate dealer, ensured his face registered nothing. Not so much as the blink of an eye. He would have made a world-class poker player. They both knew exactly why Abdel-Aziz was interested in me and hence the somewhat acrimonious dispute over price. Amongst his debauched clientele a white face on a healthy young male body, particularly a well-endowed body, was a valuable commodity and the final profit margin would be high. Every slave was expected to work, but his or her main function would be to provide for the eventual master's pleasure. True, some of the sexual habits practiced amongst the rich Arab slave owners meant a slave's life expectancy could be drastically reduced, but that depended on how valuable he was considered to be. Abdel's job and that of the several sea captains he employed was to be discreet. To ensure the merchandise arrived at the Eastern slave markets in good working order. Abdel paid them well and took care of their families, a leverage he was not above exploiting. In exchange, he demanded unswerving loyalty and total reliability. His reputation, his wealth and thus his standing in society depended upon it, as did Ahmed's. More than one captain had discovered what it meant to displease Abdel and there was never much left after the fish had done their work. The French maxim *'pour encourager les autres'* might have been coined expressly for him.

Even worse, when it came right down to it, was the go-between: Ahmed. Head of a tightly knit land-based organisation that relied almost entirely upon secrecy and its master's peculiar brand of terror. "Very well. We are agreed. I have the boy available and you can take him when you deliver the girl and her baby."

No more prone to overexcitement than Ahmed, Abdel-Aziz indicated his acceptance of the terms with the merest inclination of his head, before returning to his fastidious study of the hookah smouldering beside him. Quickly he considered the likely time it would take to produce the girl and whether her arrival could be arranged before he expected to re-join his ship, already waiting in Mombasa harbour with its cargo of South African slaves. The trade winds were set fair and, not wishing to miss them, the crew had almost finished loading the ambergris, the legitimate part of the cargo, valued for centuries as perfume although, for where it was now destined, valued far more for its aphrodisiac qualities. However, the really high-value cargo, selected slaves from the East African coast, would not join their fellow South African prisoners until just before anchor was weighed. One had to be careful, even in this benighted land. But he had a difficulty. The unsuspecting girl he had long held in mind for just such a bargaining occasion could not possibly be abducted, spirited out of her tribal lands and, together with a child still at the breast, brought nearly a thousand miles across country and down to the coast in less than three days. She was the daughter of a minor chieftain, the wife of a respected warrior, and it would require a certain amount of fast talking, bribery and heavy-handed intimidation. There was nothing for it. Departure would have to be postponed. "I will return in four days, after sundown. The cargo will keep." A captain in his own right and master of a string of dhows he might be, but Abdel was never quite able to forget that it was Ahmed's stake money as well as his human merchandise that funded his continuing lifestyle. With business complete and reputations intact, the two men turned their attention to the time-honoured formalities of Arab hospitality.

★★★

Fortunately for the peace of my already ravaged mind, I was not only ignorant of what was going on but, even in my most feverish moments, could never have guessed at the medieval ritual being played out in the intimate room far above my head. Time returned me to its mindlessly boring, foot-dragging repetition. Once more starved of light and with my watch long since rendered useless, I couldn't even take refuge in the solace of counting days. Profound silence, like a heavy, suffocating blanket, enveloped me all over again in its insidious, mind-numbing coils and I lapsed back into a semi-comatose squat, back pressed against one of the all-encompassing walls, hands spread to prevent me rolling left or right. I didn't know, had no way of telling, just how close to death I was drawing, as my mind once again hovered near the edge of sanity, this time content to stare over the abyss, fear long gone.

CHAPTER 25

It was unfortunate, Malcolm thought, that they had managed to pick a night when the moon seemed to fill the horizon, hanging low as it did over the surrounding dwellings, bathing everything, especially the stark, pencil-thin minarets of the Islamic Mosque, in its ethereal, monochrome glow. Even from fifty yards away down the dingy street fronting the high wall of his target, Malcolm could make out every detail. He had studied the sheer ramparts for some time and finally thought he'd found a possible way up in the crook of a flying buttress, the latter's hulking form in odd contrast to the lofty white walls it supported. Reaching to a point just below the crenulated parapet, it should shelter him from any cursory glance, once he'd started up the grappling-iron rope. Certainly, it would take a lucky throw, but he had expected that difficulty and now the five-pronged hook rested on the ground beside him, its long tether draped in a coil over his left shoulder.

Glancing to his left, Malcolm could just make out where Jomo was pressed back into the deep black shadows cast by an old corrugated iron lean-to. He was a lookout of sorts, but what he would do if someone actually appeared, Malcolm didn't care to guess. Nevertheless, after much urging, and clearly against his better judgement, he had been persuaded to accompany Malcolm and Roz on what he obviously considered a fool's errand. So, with too much time wasted already, Malcolm slipped out of the shadows and made his way towards the wall, moving with surprising delicacy for a man of his girth and stature. He could detect no sign of a guard and although that didn't mean there wasn't one, he hoped fervently that they would consider themselves safe from all but the most foolhardy burglar.

Tucked in below the towering barrier, he unhooked the line and examined it swiftly to make sure it would pay out smoothly, passing the first half-dozen coils through his hands, getting the feel of the light sisal cord. Then, with a last check right and left to confirm the road was still clear, he stepped back from the smooth face soaring above him, swung the grapple hard several times until it was whirling satisfactorily, then let it go on the upswing with a fervent prayer that his aim was sure and the flukes would catch first time. He could not afford an extra moment, much less a second bout of the clatter it would make if it failed to hold and fell back down on him.

For perhaps two or three seconds the line snaked out from his left hand, taking out great loops of the main coil as he watched the hook sail up and just clear the crenulations before falling slack. A definite but muted clanging thud echoed back as the grapple came up against some obstacle and he prayed ardently that it had not been enough to alert any half-asleep guard. Swiftly gathering in the slack, Malcolm pulled the hook back towards him, hoping against hope that one of the flukes would catch and hold. At least one did. Somewhere out of sight, the metal bit into the edge of a slab defining the walkway around the top of the wall and when he jerked it hard, it held. Slipping on a pair of thin leather gloves to protect his hands and improve his grip, Malcolm immediately began swarming up the rope, arms pumping as he walked his feet in steady rhythm, body held out at some forty-five degrees from the vertical. In a surprisingly short time, his head came level with the parapet and grabbing one of the crenulations, Malcolm heaved himself over the top, seconds before his arms gave out from the unaccustomed exercise.

In the mad scramble for a purchase, keeping quiet was beyond him, so he was heartily relieved to discover the compound below him was empty and apparently unguarded. Having reconnoitred, he crouched down, out of sight from below, trying to catch his breath and bring his wildly pumping heart under control. Then, rising to a half crouch, he made his way carefully towards the staircase he'd seen out to his right, excruciatingly aware of the impossibility of blending into the gleaming white background encircling him. Swiftly he dropped the first few steps towards the courtyard, knowing that if anyone cared to glance out of the windows with which he was rapidly drawing level, they couldn't help but see him. He stuck out like a sore thumb. The hairs on the back of his neck rose and the muscles around his chest tightened as he subconsciously waited for the sound of a shot and the tearing agony that would follow. He had no doubt at all that any guard spotting him would open fire. Kenyan jurisdiction wasn't famous for extending its authoritarian reach to quell the eagerness of guards on such occasions. The courts tended to busy themselves with lesser misdemeanours, preferring to allow 'enterprise' to develop with minimum interference, profoundly certain of the long-established British idiom that a man's home was his castle. Burgle it if you dare.

So, continuing to move as quickly as he could, Malcolm leaned out precariously towards the nearest shuttered window, feeling for a foothold on the narrow sill, fearful of a fall, but fully aware that to descend to the courtyard offered nothing more than a death-trap if he was spotted. Any entry would have to be made up here through a window, the only obvious weak spot. Light filtered faintly through the wooden slats and, from behind them, he was frustrated to catch a murmuring of voices. Arab voices. A language over which he had a basic grasp, but little fluency. The conversation was desultory and, as far as he could tell, innocuous. He shifted his grip and edged his weight away from the stairs and onto the foot resting on the window ledge.

As he did so, a small piece of tile dislodged, the faint thud of its landing in the courtyard coinciding with the sound of a door opening directly below him. Malcolm froze. Suspended half-way between the open steps and the window, he hung motionless, his arms beginning to screech their protest at the punishment being meted out. Mentally he cursed himself for ever having got into his present predicament and the longer the suspense played out, the more stupid the whole thing began to look. He knew it couldn't go on indefinitely – for a start his arms and legs were already trembling like a man with the ague as they reacted to the full, unaccustomed weight of his awkwardly splayed body. Below him, the guard, rifle slung over his shoulder, sauntered into the centre of the courtyard, his features momentarily caught in the flare of a match held cupped in his hand as he lit a Four Aces cigarette and breathed in deeply from the smoke and warm night air. As almost any man would, he turned to stare upwards at the stars, to savour their display, still remarkable despite the bright moonlight. It was exactly what Malcolm had feared and his heart was hard pushed to remain in his chest rather than relocate to his mouth. But even as he watched the cameo being played out in something approaching despair, he became aware of a change of tone in the conversation filtering out beside his head. Despite his predicament, he listened. And it was as well he did, because he was only just in time to catch the end of the conversation. "…tomorrow night to pick up the white boy."

Whatever else might have been said, Malcolm missed it, because at that precise point he received a rather rude wake-up call. It was presented in a form that always obtains the victim's complete and absolute attention: incoming steel-jacketed lead. And since much of Malcolm's Service career had been spent learning to allow such persuasive arguments absolute right of way, he reared desperately back and away from the flying splinters chipped off by the bullet as it slammed into the brickwork not two inches from the side of his head. The sound of rifle fire rolling around the courtyard and a simultaneous shout of warning from the guard comprehensively ruined the silence under which Malcolm had been figuratively sheltering. Barely had he begun to pull himself frantically over to the staircase when a second bullet ripped through his left side, putting paid to any hope of negotiating his way out of the mess he was in.

The shockwave as the bullet penetrated below his ribs to exit through a large and messy cavity on his right side was enough to throw him back across the stairs and momentarily below the guard's line of sight. It was probably that alone which saved him from immediate execution, because the guard was forced to run along the courtyard to where the steps reached the base of the wall, before ascending to get a clear shot. In that instant all his old training kicked in and summoning the last of his fast-draining strength, Malcolm lunged for the top of the stairs and rolled his blood-soaked body across the flat walkway.

Only adrenalin kept him moving. That and an almost euphoric feeling induced by the rapid loss of blood. There was little pain as yet. That would come. For now, all he could think of was getting hold of the grappling rope and sliding down it to the ground, anything to get away and under cover before the guard made his inevitable appearance at the top of the stairs. As he reached for the rope snaking across the walkway, his feet seemed to slow of their own accord, as if he were wading through treacle and his hands became difficult to direct. In a slow-motion dream he leaned forward to gather the rope, then stepped deliberately but unsteadily over the rampart, intending to abseil his way down.

He couldn't understand it when his legs buckled and his gloved hands began to slide helplessly along the rope. Couldn't understand why nothing seemed to work properly. Desperately, he sent an order to his hands to hold on more tightly, but for some reason they didn't want to obey. He remembered seeing the ground coming up towards him far too fast and he remembered the wildly thrashing line catching around his legs. He remembered the scything pain as one leg became trapped and he was abruptly and cruelly tipped upside down to let his whole weight combine with gravity to widen the gaping channel left through his flesh. And after that he remembered nothing.

CHAPTER 26

Roz was fretting. She had finally allowed Malcolm to convince her that acting as his driver and waiting with the Jeep warmed up and out of sight was pivotal to his plan and ultimate safety. However, what she really thought was he had come up with a relatively devious, if pretty obvious, way of ensuring she remained out of harm's way and, in particular, out of any action that might arise. She had to concede that someone was needed to drive and since Jomo couldn't talk, in the event something went wrong she might very well be Malcolm's only salvation. And now she was convinced something really had gone wrong. It wasn't that she could put her finger on it, but she was experiencing more and more often an almost tangible presence and preternatural insight whenever she really needed help. A new, indefinable spiritual sensitivity she was beginning to trust. An insight that was far closer to real assurance than mere supposition. And right now, she considered this curious awareness was of more importance than reason.

Leaning forward in the seat and looking over the collapsed windscreen, she strained her eyes and ears to pick up a clue. Nothing. Nevertheless, she eased the clutch in, slipped into first and let the Jeep teeter forward, balanced on the accelerator. No other movement, no other sound. Until with shocking suddenness and high above the throaty gurgle of the engine, the crack of two rapid-fire shots rolled around the narrow street in which she was parked. A shout echoed thinly from somewhere ahead in the direction of their target and Roz knew, beyond a doubt, that Malcolm was in deep trouble. With no thought but concern for Malcolm, she stamped on the accelerator and, barely pausing to let the engine catch up, threw the car into second gear, double declutching for all she was worth with only a yard covered, and shot round the corner into the straight that paralleled the base of the fortress-like house they were trying to access.

As the walls came into full view she was just in time to gain the impression of a falling body that suddenly jerked to a halt mere feet above street level, thereafter to slide rapidly the rest of the way to the ground as the line paid out around the leg apparently caught in its coils. It didn't take much intuition to know this was Malcolm, or that he was in desperate straits. She had seen how his arms hung slackly over his head as he dropped the remaining few feet to the ground. For an instant panic threatened to disable her, but the knowledge that she alone could hold the key to survival and would have to take charge if they were to stay alive gave her all the impetus she needed.

There were only seconds left to get clear of the walls, to get out from the predictable arc of fire. She knew beyond doubt there would be no mercy here. And with that realisation came understanding that whatever Malcolm had or had not found, this place really was tied to Paul. Desperately she stood on the brakes, sliding in a welter of dust almost broadside to the body that now lay in a motionless heap just ahead of her. Where, oh where was Jomo? She knew she would never manage to get Malcolm's inert bulk into the back of the Jeep on her own. But she needn't have worried. Even as she slid to a halt, Jomo broke cover from her left and ran straight towards Malcolm. Leaping out, Roz caught up as Jomo grabbed Malcolm by the shoulders and started pulling him round towards the back of the Jeep, legs dragging along the ground. Swiftly she bent and, gathering the trailing legs, straightened herself with a supreme effort to stagger along behind Jomo until they came up against the tailboard. There was no time to release it and, groaning with the effort, the two of them managed to roll Malcolm unceremoniously over the top, from where he fell with a dull, glutinous thud.

Apprehensive, Roz looked in and, with a sudden horror, saw a gush of sticky black liquid spreading rapidly under his body, liquid that could only be blood. Momentarily she froze again, but a hard knock against her back from a clearly agitated Jomo brought her back to reality and the precariousness of their situation. Glancing upwards, she caught sight of a head appearing against the skyline followed immediately by several others, one at least of which was aiming a rifle directly at her. Simultaneously, a stab of flame sparkled at her, but the man had been in too much of a hurry and the clang of a bullet glancing off the Jeep right alongside served only to galvanise her into even faster action.

Arriving in the driving seat like a rat on hashish and praying she wouldn't be hit, Roz began to drive as though her life depended on it, which it probably did. She heard at least one other bullet chew into the back of the Jeep before she reached the first bend, taking it so fast she slid broadside into the close-pressed wall, only to bounce off onto the opposite side of the street, before managing to straighten up and build on what was left of her speed. Then, with the engine howling, she attacked the narrow, claustrophobic streets as though all the hounds of Hell were on her tail, oblivious to anyone or anything that might have had the misfortune to get in her way. It was pure luck that after four or five minutes of this she emerged onto a street she recognised, because it was this recognition alone that brought sanity. Her foot eased away from its flat prone position on the accelerator and, with a conscious effort, she sat back in the driving seat and flexed her shoulders from their hunched concentration. Her hands were another matter and it took a moment or two to straighten her fingers and break their almost manic grip on the steering wheel. Only then was she able to turn and look at Jomo, whose face clearly showed he was less than impressed with the whole experience. If he'd ever seen a circus 'wall of death' in action, he would now know exactly how the participants felt, but Roz had no time for that. Right now she had a badly wounded man on her hands and nowhere to go. She glanced over her shoulder into the back of the Jeep, not sure whether to take Malcolm to hospital where the authorities would undoubtedly interrogate him once they discovered the bullet wound, or whether to risk the drive out to Jill, in the hope she knew a friendly doctor. However, one searching look was enough to determine Malcolm needed professional help and needed it right now, or he would be beyond anything the world had to offer anyway. In some despair, she faced forward. "Jomo, show me the quickest way to the hospital."

CHAPTER 27

Deep in the bowels of the cellar, its labyrinthine chambers excavated by slave labour some hundreds of years earlier, I was still locked in solitary confinement, sprawled in the space tunnelled out from the living rock below the high white walls. Faintly, however, my ears registered the distant sounds of rifle fire and shouting, all diffused into a soft silkiness by the solid rock and, I must admit, they barely disturbed my reverie. In any case, even if I had been able to determine what was going on, the knowledge probably wouldn't have pierced the stupefying haze that now clouded my mind, probably wouldn't even have sparked the beginnings of interest. Isolation and total blackness had long since sapped any latent effort towards attentiveness – attention to life, even. The considerations of these two treacherous companions, each one feeding off the other, had all but completed their task. By now it needed far more than distant sounds to bring me back to reality. I remember I simply kept my eyes closed. Why open them? I was in a world of my own and I doubt my eyelids even flickered. Certainly, my slow, shallow breathing was the only thing of which I was aware, as its hypnotic rhythm provided the only other sound in my universe. Days were dawning, as they must, and nights were falling, but none of this registered on my mind.

★★★

With cruel delight, Ahmed ordered the sarong stripped from the girl who stood in front of him. Her baby had already been forcibly removed and she stood with her face half turned away in shame as her nakedness was revealed. She was tall and almost too thin to be beautiful, but the high-boned cheeks and narrow nostrils marked her out as a half-breed. As Ahmed stared at her, his lust, never far from the surface, began to throb and satisfaction flooded him as he contemplated the deal he had struck. For a moment he even considered an expansive gesture of thanks to Abdel-Aziz. But not yet. Let Abdel await that moment. He, Ahmed, was in no hurry. Not with such a fine slave standing naked before him and not while he could indulge the luxury of deciding how he would first make use of her body. He let his eyes wander over her, taking in the slender limbs and milk-swollen breasts, their dark nipples enlarged from recent feeding. Like many of her kind the tight, dark pubic curls that should have been guarding her prominent mound were completely shaved away and the secret parts of her sex, meant for her husband alone, were now openly on display to the two men. Returning his eyes to her face, Ahmed thrust a callous hand deep between her thighs and grasped the labia hard, watching with amusement as she gasped and stumbled back in startled dismay. Tonight he would treat himself to something exceptional. Abruptly, he let her go and turned back to face the ever inscrutable Abdel-Aziz.

"Very well, you shall have your white boy. Barzac will bring him to the courtyard." Ahmed had no idea how this particular prisoner had fared, but then he had little interest in the finer details. It was enough that Barzac had not seen fit to report anything untoward. As far as he was concerned, delivery alive to Abdel-Aziz was all that was required. Why waste money on pampering a prisoner you would never see again? Moreover, apart from using him as a convenient source of profit, he had little regard for Abdel-Aziz and was beginning to feel that the time was fast approaching when it would be prudent to cut this particular link and seek other outlets more amenable to his little foibles. Abdel's only real asset was he usually made sufficient profit to not only reimburse the subsidy for each voyage, but enable Ahmed to fund further rounds without having to beg from the family. However, Abdel was not only beginning to demand far too much, he was getting a little careless in the way he came and went and there was no point in attracting unnecessary attention. So it might serve everyone well if he were to disappear. Permanently.

CHAPTER 28

Having been up all night, Roz was tired and, as she had long since discovered, when fatigue struck, dejection was quick to raise its ugly head. In particular, she was anxiously aware that Jill could appear at any moment. Malcolm had been alive when she delivered him to the hospital, if only just, but he had yet to regain consciousness and no one would commit themselves to a prognosis on his chances of survival. The bullet had missed vital organs, but one lung had collapsed through the shock of its passage and he had lost a considerable amount of blood. Not only that, but he had severe rope burns to his leg and had taken a brutal blow to the top of his head. There was no doubt that if his leg had not caught in the rope he would now be lying in the mortuary and Roz still didn't know what she was going to say to Jill. Moreover, she was painfully aware that Malcolm had deliberately omitted to tell Jill exactly what he was planning to do. Like many large men he had a healthy respect, bordering on awe, for his small but feisty wife. But now, with Malcolm unable to defend himself, Roz was left to placate Jill in the certain knowledge that if she hadn't made what now looked like highly unreasonable demands, Malcolm would not be facing the future as a possible invalid – assuming he made it at all. She knew Malcolm was Jill's whole world and for perhaps the thousandth time, Roz glanced despairingly through the glass at the nurses surrounding the intensive care bed where, oblivious to her misery, they continued to bustle around the bed like bees round a honey pot.

"Roz!" The sound of Jill's voice caught her unawares and she cringed. "How is he?" Not waiting for an answer, Jill swept on into the intensive care ward and marched straight up to her husband's bed. There she stood for several minutes, her animated back leaving no doubt she was questioning the nurses closely, though her eyes never left the still form of her husband. Eventually and apparently satisfied for the moment, she turned back to where Roz now hovered uncertainly in the doorway and laid a firm but gentle hand on her arm. "Come on, Roz, you and I are going to find a cup of coffee and you're going to tell me exactly what's been going on. All of it." There was a crackle of steel in her manner, but her innate kindness was mixed with the very real grief playing out in her eyes as she gazed at her young charge.

"So in the end Malcolm decided there was only one thing he could do. He had to get in somehow, or we'd never be sure and it was the only lead we had. The first I realised there was real trouble was when I heard two shots. I drove round the corner and Malcolm just seemed to fall down the rope he had been using to climb the wall. When I got to him he wasn't moving, but somehow Jomo and I managed to lift him into the back of the Jeep – it's all a bit of a blur – and then Jomo showed me how to get here. The rest you know."

Roz petered out into anxious silence, waiting for Jill to react, to shout at her, cry, do anything. But Jill just sat quietly, eyes half hooded, sifting through the events of the last twenty-four hours, mind and heart at odds while she searched for a way through the dilemma posed by her beloved husband's dreadful injuries. She knew she had to be strong for him, had to take his place somehow as she confronted the world, yet still comfort Roz. But what to do, how to respond? Should she call a halt to the search, tell Roz the two of them had done their best, but now it was time to give up on Paul? Should she rant and rave about the stupidity of their escapades – something she supposed any normal wife would do? Or should she try to take over where Malcolm had left off? Not once did she consider playing the distressed wife. For a moment she toyed with the idea of asking the medical staff to keep things quiet, but in her heart of hearts she knew that was a non-starter. Bullet wounds to white people were too difficult to explain and with the hospital involved, she couldn't hope to keep a lid on the night's exploits. Once Malcolm regained consciousness, she guessed it wouldn't be long before the police started asking him questions. And when that happened and an official enquiry got under-way, she very much doubted if it would help their efforts to find Paul. She was all too well aware they already had a good deal of explaining to do and could hardly imagine what the authorities would say when they realised who Roz was trying to find and, by implication, warn. Inevitably, the police were going to be far from pleased when they discovered the Paul in question was wanted up country for questioning about a double murder. Annoyed that she was still thinking defensively about a young man she hadn't even met, while her husband lay unconscious on his account, Jill tried to put the Moncton boy forcibly aside and concentrate on what was best for Malcolm. The trouble was she knew what would happen, if and when he began to recover. Although out of the picture for now, he would still demand to know what was being done to find Paul. Having got the bit between his teeth, he would never give up and, knowing what he was like, there was no doubt in her mind that being attacked would only stiffen his resolve.

Jill sighed and, as she did so, heard a commotion further down the corridor. Irritated, she spun round in time to see Matron firmly diverting the local Chief Inspector of Police away from the ward and into her office. The die was cast. She knew immediately that she couldn't let Malcolm down, or Roz for that matter, and would have to find a way round the dilemma posed by the officer's presence.

Whipping round she hissed "Roz, the police are here. Go now, quickly, before they see you. It's better they don't know you're here, for now at least and I need time to think. Keep the

Jeep and get on home. I'll call you when I can, but stay out of sight until we've had time to discuss where we go from here. Quick now, while that man is still in Matron's office. Use the stairs over there. Find a way out."

CHAPTER 29

Rough hands grabbed me under the armpits and dragged me upright. I suppose it's inevitable that such people never major on consideration. At any rate, I remember groaning as the blood flowed reluctantly back into my cramped limbs, forced as they were to respond to unexpected movement. Swiftly and with a total lack of ceremony, they dragged me out into the passageway and propped me against yet another wall. Then in broken English, a guttural voice ordered me to stand upright and move my legs, but like it or not, self-help was out of the question. I could summon neither compliance nor rebellion.

Slowly, involuntarily, I simply slid down the wall, unable and unwilling to command my legs or, for that matter, any other limb. Even when they began to slap me around, I was unable to react. For some reason far beyond the abilities of my addled mind to determine, I could sense the faintest stirrings of concern in their attitude towards me, but in my dream-like state any explanation merely stood tantalisingly out of reach. With no desire to influence matters, there seemed little point in staying awake and I duly let myself slide back into oblivion. Later, I have no idea how much later, the first weak warnings of distant pain reached out to me, thin tendrils of discomfort edging their way under the layers of indifference that isolated me from reality. At the same time, even my ears switched back on and although initially I remained totally indifferent, I did eventually become aware of individual sounds. In particular, that of distant slapping and pummelling, which ultimately turned into an explicit awareness that the unwanted intrusion was growing ever closer.

Then the pain hit me. It gathered in my feet first, before setting out swiftly, all too swiftly, to traverse the length of my legs, running this way and that, ferreting around in obscure parts of my torso, malevolent in its intensity, recruiting my arms in passing, intensifying yet again as it narrowed to drive up through my neck and spill into my face, before exploding at the centre of my brain, the seat of all pain supervision. There it delivered its message in one long, loud and uncompromising scream. And I know I accompanied it, because I could hear the rich tenor that my voice had but recently attained, as it rose in counterpoint to the full orchestra playing along my nerves. Which meant it wasn't long before someone forced a gag into my mouth and, despite my weakness, my whole body tuned itself to producing a physical answer to the mauling, leaving me to bite down helplessly in a supreme effort to contain the waves of nausea and pain thrusting barbed and lacerating hands into every part of my body.

Believe me, returning circulation can vault its way through every last capillary when you've been abused as I had. And yet the very pain that threatened to drown me was probably my salvation, because it galvanised me as nothing else could. In short order, the layers of indifference that had cocooned and shrouded my wavering mind were stripped away, dissolved as though they had never been. And in an experience that you might liken to birth, I shot back into reality, kicking and choking somewhat more lustily than had probably been the case on that first journey into the world. All of which left me trembling with exhaustion and the guards visibly relieved. Oddly, they relaxed perceptibly from that moment and, under the glow of a single overhead bulb dangling loosely by its cloth-covered wires, they proceeded to strip my fouled clothing in favour of a kikoi, which they wound loosely round my waist. Their ministrations didn't take long and, with my hands once more tightly bound at my back (for the life of me, I couldn't see why), I was half carried, half propelled up the steps and into the night-darkened courtyard for the first breath of fresh air in a very long time.

It was the all-pervading, never-to-be-mistaken smell of drying fish that gave me the real clue. Only minutes before, I had been shoved roughly into the cramped boot of a long-nosed Daimler waiting in the courtyard that had presented me with my last external view. I remember the car was waiting with its engine ticking over. Even I managed to work out that I was the anticipated cargo. And from the moment we turned out through the high metal gates, I tried desperately to work out where we were headed. To my intense surprise, the journey was over almost before it had begun and I felt the car respond to the brakes and roll to a stop on what sounded like rough gravel. Earlier, staggering up from my cell, there had been no hint of what to expect, but on emerging from the corridor and being pulled roughly towards the car, I had become deeply aware of a hostile scrutiny from a small knot of men watching progress from a dimly lit upstairs window. Still unable to understand the import of events, but elated by my release from the suffocating confines of the boot, I now found my thoughts turning ever more to concern over my likely destination.

Clearly, I was at the old harbour; but why? I couldn't fathom it out. Just a few steps down from where I stood, a single jetty pointed its snub nose into the rapidly shelving water. Above me, the darkened Customs shed filled the horizon, its dilapidated old gates barring entry to the inner sanctum of power like a gap-toothed old crone. Around me, the night air stirred and blew fitfully across the water from the darkened dhows riding at anchor, a stone's throw from the land. The air was warm and filled with the mingled perfume of dried fish and ambergris, whilst in the velvet blackness the sea stirred quietly against the end of the worn old stone. For a few seconds I almost forgot my predicament, momentarily entranced and at the same time stimulated by the sights and sounds all around me. Which, if you knew the old harbour, would only go to show how out of it I really was, despite the reprieve from that foul cell. Phosphorescence flickered and flared intensely white in the backwash from the jetty and, watching the ebb and flow, I had a sudden longing to throw myself in and let the layers of filth wash off my emaciated body. But scarcely had the thought formed, when a shallow outrigger canoe emerged from the blackness and brought my preoccupation to an abrupt end. The craft was no more than a roughly hollowed-out tree trunk with a single outrigger, powered by a barely discernible young man sitting in the stern. Nevertheless, its arrival galvanised my guards and a hand in my back propelled me down to the end of the jetty as the canoe swept broadside to the landing stage, to bob gently, held by a thin but muscular arm reaching up to grasp a protruding piece of wood doing time as a makeshift mooring.

No words were exchanged – something I was getting used to in this bizarre new world of mine. Just about everything was done in sullen silence, made the more chilling for the indifference or resentment I saw whenever I caught an eye appraising me. Now I half fell, half stepped into the craft and it rocked dangerously, nearly pitching me over the far side. A sharp instruction was snarled at me from the stern, but I was already dropping to my knees, aware that if I went in, my bound hands would be unable to prevent a swift descent to the seabed. Kneeling awkwardly, the hard rim of the canoe digging into my emaciated hips and thighs, I felt the familiar tug of hopelessness steal back, ever ready to beguile my mind and threatening once again to overwhelm me. But I had been there before and somehow, each new menace increased my still somewhat nascent desire to fight back. A renewed determination to keep a hold on life was stirring. Well, that's what it felt like. Dimly. At any rate, whatever was about to happen, I was sure it couldn't be worse than I had already experienced.

CHAPTER 30

With a sense of satisfaction, Israfel glanced at his companion, who acknowledged my change of heart with a nod of pleasure. For weeks now, Israfel, appointed as Guardian following my attempted suicide, had been concerned at my failure to fight back against the weight of trouble being loaded on my young shoulders. He had watched with some unease as I apathetically accepted the deterioration in my mind and body. Nevertheless, except for the original mandate to intervene over the suicide, his orders had been clear: "Don't interfere and don't alter the course of human events." Except, of course, if and when Satan clearly goaded some minion or other to overstep Heaven's well-defined constraint not to kill. At which point Israfel was authorised to take any immediate action he deemed fit.

As usual in such cases, Satan had only been given permission to torment but definitely not drive me to the point of mortal danger, where life could be lost. But just when that point was reached was a matter for the Guardian to decide. And that was why the job could be so stressful. Especially since there was always some demon or other not above trying for collateral damage that might 'inadvertently' take me out. Which was why standing back and letting me take the hits hadn't been easy for Israfel, although not for one moment did he doubt the wisdom of his orders. Like all human children, I had been assigned a Guardian Angel at conception and, like most, had been allowed to go my own way since reaching thirteen, the time-honoured and formal age of maturity. Thereafter, the presence or absence of a Guardian had depended entirely upon my general attitude. The same approach taken throughout the human race. If an individual showed a selfless interest in others, some particularly redeeming feature, perhaps some intrigue in spiritual matters, or specific angelic protection was ordered by God (which turned out to be the answer in my case), an angel might then be reassigned.

Like many, though by no means all angels, Israfel had already pulled duty as a Guardian and, having done particularly well on his first assignment, had subsequently been earmarked to undertake the Academy course for more senior and experienced angels and, in his case, this would be followed by selection for fast-track promotion. Now he had graduated and was entrusted with a second bite of the cherry – looking after me. Me, one of God's prized humans (amazing, but as I was later to discover, we're all 'prized' by God).

But back to Israfel. Only a minority of angels were assigned a second stint as a Guardian, but those who did not only generally enjoyed the experience, but usually went on to lead glittering careers. However, as always with these difficult assignments the guiding star was 'trust'. Total trust in Michael, the Captain of the Lord's Host, plus an ability to use one's initiative. Israfel could still remember his surprise and delight at being snatched shortly before the end of the Academy course to foil an apparently 'important' suicide. Clearly, he was considered one of the best, capable of undertaking delicate and discrete tasks. And to cap it all, he then discovered the human in question (me) was to become his next charge. A fact confirmed at the graduation ceremony. He would never forget the thrill of anticipation as he prepared to spend perhaps the next sixty years on and around planet Earth. Anticipation tinged only by a certain apprehension at being sent once again into the front line of the fierce battle that had been raging there for several thousand years. At least this time he was a well-taught, polished and accredited warrior and expected to have a definite edge. So together, albeit unknown to me, we began an anonymous and ultimately fateful partnership (anonymous as

133

far as I was concerned). For certain I was nothing unusual, having experienced a relatively conventional early life, except for my father and the wild life that frequented our home range. And no one could say I'd had more than the usual scrapes that any growing boy seems to attract, as if by osmosis. Nevertheless, I would have to admit that my insatiable interest in all things feral had led me and Matt into predicaments no sane human should consider. However, I'd survived without any overt help and grown the stronger for it. And now this angel Israfel was watching my progress with interest. He already knew something of why the Creator cared so much for men and women. Also, why some humans were destined for a glorious future even if, when I come to think about it, we are, by turns, both sublime and ridiculous. Anyway, here we were, embarked on an involuntary journey together.

Israfel had been briefed on the lion attack and Matt's death and why there had been no order to stop the assault. There was always great sadness in watching the end of a promising human life, even one for whom no angel had particular responsibility and Israfel knew all that lay between the atheist Matt and eternity without God was the great 'Day of Judgement'. Although it was the same for me at this point, Israfel had been given an in-depth explanation of God's future strategy regarding my case and this had apparently proved both interesting and supremely helpful in preparing for what was to come. A briefing perforce followed by an instantaneous and precisely timed return to Earth duty, in order to foil the satanic plots still being cooked up to destroy me by my own hand. Now Israfel's supreme test lay just ahead and he knew he'd have to keep his wits about him if he was to protect me within the constraints of his orders. Together with Benjamin, an angel he had met once many years before in one of Heaven's many fabulous estates, Israfel was following me across the sea, long greaved legs keeping easy pace with the canoe. Since the last fracas, at which he'd been present with Tamar and his friends, there had been little interference from Satan or his minions. However, Israfel was a warrior at heart and he knew better than to relax his guard.

Benjamin didn't have quite the same outlook. He was on a well-earned break, having recently been stood down from guarding the fisherman Kumai, now powering his canoe towards the anchored dhow. Unfortunately, although being given a chance to get out of slaving, Kumai had made an irrevocable decision and effectively thrown in his lot with Satan. But such was the fisherman's commitment to the slaver's cause (and the nature of the ship to which I was headed), there was a good chance Benjamin would be needed by the other angels for the almost inevitable fight that loomed ahead. Hence he'd been given permission to take all the leave due to him while still remaining on Earth, rather than hotfooting it straight back to Heaven for a rest. Since his thirteenth birthday, the day even his own culture had accepted he'd attained his majority, Kumai had become entirely responsible for his own destiny, but such was God's love for His creatures, that there had remained a need to help Kumai retain at least some choice over his likely future. Enter Benjamin. However, with the die cast, the order had finally come from Heaven to pull back from the young man. He had already caused too much harm to himself and others. Sadly for Kumai this meant there was now almost certainly no going back.

Up ahead, a large sea-going boum dhow, its characteristic stern bearing the famous old navigator's name *Majid an-Najdi*, snubbed uneasily at anchor and Israfel could see from the line being taken by the canoe that this was the destination. Head up, he examined the boat with interest and his hand instinctively dropped to the pommel of his sword, but Benjamin put out a swift restraining hand. "Have no fear, friend. We're to respect a truce for the time being and they know it. This boat has long been used in the vile trade of slaving and belongs to that loathsome creature Arcturus, the one you can see lording it up there at the stern. For now we are not to dispute the matter with him." Israfel relaxed a little, but was dismayed by what he saw. A noxious cloud that seemed to have a life of its own enveloped the cluttered deck and within its suffocating confines he could see shadowy figures hopping and crawling over the battered old planks. Up on the thick hemp mainstays supporting the heavily raked mast, there was a positive infestation of ugly, rat-like creatures clinging to every spare foothold, but the demon Benjamin had pointed out and who had caught Israfel's interest sat motionless at the very stern, behind the long steering oar. Fierce, piercing yellow eyes, made sinister by their characteristically vertical iris slits, tracked the approach of the two angels closely and the tightly compressed lips signalled the creature's obvious hatred of them. A huge body, with hulking muscles and long legs, singled him out as superior to the scowling pack around him. A suppressed, savage power, barely held in check for the moment, marked him as one to watch, whilst the sycophantic deference paid by the other demons confirmed him as their leader. Contemptuously, Arcturus turned his head away, as if to study matters of more importance. He knew the approaching angels wouldn't try anything and was enjoying his moment of authority over the wretches held captive in the bowels of the ship.

Israfel shuddered. The presence of so many demons was depressing enough, but the palpable air of human despair engulfing the ship set his teeth on edge. Below decks, he could see through the thick old timbers the curled bodies and slumped shoulders of the captives who lay chained and helpless. Standing well back, far beyond the reach of any of the malodorous monsters, he could also see a number of his fellow angels sitting and watching in a small group. Israfel hailed them, saluting with his customary courtesy, and was rewarded with a warm response from each in turn. Even so, assuming Paul was destined to remain aboard and sail with this ship, the next few weeks were not going to be much fun. And given the awfulness of what he could already see in the hold, Israfel knew he'd have real trouble holding his temper in check long enough to get through the journey without a fight. If it was to Arabia they were bound, the journey would take weeks and knowing what he already did about the noxious trade in human beings, the journey was likely to provoke his ire on an almost hourly basis, an effect that could eventually spill over into unrestrained anger. And then it only needed his battle sword to be unsheathed, and the flash and hiss of its extraordinary, almost unbelievable ten-foot blade would start something that, for all the demon's obvious power, could only end one way. With multiple deaths amongst the ugly horde in front of him.

In fact, he was beginning to fancy an encounter with Arcturus already, but even as he contemplated the scene, there was a stirring amongst the rank and file who had spotted my impending arrival. Several of the creatures scuttled to the side to get a better look at their latest victim. However, when they realised I was not only in reasonable shape, despite my earlier treatment, but under Israfel's direct protection (however loose), a wave of hissing and swearing broke out amongst them. Some of the more foolhardy even began to finger their weapons as they concentrated afresh on the approaching angels and recognised at least one of them as having recently been involved in the demise of several of their contemporaries. Rumour and fact had got mixed in the telling, and it was now a firmly held opinion that certain 'Avenging Angels' had been seen preparing for what the Bible referred to as the final Day of Judgement, when the Enemy had promised He would come back to Earth in all His glory. Was this one of those Avengers? He was certainly impressive. And who knew what awful fate awaited any demon faced with one of them? Legend had it (well, they hoped it was only legend) there was a lake of fire even now being prepared for them and any humans they could take down with them. Certainly there was mention of this in the humans' Bible, but their hierarchy swore the place was fictitious. False or not, the princes and powers of the underworld were in a state of near panic as rumour followed rumour and no one knew what to think anymore. And now here was an angel who looked imposing enough to actually be one of the principal Avengers. So maybe, just maybe, with enough of them available, they could even the odds a little. Get ahead of the game, so to speak.

CHAPTER 31

Below them, the incoming craft brushed lightly against the ship's hull and a shout brought two of the crew to the side. A rope snaked down and was quickly looped under my arms before being drawn tight by a sudden upward pull which, coinciding with the drop of a rolling wave, lifted me abruptly clear of the unstable canoe. I knew it was pointless to struggle. My arms were still pinioned behind my back and if for some reason I fell out of the rope, I would be in real trouble. So I contented myself with using my feet to keep away from the rough, weather-beaten planking that contoured the side of the ship. I still didn't know why they'd brought me here, but I had a feeling I soon would. And for sure I was right in that assumption. As I stepped over the low rail, an iron collar was snapped around my neck and in one practiced movement locked into place. Then dragging me by the chain attached to the back of the iron ring, one of the men led me straight down through the main hatch.

At once, the rising smell, combined with the ship's uncomfortable movement against the anchors, almost doubled me up as I fought to suppress the bile mounting in my throat. In front of me, barely discernible in the light of a single hurricane lamp, a line of bodies sat or lay – chained by the neck to a metal rail that ran the length of the hold on each side. Quickly, I noted they were mostly men, with a few women held a little apart. I didn't appreciate it then, but years later when I looked back, I realised that my overwhelming impression had been one of total isolation. Strange really, as the place was, in human terms, heavily overcrowded. But it was a place devoid of all compassion. A place of hopelessness. A place of death, where inhumanity reigned supreme. Only one of the slaves took any interest in my arrival and this was a fragile-looking black man secured at the far end of the starboard shackling pole. Despite his forlorn state, the nauseating smell and the foul conditions around him, there was something different about the man. A calmness and a peace reflecting from his face was what initially caught my attention. And unknown to me, he had also come to Israfel's notice.

At first, the angel had missed the obvious signs when looking through the hull, but now he gazed in frank admiration at the courageous young black man sitting bolt upright in the midst of real squalor and uncertainty. Ripped from his home, dragged like an animal to an uncertain fate and held captive against his will, his demeanour still spoke of strength and purpose as he sat staring quietly and without fear, looking straight at me and my gaolers. What I could not see, and Israfel could, was a slight iridescence, a delicate, almost imperceptible shimmer of light emanating like a halo from within the man. It wasn't much, but the demons had certainly noted it and they were keeping a prudent distance. Not one of them dared step within that pale glow, because they knew exactly where it originated. Feeble or not, it confirmed the presence of their arch-enemy. Or to be more precise, the Holy Spirit, being the manifestation of Jesus Christ, the humans' promised Saviour. Which amounted to instant death if they so much as laid a finger on the man without express permission. And not just because of the awe-inspiring angel with the forbidding look now standing well within striking range. To touch a favoured human at any time without God's permission was to invite instant retribution, no questions asked and no quarter given. Besides, heroics were never high on their list of 'things to do'. Invisible, they contented themselves by watching, with some relish, as my body was forced down far enough to allow the crew to lock my chain onto the rail. Allowing them to dispense with my temporary bindings as I found myself kneeling right beside the man I had noticed whilst descending the gangway. Nevertheless, for a while sheer burgeoning, hopeless terror kept me quiet. I just knelt there, my breathing shallow and ragged, trying to control the horror rising like a tide within me. With complete awareness and awful clarity I now knew exactly why I was on board. I was destined to live a nightmare, something I'd only heard about once or twice in my life while at school, studying slavery as a footnote to history. Now I was an integral part of what I had mistakenly assumed to have been consigned to that very history and, what's more, I was definitely on the wrong side.

Shackled in a medieval slaving ship, totally alone and, to all intents and purposes, dead to everything I held dear, the world once more came crashing down on me. A life sentence of slavery, from which I sensed there would be no remission, stared me in the face, stretching out into darkness as far as the eye of prescience could see. And judging by events so far, there was little I could do about it. Despite the heat, I began to shiver deep within myself and before long I was shaking from head to toe. A mixture of the obvious misery surrounding me and the stinking bilge water that slopped about my knees, containing who knew what in liquid form? That, certainly. But it was more than that. Something far more profound was in the air. Lying like a pall over the ship's hold, it held the chill of utter hopelessness and abandonment. That brace of capricious creatures that creep into the soul, forcing one to contemplate both the present and the future with absolute honesty. And whichever way one looked at it, my destiny since leaving home had displayed all the hallmarks of disaster. Now painfully clear before me lay the full horror of the depths to which I had been dragged and, in response, I felt rising within me a desolating rage against the inhumanity of the men who had determined my every move since I'd first stumbled into that train carriage a full lifetime ago. Rage against a gang who had seen me only as a useful commodity to be sold for who knew what price? A round of drinks, another night on the town? At the same time, more miserably alone than I'd ever felt before, I sensed rather than heard a stirring beside me, followed by a sympathetic hand closing over my dangling arm. Mysteriously, with this stranger's hand came the first vestiges of peace in a long time, an unfamiliar tranquillity, something strange and exotic that stole over me like a warm blanket, quietening and stilling the trembling, leading me back from the fearful yet now familiar abyss beyond which lay insanity. Gradually, I remember becoming aware of a friendly voice speaking words in a dialect past understanding. The melodious sounds had an odd cadence, as though the speaker was talking to someone else I couldn't see, although somehow I didn't mind. From somewhere far beyond me I could sense a deep reassurance, as though someone actually did care about me. Strange. But who or what it was, I couldn't tell.

The demons could though. Even Arcturus, for all his posturing, was getting profoundly agitated. What I didn't realise, couldn't see and wouldn't have understood anyway, was that the young man sitting beside me had begun to pray to the Living God and in the unseen world around us, the weak aura emanating from within him had begun to strengthen until it flashed into a brilliant shaft of pure white light stretching straight up from the hellish hold to the highest Heaven. And to make matters worse, the group of angels encamped just off the ship had all leapt to their feet and begun to join in, their voices rising in a great shout of triumph and praise to the God of Heaven and Earth. As the rolling thunder of their proclamation and the swelling sound of intense prayer resonated throughout the dhow, demons came tumbling out of every corner like the proverbial rats leaving a sinking ship, frantic to get out of range. Diving out of the darkened hull straight through anything that got in their way, they rushed around, shrieking in abject terror, clutching their ears in a doomed bid to shut out the awful sight and sound of holiness.

CHAPTER 32

Totally unaware of what was going on in the spiritual world around him, Abdel-Aziz was approaching in the ship's lighter, accompanied by his chief mate and a leather satchel that was never allowed to leave his side. A hail to the deck produced a rope ladder and Abdel swarmed up with surprising alacrity for a man of his size. Dawn was not far off and, with the tide on the turn, he wanted to make the most of the slight off-shore breeze, weighing anchor while the sea still favoured a dash for deep water. No dhow could tack much to wind – the lateen sail and shallow, flat-keeled bottom preventing anything approaching the closer hauled beats to windward available to even some of the old western square riggers. Nevertheless, he and his crew were competent sailors and would make the most of the ship's strengths to haul clear of the many reefs in the area. The intention was to head northeast, if they could make it, until they had blue water under the keel. Then turn north, running before the southerly monsoon some two to five miles off shore. From there he could be sure of clearing any coral outcrops, but still see enough of the land to ease the navigation of a route that had been sailed in much the same ships and much the same way for many hundreds of years. So it was that with the ship still swathed in early morning darkness, I was jerked from a fitful sleep by the sound of running feet overhead and the occasional shout of command.

All too soon, we experienced the inevitable change in rhythm and felt the bilge water slapping to and fro. My head suffered as though it was in a vice, splitting with pain from dehydration and the foetid air in which I sat incarcerated. But empty belly or not, it didn't take long for the stench of my renewed retching to join the general malodour. There was no privacy, no nod in the direction of dignity. I might as well have been a feral animal, for all the esteem I was likely to be accorded as a human being. At least they probably wouldn't let me die of thirst, even if it seemed as though we lay forgotten in the general rush to make sail. Beside me, my newfound friend, whose name I'd discovered was Fenyang, stirred and muttered in his sleep, a veteran already, having been brought aboard at Durban, far to the south.

Close to midnight following my arrival and with sleep no more than a distant hope, I had begun to question and to listen, to be interested in the extraordinary man beside me, drawing comfort from his presence, probing him and mulling over his story as he replied in occasionally awkward but usually understandable, if heavily accented, English. It seemed he had been rescued from the aftermath of a massacre and brought up as an orphan by white missionaries, who had also given him his more memorable, anglicised name: Adam. They had treated him as family, providing unsophisticated schooling from their rudimentary means, basic medicine and undoubtedly more food than he could have hoped for elsewhere. When, finally, he had reached the age at which most young men went their own way, he had been content to stay and work for his adoptive family, acting as a go-between with members of his own tribe, bringing them into contact, often for the first time, with the Christian Gospel embraced by his foster parents and which he had eventually accepted for himself. Which was precisely why he now found himself shackled in a slave ship.

His privileged background and acceptance of the 'white' religion had angered some of his tribe, particularly the local witch doctors, who had encouraged tribal members to sell Adam into the sinister world of slavery. Not needing much encouragement to make a rand or two, they had come for him one night, just after midnight, and he hadn't stood a chance. Now all he had was faith and an absolute and intriguing trust that God would not abandon him. I have to admit, I was momentarily interested, despite myself. True, I'd never had much time for religion, particularly the sort peddled by the school chaplain, virtually the only time I'd come across such matters. As a result, I certainly didn't expect religion to play any part in my present predicament. Although I'll be honest, I couldn't help but notice the difference between Adam and the rest of the wretched cargo. He definitely had something, although what it was precisely, I couldn't tell. With the ship beginning to roll and wallow against the conflicting pull of southerly wind and westerly wave, it was sufficient just to be chained next to him and not alongside one of those who were clearly suspicious of my white skin, despite the shackles. In any case, at this point explanations were way beyond me. Although I couldn't help but remember what Adam had said about relying on God to carry you through adversity. And something about giving your life to His Son, Jesus, who had tasted death on our behalf and now extended a warm welcome to anyone who would believe in Him.

CHAPTER 33

Roz slipped quietly down the stairs, desperate to keep out of sight, feeling suddenly wracked with guilt and acutely aware she had become part of what could almost certainly be construed as illegal – perhaps even a full-blown conspiracy against the forces of law and order. And it was now all spiralling out of control. Quickly, she threaded her way along the unfamiliar corridors, taking care not to follow the 'way out' signs, just in case they led her straight into the arms of incoming police. For all she knew, there were plenty more of them waiting at the entrance for just such a dash. However, within minutes she had found her way through the labyrinth of corridors to finally step into the sun-fired heat brewing in the courtyard behind the kitchens. From there she turned left and made her way round to the car park, trying hard to look as though she was a member of staff who always approached the car park from the back of the hospital. Which was just as well, because there were a couple of Askaris sitting in the back of an open Land Rover, parked alongside the main entrance. Admittedly, they were leaning back in what could best be described as the supine position, but a young white girl on her own was unusual enough to be remembered. Particularly one with such striking good looks. It's the same the world over. Only really comatose men fail to notice a pretty girl.

★★★

By the time Roz arrived back at '*Kwetu*'[(1)], the Jouberts' home, Jill was not only feeling decidedly uncomfortable, but was only too well aware of the choice she faced. She didn't like the way the rather sweaty individual now lounging in front of her was eyeing her legs either and, despite the heat, she was beginning to wish she'd worn something less revealing than the skimpy shorts guaranteed to produce admiring comments from Malcolm. Terence Foley, Superintendent of Police, Mombasa Division, leaned back in his chair and watched with interest the effect he was having on her. He had made it exquisitely clear. She could either co-operate, in which case he might put one of his better detectives on the case to see if they turned up anything on her husband's would-be assassin. Or she could continue to obstruct him by insisting she knew nothing, in which event he would ensure the full weight of the law was brought to bear on them in his own inimical fashion. Not to mention what he might do specifically to Malcolm when and *if* (the emphasis could hardly be missed) he got off the critical list. She was wavering, he could tell, but he kept his face a mask of indifference, keenly aware that in the game of bluff and counterbluff most women had an almost preternatural ability to sniff out prejudice and insincerity, particularly where he was concerned. And he was certainly prejudiced. He'd be the first to admit that – in the right, all male, company, of course. Quite proud of it, really.

Throughout his life he'd been rejected by women just like the one now standing in front of him. A trim body, especially the legs, he thought, the sort a man could take real pleasure over. Well spoken too, despite the accent. Probably more than enough money and no doubt at ease wherever she found herself. Except not when he was involved. He could depend on it. Five minutes after he'd started a conversation, offered to buy a drink, or tried one of his fatally flawed chat-up lines, women like her would be looking for a way out, an excuse to get shot of him. And he hated them for it. Looking back at middle age from the wrong direction and with the only girls available being the kind you bought, every encounter, every negative reaction, merely reinforced his misogyny. So much so, there was no longer anything he could do to amend his attitude, even had his long exhausted conscience managed to prick him. For years now, he had lived for each moment when he could play the 'authority card' with a woman like this. Letting them out and reeling them in, like a cat playing with a mouse, until they became so desperate to get off the hook they almost begged his help. And that was what he waited for. The moment he could offer them hope. Off the record, deniable of course, but which would begin with a casual offer to 'revisit all the facts'. Perhaps over a drink or a meal in a secluded bar he knew of, where he would listen outwardly, but inwardly prepare for the end game he knew was coming. It was all done with such an appearance of genuine concern. They never suspected he was the reason behind any lack of progress, preferring to grasp the straw of hope that, yes, there might be a successful conclusion to their 'difficult' case. But it never ended there, not for either of them, and it wasn't until the victim woke up in some cheap hotel room with a splitting, drug-induced headache and no recollection of how she got there that the 'price' was fully understood. And now Foley was once again on the prowl and intending to savour every moment. He could already feel the prurient excitement rising within him which, had Jill but known it, heralded an ugly prospect for her somewhere up ahead. However, even Foley hadn't bargained on just how high profile this story was going to get.

"So that's all I know. Paul was supposed to be staying with us and when he didn't turn up, we started asking around and finally discovered he was last seen in a truck driving towards that large white building near the old harbour, so Malcolm went over to talk to the owners. Although he tried a couple of times, he couldn't get anyone to answer the door, so he apparently took it into his head to climb over and have a look. Our houseboy tells me that's how my husband got shot and that he's the one who brought him to the hospital."

Jill was only too aware that her on-the-spot concoction sounded pretty lame (well, lies usually do) and decided her only hope was to go on the offensive.

"Obviously, there has to be something pretty nasty going on in there and I don't know what it is, but I think you ought to investigate." Every alarm bell in her head was sounding off as she faced Foley. Notwithstanding the sudden rush of loathing she felt for the creep (she had already begun to think of him in these terms), she was beginning to realise that with Malcolm so dramatically and convincingly out of the equation, they had seriously overrun their luck and were going to have to find some help, however reluctantly. Moreover, if she was going to keep Foley off the true scent, she had to make sure he didn't interrogate Malcolm, who would probably give something away in his disastrously weakened state. So, by the time both the cat and the mouse had stepped into Matron's office, mouse had already resolved not to mention Paul's surname, to be as vague as possible and not let on to any more detail than she could possibly help. Anxiety slipped a cold arm around her shoulders, but she was smart enough to use just enough truth, for now, to ensure neither the family nor the house servants inadvertently used a name with which the police were unfamiliar. Hence the use of 'Paul', a name that had been bandied around sufficiently often for every one of the servants to remember. Finding out they had been given a wrong name was likely to have aroused immediate police suspicion.

If she could just get through this interview, there would at least be time to come up with an agreed story and maybe even an alternative surname for Paul. It was just possible that they could still find him without giving away his true identity. But she knew that wasn't the only problem. It was highly likely that Malcolm's assailant would come sniffing around the hospital to find out exactly who he had shot. She had been reluctant to mention it to Roz, but for some time now she had harboured a shrewd suspicion that I was a victim of the age-old but still quietly thriving slave trade. Young white men didn't usually just vanish and, if she was right, she knew they could all be in for a rough time. She had heard whispers of what happened to those who crossed the slaving gangs. All she needed now, she thought, was the ill-mannered lout still lounging arrogantly in front of her to give her a hard time. So it was with some irritation that his words, purring in her ear, brought her abruptly back to the present.

"OK. By your own admission, your husband was breaking and entering a house at night. And we both know perfectly well the owner is going to claim he was concerned for his own safety, and I can assure you the court will accept that. We seem to have a *prima facie* case against your husband, Mrs, ah…?" Foley slipped a pen and pad out of his bush jacket and sat poised. Reluctantly, Jill gave him her surname, address and telephone number, bridling when he went on to ask for her age. Finding it difficult to keep the anger out of her voice she dropped a few years (to forty-three) and then fell silent. "Mrs Joubert, your husband gets himself shot being stupid enough to break and enter at night and you want me to use up valuable police time just because you think something is going on in there? You want the law to start poking about in Prince Ahmed's house – yes, I know who lives there and believe me, he's well connected – simply because you think a friend of yours was taken there against his will?"

Jill was stunned, but tried desperately not to show it. She had met Ahmed on several occasions, but always at public events. Who had not heard of the sophisticated, urbane man in his flowing Arab dress, with a reputation for generous alms giving and a notoriety for expecting certain unspoken favours in return? "No, I don't want you to do your job because I think something's going on. I want you to do your job because my husband was shot and I know there's something going on. Something that this Prince Ahmed apparently doesn't want anyone to know about. And I don't care how well connected he is."

Foley glowered at her for a moment, not sure how to react to the implied criticism, but certain he would make her pay for it. "Alright, suppose I send some men round there and they find nothing – which, quite frankly, is what I would expect to happen. Then what? You can hardly press charges, since your husband was acting illegally and burglary is still a crime, even if Prince Ahmed is as bent as a paper clip. And where would that leave me? There has to be a better reason for searching his house than just a feminine hunch." Foley gave her a long, slow look and let his words hang in the air while he gauged her reactions. Had she but known it, Foley was already as certain as he could be that Ahmed was up to no good and something really was going on in there that the police weren't supposed to know about. Because he kept a tight hold on his 'patch' he also knew Ahmed had recently absented himself, although annoyingly in this instant, he didn't know where he'd gone. But Jill didn't need to know that. Foley's real problem was that until now he'd failed to come up with a good enough excuse to merit the issue of a search warrant against Ahmed. However, if he played his cards right, this woman might provide him with the very justification he needed, particularly while Ahmed was away and probably couldn't interfere. Moreover, if it all went pear-shaped and Ahmed came up clean, he could always make sure Jill was the one left twisting in the wind.

CHAPTER 34

When it came, the raid by Foley's hand-picked men was well enough executed and the one caretaker left in the building had little or no chance of escape. Dark and wraith-like in the early morning light, he was caught before he got halfway across the courtyard and laid out cold with a ruthlessly swift blow to the back of the head from a short rubber cosh. Dragging his heels through the dust, the strike team pulled him into the building, there to work on him at their leisure, once the building was declared secure. For the rest, searching the almost empty building was the work of minutes and when the entrance to the underground cellars was discovered, the powerful stench of human faeces and rotting food told them exactly what the subterranean vaults had been used for. Their problem was, by the time they arrived, all hope of finding any slaves, or of tracing Ahmed's financial dealings through his records, had clearly disappeared, along with their erstwhile owner. He might as well not have existed, for all they could turn up, so there was little to be gained.

Which left their supine prisoner, head and neck now caked with drying blood, and the first signs of returning consciousness beginning to animate his face. A suitable object for Foley's legendary wrath. The superintendent was as much feared by his own men as he was loathed by the local criminal fraternity. His reputation was second to none when it came to extracting information and it was rumoured several prisoners had died under his ministrations, especially once they had nothing left to tell. So when Foley turned the man over with the toe of his boot and ordered a start on softening him up, no one thought to object.

Even when the ragged and tormented shrieking began to penetrate the thick walls they still kept at it, working their victim over from head to foot with all the studied indifference of those long used to getting what they wanted. Just a light beading of sweat to mark out the men whose enjoyment of the process spurred them to ever-greater efforts. The irony of policemen aping the very behaviour for which they were hoping to prosecute Ahmed completely passing them by.

But while Foley was hated for his cruel indifference, such feelings paled into insignificance beside the terror felt by those who worked for the Prince. Not for nothing was he recognised as the very personification of avenging malice. If even a hint of treachery reached Ahmed's ears, his reputation alone was enough to drive strong men to suicide, rather than face the lifelong threat of the unknown behind every pair of eyes, every street corner. The Arab racketeer never gave up, never turned aside from his patient tracking of the object of his wrath until, eventually, there was no place left to hide. And Kijone, his long-time valet and now rapidly swelling object of wrath, was more aware of this than most. So he had no option but silence. All he could hope for was a merciful death before they either forced him to talk, or crippled him for life. And he almost got his wish. A blow to the side of his face delivered with too much enthusiasm, too much masochistic delight, split his skull, broke his cheekbone and sprayed blood and teeth over the surrounding floor. Foley turned away in disgust, convinced the blow had ended all hope of progress, angry with the over-zealous fool who had brought the interrogation to such an abrupt end, before even a word had been extracted from his only possible source of information. A finger jerked savagely in the direction of the offender ensured Foley's sergeant would soon visit the Superintendent's displeasure on the miscreant.

"Call in a team to dump the body and clean up. We have work to do." And with that, Foley strode out of the room and down to his waiting car.

Jill had no idea who could be calling so late, but she took the precaution of sending Roz out of the room before moving closer to the chained and bolted door. "Who is it?"

"Superintendent Foley. You can open up, Mrs Joubert, it's alright."

Momentarily rooted to the spot, Jill felt the hair on the nape of her neck rise. There was just something about Foley, his voice and mannerisms that made her skin crawl, but she knew it was pointless denying him entry, so with an arched eyebrow in the general direction of Roz's disappearing back, she threw the bolts, drew back the chain and let him in. Foley stepped swiftly over the threshold, his gaze sweeping the room, senses missing nothing as he noted the two glasses and the fading swirl of a perfume Jill wasn't wearing. Turning, he contemplated her for a moment with some pleasure, mentally removing the flowing silk dress and imagining what he would do with the full breasts and slim hips.

"I thought you would want to know we've had a good look in Ahmed's house, but found nothing. He's disappeared, cleaned the place out. No servants, no papers, no evidence, nothing. So there's little I can do beyond opening a formal enquiry into the shooting and, of course, your husband will have to explain exactly what he was doing there in the first place." He let the import of his words sink in, pleased with her reaction, because he could tell his presence was unnerving her. Not just his presence, but something more. She was hiding something, he was certain, and not just the woman who had obviously left the room in a hurry. He made no assumptions, but why the secrecy? What was he missing?

Listening from behind the flimsy door, Roz could hear Foley quizzing Jill. He was obviously suspicious of something and now he was asking her who else was in the house. With a start she realised he might even demand to be shown around and if he gave kitchen staff the third degree, he would be on to her immediately. She knew there was no chance of Jill giving her away, but she was equally aware that her only prospect of finding and protecting me lay in remaining free and able to reach me before Foley did. And that meant staying out of sight. Having so recently heard Jill wax lyrical on the subject of the 'odious little creep', she was even more afraid of what would happen if and when the police caught up with me.

If Ahmed's white house was empty tonight, she decided, she might as well start there, because there was nothing else to go on and it was just possible the police had missed something. Moving carefully away from the door, Roz made her way to the back of the house and out to the stables. She prayed silently that the house fans would cover the sound of the Jeep engine as she turned it over and was relieved when it started first pull. It didn't take long to clear *Kwetu* and soon she was well underway, weaving a path across town to the white house, where she parked a street away, trying not to arouse suspicion. The large gates were standing open when she arrived, creating a forlorn and abandoned look, obviously ignored by the police team in their haste to leave. Even against the glimmer of white walls, the courtyard beyond was a black and forbidding void. Summoning all her courage, Roz slipped quietly between the gates and, staring hard, tried to penetrate the enveloping darkness. At least her night vision was good, so it didn't take long to locate the darker shadow of a door. Once inside, she snapped on a torch and, filtering the light with one hand to prevent the beam from betraying her presence, she began to carefully climb the stairs. In her soft sandals little sound betrayed her progress and her pulse was just beginning to drop back below a hundred, when a deep groan somewhere up ahead froze her dead in her tracks.

The sound, which carried a mixture of desperation and almost animal pain, trailed away in the surrounding darkness, taking with it any hope of controlling her heart rate. But the strains of anguish overlaying that single cry echoed in her mind, the perpetrator's obvious torment dissipating her fear, until once more she could pick up the pace and move quickly on upwards. This time, she didn't worry about noise and soon her bobbing light picked up the outline of a man spread-eagled on the floor, black, sticky blood oozing from his head and face, spreading in streamers across the boards. Whoever it was lay still, only his eyes giving any indication of life, as they turned slowly towards her, the whites glittering briefly in the torch glow. Swiftly, Roz knelt beside him, biting back the nausea and cradling his head with her hand while she reached for a handkerchief in the hope of staunching the slow trickle of blood from his nose, ears and mouth. There seemed little she could do for him, but spotting a carafe of water on a low table, she eased his head up and tried to pour a little of the liquid into his mouth. Which only caused him to cough and splutter horribly and, in fright, she swapped to simply dowsing the handkerchief and wiping his blood-spattered skin. Slowly, he regained a little composure, but his swift, shallow breathing gave little hope he would ever recover. Grateful eyes stared up at her and, speaking gently in Kiswahili, she tried to soothe him. She could see more clearly now and could trace the dreadful swelling across the side of his face, reaching up to his skull, where a suspicious depression explained why he was in such dire straits. Even with her lack of experience, she knew he was dying and, looking into his eyes, she could discern his own realisation there too. But there was nothing effective she could do. Nothing useful she could say. Nevertheless, unwilling to remain passive in the face of his slow passing, she rocked him gently in her lap and, for want of something to say, began to tell him why she was there. Who she was looking for. Describing me in detail.

After a while, her words dried up and in the silence, she simply stroked the caretaker's swollen face. Tears began to fall, wetting the drying runnels of blood. She wasn't sure how long she had been kneeling there, but into the silence a voice whispered and, with a start, she realised he was speaking to her, the man whose name she didn't even know.

"The young man you seek, he was here. Ahmed has sold him to Abdel-Aziz, the slave trader, and he was taken a few days ago. He is on a slaving dhow and he will sail first to Somalia and then probably Yemen. You can easily recognise the dhow by the bright copper post just in front of the main mast. No other dhow in these parts has such a post. It's where Abdel-Aziz ties the slaves he wants to whip. If you hurry, you may find him. They will call at Malindi to take on water."

Barely able to believe her ears, Roz looked down at him, whispering her thanks. As she did so, his eyes clouded and his head rolled slightly towards her, seeming to nestle closer into her lap and she felt the warm breath spill out of him for the last time. Looking at this nameless African, she felt a great wave of compassion reaching out to him and from somewhere within her childhood memories, a half-forgotten prayer fell from her lips. It was such a miserable ending, she thought. Who knew how long he had been lying there in pain, unnoticed and unmissed. Was that the way everyone went in the end? Sordidly, slipping away into nothingness – a lifetime spent in doing what, going where? She hadn't known him and now she never would. He had passed unremarked and, for all she knew, unremarkable. Looking at him, the enormity of her situation beginning to dawn on her, she felt the tears slide more freely down her cheeks and as she stared down her eyes lost focus, her mind fled to memories of me, and her body suddenly longed for the comforting touch of my hand (oh, the opportunities lost through my stubbornness). And in the midst of her reverie, gaining ground from tiny seed to full-grown thought, the knowledge of where I might be finally burst into her consciousness and despite the desperate circumstances she now knew me to be in, the agony and fear that had been threatening to overwhelm her receded like a tide on the ebb. At last, there was a real chance she would find me. As gently as she could, she slid the cooling, lifeless head to the floor and closed his eyes. There was nothing further to be done and she was far too practical to waste time wondering if she should go for help. One word to the police that she had been there and it would only be a matter of time before they made it their business to find out why. Besides, she thought suddenly and with surprising perspicacity, what if it was the police, under the command of that awful man, who had done this?

CHAPTER 35

Reaching the edge of town from where the narrow ribbon of tarmac trailed away behind her and only murram lay ahead, Roz put her foot down as hard as she dared, driving into the soft velvet of the moonlit darkness stretching out ahead. At last, there was a definite purpose behind her movement. Driving hard, she could hope to reach Malindi in four to five hours, even if she was slowed by the usually tardy hand operated cable ferries that spanned the creeks. And the unpleasantness of the road, which she could already taste in the dust sucked through the open sides of the Jeep, wasn't likely to impede progress either. Added to which, the thought of going back to her beloved haunts was enough to lift her spirits in a way they had not been aroused for weeks.

For a brief while, as she drove back through the narrow streets of Mombasa, Roz had vacillated over whether or not to call Jill. To let her know what she had found. But the more she thought about it, the more she realised her friend had enough to cope with and what Jill didn't know, Jill didn't have to keep secret. Thoughts of the dead man she had left behind bothered her too, but soon they were pushed aside as she gave her mind over to calculating the ship's likely progress. When exactly had it put to sea? What was the wind like out there? How long would a dhow need to replenish food and water for crew and cargo? She couldn't imagine it would be long, or that it would take many days to make passage to Malindi. However, she eventually stopped fretting, accepting she would either be in time or she wouldn't. And if she wasn't, she really didn't know what she would do. But then, when she thought about it, she didn't know what she would do if she was in time. And anyway, assuming the dhow did show up, how would she reach it? There were usually at least half a dozen dhows in the port area coming and going about their business as they scurried up and down the coast, and Roz knew that none of them would welcome an infidel woman on board. So it really wasn't worth worrying about. She would just have to drive until she reached civilisation, enlist some help and ease down to Port Malindi to see what would happen from there. At least she knew where she could get breakfast and where she would find a welcome.

CHAPTER 36

In the sunless hold the days and nights rapidly melded into each other as the heavy dhow wallowed its ungainly way northwards. It rolled like a pig and the stench of the mounting volume of human excrement merely thickened the already foetid air of our cramped prison. It hadn't taken me long to give up on the struggle to keep clear of the surging bilge water with its nameless contents but, much more importantly, I was determined, desperate, to gain some respite from the lurching, staggering gait of the lateen-rigged vessel. Ungainly and heavy, the old slaver slammed into, or rolled over, rather than with, the long ocean breakers hunching themselves into towering slopes as they were forced up by the slowly shelving shoreline. It didn't matter where you were on the eastern seaboard, from several miles off-shore the floor of the ocean bed angled steadily up towards the jagged coral banks and creamy beaches of the brooding coastline. So, for the most part, my fellow sufferers sat in sullen, unresponsive silence, simply staring towards the only source of light that streamed down through the open hatch. Hopeless it might have seemed but, despite everything, I was just as unready to give up as my newfound ally, Adam.

Between us, we had managed to persuade the crew that letting the prisoners go up, a few at a time, to the rope-cluttered deck, would be good for the health of the ship. In any case, those few precious minutes exposed to salt-laden air that tasted like a rare wine as it was sucked greedily down into our overwrought lungs was worth any and every effort. Even the harsh glare of the sun slitting our eyes as it glittered off a thousand facets of the deep-blue jewel on which we floated, gave welcome assurance that the Hell below was not the only reality.

And it wasn't long before the two of us, ears cocked warily towards the hatch, were raking quietly and earnestly over the information we had gleaned about the crew. We debated endlessly around the option of jumping overboard, but were always forced to face the inescapable – even if we survived the ubiquitous sharks and managed to stay afloat long enough to reach land, there were very few breaks in the reef stretching hundreds of miles to north and south of our supposed position. One raking wave tumbling us across the razor-sharp coral, not to mention the serried ranks of long-spined sea urchins, would be enough to abruptly terminate any foolhardy venture. In the end we had to reluctantly agree that going overboard was tantamount to committing suicide which, to some of our fellow prisoners at least, might well have held some attraction. But neither of us was yet ready to concede defeat or bring others into our confidence. The more who knew we were even contemplating escape, the more chance someone would buy themselves a short-lived respite in exchange for the information. As it was, I was taken aback by the latent hostility still being shown towards me, despite all my efforts on their behalf. Being white obviously had its drawbacks. Still, of one thing I was certain: the crew's demeanour showed they were confident there was nothing to fear from their slaves. No particular watch was kept and even when batches of us were allowed on deck, little was done to restrain or police us. I could only presume these slavers had never faced organised rebellion. A status quo I had every intention of changing.

And to that end, I remember outlining a recklessly simple plan to Adam, merely trying to gauge his reaction. "We can't swim for it, so there's only one other option. We have to seize the ship. We've only seen one guard topside, and he's armed with a rifle. Both times we've been up he's been sitting by the starboard rail, keeping in the shade from the sail, and I could swear he was asleep last time. Apart from him, we've only seen a half-dozen or so crew, plus the one at the stern behind the steering oar, who looks like he could be the owner, judging by the way he's dressed. We must assume he's armed as well, so I couldn't deal with both of them at the same time. To have any chance, there have to be at least two of us involved and none of this other lot looks as if they would know which way is up, no matter what the stakes. Which means, either you go for the owner, or I'm the one who has to hope he can't shoot straight. I know I'm getting weaker with each day's passing, so I'm going to try to persuade them to let us up on deck when they come to feed us this evening, just before sunset. Then, if there's still only one guard, I'm going to have a go at him. Adam, I don't know about you, but I don't think we can afford to wait another day. So, just let me have a few seconds without interference and with luck I can dump the guard overboard. If we pick the right time, darkness should at least work in our favour if it comes to a shooting match. I'm serious, Adam. I'll do it anyway, but, if you'll help, we have a real chance of pulling it off. That rifle is the key. Get it and there's a likelihood we'll succeed. Believe me, I'm a good shot and I won't hesitate to kill. They'll know we're desperate, especially when we free the other slaves, and we'll demand they take us in through the next break in the reef, or I'll threaten to shoot them one at a time and, if the worst comes to the worst, take a chance we can sail this thing on our own. At a guess, we must be somewhere near Malindi by now. So what do you say? Are you with me?"

I watched Adam hesitate. Actually, I could see the shadows of doubt flickering across his expressive face. "Come on, Adam, what've you got to lose? Once you're sold on, you'll probably die anyway. Isn't it better to die trying to get free, rather than be worked to death because you chickened out when you could have done something?" Desperation can make fools of us all and selfish fools at that.

I'll never forget it. Adam looked straight at me and sighed.

"Paul, you haven't heard me, have you? I've already told you, I will not kill or put anyone's life at risk for the sake of my own freedom. If I am to die, so be it. What really matters is that my spirit is already free. Yes, they can break my body and I can't stop them. Does that make me afraid? Yes, it does. But they can't touch what really counts. My spirit. They can't do that, because I belong to Jesus Christ, the Son of the living God, and he will look after me, even if that means death at the hands of some slave owner. Death in this world is really only the beginning of real life, not the end."

As I looked at my new friend, I wondered if he had lost his sanity. I had listened to him many times since my arrival on the ship, but I still didn't believe what he had to say about this God thing. Certainly, Adam was a good guy. There was no doubt in my mind about that. Possibly a little deluded, even though he had a strange knack of calming everyone around him (not just me). Even when things took a turn for the worse, he seemed to bring hope just by being there. That was the stupid thing. One part of me really wanted to believe Adam, to accept what he had to say and to fall under his spell, to let his tales of a God who cared become the reality that Adam said He was. But there was only one way to act now, as far as I was concerned, and that was to take any and every opportunity to hit back, to gain the upper hand, to determine my own fate, particularly if there was even a halfway chance of success. I couldn't help it. With the passage of the last few days that initial, half-felt rage had blossomed into an all-consuming hatred that was eating me up. It was no longer 'half-felt'. Fury at my perceived fate was almost overwhelming me. Anger against those whom I perceived to be the cause of so much trouble, coupled with a burning determination to get my own back, was informing my every thought. So, in disgust I shook my head at him and dismissed him with a shrug. The self-styled all-action man, I turned back to contemplating the hatch with its beckoning beams of light.

The odd thing was, when it came to the time, it was

surprisingly easy to convince the crew to let us up on deck again and once there, I stood looking around me, aware of Adam's presence within an arm's length to my right with two other nameless prisoners standing behind him. True, the guard was awake, but his weapon was leaning against a nearby cask, whilst he sat on the gunwale, leg wrapped firmly round a convenient stanchion. I watched him idly applying himself to plaiting one of the palm leaves kept on the deck for use by any crewman who needed shade.

Slowly, under the pretence of looking to see what he was doing, I eased myself closer. I didn't dare get too close for fear of alerting him. Glancing aft, I was able to see the owner still up at the stern, but standing now, eyeing us through the rapidly encroaching darkness as the sun slipped below the horizon. For a moment my courage deserted me and I felt my hands beginning to tremble but, even as I did so, a hand pressed my arm and Adam's voice whispered encouragement. Unable to turn around, I could only listen as my friend pledged himself to draw fire, anything to give me a fighting chance. And in that instant, I knew he was offering to die for me. For a moment there was stillness around us, only the soughing of wind in the rigging and breaking water slapping at the hull disturbed the tableau.

Standing loosely, feet spread against the ship's roll, I felt overwhelmed, but knew it was now or never and so, balling my fists, I gave Adam a grateful glance and a whispered command to "go" before stepping swiftly across the short distance separating me from the guard. Surprise was complete and the man had time only to widen his eyes as my shoulder took him full in the chest and he flipped backwards, arms flailing as he swayed too far over the railing on which he had been sitting, and which now simply added to his balance problem. Even as he went over, I had already turned towards the rifle, aware of a rising crescendo of shouts towards the stern. Grabbing the gun, I levered the action in one smooth movement, back and forward, automatically checking it was cocked and loaded even as I was bringing it level with my shoulder. In the few seconds that had elapsed I was almost surprised to see how far Adam had got, but even as I sighted down the rifle, I knew I was too late.

Abdel-Aziz was facing Adam, balance thrown forward onto the balls of his feet, right hand stretched in front of him, a pistol pointing directly at the racing form coming directly towards him. There was no fear, just a tight look of anger etching his face and even as I took it all in, a gout of flame lanced outwards directly towards Adam and the gun-wielding hand started tracking towards me. Desperately, I pulled the rifle's trigger and watched the shot tear through the man's left arm, but it didn't stop him. As the pistol came into line with me I heard the crash of its explosive force and felt the momentary tug of a bullet passing through the fleshy part of my thigh. The blow knocked me sideways, staggering against the roll of the ship and throwing my aim too far left to draw down on the man at the stern, and as a combination of pain and ship's movement delayed my reactions I could hear the slap, slap of swiftly running feet coming from behind. Feeling as if I was swimming in molasses, I turned my head in slow motion towards the sound, only to discover I was way behind the curve ball and the last thing I saw or felt was the clubbing fist that caught me squarely between the eyes.

CHAPTER 37

For all that it was considerably less than a hundred miles, the journey had seemed never-ending, particularly as she'd had to persuade the two ferry operators on the route to open up, despite the late hour but, as dawn opened its first bleary eye, Roz was finally able to relax and wriggle her shoulders to ease the tension. Slowing for the first time in some while merely allowed her teeth to stop rattling in sympathy with the rough corrugation patterning the mixed grey and white coral dust road that wound in and out of the never-ending coconut plantations Every turn faithfully reflecting the meandering coastline. She longed for a drink, any drink, to relieve the burning dryness of her throat and wash away the vile metallic taste of dust. It was everywhere. In her hair, her clothes, gritting her eyes. Every crease on her sweat-cooled body sported a dark line where the dust had coagulated – and light khaki shorts and a short-sleeved shirt hadn't helped.

Leaving in a hurry had seemed a good idea at the time, but she had failed to bring even the basics of food, water and mosquito-proof clothing. A fact she had spent most of the journey regretting. Being night, she couldn't even rely on the ubiquitous totos[1], who usually lined the route wherever it passed through a village, desperate to tout their wares of sweet-tasting green coconuts and roasted cashew nuts. She loved their eager smiles as they stretched on tiptoe, trying hard to peer into passing cars and wishing they were old enough, tall enough, to see into her adult world. But, despite their absence, she was already beginning to feel better as she recognised the palm-fringed outskirts of Malindi. Drawing level with the first outlying shack, she soon spotted the unmarked trail that would lead her down its rutted, coral-strewn pathway to her old home. For a moment all weight of concern lifted from her shoulders and a small smile played around her lips, lighting up her clear blue eyes as they drank in so many familiar childhood scenes. It was too early for the compound's white tenants to be up and about, but from within the line of servants' quarters she could see early stirrings as families she had known most of her life rose to greet the new day, handfuls of kindling and larger sticks already gathered to revive the slow-burning fires banked the previous evening against the dew-laden night air. She let the Jeep rock to a halt, killing the engine as heads turned to stare inquisitively at this unexpected intrusion. She could sense the uncertainty quivering in every line of their suddenly nervous bodies, until one by one they began, hesitantly, to recognise her.

The change, when it came, was complete. With real joy lighting their friendly faces, the whole group relaxed, to gather swiftly and noisily around her, hands outstretched in greeting as the haunting cadence of a true and heartfelt African welcome roused even the laziest children still playing possum under the soft skins thrown casually across their Spartan cots.

"Eh! You come back, Memsahib kidogo"

She was much too tired and too relieved for even a hint of annoyance to develop over the reminder of days long gone, when she really had been 'the little lady'. "*Anyway,*" she thought, "*it's only a term of endearment.*" More importantly, she could see the unspoken question in their eyes, but the conventions of African courtesy forbade asking until the guest was well settled and immediate needs addressed. Which, if she allowed them free rein, could take half the morning. Nevertheless, she was more than grateful for their consideration and sank gladly onto a log while Mama M'baneo bustled around preparing an impromptu breakfast of fresh pau-pau, posho[2] and dark, steaming coffee. There had been plenty of time on the journey to think through her next move and the realisation that these old friends were her main if not only hope had long since settled any doubts. They of all people along this hot and humid coast would know what might be done. Of that she was certain. Flicking back her long blonde hair, she let the worries go and gave herself over to their warm ministrations.

"There are nearly always dhows in the harbour, Memsahib Roz. At this time of the year, with the trade winds blowing, they come and go every day. They say some have slaves on board, but no one can be certain which, because they keep the slaves hidden. But if the dhow with the copper post comes in, we will see it and if we do, we will let you know. What you do after that will be for you to decide. It will not be easy to get on board, but we will do what we can to help you. Kimau's uncle is a fisherman and he has a fine boat. If you like, we will talk to him and try to persuade him to take you out, but he will only go at night after he has finished the day's fishing. Anyway, night is the only time it might be safe, as the Arab slavers carry guns and they are not afraid to use them."

Roz smiled her gratitude and ducked her head with pleasure at their immediate and unstinting support. She didn't want to get them involved if there was any danger and just their offer to keep an eye out for this one particular dhow was enough for now. "You haven't asked me why I don't go to the police for help and I am grateful for that. I can't tell you at the moment, but believe me, it's important the police do not reach Paul before I do. However, if we don't find him in the next few days or if, when we do, it all looks too dangerous, then I'll have to ask for their help. But it will only be as a last resort."

Several heads nodded. They had little love for their local police and most of them would rather run a few quiet risks for their *memsahib kidogo* than give the police an excuse to crawl all over them. With the day now firmly established, the ubiquitous heat was beginning to build and Roz felt she had rested long enough. She knew it wouldn't be long before uncertainty would once again start to tap-dance its way around her consciousness and the inevitable emergence of the family renting the main house would quickly 'up' the ante. It was time to get going.

Standing, she beckoned them closer. "I don't know how long it is since Paul left Mombasa, but there's really no time to waste. Please, Kimau, will you and N'jerogi come with me now to the harbour so you can speak to your uncle? For all I know, we may need his boat tonight. Once we've dropped you off, Kimau, then N'jerogi can show me the best place to keep a lookout for this dhow."

CHAPTER 38

For all her optimism, two long and frustrating days were to pass
before word came of a dhow with a copper post edging into the
bay just ahead of a swiftly darkening sky. One thing was certain.
It had come from the south, the right direction, and it obviously
had no wish to attract attention, because it had dropped anchor
well away from the beach. Clearly, there was no run ashore
planned for this crew. Kimau found Roz down by the mole that
marked the end of Malindi harbour, her bare legs hanging over
its edge, suntanned heels kicking up and down as she squinted
morosely out to sea. He squatted down beside her and didn't have
to tell her why he was there.

"Where is it?"

"Not far, just around the headland there. It will not take us
long. You can't see it from here, but it's definitely the one you're
looking for. Come, I will show you."

Roz scrambled to her feet and followed him eagerly, almost
running to keep up with his long, loping strides until they
rounded the small point and stopped. The soft, still warm sand
trickled through her bare toes as she stood facing the sea, one
hand shading her eyes against the dazzle of the undulating water,
sparkling with the last rays of the lowering sun. Just inside the
line of the reef, its great sail furled, a nondescript dhow rode at
anchor. Completely unremarkable and, like all of its kind,
completely devoid of paint, it could have been any one of the
thousands that endlessly processed along the East African coast.
Except, that is, for an unusual, sturdy and highly polished copper
post fixed mid-ships, which even now appeared to have someone

or something propped against it. But even for her young eyes, the shape was impossible to make out from that distance and elevation. Roz stared hard at the isolated boat bobbing and ducking to the roll of the incoming waves, snubbing at a long coir rope that no doubt ended in a rough-hewn block of coral doing duty as an anchor somewhere ahead of it. She could see no activity, but that was hardly unusual for the time of evening. Eyes narrowed, she thought hard for a moment. How long was it likely to stay? The tide would turn favourable for departure in an hour or so, but would she set sail in the dark, or wait till morning, when the tide would once again favour the ungainly vessel and the swiftly growing light would ensure an easier passage through the treacherous reef? And how many crew were likely to be on board? She knew that a four-hundred ton boum dhow would normally carry between eight and sixteen crew, but it was already getting too dark to make out the details. So could she really risk boarding in the face of so many unknowns? She was at least certain Kimau's uncle would now take her out, but he was equally adamant in his resolve to stay clear of any likely fracas, already considering any attempt at a rescue to be foolhardy in the extreme. There was no doubting the crew would treat any infiltration on board as a threat to their lives, never mind their livelihood, and it was predictable that they would act accordingly. Little mercy would be given or expected in the dark and confusion of night. And Roz was almost convinced that at the first hint of mayhem, her transport would leave. In any case, with the stakes so high, she couldn't expect the others to get involved. After all, with the sole exception of Kimau, who might be persuaded to 'volunteer', they had their own lives to lead.

Surreptitiously, she glanced at her companion, who was also trying to make out details in the fading light. She hadn't broached the subject yet, but was acutely aware she would need his help if there was to be any hope of a rescue – always assuming this was the slaving vessel she was after. So far she had no weapons, no backup and little idea of how to get on board. The only positive attribute she had going for her was iron-clad resolve. But what was that worth against well-armed men? Squinting at the distant hull, any clandestine attempt to get on board seemed like a hopeless recipe for disaster, and she knew it. But for all that, she had no intention of backing down. She would just have to improvise as she went along or become one more member of the cargo if it all went pear-shaped. The gathering darkness finished its rapid slide across the water, frustrating any further hope of observation, and the urgency of the situation once more pressed in upon her. Her mind made up, she swung towards Kimau and put him on the spot.

Kimau's uncle was old and grizzled, but with Kimau's aid he worked the sail with a dexterity that brought the little craft to a dead stop, head into wind and a mere foot or two from the wooden hull looming over their flimsy craft, its slick sides reeking of rotting seaweed, stale fish and something indefinable, yet deeply disturbing and nauseous, all at the same time. Apart from the hiss of water forcing under the keel and the creak of wood on wood as she pitched against the waves coming from her bow, there was little sound, certainly nothing emanating from the deck above to startle Roz. It was shortly after midnight and their objective had remained swathed in its pitch-black mantle, her raked mast blotting out the stars one by one as it swung in lazy circles against the night sky. No light pierced the darkness around the ship, which seemed to drain even the little light the sea did manage to reflect. There had been no sound and no obvious movement to disturb the deceptive stillness as they warily approached the dhow from the west, close in to the beach and taking advantage of the off-shore breeze. A breeze that had, by its very direction, forced them to risk being spotted against the white sands gleaming softly behind them in the pale starlight. However, had they but known it, there was no immediate danger from the crew who, to a man, were stretched out comatose on the cluttered deck, taking what rest they could.

On the other hand, the wraith-like creatures infesting every square inch of the floating nightmare were very much awake and watching with mounting glee as the tiny craft slowly crept towards them. With Roz now right below them, desperately searching for a foothold against the heave and pitch of her fishing smack, a ripple of evil anticipation flickered along the deck like the sigh of a morning breeze riffling through stately palms. Now – now was the time to rouse the crew, to stoke their deepest fears, to wake them suddenly with a half-remembered whisper of danger in the far recesses of their sleep-dulled minds. To thus goad the sleeping crew was meat and drink to the reptilian onlookers, forever lusting after the life-force of their potential victims. In their swarming hoards they hung boldly above the sleeping crew, confident their long-practiced intervention would trigger an immediate and deadly outcome. Cravings already whetted that day, they had watched me writhe and moan as I begged the owner to stop the merciless lashing that drew yet more blood from dozens of deep cuts all over my body, arms and legs. And now here was an opportunity to witness, to even initiate, guaranteed butchery and probably get away with it, as far as Heaven was concerned. All it needed was the right trigger and the nameless guilt and dread in which all the crew were steeped by the horrors of their trade would quickly do the rest, driving them into a frenzy of activity, sufficient to overwhelm any stranger daring to step onto the ship's deck. At which point, virtually nothing could halt the killing of someone like Roz, who surely had little or no chance of defending herself against fully grown men.

The heave of a passing wave coincided neatly with her furthest stretch and suddenly Roz found herself treading air as the wave receded, the fingers of her right hand the only means of preventing a dangerous and ignominious descent back to the sea that had already drenched her. Clutching the mid-ships guardrail with all her strength, and fighting desperately against the combined lurch upward of the dhow and the downward pull of gravity, Roz forced herself to lunge with her left hand towards a rope end flopping backwards and forwards just above her. The roll of the ship dangled her helplessly outwards, but its reverse pitch brought the rope within momentary reach and, with a barely suppressed gasp of relief, she began to pull herself upwards, feet scrabbling for purchase against the rough planking.

CHAPTER 39

It wasn't so much the barely perceptible change in the background noise that triggered the preternatural alert. Rather the instantly suppressed glitter of an impossibly white light sparkling off a small patch of worn grey sail sagging from the end of the dhow's uneven boom, still secured where it had been roughly lashed as the anchor went overboard. The flicker was so quick that the scattered photons of ethereal light were gone even as they registered, but the devils' leader, Arcturus, caught the mistake as his eyes roved the deck, impatiently waiting for the right moment to give the command that would start the intended riot.

The brief warning had barely faded from his retina before Arcturus knew for a surety what was coming. It wasn't that he'd made any particular mistake, or been foolish enough to let down his guard. Long eons of time had taught him that, in his book, the Enemy never did play fair. God was just as likely to materialise a whole regiment of warrior angels right on top of the dhow as allow Arcturus to get on with his business undisturbed. That was the problem. You never knew what the Enemy was up to, or where He would stir up the next dispute over His beloved humans, or even over territory. And as for Arcturus' own supreme commander, Lucifer, if you happened to be in the wrong place at the wrong time and lost any of his territory, you were damned. Literally. There was no alternative. Particularly if you were in command: you fought to the death, or you faced certain conviction and at best exile, probably attended by the rest of your outraged company. Rumour had it that Lucifer had even begun using the Enemy's own invention for his own ends, the gruesome annex to Hell referred to in the Enemy's writings as the bottomless pit. Apparently, it had recently become his weapon of choice for destroying those unfortunate enough to cross him. There was no appeal and once dispatched no one had ever returned. Arcturus shuddered, but this time he did at least have an edge. Not much perhaps, but hopefully just enough. At a guess, the angels shadowing him and growing in numbers ever since the slaver had set out from Durban, had been ordered in because something had changed and right now that could only mean the recently arrived boat with its lone female, who was in the very act of slipping silently over the port gunnels. For the life of him, he wasn't sure why this puny entity was worth any bother, but something had obviously stirred the Enemy and He was clearly displeased, or He wouldn't have ordered an attack. For centuries Arcturus had been pursuing his grisly trade unmolested, even before the fiasco on the west coast of Africa during the 1740s, when he had first come to Satan's attention by losing John Newton, a prized slaver captain. If that hadn't dragged out over several years of administrative incompetence involving a few arch-demons, he would have been summarily executed there and then. However, as fate would have it, there were enough of the hierarchy involved to ensure others took the rap, allowing him to escape execution. Just.

After that it had taken years of assiduous work but, with precisely the right mixture of subservient depravity and brazen arrogance, he had advanced far enough up the promotion ladder to come to the attention of Satan's inner court and, despite what his immediate superior thought of him, he was sure he was now considered almost useful within the upper echelons of Hell's hierarchy. Moreover, as a relatively senior commander he could, if all went well, expect eventual access to Hell's presiding council and perhaps even participation in the sort of acts of depravity over which, as yet, he could only dream and slobber in eager anticipation. If only he could manage to keep a low profile in the meantime. Almost hissing with rage he watched carefully as the angels approached.

From where they had been trailing him, just off to seaward, he knew they could easily have reached the dhow undetected if one of them hadn't made the elementary mistake of easing sword and scabbard too early. But as far as Arcturus was concerned, that was one mistake too many. The razor-edged blades they wielded were fearsome, but they were only ever as good as the warriors who sported them. And it didn't take much light to pierce the thick pall of darkness surrounding the dhow, which any angel worth his salt would have known. With long years of campaigning behind him, Arcturus recognised instinctively where the weakness lay. Experienced warrior angels, any one of whom could match any ten of his own veterans single-handed, didn't make elementary gaffes of that nature. So, with at least one of the angels short on experience, there was every reason to suppose their line of advance could be turned, provided he was off the mark fast enough. Yet even as Arcturus began to relocate his forces, Numibia, the dark-skinned and supremely athletic angel in overall command, was weighing up the odds on just that likelihood. Numibia knew they'd blown it. Like the rest of them, he had to admit to a certain inexperience, but that didn't mean he was irresponsible, or that he would simply ignore the mistake. None of the angels now under his command had been assigned to Earth very long and, so far, they had been spared the raw power and ugliness of Earth-side skirmishes, most of which, by all accounts, tended to be a far cry from the set-piece battles junior angels studied and war-gamed back in Heaven. There, the King's armies had instant access to overwhelming force wherever and whenever it was needed. War in Heaven exulted in the sort of backup system guaranteed to thwart even Satan's evil genius, and it always struck terror into the hearts of his fallen troops, driving them to a fever pitch of useless speculation whenever battle was about to be joined. Hard as they might try to guess where the next assault would materialise, God merely had to speak a word and any one of a number of distinguished squadrons would materialise instantly, exactly where required. Hence the demon's poor morale and often careless tactics. But here on Earth it was very different, and Numibia had begun to wonder why he, of all unit commanders, had been given charge of this motley bunch of raw troops. Somehow, it seemed none of them had previously graced a frontline squadron on Earth detachment, which meant he was immensely grateful for Israfel's presence.

As far as Numibia knew, his warriors hadn't even managed to earn distinction in the regular but less demanding warfare that had for so long marred the plains of Heaven. About which his human charges understood little. Trapped within their restrictive dimensions of time and space, they had only a minimal grasp of reality, believing Heaven to be 'up there', somewhere above what seemed to them to be empty, inhospitable space. A belief of immense surprise to angels on their first Earth posting, as they began to learn more about their sassy, egotistical and highly valued charges. How could the pinnacle of God's creation, with few exceptions, be so ignorant? Of course, it didn't take long to understand why humans thought of space as no more than a vast emptiness or why, in their almost total ignorance, they assumed there was nothing 'out there' except distant galaxies, stars and planets. But it did take quite a while to acknowledge, even to themselves, that virtually no human understood anything of the real universe in which they existed. Operating with a mere five senses was clearly a hindrance, barring all but the chosen few from even beginning to comprehend the reality of the Heaven that lay all around them. True, they were separated from this reality only by a thin veil, yet the completely incomprehensible dimensions that formed the full or 'real' universe remained far beyond the understanding of most. But enough of human error. Back in the present, eyes narrowed, Numibia peered intently as he neared the slave boat, waiting for the inevitable response to their blown cover. Nevertheless, he had almost begun to believe they might have got away with it when the dhow erupted. Before he could shout a warning, a phalanx of black forms exploded outwards from the wooden hull and threw themselves savagely against the startled angels.

Arcturus, battle plan full formed, had telepathically accessed what passed for minds amongst his ill-disciplined horde and ordered a number of them quickly forward to disrupt the angels' advance. He had decided to buy more time for himself to organise an effective defence by first sacrificing a few of the less useful thugs under his command. A sacrifice he could afford to make at this stage. A nominal force of demons mixing it with even halfway determined angels would guarantee defeat, but that wasn't his concern. For now, at least. He was much more interested in taking down the young woman, because he had an idea that killing her would thwart the Enemy's plans, and that would certainly get him recognition. Provided he survived.

Wide on the flank, Israfel saw them coming even before Numibia. As one of the few who had any previous experience of fighting on Earth, the Guardian had been automatically asked to captain the right of the line, drawing it round in a sweeping pincer movement. The move was aimed at encircling the ship and forcing Arcturus to spread his troops along several fronts at once, or lose all hope of repulsing the angels as they moved swiftly forward in their thin but disciplined line. After some days of being obliged to watch from the side-lines as Paul suffered, Israfel had been itching to have a go at the sinister militia that not only swarmed all over the dhow, but could regularly be seen leering and gesturing as they freewheeled above the angel camp in an arrogant but ultimately pathetic display of strength. For what seemed like ages now, Numibia had also waited restlessly for the command that would rescind the embargo on pre-emptive strikes. Since the day the slaver had cleared the South African port on yet another of its lethal trading voyages, there was not an angel among them who hadn't wanted to take the fight to the enemy. But direct intervention had been expressly forbidden. Until now, their orders had allowed retaliation only if directly attacked. Not that it stopped them from meting out the occasional sharp reminder of exactly where everyone stood in the pecking order. Usually with individuals who got too close, or grew too cocky, clearly labouring under the mistaken impression that a lack of action implied weakness. Now at last, Numibia was about to discover exactly what Earthbound combat would be like with at least one, maybe two full legions of demons under the command of an able, ruthless and determined leader. Not that he was going to take any great pleasure in close-quarter fighting. Quite the contrary, because he, like Israfel, found their foetid smell and endless stream of coarse invective somewhat unnerving. Nevertheless, both had seen and heard sufficient to strengthen their resolve and, in Israfel's case particularly, enough to leave him seething with anger over the way Paul and the rest of the human cargo were being treated.

A sharp call from somewhere to the left cut through these reflections and, in a single smooth and practised movement full of deadly promise, Israfel drew his main weapon and let its light flash on the contorted features of the nearest assassin diving at him from slightly above and to his left. Apparently relying on height and speed to give momentary advantage, his opponent had committed himself with unusual and surprising haste. Israfel didn't bother to swing at him, contenting himself with a swift step forward and down to use the creature's own speed to his advantage. In free flight, unable to stop and too close to the next angel to risk a banked turn that would expose his vulnerable flank, the demon's underbelly was inevitably and dangerously exposed to Israfel's upturned sword. Having repositioned, all Israfel had to do was angle his sword upward and wait. The sudden countermove caught the onrushing demon by surprise. It was either inexperience, or sheer carelessness but, by the time comprehension dawned, it was never going to matter which. The razor-sharp tip, honed to the width of a single light photon, simply vanished into the creature, more or less where his navel would have been if he had been born in the sense that humans understood birth. But of course he hadn't. Eons before, God had simply spoken and he had appeared instantly, full formed, a magnificent, radiant angel, created to stand in the ranks of the favoured, ablaze with an intense inner light and appointed for an incredible future. That is, until he gave in to pride and threw in his lot with Lucifer. Lucifer, the most beautiful of all God's creatures, who desperately wanted God's throne for himself and who was prepared to provoke mutiny to achieve his fantasy. This weaver of dreams, this arch-liar had enticed away nearly a third of the angel host with promises of higher rank and greater status in his new, 'independent' administration.

Now, as with all those who had given way to that temptation, the years of self-indulgence and separation from God had taken their toll. Chevin (for that was the demon's God-given name), reduced to a lowly captain of a burned-out platoon, had grown ugly and spiteful over the years, reflecting outwardly the vicious hatred spawned in his spirit, which now burned unchecked, as he continually contemplated the depth of his awful, decisive and irreparable mistake. Ruthlessness and an unspeakably cruel attitude had replaced a once gracious disposition; spite coloured everything; depraved lust informed every decision; and only the depth and intensity of his despair marked him out from a thousand wilful colleagues. But above all his anguish had found focus in an implacable hatred for his chosen champion, the Prince of Darkness. Satan, from whom there was no escape. The one who had already ensured his own eternal damnation in the lake of fire, the final fate for all of Hell's denizens and certain humans. And now in the instant of joining battle, those distant fires were beckoning. Sick with the realisation, Chevin sensed rather than felt the unbearable light flooding him as the blade sank deep, piercing to his very essence. For a creature nurtured in profound darkness, light was the one medium against which there was no defence.

Which was precisely why the angels needed so little armament, yet remained so confident of ultimate success. They knew darkness cannot stand against light. Even a single candle in a dark room will destroy darkness. A sword, whose nearest description in human terms was a laser, but which surpassed any laser much as an interplanetary rocket might outstrip the first steam engine, was a virtual passport to victory, even in the hands of an apprentice. Almost, but not quite. And it was the 'not quite' that, against all the odds, kept alive a slender, albeit continually frustrated, expectation amongst the fallen angels that they might, somehow, somewhere, get lucky. To his left, Israfel could see a darting mass tearing into the thin line of angels and then breaking up as combatants squared off, with up to half a dozen of the black-shrouded fiends swarming around individual angels. Here and there, a pair would emerge from the fray locked together in mortal combat, shooting up or down, it made no difference, trailing fire as sword met sword, the picture of temporary chaos which, as always, permitted that tiny element of doubt as to the eventual outcome of the battle. An impression that lasted barely as long as it took to take in.

For the moment, however, Israfel found himself unopposed and, glancing towards the dhow, was just in time to spot Arcturus rousing the sleeping sailors, all the while re-disposing his forces in a furious effort to keep the angels at bay and deal with the matter that he still thought of as 'the prize' in all this: Roz. His gaze sweeping the deck, Israfel observed the girl swing herself carefully down from the main stay to the deck, only to lose her footing and stumble on a coil of casually discarded rope. Harried by their demons, the crew was beginning to stir and Israfel could see there was little time to waste. Without hesitation, he projected himself forward, straight towards Arcturus, who was still choreographing his forces from the high stern, but with his attention fortuitously distracted by a lone angel loping forward from just off the port beam.

CHAPTER 40

Considering it was a balmy tropical night, Roz was surprised at how cold she felt as she swung warily down, palms clammy with tension and her heart in her mouth. Every sinew in her arms and legs was as taut as a bowstring, but with any alien sound likely to bring the crew running, there was no chance to relax. Coming over the side, she had just caught the comfortable breathing and occasional mutter of sleeping men off to her left and was now desperate not to disturb them. With her foot extended as far as it would reach, she felt for the deck that lay somewhere below her, unseen in the pitch black but, outwitted by the ship's roll, her body swung too far and her left foot wedged in what felt like a coil of rope. Hands slipping on the thick stays and unable to stop, Roz stumbled forward only to pitch her full length across the unseen mound, making what seemed to her overwrought senses more than enough noise to wake the dead.

Fortunately, whatever it was snagging her foot was at least soft enough to avoid any broken bones and, despite the ungainly arrival, the rope mound even contrived to deaden the sound of her fall. Terrified, she froze. Every sense straining to catch the slightest nuance of change, to detect the first uneasy stirrings of the nearby sleepers. But nothing gave cause for alarm. Only instantly recognisable creaking and rubbing disturbed the night, as the old tub sought to accommodate herself to the rise and fall of the steepening waves. Gingerly, Roz picked herself up and stepped warily towards the main mast, hands outstretched in front of her in the vague hope of making up for what her eyes were missing. As she moved, she heard for the first time the eerie, muffled sounds of human hopelessness drifting up through the decking planks beneath her feet. There was such bleakness and misery interlaced with melancholy bound into the muted weeping, that the hairs on the back of her neck stood on end and her skin crawled as though touched by something unclean.

Slowly, her eyes grew accustomed to the lower light levels in the well of the ship and she began to make out more and more of the obstacles. Most noticeably, the post just ahead of the steeply canted mast swam into view and with it came the smell of unwashed humanity, all mixed with the sickly smell of dried blood. Dimly, she could make out a human form slumped against the post, presumably the lump she had first spotted from the shore. The body clearly had life, although by the look of it, probably very little. Slow, laboured breathing bubbled through slack lips and the man's head swung gently with the movement of the ship. Dark rivulets that were presumably blood dribbled down much of his naked body, except for his arms, which were stretched rigidly above him and lashed to a ring in the copper post. Briefly, Roz let her eyes play over the man's body, but not recognising him, she turned to look elsewhere. Other than the sleeping crew, some of whom she could now make out in the pale monochrome light, there were no others on deck. Which meant she would have to venture down into the hold, to what was clearly the source of the low moaning echoing through the ship. Roz shuddered. If there was one thing she did not want to do, it was to go anywhere near the source of that noise, which carried with it the frightening possibility of becoming trapped in the hold if the crew woke up.

Nevertheless, she turned and, screwing up her courage, began to pick her way towards the hatch, which seemed to awaken something in the beaten man she'd sidestepped, because he stirred and moaned loudly. Alarmed that he might wake the nearby sleepers, Roz stepped swiftly back to him. Stooping, she instinctively placed a hand firmly over his mouth and nose, to choke off the sound. Immediately he stiffened, writhing backwards, hunting for air, ready to cry out. Desperate, Roz bent closer to hiss "Kuwa Kimya"[1] in his ear, relying entirely on the poor wretch being able to speak the *'lingua franca'* of the area, rather than any of the numerous coastal languages. At any rate, it seemed to do the trick and slowly, she was able to relax her grip on his mouth, her eyes drilling into the stranger's, daring him to make a noise. The face was puffy and probably unrecognisable even to his mother, she thought dispassionately, so hard had he been beaten. But, as she continued to stare, she saw something begin to light up in his eyes, to come alive, as I stared incredulously back at her. Warily, she watched my lips trying to form themselves, as I tried to speak to her, tried to reveal who I was. Irritated with the delay, she shook her head and made to step back, but in doing so caught against my foot, which I had desperately curled around her ankle, endeavouring to restrain her departure. At this point, even in her rush to get on, Roz noticed my curious agitation and the effort to communicate seemed to her to contain something strange about it. Accordingly, she bent reluctantly towards me again, if only to ensure I didn't rouse the crew with my efforts. At first, she could only hear a stifled, formless whispering, accompanied by a fine spray of blood and spittle, which drifted stickily into her face. But screwing up her nerve she leaned closer, the quicker to end the interference.

"Rzz," she heard. "Rrzzz." And finally, after a supreme effort: "Rozzz."

And that sound was close enough to her name to spark the connection. I could see her mind struggling to understand how I could possibly know who she was. If, indeed, it was her name I was trying to say. And then I saw it hit her, like a thunderbolt straight between the eyes.

Gasping in dismay, Roz drew back, the better to look at me afresh, to try to see through the swollen, distorted flesh, to discern some feature in the darkness, some recognisable hint that it really was me. But she could see very little. Not even the colour of my hair. Quickly she touched her hand to my extended foot.

"If you're Paul, push my hand twice." Hardly daring to hope, she waited while I laboriously pushed once, then twice, before my foot slipped back in exhaustion. As she felt the downward pressure of the second push, her heart had leapt and for a second, as the tears sprang unbidden to her eyes, she had felt giddy with relief. She had found me and I was alive. I remember seeing newly formed tears glistening on her cheeks. Then feeling her push the hair back from my face where it had fallen forward as my head once more hung down. Gentle though her touch was, it drew a moan from me and the cold reality of our situation, our exposure, almost overwhelmed her with its choking waves. She was under no illusion as to what the crew would do to her if they caught her and nor was I. Her life would be worth next to nothing and it was highly probable her death would neither be swift, nor easy.

However, necessity did what hypothesis could not, and drove all thought of failure from her mind. She realised immediately that there was nothing I could do to help myself and she was equally certain there was little time left to get me safely off the dhow and away. Quickly, she drew the knife she had secreted at her belt, slashing at the rope that bound my wrists to the post. As she did so, she half heard the sound of someone moving in behind her and turned, barely in time to dodge the hand stretched out to clutch her long hair, its owner obviously intent on getting himself a rare treat on this dhow – a white girl who, judging by her slight form, would not prove too difficult for a man long-familiar with humiliating female slaves in the ship's hold. Probably it was that very experience that caused his downfall. How could he know this was no cringing captive overwhelmed by hopelessness and intimidated by repeated rape? As he lurched forward, deeply aroused, to make another brazen grab, this time for her breasts, he was surprised to find her stepping towards him. Unused to such a response, he dropped his arms towards her hips, welcoming her apparent acceptance, only to allow the opening she needed to slide the wicked little stiletto blade safely between the third and fourth ribs, before angling slightly upwards towards the pump throbbing at the centre of his chest. Surprised, he felt nothing, registering only a great and fading disbelief as his strength drained nearly as swiftly as the black rivulet of life flowing down her arm, to cascade in gelatinous streamers along the darkened deck. Even as his legs began to fold, Roz whipped out the blade, catching the falling man by his clothing, determined he would make no noise as he hit the deck. Had she taken time to think, she would have been surprised at herself, but then there had been quite a few things happening over recent months that would have astonished her former character, given any sort of self-examination. Actions and attitudes a world away from her previously sheltered existence were becoming almost commonplace.

Barely had she slid her erstwhile assailant to the deck, than she was back to attack my bindings, springing towards me with all the intensity of a mother tiger defending her cub. Unable to help, I could only wait and watch in befuddled apprehension, while Roz once again slashed at the ropes above my head. As they fell away, releasing my arms, I was forced to make a supreme effort to swallow the yelps of pain in response to the rapid return of feeling within my so recently anaesthetised limbs. Blood once more coursed around my body, my head whirled from the combination of pain and water deprivation, and I sensed myself being pulled upright by an almost superhuman strength, before being dragged across the short width of deck to the side of the ship. Even as Roz struggled to get me there, a shouted command froze her momentarily in her tracks before galvanising her into a last frenzied effort. I tried to help, but found it impossible. Neither my arms nor my legs would respond to instruction and I couldn't even force myself to stand upright. Everything that could drag was now dragging and the railings still seemed impossibly far away.

I could hear pounding feet not far behind me, and I willed a response with all the means I had, frantic to reach the rails before whoever it was caught up, but I have to honestly say, I had no idea what would happen when we got there. I knew nothing of the boat, of any rescue plan. Of any hope. But I reckoned without the steely determination that was gripping Roz. With a last heave she rushed me against the side, pushing upwards with all her strength and rolling me sideways across the top of the rail to give a final shove that sent me plunging straight towards the sea. And as I fell away in what seemed like slow motion, I was aware of a scrawny arm snaking around Roz's neck. And dear girl that she was, one more sailor discovered that an arm lock around this feisty lady brought with it an immediate invitation to meet his Maker, because adrenalin had lent her wings. Once more the knife arced, this time backwards towards the exposed belly behind her and, as he grunted with a pain that forced a momentary relaxation of his grip, she spun away and back-flipped over the rail, oblivious to where her transport might be. One aim and one aim alone gripped her whole attention: to get off that dhow, then find and keep me alive until Mbogo reached us. And not for a moment did she doubt that her friends would still be there.

CHAPTER 41

As the warm, clean waters closed abruptly over my head, the sting of salt in the open wounds criss-crossing my entire body fired a bolt of raw energy into the mush that was doing time as a brain, forcing a response. I remember instinctively angling for the surface, every reflex kick and lunge an antidote to the paralysis that had been gripping me since I'd first been tied to that post. The sea that had swallowed me whole when I dropped like a stone headfirst into the hollow of a passing wave, then decided to boost me skywards with equal indifference, spewing me up towards the water-shattered moon shining brightly but intermittently through the stippled surface. Even in the few seconds the plunge lasted, I could feel my nearly empty lungs beginning to burn, but the unfamiliar exhilaration of freedom coursing through my veins gave me the injection of adrenalin needed to keep going. For the first time in a very long while I had some control over my destiny, even my very existence. Not much, true. But even a modicum was welcome, just enough to momentarily overcome the ravages of my recent whipping.

Only the blood, trailing and dancing behind me as it was expelled by the movements that flexed my weeping wounds, gave the lie to this supposed freedom. For all down the food chain little welcoming signals must have been sparking off olfactory receptacles, each sensitive enough to pick up one part of blood in every million parts of water, and each stimulating certain owners into a shiver of gastronomic anticipation. Looking back, I'm pretty sure I know what happened. Several hundred yards off shore, invisible in the night sea and hunting as accurately as though it were on a well-lit and familiar village street, a tiger shark turned west, wound up the spring and began to cruise shorewards with a concentration that brooked no interference.

When Roz hit the water feet first, she very nearly took me down with her but, fortunately for us both, only her flailing hand made passing contact with my shoulder, pinpointing her arrival in the blackness of the heaving, noisy sea. The stinging crash of her fall and the flood of water into her eyes, mouth and nose drove the breath right out of her and she couldn't stop an involuntary gasp that brought in what had seemed like half an ocean. Plummeting on down past me, her lithe body offered little handhold as I stretched out for her, grabbing for anything I could reach until the effort was rewarded with a handful of hair billowing in her wake. Supremely conscious of my weakness, but more concerned that simply trying to hold on might well scalp her, I forced myself to duck-dive and allow her weight to pull me along, matching her rapidly slowing descent. But by the time I could turn and kick frantically for the surface, my own lungs were desperate for air, whilst her body seemed almost lifeless. However, one last heaving wrench got us there, and with my lungs no longer threatening to burst, I propped her head against my shoulder and wound my now loosened arm tightly round her waist. After that, all I could do was let the backwash of waves that were breaking against the pitching dhow propel us rapidly away from the solid wall of wood, rolling and plunging dangerously close to our right. I distinctly remember the desperation borne out of my rapidly waning strength as I kicked myself round, searching the near horizon. I had realised by then that Roz must have come by boat and unless she had come alone, which was highly unlikely, it had to be somewhere near.

But so was someone else. Unknown to me, Ahmed's nephew, a man many had found to their cost could be deeply dangerous when crossed, had almost caught Roz on deck, only missing her by a hair's breadth. His reward, a tantalising glimpse of long white thighs drawn to a dark V as she went over backwards, the already wet material of her tight shorts singularly failing to maintain more than a modicum of modesty. But that glimpse alone would have been enough to drive Abdullah headlong in a frenzy of lust. Certainly enough to drain all sense from his mind. I can picture it now. He probably hadn't had a woman, never mind a white woman, in a long time and the way she had filleted that fool of a sailor just ahead of him had only intensified his lust, to the point where he could no longer think straight. If he had, he would never have risked following her into the water. As it was, he used some sense in waiting until we resurfaced and he could see our upturned faces against the black water before taking a running dive over the side. Certain he could catch us. Certain he could deal summarily with me, and then get her back on board. Already enjoying the thought of what he would do to her throughout the rest of the long night. No doubt he was contemplating that pleasure even as he hit the water.

Through all this time, Roz was becoming heavier. To the point where I knew it was but a matter of seconds before what little strength I had left finally gave out. It might only have been her head I was cradling whilst the water took most of her weight, but I was forced to scissor my legs frantically just to keep my own mouth above the water, never mind Roz's. I knew the battle was almost lost and had begun to claw frantically at the sea with my remaining arm, reaching towards where I thought the shore ought to be, when the inevitable happened and I simply ran out of energy. As a result, my mouth sank so low that every gasping breath sucked in rather more water than air, although at least this had the merit of concentrating my flagging mind. So it was fortunate that even as I ran out of every last alternative, a deeper, boat-shaped blackness arrived out of the all-pervading dark, almost running us down in its eager charge. Moreover, the two brawny arms arriving with it managed to grab and lift Roz halfway over the side all in one quick heave. Grateful, I remember treading water with a last burst of transformed energy and clutching at the lowered thwarts that wallowed backwards and forwards in unison with the rapid shifting of the unknown rescuers tending to Roz. Unable to do much more than hang on even though stripped of the added weight, I was impatient, willing them to hurry, desperate to get out of the water. And then the unthinkable happened and it almost stopped my heart. A hand rose out of the water behind me, strong fingers gripped my upraised arm and a face, its mouth fixed in a fierce snarl, burst out of the water alongside me. To say that time stood still is no exaggeration, but even in that split second of utter paralysis, the boat dipped abruptly and strong hands reached down to grasp me under the armpits. Kicking weakly, I tried to shout a warning of the danger and tried to help them by adding my last ounce of strength, but in the instant of doing so, the face at my side went from triumph to total bewilderment. From below us both, something solid rose like an express train and before I could even begin to respond, whatever it was crashed into me like a giant, solid lump of sandpaper, propelling me abruptly upwards and sideways along the length of the boat, there to crash back against its rolling side much nearer the stern, from where my rescuers, almost as stunned as I was, but thinking faster, managed to drag me to safety. Behind me, a shout was cut off almost before it had begun and a great drenching splash signalled the shark's vigorous passing.

For my assailant, the nightmare was reasonably quick, a clemency I doubt he'd ever shown his victims. As with me, his first indication of the shark's attack was probably an extraordinarily heavy thump in his side. Probably like me, he had registered little pain. Just 'something' he could surely live with. But that's where the similarities ended and, for him, there began his own last drear journey. It must have been only nanoseconds before recognition dawned that 'something' was, after all, very wrong. 'Something' was missing. For some reason his body was bending in a very strange and sinuous way. Almost as though there was no skeletal structure. Which wasn't that far off the truth. In fact, had he been able to see into the rapidly reddening water, he would have noticed that most of his right side was missing in a ragged arc that reached from hip to shoulder and from the waist inwards, almost to his backbone, leaving his remaining entrails to wash out into the heaving waves in a long, slippery line. But he couldn't see any of this and so was probably unable to understand why it was that he was slipping so quickly into sleep at a time when he should have been totally alert. It wouldn't have made any sense. That is, until a great, tooth-lined mouth, water gushing away to either side, opened wide in front of him as it returned to reach for the head. The clamping jolt of multiple rows of serrated teeth around his neck and face would have been pretty close to the last thing he knew. But I've been rather hoping that his very last thought was one of total, shattering fear, as he remembered what his own religion would have told him. That all men must face the Supreme Judge. And in the same instant that the shark started chewing, he would have known, with crystal clarity, that he could expect no mercy from either source.

CHAPTER 42

Fired by the sudden release of adrenalin that accompanies such unexpected frights, the fishermen chased the shark's passing with a stream of expletives that did little to compensate for their shock, but much to boost their confidence. Familiar as they were with the slashing teeth of their chosen trade, the narrowness of their own escape was not lost on them. For my part, I simply lay on my back in the fish-slimed water slopping around the bottom of the boat and let myself go, shaking from head to foot with a mixture of cold, exhaustion and fear. And adding to the general chaos as I retched and urinated weakly.

Almost immediately, however, I felt the uncomfortable, choppy motion of the boat steady as she rolled onto her beam and lay across the wind, pulling against the large sail I could now make out, drawn taut above me. Once it had probably been white, but now the moon's clean glow could raise little more than a pale flicker of grey as it pulled my rescuers ever more swiftly into the surrounding night, away from my prison of the recent past from where, even now, I could hear the sound of furious imprecations falling swiftly behind.

Except for the sibilant hiss of water running down the boat's thin hull, the silence closed around us and, staring intently, I was able, for the first time to take in my surroundings. So far, few words had been exchanged, but that was hardly surprising, given the effort involved in getting away before we snagged against the dhow or were hit by gunfire. Suddenly anxious for Roz, I remember twisting round, desperate to see her, and unexpectedly aware of the painful tenderness that attacked every part of my salt-cleansed body. The intensity of wanting to hold her, wanting to be sure she was OK surprised me. The darkness didn't make it easy, but the pale glow of her exposed flesh drew my eyes to the foot of the mast, where she appeared to be distractedly tying down a bundle of loose rope. As if aware of my gaze, she turned towards me with a smothered exclamation: "Paul, are you alright?" Trying to favour just about every part I could think of, I dragged myself into a sitting position, unable to prevent a grimace, which I know always makes me look as though I'm angry and which, in this case, I certainly wasn't.

Suitably propped, I managed to whisper back: "I've been worse." I could see, even as I spoke, that the response was enough to drain the tenseness out of Roz and reassure the two men and the young lad now sitting almost immobile in the stern. There, the oldest of them leant against the tiller, leaving the others to attend to the set of the sail as the wind and sea combined to throw my newly acquired transport from side to side. I could tell pain wasn't about to get a holiday, but later I was to vaguely remember the sweet relief of fresh water held to my lips by a hand to which I owed everything.

Unable thereafter to do much more than lean against the hull and catch my breath, I waited as the boat put rapid distance between us and my nemesis. Away to my left, I could see the twinkling lights of a swiftly retreating settlement, which I presumed to be Malindi. I had little idea of my location, but it was quite clear that we were not heading towards the shore. Indeed, if anything, we seemed to be setting a course designed to take us back out beyond the reef and well clear of any obvious help. The shoreline, bright though the sand was in the gleaming moonlight, was already beginning to fade and the swell under the boat was once again lifting me with the hypnotic rhythm to which I had become so accustomed over the previous days. With the dhow lost in the darkness, the danger of being tracked by sound had passed and although there was little sense of elation, we could at least talk normally and, in so far as the small craft allowed it, we could rearrange and settle ourselves more comfortably. And this change in tempo and all that it meant brought with it a renewed surge of hope, which galvanised me into easing gently towards the mast, there to reach for Roz's arm. "Roz, where are we going? How did you find me? What are you doing here?" I could hear the words tumbling out, easier to understand now that I was no longer suffering quite so badly from the incipient lip stall of utter fatigue, but only just comprehensible for all that. But then, my thoughts were also lurching around with an associated lack of rationality.

For the time being, though, it was enough that I had the freedom even to ask. Eyes screwed up against the salt now drying rapidly on my eyelids and beginning to pulsate in the open wounds on my back, sides, thighs, in fact pretty much everywhere, I tried by the wash of moonlight to study her expression. But it was no good. I had to make do with an almost disembodied voice, soft and full of relief.

"I'll tell you all about it later and to be honest, I'm not exactly sure where we're going, but I trust Mbogo. That's him steering and he's the owner, so I know we'll be safe. The young one is my friend Kimau. All I can tell you is we're heading up the coast to a small settlement that Mbogo says is just beyond the Sabaki River and well hidden. They've little love for slavers there, as the tribe's been attacked themselves. He says we'll be safe and we're to wait, maybe a week or so, until the slaver is well on its way north. He doesn't think they'll waste any time looking for you, but it's better to be safe than sorry."

I was confused. Why couldn't we just sail into Malindi, approach the police and then get in a car and either drive to the nearest hospital, or back to Mombasa? Surely, we'd be as safe there as anywhere, once we'd told the police the story? And at least I'd get some proper medical attention. What was the problem? Was there something more I didn't understand? There was so much I wanted to ask and say, but now didn't seem to be the time. And come to think of it, there was probably quite a lot I had forgotten, either wilfully or simply from sheer fatigue. So I just reached for her hand, squeezed it and eased myself back against the planking, before lapsing into silence, trying desperately to order my thoughts. But as I did so, a profound and welcome lassitude stole over me, leaving me to drift quickly away into unconsciousness. The last reflection being of a girl, beautiful, vivacious and feisty beyond belief.

CHAPTER 43

Speed is a relative term, but no human could possibly have followed the cut and thrust of what was about to happen. Neither Israfel nor Arcturus was confined by the parameters of an Earth-bound existence, even though dealing with humans meant they were regularly forced to combine elements of their two very different worlds. Usually to the greater detriment of the angels who, unlike their planet-favouring opponents, spent less time in the company of humans, with all its attendant limitations.

However, right now whether operating in the physical or spiritual realm was an irrelevance and their entire concentration was focused on each other. A concentration born out of the oldest enmity in creation and honed by millennia of malevolent war. With the eighth of his many senses highly developed by these conflicts and the sheer effort of staying alive in an environment plagued by armed angels, Arcturus had realised immediately that whilst the patrol now approaching openly and almost casually from landward might well pose a threat in due time, their purpose in life right then was simple distraction. Which, to Arcturus, inevitably meant his back was exposed. Snarling, he whirled instantly and his angled blade, following the line of rotation, parried the thrust meant to fillet him. With a sound no louder than a sigh, their extraordinary weapons bit and slid against each other, until the hilts met and the pommels locked. Each was instantly aware that neither sported another weapon, or the fight would have been over for the other, so there was no need for immediate disengagement and for a moment they stood swaying, eye to eye, testing resolve and strength.

At any other time, the stench in Israfel's nostrils would have been enough to make him gag, but imminent danger held every muscle, every involuntary reaction in check. He had never been this close to such a high-ranking demon, but he knew enough about its past to be particularly wary. Unlike the rank and file with whom he normally dealt, this one would be no pushover. More calmly than he felt, he looked deep into Arcturus' livid black eyes, where the vertical yellow pupil slits failed to mask the furious hatred crouching behind the ugly mask that had once been a gloriously handsome and well-loved face. And deep in the lower recesses of his evil conscience, slithering almost out of sight like an innate canker, lay the all-pervading, insidious, virtually overwhelming fear to which Arcturus would never admit, but which at times could leave him gibbering. The dread that if it all went wrong one day, he could finish up in the hands of the living God.

For Arcturus, too, this duel was something of a first. Having been elevated above the rank and file and into a position of command for some considerable time, he could barely remember the last occasion on which he'd been forced to compete in hand-to-hand combat against a serious opponent, and he knew immediately that his adversary had every intention of fighting to the finish. The implacable planes of the face mere inches from his own were reinforced by a righteous anger reflecting through eyes that burned so bright, he was almost blinded. Arcturus knew himself to be an imposing warrior of considerable standing amongst his own kind and there were few within the ranks who would dare challenge him, but for a fleeting second even he felt the worm of doubt stir fitfully. And he knew the angel had seen it. Cursing, he flung himself forward, trying to impose his superior size to break the impasse of the interlocked weapons. And, for a moment, Israfel was caught off guard. Staggering back under the unexpected weight, he was forced to drop to one knee and parry two lightning-fast thrusts that came from the hands of a master swordsman. Giving ground, he managed to regain his balance and, using a helpful roll as the ship leaned to port, exploit his marginally superior speed to momentarily dominate the fight, advancing one step at a time, all the while spinning his sword in quick, flashing arcs designed to keep Arcturus off guard and powerless to mount a counterattack. It worked for a few seconds, but it was never going to completely subdue someone as astute as Arcturus.

Slowly, but with increasing confidence, Arcturus began to use Israfel's forward momentum to his own advantage. Using all his considerable skill to parry and redirect the lethal rain of blows aimed at his head and upper body, he allowed himself to drift almost imperceptibly backwards, drawing Israfel after him, encouraging the tide of battle to take them closer and closer to where Roz was still frantically trying to free her boyfriend. For by now Arcturus was confident Roz held the key to the current mayhem, and provided she was taken down in full view of his Angelic opponent while she and the boy were still on his territory, he could no doubt handle the consequences. And he was certain he could achieve the aim, despite the weaving and spinning of an almost mesmerising rain of light from a blade that danced lethally close to his body. But Israfel was no more stupid than Arcturus. It didn't take him long to work out why he was being drawn ever closer to Roz and he knew that if Arcturus intended to kill her himself, then at some time he would have to risk exposure as he reached into the girl's spirit to choke off her life. Whilst it was the only opening Israfel would need, he wasn't going to let it happen in the first place. But he had reckoned without the demon's guile.

As they continued inching towards Roz, Arcturus suddenly called out to a demon controlling one of the men: "Santo, get your man up and let him know there's a white girl begging for it, if he's quick enough." Arcturus allowed a leer to play across his face as he stared at Israfel. "Thought you'd take me down when I was occupied with the girl, did you? There's no need. That human can do the job for me and he'll love it. Which means your code of moral justice can't touch me. Just watch."

And with that he shifted to the front foot and began to show exactly what he could really do with a sword, forcing Israfel to skip swiftly away from Roz and any hope of providing direct protection. But he needn't have worried. She was far more resourceful than either of them had given her credit for. From beside the taffrail to which he had beat a hasty retreat, Israfel watched as Roz filleted her first opponent with almost practiced ease, barely pausing before turning to manoeuvre Paul over the ship's side. Profoundly agitated for the first time, Arcturus began to realise the awful possibility that for all his scheming, she might yet get away. Spitting a stream of invective, he began yelling at the only forces he had left who were not directly occupied by the battle. Those still riding the backs of individual crew members, their talons locked deep into flesh and spirit. It took far too long, but finally the fools got a few of the crew moving, only to find the first to arrive fared no better, ending up clutching at a stream of blood coursing from his belly. Which left Arcturus so incensed that he even risked a sideways swipe at one of his minions as it skittered past, effectively doing the hotly pursuing angel's job for him. And in that instant, the flat of his blade being nearest, Israfel caught Arcturus across the head with a double-handed strike, dumping him unceremoniously onto the deck, his sword sliding momentarily out of reach. Immediately, Israfel sank the tip of his blade into the now exposed throat. "Be still or die," he commanded.

Working on the equivalent of catching his breath, he watched carefully as Roz disappeared over the side, savouring the moment when he would put an end to Arcturus, only momentarily concerned as yet another sailor took too close an interest in the girl. But with the two youngsters gone, clear and incisive, the whole squadron heard their Commander-in-Chief's voice: "Enough for now. No further killing. Pull back and well done."

Disappointed, Israfel replaced his sword with a foot and leaning down towards Arcturus, looked intently into the wildly glaring eyes that were still waiting for the death stroke. "This time, excrescence, you are spared. But if we meet again, you will surely die." And with that Israfel was gone, leaving Arcturus to compensate for loss of face in the only way he knew how: personally eviscerating any of the troops he thought had witnessed his shame and vowing to pursue and kill the angel in question if it took him all eternity. But, given the significance of what the future held for him, he would have done better to apply himself to considering exactly why the angels had attacked.

CHAPTER 44

It was a change in the rhythmic roll of the boat that brought me to my senses. That and the dawn light pressing through bleary eyelids. As I tried tentatively to ease away from the boat's side, I felt some of the wounds on my back shredding open, the dried blood having stuck as firmly to the planks as it had done to me. Which was why I couldn't suppress a groan. For her part, Roz had apparently been watching me most of the night as we continued to sail steadily north, the lateen sail pulling strongly in the unremitting monsoon wind, which seemed to have strengthened, almost as if it wanted to lend its own helping hand. Mile after mile had been added to the gap between us and the much slower dhow, always assuming it had managed to mount a chase. Once clear of the reef and the protection of the land, the wind had even strengthened sufficiently for Roz to relax and start congratulating herself, the feeling of euphoria lasting the rest of the night, only to intensify as dawn arrived, bringing with it the welcome sight of a completely clear horizon astern.

As soon as she realised I had dropped back into oblivion, Roz had carefully braced me whenever I had seemed in danger of falling sideways. After a while she had apparently slid down beside me, to let me rest against her, my unconscious head on her shoulder, although she didn't quite dare to place an arm around me, lest she be the cause of even more pain. Now alerted by my groaning, she stretched with relief, helping me to sit awkwardly forward, every tentative movement I made designed to minimise the pain and favour the plethora of open wounds, but there were too many. A smile of pure relief lit her face and she leaned forward to kiss my cheek.

"Hi! I've definitely seen you looking better." Lightly and lovingly, she stroked my battered face with the tips of gentle fingers and watched as my eyes adjusted sufficiently to focus on the thwarts and strakes surrounding me, before finally turning back to face her. At first, I was nothing but inept, finding the situation difficult, embarrassing even, and so I suppose in those first few minutes, I made something of a fool of myself, probably appearing rather less than approachable. But the softness of her hand as it continued gently to trace the contours of my face and the obvious love in her gaze rapidly dispelled even my awkwardness.

"Roz, I'm so sorry, I must have dozed off. You were talking to me and I remember you said we're going to a settlement that your friend, err, Mbogo, knows. I guess we've been heading north all night, but why didn't we just go into Malindi?" As I spoke, I turned slightly to track the adjacent shore and emphasise the obvious connection. We were paralleling the coastline but had evidently crossed into a lagoon again and it was this change to calmer water with its altered tempo that had woken me.

A few hundred yards off to port, the dark green of close-packed trees swept down to the water's edge, forming what looked like an impenetrable barrier to the hinterland. Fast disappearing behind the boat's wake, an indentation in the land revealed the mouth of a river and the source of the fresh, light brown water that was the reason for the reef's gap. Ahead of us stretched a lagoon of purest aquamarine, shading to the white of coral sand within its shallows, with occasional coral heads poking through the calm surface. Enough to keep Mbogo on the alert as he threaded his way carefully between them at what was still a respectable pace.

"Paul, there's so much to tell you and I want to hear your story too. But perhaps I should start."

At that I turned back towards her and settled myself carefully against the thwarts, eager to listen. "Yes, but most of all, I want to know how you got here and how you found me. I didn't think anyone could possibly know where I was. In fact, how did you know? When I was dragged onto that slaver, I thought I'd finally had it."

Roz leaned forward and took my hand carefully, something I found strangely comforting and, smiling with appreciation, I nodded for her to continue. Thinking quickly, she determined I would have to know everything, even her deepest feelings, so she decided there was nothing for it but to go all the way back to the last time we'd been together. Sparing nothing, but beginning with her deep hurt at being told she wasn't wanted, she related in detail all that had happened between my flight from Eldoret and her appearance on the dhow. Astounded and somewhat ashamed, I listened in silence as she told me of her defiance in the face of despair and of her determination to find me, whatever it might cost. And paying close attention, not only did my admiration for and delight in this extraordinary and selfless girl grow steadily stronger, but the fragility of my position hit me full and square between the eyes.

Now, for the first time, I could begin to appreciate the whole picture and to understand why we hadn't just sailed into Malindi and gone straight to the police, or at least the nearest doctor. From what I was hearing, a visit to the local police station would simply have ended in our arrest, questioning and no doubt impossible demands for proof of innocence. And virtue was the one thing I couldn't prove without corroborating evidence from at least one of the many crooks with whom I'd been in contact. Without them to confirm what had happened, how likely was it that I would be believed and so avoid yet another spell in yet another gaol? After all, from where would the proof come, when the only tangible part of the whole chain of events was probably already on its way north to Somalia? Obtaining corroboration would require more help than the police force was likely to provide. Slavery behind, gaol ahead. It was going to be down to me alone, I thought. Anyway, for now it seemed like an impasse and too great a problem to even begin to consider. So when I did eventually come to it, I'd have to be a bit sharper than I currently felt. Besides, right then there wasn't a single part of my body that wasn't in active rebellion. From my throbbing head to my lacerated feet, everything hurt and that ensured the impossibility of rational thought. So, thrusting the quandary weakly aside, I took refuge in closing my eyes and leaning carefully back against the thwarts. Not forgetting to roll my head onto her shoulder.

Was it only a heartbeat, or was it hours later? I couldn't tell but, warmed by the regular shift between sail shade and beating sun, my grateful body had relaxed, lulled by the gentle, insistent rocking of our transport. With the advent of a slight breeze coming off the land, there was change in the air temperature too but, even better, I could detect a definite, if modest, lessening of pain. Always assuming that wasn't just down to lack of movement. Whatever else, I felt a sense of detachment: of being safe, hidden in a womb, of being protected from anything that could offer further hurt. A sensation I hadn't experienced in a very long time. If ever. Almost immediately deep and irresistible sleep drifted back over me and with it, a further unknown passage of time. So, just as before, I was unable to determine how long it had been before I felt the gentle scrape of the boat's keel against soft sand and heard the altered sound of water lapping against a beached object. Strong hands lifted me and momentary shafts of flashing pain rippled down my back and thighs. But that didn't last long. Despite the transfer from boat to hut, I quickly and firmly faded into oblivion again and was aware of nothing further until thirst drove my body reluctantly back to consciousness and to that now familiar feeling of being closely watched. Albeit and unknown to me, Roz wasn't the only one doing the watching.

CHAPTER 45

"So what", the sibilant, baleful, almost whispered demand taunted, "So what exactly kept you from reporting your incompetence immediately?"

Still seething from the way he had been virtually ignored by the commander's Aide-de-Camp (a useless lackey if he'd ever seen one) but inwardly quaking with fear, Arcturus waited in the certain knowledge that this time, without some sort of a miracle (detested concept put about by the Enemy), legendary legion commander though he felt himself to be, he was nevertheless doomed. Surreptitiously, he glanced around at the almost familiar surroundings. He'd been here before, but if ever he needed his wits about him, it was on this occasion, because there was no doubting the supreme danger facing him. True, he'd been centre-stage before, ranged in front of the same high-ranking demon, the same dark power. However, in the past he'd always been here to receive some reluctantly offered accolade or other (why was success so resented in Hell's corridors?). Sometimes he'd even been here to receive a begrudged promotion, following the extermination of yet another superior who had fouled up, just as he now stood accused.

Exposed and unarmed, Arcturus waited in the middle of the vast and threatening cavern, whose deep shadows masked its far reaches and whose sparsely furnished galleries hung heavy with an eerie stench of sulphurous death. A bouquet that pervaded any and every stronghold belonging to his satanic lords and masters. Senses honed from eons of in-fighting, Arcturus didn't need to be told that from within the darkness several pairs of scheming eyes, vertical slits narrowed by anticipation, were staring in unblinking calculation and cruel expectation, as their owners waited for the expected charade to play itself out. Eyes that belonged to impatient and ambitious contemporaries, every owner as ready and willing to run a blade through the ill-fated legionnaire as spit, if they thought it would further their own dire cause. For them, Arcturus simply represented a block on the promotion ladder. For him, they symbolised death. All they had to do was wait and, when the commander gave his usual 'thumb parallel to the floor' signal, Arcturus would be dispatched in a few gory seconds. They knew it and he knew it. Yet here, in front of him, the emaciated old putrescence that was his commanding officer remained utterly still. To Arcturus, he seemed almost hesitant, leathery old wings that denoted a once high and glorious rank within the Heavenly host wrapped tightly around his scabby back. Curiously, eternity had been far less kind to him than to most of them. Almost as though he had somehow been infected by the humans' problem of ageing.

Yet for all his vacillation, Josephus remained a terrifying threat. Prescience gripped him and Arcturus shivered with fear. There was a well-documented and, for the moment, tightly controlled ferocity reserved within that tense, uncanny and completely uncharacteristic stillness. Undecided his nemesis might still be, but involuntary shivers of dread continued to course through Arcturus who, despite or perhaps because of the circumstances, still fought to hide any hint of weakness. It was a very long time since he had himself first waited and watched from that very gloom, slavering just like the ones he couldn't quite see, as his erstwhile squadron commander had stood where he now stood. A very long time since he had first observed the blind rage that underpinned the nightmarish hierarchy constituting all authority in the kingdom of the fallen. And yet, was it possible he really had detected a momentary indecision, perhaps moderation in the well-practiced malevolence? He could only hope (dread word that, mostly confined to the humans he so despised). And for his part, watching the terrified legate standing to attention in front of him, Josephus was surprised to detect few obvious signs of the fear he normally instilled in subordinates. Clearly, this centurion was different, although why, he could not for the moment fathom. But it gave him pause to think, to reflect for a while on the millennia he had been in control, the countless times he had initiated deliberate mayhem and untold obscenity from this very office, this epicentre of his power. The arch-demon swayed slightly, hunching low behind the huge ebony desk that hid his twisted, almost useless legs from the gaze of the helpless offender, still braced stiffly in front of him.

Sweat was beginning to bead Arcturus' temples, but given the threads of heat emanating from the ground beneath him, that was hardly surprising. Below him waited a drop too awful to contemplate and, worst of all, he had no hope of taking anyone else with him. When you get right down to it, misery really does love company. And Arcturus knew, without a shadow of a doubt, that as soon as his commander gave the signal, nothing could stop the inevitable and devastating attack with which the spectators would react. First disembowelling him, they would then slowly and ostentatiously open the covers to the awful pit from which there was never any return. And watch with ghoulish fascination, as he took the last long fall to his doom. Not for the first time in his existence, Arcturus despaired. The awful nature of his treachery towards the God of the universe, perpetrated in those far-off and heady days of rebellion, once more crashing down around him. How often had that happened? He had no idea. So often in the early days he had dreamed of reversing that offensive and precipitate decision, of throwing himself on God's mercy, but he'd always known in his heart of hearts that the very luminosity of Heaven would destroy him. The rebellion had wrought its devastating and irreversible changes. He had fallen from grace and that was that. From that very first moment he had known he was incapable of going back, of surviving in divine light. Darkness suited his fallen nature and his conscience was now too seared to recognise or even properly remember the gratuitous and utterly destructive error that had led to his ruin. The original decision to throw in his lot with Satan. There was simply no way to make amends, no way to regain the beauty of the Heavens he had once known, the endless peace and rewarding purpose he had once experienced in such incredible abundance. And that embodied the very nature of his personal Hell. To know for all time, for all eternity, that on the one occasion when it had mattered, really mattered, he had made the wrong choice. And how he had paid for that since. Paid endlessly for what he had immediately afterwards realised was almost unimaginable stupidity. Once again, misery wrapped its ghastly chains around his desiccated heart, and hopelessness skittered across the cesspit of his mind, dragging him ever further into wretchedness. What could be worse than being condemned to live on throughout eternity, weighed down with burning chains, ordained to maintain consciousness indefinitely, unable to pull down the final curtain? Ever. Moreover, to be mired in the fiery pit that allegedly awaited him was utterly beyond his comprehension. For despite Hell's official position on the matter, he was certain this was indeed the pre-destined fate they all faced. Only in his case not yet, please. Not yet. To forever know you were locked into the single most stupid decision it was possible to make in this universe and burn for it? Truly, that was Hell.

Then, cutting through his fevered reverie and as though from a great distance, Arcturus caught the feral menace of his inquisitor. "Tell me exactly why you lost Paul, excrescence? And tell me in a way that doesn't leave you dangling on the end of my sword."

For sure the last thing Arcturus needed was to remain preoccupied, but true to form, his commander's words concentrated his mind wonderfully. Only why was the chief concerned about the young man? Surely the problem had been the woman? Hadn't the angels left him alone right up until the time she had appeared below the slaver? As far as he knew, they had never shown much interest in the young man called Paul. Yes, the girl was interested in him, but these humans, especially the young ones, were always showing an interest in one another. In fact, it had long been his job to spoil such interests wherever he had found them. To sour relationships whenever he could or, at the very least, to break down trust, especially by diverting them into perverse sexual cravings. Above all, to ensure they didn't accept the Enemy's open invitation to ditch their allegiance to Satan and place their hope, their future, their trust in Jesus of Nazareth, the Creator's Son. That was basic to any demon's mission. But was it possible that, too caught up in the fundamentals of what he was supposed to be doing, he had missed the obvious? Laid himself open to the most dangerous charge of all? The loss of a soul to the Enemy. Yet even in his extremity, Arcturus recognised he was being handed a sliver of hope, a possible amnesty, and a future that hadn't been there seconds before. He had actually been invited to provide an explanation that might not signal his immediate death. Why, he had absolutely no idea, but that hardly mattered. If the boy really was the problem and Josephus was still talking to him, it was highly likely Paul hadn't changed sides yet. There could be a way out. His particular skills must be needed if the boy was to be terminated without arousing Heaven's ire. It was the only rational explanation.

Thinking with the lightning speed for which he was duly notorious and rapidly factoring in the assumption that it was the boy who interested the boss, Arcturus launched what he saw as his only chance. To plead mitigation on the grounds that he'd kept the boy from fulfilling Satan's worst fears (a pure guess); that the boy and the girl were now together where he could, so to speak, kill two birds with one stone and the legionnaires assigned to him had been far worse than any he had been saddled with before (no lie there, by way of a change). Yes, there was possibly a 'get out of gaol free' card somewhere in there. So he'd better keep some of that powder dry for the denouement. A bit of clever nuancing of the fact that not only had he been understaffed and saddled with a completely useless guard force, but his present circumstances were the direct result of decisions made by a demon Arcturus knew to be currently out of favour (a master stroke!). But he would have to begin by assiduously stroking the commander's massive and perverted ego.

"Honoured Commander-in-Chief," he began: "Since the dawn of that wonderful day when you stood firm with our supreme lord and master, His Satanic Majesty, the great Prince Lucifer, and together with him, founded this invincible kingdom, you will know that I have served you loyally and with every ounce of my being in the many ranks you have seen fit to bestow upon your humble servant...."

CHAPTER 46

Josephus' eyes closed momentarily as the opening words stroked his battered psyche and provided a certain balm to the juddering waves of foreboding that, for some considerable time, had been coursing through his depraved spirit. Allowing his attention to wander, his mind fled to the ill-received tidings of particular adjustments in the Heavenly realm brought to him recently from the outer reaches of the empire. Tidings that had not, could not, remain secret for very long and that, he suspected, were even now sweeping the corridors of power, in the guise of whispered outrage. Outrage that would gain in strength with every repetition. Rumour following upon rumour, no doubt accompanied by nervous eyes darting to and fro, limbs trembling and hearts failing as the dreadful possibilities behind the gossip expanded rapidly from imagination to received fact. If things ran true to form, someone, somewhere, would yet again start putting two and two together to make five, having noted, with growing panic, the seemingly inexplicable and substantial increase in Heavenly activity.

True, such rumours were forever sweeping the satanic courts. Equally true, one day there would be real reason to panic if the Creator's special book, that odious collection of sixty-six texts they called the Bible, perversely enough brought together under one cover, was actually reaching its prophesied conclusion: utter humiliation and catastrophe for Lucifer and his kingdom. There couldn't be a single one of Lucifer's hangers-on who didn't know what those Scriptures foretold, who hadn't surreptitiously read the script, even if very few would admit to the act and even fewer to giving the writings any credence.

In official circles the Bible was only ever referred to as "that monstrous manuscript" and it was unanimously loathed and formally distrusted, if for no other reason than it had been presented as a gift to what God considered to be His foremost act of creation: His beloved humans (which left them, the 'fallen angels', where exactly?). Humans considered it to be 'their' Bible and those Satan had once been entitled to hold captive as his personal slaves, with no hope of remission or pardon, now claimed it set out the terms for their manumission or liberation. All tied up with Jesus, that embodiment of God, who they'd managed to crucify just outside Jerusalem. Josephus still shuddered at the memory. Until that terrifying day, every human had been Satan's by right, each one of them having forfeited their freedom by willingly and/or knowingly rejecting God as their king. And yet, for some unfathomable reason, those same humans had remained the singular and all-consuming object of God's love. The ultimate reason behind His every act of creation and preparation, as He structured the universe for its final destiny. Namely, the honouring of humans as restored members of His family, fellow heirs with Jesus to the riches of Heaven. The very person whom Satan had had killed, but whom he hadn't been able to stop rising up from the grave three days later.

And there was the nub of the problem. One which he, Josephus, had never been able to fully grasp. Despite his and Lucifer's every effort to disparage and destroy the God/man relationship, uncounted hordes of the despicable humans still put their trust and hope in His Son, Jesus. And the idiots were forever quoting the Bible. Which, many were convinced, set out history from God's point of view, together with an account of His merciful love for them. And they referred to this book as 'His Written Word', and to Jesus as His 'Living Word'. And if neither he, nor Lucifer (indeed, none of the hierarchy) could fully comprehend the deal, then it was surely no coincidence that their minions, Hell's apathetic denizens, showed even less understanding. How could the prophecy that mankind would one day attain to higher rank than angels be allowed to happen? Why, it would mean they might even have authority over Satan, the greatest sentient being ever created. Sacrilege! Even God had once called him 'the Bright Morning Star'. Which Josephus knew was still able to stiffen Satan's spine ever so slightly, whenever the subject came up. Before his mood inevitably turned, yet again, to fury over his spectacular fall from grace and his eternal exile from the real corridors of power. Annoyingly, even the humans Satan had managed to turn back from worship of God to a worship of himself, far too often acknowledged (despite themselves) that the Creator's book retained a certain life and truth of its own. No matter what Hell did to offset its influence, that 'Book of Books' still spoke to all men everywhere about the One who had made them, and to whom they owed their true allegiance. Disgustingly, it even majored on sacrificial, romantic and all-consuming love (And how could anyone continue to believe such things in the face of all that Hell put out to the contrary?).

However, in the end they were always forced to consider the inevitable question: was this, finally, the event promised from the dawn of time (Satan would always strenuously deny it, but everyone knew he was the father of lies), when God would banish them and anything evil to the so-called 'Hell of fire'? Permanently. Fortunately, humans didn't generally believe in such a fate either, which made them easier to control. But there wasn't a single one of Satan's minions who didn't feel he knew the truth of it (whatever they might admit to). A reality with which they were faced every time one of their own forfeited his life and was banished to the lower and definitely hotter regions. In particular, that wretched Book prophesied a time of increased activity in Heaven and on Earth just prior to the ultimate Day of Judgement, after which God would apparently fashion a new Earth and a new Heaven. Neither of which would contain anything bad or, incredibly, any of their own kind. Hence the panic.

So, all things considered, perhaps this was a time when it would be better to retain every well-tried warrior for employment on the front line. After all, they weren't just fighting on one front. No. Regular squadron detachments still had to be arranged to maintain hostilities on Heaven's rolling plains, no matter how much the rank and file might rebel against exposure to its painful light, attenuated though it was by their special armour. Absolutely no doubt about it, Arcturus deserved a suitably gruesome disembowelling, followed by banishment to the tender mercies of Abbadon. Indeed, it was true that he, Josephus, got a great deal of satisfaction out of pronouncing such fateful punishments. An immense and continuing pleasure from sending these failures, these useless and depraved spirits who had the temerity to fall short of his demands, to the hidden delights of the pit. So, yes, perhaps in this case he could kill two birds with one stone and add considerably to his overall gratification in the long term. All he had to do was let Arcturus know that his guilt was decided and his expulsion to the pit inevitable and, at the same time, delay the date of execution. Certainly until after Paul Moncton had been dealt with. Perhaps longer if the rumours persisted. That way, he not only kept a particularly experienced legate who could still be useful, but he would be able to revel in the knowledge that Arcturus would have his ultimate fate constantly in mind, with all the terror that would inspire. Machiavellian!

What's more, he could also confirm to colleagues and superiors alike just how shrewd he really was. Of course, what neither Arcturus nor any of the dolts he commanded knew was that something had finally been put right by management and reports were, at long last, filtering up to those who needed to see them. And the name of Paul Moncton had featured on a number of occasions. Which meant Heaven really was interested in him. And if Heaven wasn't soon thwarted, the boy could clearly cause trouble. So, pre-emptive action by Josephus might provide a sop to the usual seething anger and screaming frustration that accompanied encounters with Lucifer. And he could report that for some time he had been preparing to frustrate Heaven. It wasn't often he could beat Heaven to the draw, but this time he was sure he had exposed one of their favourites before any harm had been done. Reporting this with due solemnity to Lucifer would surely earn him some accolade? After all, Machiavelli might have been viewed as exceptional, but where had he learned his trade? At the hands of the supreme leader, Lucifer, of course (with perhaps a certain degree of help from his evil self). Yes, a good plan. Grunting with the effort, Josephus shifted, opened his eyes, glared at Arcturus, raised himself to his full if rather diminished height and, waving his right hand dismissively, cut Arcturus off, just as he was getting into his stride.

"Enough, fool! There is no more to be said. You will show Abbadon what a useless blemish you really are… but not quite yet." Ah, yes. It was all in the timing and he was still a master of the art. As he spoke, his out-of-sight hand signalled with a thumb held vertically downwards, and the demons waiting for the announcement to strike merely shrugged, hid their disappointment and drew their swords with as much noise as they could generate, still happy to teach Arcturus a lesson. Unfortunately, restricted to the flat of their blades on this occasion. Which didn't stop Arcturus, who hadn't seen the thumb gesture, or worked out what had really been conveyed, from beginning to wail in abject terror. It was only much later, as he nursed his bruised body and damaged pride that he discovered the precise nature of malevolence intrinsic to an indefinitely delayed sentence of execution. Coupled with his 'temporary' assignment to ensure Moncton didn't change allegiance, the whole bound up with orders to frustrate Heaven. A death sentence, whichever way you looked at it.

CHAPTER 47

Watching me out of the corner of her eye during our first night ashore, Roz had concluded, beyond any shadow of a doubt, that she loved me. Nor would her passionate nature brook any intervention in the matter. A nature which adversaries had learned to disregard at their peril (no doubt there were those who could testify to that amongst the crew of a certain dhow). Throughout the night she had stood close guard as I lay, oblivious to the world, stirring fitfully and snoring gently through slightly parted, heavily bruised lips. And during those same hours her love had not only matured, but successfully countered its own uncertainties. Hence, with the dawning of a new day and a long, sleepless night of reflection behind her, she was able, finally and fully, to acknowledge to herself that she could conceive of no desirable future that failed to contain me. So there she stood, in love with a man who had so far given her little cause for hope; a contemporary by birth, but one who might as well have been an alien for all she knew of attitudes and outlook, hopes and fears. Nevertheless, one whom she was convinced held the key to her future. The only obvious problem being whether I would be equally convinced.

And what of me during all of this? How often in those early days of liberty did a return to consciousness simply mean a resurgence of the all-consuming pain that flooded my slowly healing body? I don't suppose I ever managed to stir without reopening many of my wounds. And that first morning ashore after we'd landed definitely set the standard. Less than twelve hours after what can only be described as a miraculous rescue, everything hurt. My whole world was bound and informed by pain. But at least I was free. Slipping in and out of consciousness, every return to awareness involved a slow, careful stretching of a tentative hand towards the smiling face always ready to welcome me back. She was my first clear, radiant promise that there really was a welcoming humanity out there, and in this case, a promise intertwined with breath-taking beauty. As I continued to feast my eyes on this dazzling image, I realised there was no comparable vision upon which I could hope to focus then, or at any time in the future. Only the deep shadow of the hut in which I lay spared my considerable blushes around this time. And as the days slipped by, I came to realise that I lived for her appearances. When she was not there, I was bereft. When her light footstep sounded on the path outside, my heart leapt for the anticipation of seeing her. I could not get enough of her. Simply to hear her voice was sufficient to make my heart skip a beat.

Straddling the equator as it does, the central African coastal heat seldom, if ever, lets up. From six in the morning until six at night, day after day, the sun beats down with uncompromising strength. Glaring at the landscape out of a burning, cobalt sky, it turns already arid ground into an iron-hard, dust-smeared radiator. Raising mirages, spawning dust devils, the tropical sun simply drains the life out of virtually anything that lacks a deep root. However you dress, wherever you go during the burning day, the best you can hope for is the relief of a good shade tree, perhaps the thick leafy canopy of a cashew nut tree, or the lighter green of a mango and, if you're really fortunate, a spot that luxuriates in a fitful breeze. Perhaps a cool veranda accompanied by an ice-cold drink. But not so for me. Not in my recuperation.

Unwilling to even stir, I was firmly anchored to a fire-hardened wood and sisal cot in the back of an African fisherman's simple thatch, wattle and daub home. But, wrapped in darkness, I could at least gain some relief from the relentless glare outside;

little enough, but certainly all I was likely to get before evening. And with it, courtesy of my host's trade, came the overriding stench of rotting fish, permeating everything. Something I can still smell to this day. That cloying aroma triumphed over my nostrils, trickled across my tongue and even managed to suffuse the parrot cage that, for all its foulness, passed as my mouth. A part of my anatomy that hadn't been graced with a clean-up in months. No breeze stirred in that hut to dissolve the nebulous perfume of fish and I remember the ribbons of sweat trickling like transient spiders as they ran coldly down my back and sides, before combining into small streams of moisture that gathered around and under my legs, armpits and buttocks. At least I was only wearing a kikoi, the grip of the folds wound around my waist providing my one assurance of modesty. Not that I would have minded the alternative particularly. Somewhere in the preceding days I had managed to lose so many of my childish inhibitions, or perhaps they had simply been beaten out of me.

Thus sheltered and lying quietly, covered in some nameless and presumably antiseptic ointment provided by my carers, a liniment that somehow kept septicaemia at bay, I could hear the endless, lazy rumble and hiss of waves kissing the shoreline hard by the hut. At a guess, no more than a hundred feet from the simple cloth covering at the entrance, thus remaining frustratingly out of sight beyond the foot of the bed. Closer in, the rustling of palm fronds in the ubiquitous coconut palms that stood guard around the loose scatter of mud huts provided the tiny community with an incessant but strangely comforting lullaby. Weariness kept hitting me between the eyes and every so often its inexorable and unavoidable lassitude once again stole quietly over me. Despite the passing of days, perhaps weeks since my rescue, it seemed I was still ready to drift in and out of consciousness at the drop of a hat. Always moving as carefully as I could, I would inch onto my back, from where I could glance upwards to catch the only view available, through the small hole at the roof's apex, where smoke from the perpetually burning fire drifted off into the brightness of day. Below this obligatory opening, darkly discernible poles, constituting the roof's circular skeleton, supported an equally blackened thatch, the whole rendered into one by the ubiquitous soot. Still, whilst the days themselves melded into a single, vague shadow, each and every one of them contained that refreshing, vivid spark that maintained my sanity. And had she but known it, she was all I needed, then or now.

CHAPTER 48

There were so many delightful qualities to relaxing in one of the King's dazzling gardens, but chief amongst them was the sense of utter safety and serenity. Wherever he looked, the Archangel Michael could see the most exquisitely beautiful and extraordinarily diverse flowering plants and succulently leafed trees. Whilst Heaven was remarkable for the incredible variety found in every one of its many dimensions, it was the fact that most of Heaven's citizens chose to operate in this particular dimension that captivated Michael. As one of God's Angelic princes, with a seat on the Inner Council, he was charged with assisting in the smooth running of the Universe, which in his case meant keeping Satan's hordes in check. Thus, his main responsibility revolved around the exercise of strategic and tactical deployment amongst Heaven's warriors. To his constant delight, the garden stretched away as far as the eye could distinguish and every time he looked up, his visual senses were assaulted by sensuous colour streaming towards him in every conceivable shade and tone. Exhilarating, awe-inspiring, coruscating, ever-changing pigments that were cast in hues far beyond any range the human eye could perceive or mind conceive. A soft, scent-laden breeze wafted gently through the branches of the tree under which he sat, accompanied in its passing by the sound of one of the quietly flowing streams irrigating the flamboyant grounds.

Everything bore the Maker's stamp of extravagance. As if to reinforce the point, high above him a jewel-like bird, flashing iridescent in its electric blue, green and virulent red suit, trailed into melodic silence as Michael turned to watch. The echo of its thrilling notes dropped swiftly away as it drew breath for the next exhilarating stanza, the next harmonic verse that would pour unconstrained from a heart made euphoric with love for its Creator. Like every one of the myriad creatures winging the high soaring realms of Heaven, it was an artiste of song *par excellence*, particularly when expressing itself in paeans of praise. As if to complete the picture, and some distance away, another angel quietly tended to the ripe fruit of a mature old fig tree. And everywhere a mysterious, delicate luminosity suffused the garden, picking out every detail of the exotic foliage in crisp and astonishing clarity. Heaven had no need of a sun to light it. The Glory of God Himself was its light, permeating everything.

Letting his gaze wander, Michael mused for a moment on how he had used these tranquil grounds almost as his own since the dawn of time. From that first unforgettable moment when he had sprung full grown into dazzling and astonishing existence, conscious that not only was he an extraordinary warrior straight from the hand of God, but aware that he was fashioned as the equivalent of a 'four star' General, with the unique and vital responsibility of leading Heaven's armies. Angel troopers who were even then appearing full grown around him. From shortly after his creation, although held back from providing the outright victory he yearned to deliver against the perfidious traitor Satan (a victory that he knew to be within his grasp), Michael had revelled in his unique assignment. Whether it was dealing directly with Heaven's enemies, or serving humans, he approached each and every mission with the utmost attention and delight. Never failing to deploy his squadrons to singular and devastating effect. Almost always several steps ahead of the arch-enemy Satan. And continuing to look around, Michael recognised, beyond a shadow of a doubt, he would never grow tired of this role. Or his place in the Kingdom.

The apparent privilege of such a glorious yet solitary setting was merely to afford him the space to plan effectively. The only way to counterbalance the distraction of Heaven's happily uproarious citizens. But no matter where he was, the light of God permeated everything. Although, even as he sat considering his most recent orders, it would have seemed to the uninitiated that Michael was himself ablaze with the fire of Heaven. Light flooded out from within his flowing toga and radiated from every pore of his perfectly poised body. An intense, vibrant luminosity, which, from time to time, seemed to flash outwards as if to engulf the careless observer. A white light of holiness, which, for the unclean, came close to being unbearable in its intensity. Which was exactly Lucifer's problem. For some reason that he could never quite fathom, he and his armed forces were still allowed an almost unimpeded run of Heaven. Under certain strict conditions, he had even been allowed to retain his *entrée* to the Inner Council. But now, far from being a joy, such remaining hints of intimacy were frightening in the extreme, although he did not dare to question the arrangements. Reason told him that the moment he stepped out of line anywhere near God's throne, he would simply cease to exist. Yet it was utterly infuriating to know that every citizen of Heaven had been briefed to allow him to pass unchallenged. To be accorded the utmost, if somewhat icy, courtesy, whilst knowing that he was considered no better than dog food, was devastating. To Lucifer, such discrimination was nothing short of humiliation, utterly demeaning to an individual who had once held the highest rank bestowed by Heaven. An ignominy compounded because, what might otherwise be considered a flattering right of access, was quite clearly designed to be a two-edged sword. And every angel, every redeemed human, every animal in Heaven knew it.

Nevertheless, there had been real moments to savour when he had actually been given permission to meddle with certain humans. Right up to the instant before death. Sadly, seldom beyond that. So far. They readily killed each other, but he could normally only encourage such actions surreptitiously. He and his followers could invade minds unchecked, but they couldn't indulge themselves physically. He knew, too, that somehow he'd been 'blinded'. He, who had been the pinnacle of creation, could now only see into a couple more dimensions than the humans he so despised. And always, rankling in the back of his mind there lurked that annoying character, Job. A source of very public embarrassment, every time he spotted the wretched man walking the highways of Heaven. How could he forget how comprehensively he'd been outsmarted on that one, although even that paled into insignificance beside his mistake at Calvary, just outside that scruffy little town of Jerusalem (why did God rate it so highly?). He really thought he'd nailed God's only Son that time. And then Jesus of Nazareth (as the humans called him) had had the temerity to walk into Hell and tell him, Lucifer, where to get off. There had followed an appalling three days of intense light (light!) lancing through the farthest reaches of his dark kingdom, causing uproar. Something from which Hell had never really recovered and, worse, aware of his extreme embarrassment, something his senior commanders never let him forget.

Lucifer growled involuntarily as he eyed Michael. One day. One day he would prevail over this angel, even if he'd shown himself to be completely helpless against God. Come to think of it, once he'd nearly stolen a march over Michael. He'd been visiting Persia at the time, organising his incompetents to oppose yet another irritant, a praying Jew named Daniel. And he'd caught a complacent Michael on the hop. Very nearly removed his head with the first swing of his blade as he stepped from what he could only describe as a devilishly cunning ambush (no pun intended, but he did rather fancy himself as a wit). Yes, one day he would succeed. Of that he was certain, despite all the obvious indications to the contrary. Had not Jesus once acknowledged that because the first human, Adam, had rebelled against God, he had essentially transferred his authority over planet Earth to himself? Effective, right up to the time he had masterminded that ill-conceived crucifixion (no disguising the fact of his involvement). And three days later his army of fools had lost the plot and let Jesus walk right back out of Death Valley (or Hell as he preferred to call his domain), totally unmolested and taking some of the supposedly condemned humans with him. Finally to reappear in front of His human followers, claiming victory over death and declaring that from then on, humans who believed in Him and were content to acknowledge this before others would be freed from Hell's grip.

Shrugging irritably, Lucifer let his hand wander to where his weapon should have been. The trouble with visiting rights was they required him to disarm and partly disrobe on arrival. Two requirements that caused him particular misery. The foremost being that, whilst exposure to Earth's sunlight was bad enough, exposure to God's unique light caused him nothing short of intense and virtually constant pain. Particularly to his eyes and the skin of his face and arms which, by decree, had to remain uncovered. He had long since assumed this to be one of Michael's arrangements, issued under the dubious pretext of security, because every angel was perfectly capable of seeing straight through any disguise he might employ. And that, of course, served perfectly to rub his nose in it. Exactly as it was designed to do. Although it wasn't all doom and gloom. At a stretch, there was a plus to any visit. An aspect that made the humiliation and pain almost worthwhile. Forays into Heaven provided a reassuring side effect when he returned to the dark corridors of Hell. An immediate and satisfying whiff of terror amongst his nightmare attendants, as they fought to retreat from the fading glow of his exposure. A 'cause and effect' that never failed. But today was one of those occasions when it was more important to gather information than relish the idea of future pandemonium. And the only way he was likely to succeed was to crawl to his erstwhile comrade in arms, Michael. How he hated these occasions. He,

Satan, the once noble Jewel of Heaven, forced to grovel to a mere Archangel. But there was little choice, given Heaven was evidently plotting something that apparently involved a certain Paul Moncton. An individual who was already beginning to prove a nuisance to Hell's executive. He knew something was happening and whilst he was pretty sure he knew what the final outcome would be, he could never quite rid himself of the urge to upset Heaven's confidence. And anyway, the matter was beginning to exasperate him. It was one of the drawbacks to an unsuccessful rebellion. You lost every last vestige of peace.

So, trying to effect a confident swagger, Lucifer marched straight towards Michael from behind, hoping to catch him unawares. Stupid, he knew. But at heart he was a brawler, a chancer, and he simply couldn't help himself. But as if to compound his frustration, Michael didn't even look behind him.

"Morning, Lucifer. I didn't think it would take you long to get here. I've noted your recent interest in the East African coast. So, let me guess. You want to know what we're planning and where Paul Moncton fits in."

Grinding his teeth (he just couldn't help it), Lucifer stopped and drew himself to his full, repellent height. How did Michael always know? It was nauseating, but he was forced to listen as Michael continued unhurriedly.

"As I'm sure even you have realised, I cannot divulge our overall plans, but I will say that Paul's progress and life are of great importance to God. There are a number of steps young Paul must yet take before he acknowledges God's Son, Jesus, as the Supreme Being. So, God has ordered that not only is Paul to be protected from physical death, but no demon is to possess him again. Harass, yes. Possess, no. You would do well to remember that. And no. Don't even think of trying to jump me. You wouldn't get half a pace before I skewered you like the parasite you are. Look around you, Lucifer. Are you now so blind that you cannot see my companions, my guards?"

Michael's hand motioned the space around him and although Lucifer knew he would not lie, he still couldn't see. Frustrated, he waited as Michael calmly pointed out that not one of the sentries loitering in a separate dimension would hesitate to materialise and deal swiftly with such a prize, the moment he stepped out of line. The protection was discreet but no less effective for all that. And Lucifer knew it.

"But back to Paul. The Lord God has decided that you may get up to your usual devious tricks and may allocate demons to test Paul. Moreover, they may even do to him as you wish, except, I repeat, under no circumstances are they to hound him to the point of death. As for Roz Lescal, she is also given into your power for a short time, but, again, her life may only be taken by another human. Certainly not one of your sidekicks. Is that quite clear?"

Faced with the implacable and menacing nature of Michael's deceptively mild delivery, Lucifer decided to make a conscious effort to uncurl his hands and relax his tense muscles. Michael was acting unusually. Normally he was urbane charm itself, poised elegance personified. So, clearly, Paul Moncton was important and would have to be watched, which meant he'd better find out who had been assigned to meddle with him. *If anyone, given Hell's ramshackle administration*, he thought sourly.

CHAPTER 49

If ever there was a saying that suited Ahmed's foul mood, heightened as it was by the irritation of lost assets, it was 'spitting feathers'. That he'd probably lost a white slave was the height of stupidity, especially one who had apparently defied Abdel-Aziz in the process and over whom he'd clearly lost a substantial sum (even the female provided in exchange was no compensation as she'd died shortly after arrival, forcing him to modify his particular vice). But, as if that wasn't bad enough, he was now being forced to join Abdel-Aziz in the godforsaken hole they called Malindi. At least the boy had paid a certain price before escaping, having been whipped to within an inch of his life. A stark warning to any other slave who might be foolish enough to consider mutiny. Add to that the loss of three of the crew at such an early and crucial point in a transit voyage and he was looking at little less than financial catastrophe. But all else paled into insignificance besides Abdel-Aziz's failure to return with his nephew, Abdullah. That unexplained disappearance could spell disaster when it came to the continuing support of his invaluable source of ready funds, the family fortune.

Upon such infuriating events did a lifetime of investments turn. The real problem was that whilst his easy-going grandfather was the nominal head of the family and supposedly in charge of its considerable wealth, the actual power behind the throne (though never admitted in polite Arab circles) was his aunt, Buhaysah (named even from her youth for 'walking with pride'). Not for nothing was she known for her almost homicidal, usually unreasonable and always direct response to avoidable blunders.

Especially if she felt there might be a personal insult involved. Something she would assuredly believe in this case, given her favourite grandson was one of the missing. And if Abdel-Aziz didn't provide a satisfactory answer to the matter pretty soon, then his demise was unlikely to be much delayed. Captain or not. Of course he, Ahmed, had not the slightest concern for his nephew per se. It was just that he had guaranteed safe passage and so found not only his considerable reputation in possible jeopardy, but an unexpected frisson of fear pricking his mind at the thought of eventually having to face his imperious aunt. And his aide's immediate enquiries amongst the crew had determined that nobody had seen the young fool alive since they'd all turned in on the night of the raid. For which there could only be one explanation. He must have been snatched by the scum assisting the girl. Had she not displayed the sort of impudent temerity that only a white girl could, by stepping uninvited onto one of his ships? A ship that, true to Arab tradition, had never been sullied by an uninvited female foot. Invited, yes. Uninvited, no. Over many decades, the decks had no doubt hosted a far from inconsequential stream of harlots and ladies of a certain ilk, all bent on providing suitable and erotic entertainment for the crew.

But enough of such distracting thoughts. Angrily, Ahmed had had Abdel brought before him. "Aziz, you will return to your ship immediately and this time you will find Abdullah. Allow me to assure you that if you do not return with him soon, it will not be long before you join your ancestors."

Abdel-Aziz knew this was no idle threat, but equally he understood that if Abdullah had been unable to look after himself thus far, then it was highly likely there was absolutely nothing to be done for him now. Either he was already fish food, or he was a prisoner and thus a useful hostage who would not be surrendered lightly. Whichever, right now Aziz knew he could do nothing about it. Except, of course, look as though he actually gave a toss and head north on the assumption the man had been taken prisoner. Muttering and cursing under his breath, Abdel had left to begin the task of putting to sea once more, issuing a stream of orders to set course safely through the reef gap and on out into the great Pacific rollers, before backing the dhow once again onto a northerly track to retrace the assumed route of the fleeing bandits. Finally clear of the reef, his ship had strained eagerly forward into the steepening undulation of an on-shore swell and the hiss of water gathering pace under her bluff stem was at least comforting. Not that it made any marked difference to the crew's demeanour, because they were already disgruntled enough and now knew for certain there was unlikely to be a pay day following this year's efforts. Moreover, they couldn't be less interested in Ahmed's relative, as no one really cared a hoot for anything other than the money the escaped boy and remaining slaves represented.

And sailors, unlike land-based traders, know there is nothing to be gained from trying to outsmart wind and tide. Or find missing crewmen off a shark-infested African coast. Moreover, to try fighting the wind merely to look for a missing sailor was not a matter to be taken lightly. Clearly, it was going to involve the better part of a week searching north before beating back to Malindi, always assuming they even managed to find Abdullah, or recapture the escaped slave. A state of affairs that meant at the very least they faced rampaging sickness amongst the cargo, as the old scow squandered time, bucking and rolling against the set of wind and wave. Perhaps even the death of some captives. It wasn't just Aziz who was beginning to heartily regret ever setting eyes on the white boy. It was every man-jack of the crew.

CHAPTER 50

On the day my body finally began to register some genuine improvements, I remember stirring very carefully as I came round, there to find to my delighted surprise that movement was no longer quite the ordeal to which I had grown so wearily accustomed. An experimental foot waved in the general direction of the floor completed the initial appraisal and I found I could move within a controllable level of pain, and this, coupled with the gradual realisation that I was far more awake than usual, proved to me that I really must be on the mend. How many days had I been lying there semi-comatose? I still had no idea, but it was clear from the angle of the sun streaming through a gap in the wall that already this particular day was wearing away, the sun heading inexorably towards late afternoon or early evening.

Whatever the hour, I felt a distinct surge of renewed energy, which in turn fuelled a fresh sense of purpose, and such was the degree of change that I needed to tell someone about my progress. Preferably Roz. Opening my mouth to call her only led to the discovery that I was beyond dry, my tongue being firmly stuck to the roof of my mouth. Which put an immediate end to any hope of shouted communication. With no alternative but to get myself up, I rolled gingerly towards the edge of the bed frame and dropped to the floor on hands and knees, before hoisting myself upright with the aid of an obligingly placed stool. That was the easy bit. The real effort came with hauling myself outside in a bid to start looking for Roz. Where I soon discovered that not only had she disappeared, but so had every last member of the community. Presumably to engage in that stalwart of the *mañana* society: horizontal PT (under the shade of some handy palms). Fortunately, given there was no one in sight, it wasn't long before I picked up on the distant sound of laughter, which proved easy enough to follow as I lurched away from the settlement and towards the area of beach over which I vaguely remembered being carried ashore. The problem wasn't so much my innate physical weakness, more an inability to move with any enthusiasm without first taking in some much needed water. The very reason I had been forced to stagger out in the first place. Consequently, I not only started to feel distinctly lightheaded, but soon had to endure the onset of a blinding headache. Still, gritting my teeth, I managed to totter slowly in the general direction of the noise, sustained by little more than a fervent hope that I wouldn't collapse along the way.

They weren't too far, but my somewhat unstable arrival produced an eminently satisfactory reaction within the gathered throng. Roz came running towards me from somewhere in their midst, arms outstretched, presumably the better to catch me, as I was beginning to tip forward on the distinctly uneven sand. But for all I cared, that sand was welcome to do its worst, because I don't think I'd ever seen Roz looking more beautiful. I can still conjure that vision to my mind's eye, as though it were yesterday. She could have been wrapped from head to toe in a sheet and she would still have been stunningly beautiful. But on that late afternoon and in that place, she was in perfect harmony with her surroundings. And, to my further enchantment, wearing little more than her obvious concern. The ubiquitous khaki shorts were rolled down at the waist and up at the leg, the better to maximise the tanning of her honey-coloured skin. Above them, her slim stomach took a long inward curve past the delicate valley of a finely shaped, elegant belly button, the whole lightly dusted with delicate blond hairs. Just above the rib cage where her flesh began to sweep upwards and outwards in fine counterbalance to the fulsome curve of her hips, a startlingly white bra cupped high, tight and delightfully rounded breasts that would have been the envy of virtually any woman on the planet. And certainly the desire of any man. Graceful arms and finely turned legs, the latter seeming to sweep all the way to her armpits, completed that enthralling, never to be forgotten picture of beauty. The whole set off by the most attractive face I had ever seen. And all topped with a long blonde ponytail that swept back and forth across those lissom, tanned shoulders, responding as if imbued with a life of its own and swaying in time to the easy, graceful lope that brought her ever closer to me.

I think I can measure my total enchantment in this delightful lady and my absolute and undying enthralment from that precise moment. It was the instant when every feeling I had ever had for her, both physical and emotional, crystallised into a grand passion that would forever dominate my life, never fading, only deepening. I was captivated. Fortunately, she caught me before I hit the deck and if I ever needed confirmation that the Moncton juices were back out in force, it was established in the sheer ecstasy of erotic feeling that raced through me as her strong arms and soft hands wrapped around my naked torso, stabbing me with all the electric excitement of physical contact that one of the opposite sex can impart. Even with still bruised and beaten skin, the sensation of sliding against a warm, scented body was utterly enthralling. Of my own hands, suddenly allowed to follow the play of muscles bunching and relaxing down the length of her supple back, I can only reminisce. Of firm breasts pressing against my chest as she fought to keep me upright, I remember thinking that Heaven had nothing finer to offer. Before having to turn half away as my unruly and unfettered member let me down in a fundamental and embarrassing manner. Which she judiciously ignored.

"Paul, it's great to see you up, but please be careful. You've been off your feet for a couple of weeks now and I'm so sorry I wasn't there when you woke up."

What is it about love that changes everything? One minute you're sane enough and concentrating on *numero uno*. The next you're completely disorientated, hooked by a retroussé nose, and a look that can only be described as 'one to die for'. Lost in a tender world you could never have imagined, even had you tried. If I'd been more a man of the world, I would no doubt have seized her then and there, laying my mouth on those lips placed so close to mine it almost hurt. But, as yet, I was unschooled in such matters. Perhaps fortunately for my esteem, it didn't seem as though I was expected to say or do anything much and so the moment passed and I relaxed, seizing the welcome opportunity to enjoy every lingering second of surreptitious and continuing contact. And to pretend a little regarding the matter of energy and ability, because simply being near her had already given me all the stamina I needed.

How things do change. Physically and mentally. Most of my pretensions and preconceptions had been stripped bare in those past days of imprisonment and 'not knowing'. Days of fearing for my life. Days that had turned to weeks then months, during which I had been forced to reconsider all that I held dear, to confront every previous assumption and face down each dread as it arose. And had I but known it, I had already sunk to the root of all that mattered. Somewhere between Matt, Giuseppe, Ahmed, Adam and Roz I had grown up, matured and entered into that other reality, the world of adults, light years from youth's dream. A world so packed with injury and destruction (for me at least) that the average individual could probably never envisage it, never confront such choices, no matter how long and varied life might be. A world of danger and hardship, of indifference, of participants too cold and devoid of basic compassion to be considered fully human, but yet a world in which unknown and unsung heroes were prepared to give their very lives as the price for a stranger, or two people could become more than the sum of their parts by falling in love and learning to share in everything. But dreams are there to be shattered and I should have known my idyll was never going to last. At any rate, that was what the world had clearly been bent on teaching me. Perhaps I just hadn't learned the lesson. Regardless, I still had a few delicious hours in which to cement the love I not only owed Roz but longed to confirm for her anyway. And it would not be very long before I became aware of the fly in my particular ointment.

CHAPTER 51

A fly already hovering only a few yards from me. Even then. And leering. Re-armed after his run-in with Josephus and ready for action, Arcturus was beginning to recoup his somewhat battered self-confidence and, having accepted his assignment (what choice did he have?), was taking the time to think through his new project with some care. Sifting across the outer reaches of my mind, Arcturus had been slightly alarmed to discover a noticeable maturity of attitude, a refinement of principle and ethical development, principles not found in many of the humans with whom he had previously dealt. Presumably developed in the hardships I had recently undergone. Experience had taught him that most humans bumbled through life seldom, if ever, concerned about morality or principles, even when push came to shove. Which made a demon's job that much easier.

But this one (me) had, apparently, managed to compound the immediate problem by succumbing to possibly the worst pollution available to the human mind. Excited, outgoing love. Carnal, yes, but rapidly adding overtones of affectionate, unselfish empathy. As far as Arcturus was concerned, if you had to have anything to do with love, then self-love was as good as it got. Self-sacrificing affection was potential disaster. Having said which, by definition, human lovers opened themselves to sexual manipulation, which would probably give him the opportunity to engage a particularly exquisite torment he'd managed to perfect. Indeed, the manipulation and exploitation of human lovers in the hands of someone as gifted as himself was usually pretty straightforward. Revolted though he was by proximity to genuine love of any sort, Arcturus nevertheless needed to evaluate my mind more closely. To seek out and assess the weak points, obsessions, corrupt or offensive habits from the past, anything that could be exploited to his own sordid ends. And inevitably there would be some, but the sifting would take a little time. Worth it though, if the result of his investigations meant he could select the perfect poison to bring about my swift and final self-destruction.

Whatever Heaven might be planning for this creature, Arcturus felt, it was essential that he quickly destroy any hope he might have gained, demolish any trust, twist the friendship and above all spoil any burgeoning love for the female, Roz. And Arcturus knew from long practice that he was as slick as it got when it came to that sort of creative malice. As far as he could tell from Josephus' short, sharp briefing, which was actually designed to confuse rather than enlighten (who knew what went through whatever passed for the commander's mind?), he, Arcturus, was now fully aware that sooner or later he could expect Heaven's intervention. Why, he wasn't entirely sure at this juncture. But he was used to such uncertainty and actually more than content to simply be a free agent once again, released from having to take responsibility for the usual swarm of irritating sycophants Hell tended to foist on him. The best of whom could never seem to accomplish the simplest of orders. No, he was probably much better off alone on this mission, even though the threat of death still hung over him. And, who knew, he might yet earn himself not only a reprieve, but promotion and some worthwhile prize to boot.

Continuing to watch, he debated his best course of action, becoming slowly aware that, for some reason or other, there were no warrior angels, never mind Guardians, anywhere in sight. Interesting, and a point worth bearing in mind. Those miserable Guardians seldom left their charges alone without good reason.

And it certainly hadn't escaped his notice that there were hordes of the human blemishes everywhere he looked. Quite a few of whom could normally expect to be on some angel's radar. Suspicious and keeping his eyes peeled, Arcturus unsheathed his sword, pointed the sharp dart of a tip towards his assignment and drew back his arm as though to strike. And, with enormous satisfaction, observed an anonymous angel materialise immediately opposite him, obviously intent on parrying the simulated blow. Smirking, Arcturus lowered the blade and leaned casually on the pommel. "That's all I needed to know for now," he said to no one in particular. Content simply that the obviously inexperienced angel (new Guardian?) did now fully appreciate the extent to which he had been deceived and the ease with which he had been drawn into an embarrassing overreaction. A disdainful glance was all it needed to underwrite the contempt. Thereafter, he simply filed away the useful snippet of information that Paul's previously assigned Guardian, the warrior with whom he'd already crossed swords, was absent. On a new mission? Or being updated on this one? If the latter, then this was likely to become more interesting than he had supposed, as everyone knew Heaven only called face-to-face briefings on exceptional matters.

Of course, if and when Israfel did return to duty, he would be much harder to deceive than the inexperienced minion currently assigned. Of that Arcturus could be entirely confident. So, turning back to his target, Arcturus resumed the task of sieving through the outer reaches of the mind laid bare before him (frustrating that he wasn't allowed to tamper with the core of it), looking for a clue as to the best way to reactivate the self-destruct button, a ploy that had so nearly succeeded earlier. All coupled with finding a means by which the specific restriction on killing, already announced by Heaven (at least Josephus had included this in his briefing), might be judiciously circumnavigated. Inevitably the best way to curry favour with his masters. Of course, persuading another human to undertake the killing could be difficult. But Arcturus was under no illusion. Any attempt by him to exterminate Paul himself would be met with instant retribution. Something he was determined to avoid.

CHAPTER 52

A soft evening breeze stirred the hard, dry fronds clustered in a neat spiral around the top of each elegant palm trunk. Arched spears of evergreen leaves click-clacked their way into the soft onrush of night and rendered the purple shadows the more attractive for their soothing murmur. Dancing to their own primeval tune, they managed to harmonise the casual randomness of cooling gusts of air into an almost symphonic melody. So much so that, from the soft sand where I lay staring up into the star-glazed sky, their serenade provided everything a young man in love could wish for on his first, unchaperoned tryst.

Only an hour or so earlier, Roz had finally managed to wrestle me back to the hut, surprisingly little the worse for wear. And not before I'd extracted a heartfelt promise to meet me later at the beach. Now, stretched out on the cooling sand, I found to my delight that even that short, earlier excursion had produced a benefit out of all proportion to its content. Perhaps it was simply the effect of stumbling and stretching, or perhaps it was down to victory over a psychological barrier, but, whatever it was, the past few hours had produced a sea change within me and the blood had begun once again to course through my limbs, not out of them. Not without pain, I hasten to add. Nevertheless, it was progress and marked progress at that. So much so that, not long after I had been unceremoniously dumped back onto the charpoy that had acted as horizontal brace and virtual prison for the last couple of weeks, I was able, like the proverbial phoenix, to rise once again to my feet. Not only that, but able to rejoice in a considerable degree of returning dexterity, something I had begun to fear permanently lost. Now I waited at the edge of the palms, right on the line between the grey, dusty inland soil and the whitewashed beach sand, ears straining to catch the first footfall of the girl whose very presence could overwhelm my senses. How heady that moment, forever etched in memory. How my heart leapt and somersaulted in contemplation of such beauty, such untrammelled delight. Had I ever previously given thought to how love might feel, I would have fallen so far short of reality it would have been ludicrous. I would not have had the remotest understanding of how unadulterated joy could flood one's veins. My heart sang while my mind delighted in contemplation of that dear girl and of how she would affect my future.

Her voice, when it came, was cool and lilting, and to my waiting ear was like oxygen to a drowning sailor. I don't remember the words, just the thrilling sweetness of her tone. The open, innocent calling of a young girl in the first flush of feminine maturity, calling for her love, knowing I would be waiting exactly where I had promised. Turning and raising myself up on one elbow, my heart went into overdrive as I caught sight of her shadowy outline in the light of the last rays of a sun that was already well below the horizon. She moved as gracefully as a faun across the open ground that fronted the hut she'd made her own. Even in the lengthening shadows her silhouette traced a heady mixture of style and leggy coltishness. I thanked all the gods I could think of that despite the restless off-shore breeze, the temperature remained overly warm and was no doubt the reason she wore even less than before. A red and gold sarong wound tightly around her breasts fell in loose, flowing pleats to mid-thigh, beneath which the skin of her legs glowed dusky white, in counterpoint to her bare, brown shoulders.

Gently, I answered her call and watched as she responded by swiftly altering her path directly towards me. I stared enchanted as she drew near and plumped herself down, while small puffs of sand thrown up by her passing splashed carelessly out around her bare feet. Every move she made, from the sway of her hips to the toss of her long blonde hair, seemed to me to be the personification of elegance and beauty. Such was the overall effect of her exquisite allure that the breath caught in my throat, my heart started thudding like a trip hammer and the boisterous susurration of blood coursing through my ears all but drowned the soft sounds of twilight. As she came to rest beside me I was certain she, too, must be able to detect something of the confusion her very near presence (and my overworked imagination) was developing. But if she did, she said nothing. So close was she that her natural fragrance filled my nostrils, even as the added electricity of touch almost gave me a heart attack.

"Hi, and how is the patient?"

By then I could barely speak, such was her overwhelming effect on my confidence. But I finally managed a weak and doubtless inane response. At any rate, we both broke into nervous, if somewhat relieved and delighted, laughter. Mainly, I suppose, because the simple sound of words was enough to discharge the tension between us. Both of us revelling in the fact that I was free and healing rapidly, but mostly in mutual recognition that we were alone, with the whole night stretching out in front of us, to make of it what we wished. And with the draining of tension came the contented and joyful acknowledgement of a shared love that, whilst it had certainly begun to mature, had by no means yet achieved its apogee. Released, we filled our world with speech that tripped easily off the tongue, sitting close together, side by side, thighs and arms touching gently but deliberately. Inwardly, each exploring our own very different sexual responses but, outwardly, filling in something more of what had been happening to each of us over the preceding months.

For my part I discovered, for the first time, that what had seemed to me to involve a complete lifetime had, in fact, only been the product of little more than five months. Five months. Less even than half a year, in which not only had my whole world

245

been turned upside down, but my life had several times hung by a mere thread. Moreover, both psychologically and emotionally in that short time I had grown further and faster than I had dreamed possible. Above all, the innate trust I'd had in the world around me, that modicum of confidence in the grown-up world most young men of my time retained even on the verge of their own adulthood, was gone forever. In its place had developed a brittle, cynical understanding that you lived and survived by your own cunning, your own abilities, or you went under. And I still seethed with the bitter knowledge that the law of the jungle was the only law that seemed to count. True, the excruciating pain of utter betrayal had dulled as I had grown more resilient. But just as shockingly, I had discovered that even Matt had receded in memory. And, with that awful realisation had come a cold and secret resolve to somehow erase my debt to him, if such an outcome was possible. I would overcome the fear that had left him to die alone and in some sort of recompense, would hunt down those who had not only abused me but, just as importantly, had put so many others through a living Hell. Not least, the gorgeous creature now sitting beside me. And with that resolved, I gave myself over completely to the most beautiful girl I would ever know.

Slowly, inevitably, our physical closeness had begun to fill the world of conscious thought. At first, it had been almost incidental, especially while we had so much to say and to absorb. But the companionable warmth of contact, skin to skin, had inevitably burgeoned into a positive and electrifying heat that neither of us could hope or wish to deny. Conversation flagged as so many new and untested sensations coursed through our youthful, virgin bodies. For both of us, they distilled into an almost overpowering sexual desire, a wordless drive to move closer still, until our bodies were touching along the full length of oh, so casually, outstretched legs. Pressed together at the hip. Arms deliberately entwined and rubbing silkily all the way to our bare shoulders (how did that happen?). Such was the power of raw emotion flowing between us, I thought my heart would forget its function or, at the very least, my lungs neglect to breathe. Whichever might happen first, it was likely to be a close run thing. And by this time the last stray signs of evening light had gone and the deep shadows of night had wrapped themselves around our al fresco couch. Behind us, muted by distance, the low and comforting sounds of domesticity carried faintly from the circled huts, where fires winked in staccato rhythm as door hangings moved to and fro in response to the passage of resident and visitor alike.

No one else had even a passing interest in our encounter and it seemed to us as though we floated free in a world of our own. Nearer to hand, the ceaseless advance and retreat, rush and hiss of the gentle lagoon surf on sand beat a rhythm as old as time itself. On the softly sloping beach laid out below us, ghost crabs flitted rapidly about their business, forever hungry, forever afraid. Overhead, the light of a million stars whitened the sky and in the subdued waves phosphorescence gave sudden and eerie glow to the tide line. All a mere backdrop, a spectator to our growing passion.

Utterly absorbed, we had eyes, hands and hearts only for each other. How could I ever forget that first sublime kiss? My first entry to the world of real, life-affirming, enduring love. Seemingly on impulse, we had gently rocked back onto the cradling sand, turning almost by instinct towards each other, our breath intermingling, our noses almost touching, each supremely aware of the other. For a silent moment we had stared deep into each other's eyes, every limb utterly still, savouring the moment. Unwilling to shatter the magic. Our eyes had locked, even though all that could be seen in our night-shadowed orbs was a faint reflection of starlight, but it seemed to me as if I was falling headlong into a well of delight from which there should be no return. With a new urgency our suddenly hungry lips mashed together, the gentleness of our first encounters forgotten and I remember thinking someone must have coupled me to the mains. Nothing further was said. Nothing extra needed to be articulated. How long had those first, lingering and gentle touches lasted? I have no idea. All I can tell you is that as I tasted her and felt for the first time her small, even teeth sliding silent against my tongue, I knew beyond doubt that here was my soul's lifelong companion.

There are no words to adequately describe the impact of a first kiss with someone for whom you have developed an overwhelming love. No words that can do justice to the initial response of the heart, the irrepressible intention and purpose exploding within you, as it seeks to protect and nurture, but also to explore the object of that love. If you have never experienced such an emotional awakening, you cannot hope to understand. And on this night to remember, for us there was also the first arousal and experience of sexual pleasure. Is it any wonder that love holds all the trump cards? To a frisson of almost overwhelming pleasure, I soon discovered that Roz's sarong was her only covering and as my nervously exploring hand slid along her velvety, shapely and athletic thighs, I discovered that there is more excitement to be found in a pair of silky smooth female legs than any parental pep talk or scholarly discourse can hope to prepare you for. And when that first and simultaneous climax exploded around and within us, it did so as the culmination of a frenzied, passionate and almost primordial coupling that left us both drained and gasping for air, our suddenly naked and sweat-slicked bodies drenched with the dew of lovemaking.

CHAPTER 53

Abdel-Aziz had finally worked his ship back to the natural break in the reef that signalled the entrance to the old port of Malindi. Only to confirm, as anticipated, that his was now the solitary sea-going dhow using the almost deserted port. Quartering the area just north of Malindi with some difficulty, they had wasted several days looking in vain for their attackers and the erstwhile Abdullah. Watching with extreme irritation as the last of the identifiable dhows had slid silently past on their north-bound journeys, long, sail-strained spars soaring and dipping in time to the rise and fall of the ocean rollers. Thoroughly enraged by the delay and barely able to contain himself, despite his innate and not unreasonable fear of Ahmed, Abdel-Aziz fought to contain his fury as he contemplated the wasted journey on which he had been sent by his long-time paymaster.

Afraid of him or not, he knew there was no point in continuing to search for someone who, for all anyone knew, was providing a feast for the local crabs since, like many Arab sailors, the fool probably couldn't swim anyway. Either way, abducted or dead, any dimwit could see that wasting further time searching the glittering, empty sea would lead to one thing only: fractious, unhealthy slaves, whose chances of developing devastating diseases or simply dying from fear or thirst were increasing by the minute. And some already had. Which also meant any chance of a profit from this futile voyage was slipping inexorably beyond his grasp. And whoever the scum were who had invaded his ship, neither Ahmed nor Abdel were prepared to accept that all the mayhem had been the work of just one white girl, teamed with a couple of companions who hadn't even come aboard. Despite the crew's vehement protestations to the contrary.

And in the Captain's view, whether by day or by night, keeping a slow-moving, heavily laden and lightly armed dhow meandering around just off the coast offered easy pickings to any one of the flimsy yet highly manoeuvrable local fishing boats. Particularly if the original, miserable pirates took it into their heads to return for another attack. So, anchored back at Malindi and with all hope of finding Abdullah now gone, he had found that fury had begun to get the better of fear (and common sense). And since Ahmed also lived in a degree of fear over his scheming aunt, he was prone to strike the nearest offender without warning when things failed to run to plan. Especially where money was concerned. Something Abdel-Aziz would have done well to remember.

Yet it remained a mystery to Abdel-Aziz as to why, with a cargo of prime slaves at stake, Ahmed had persisted in demanding the search for his cousin continue. Even the most amateur of sailors knew the southerly monsoon only blew for a limited period each year, after which it was pointless trying to take a cargo north. And that meant Abdel remained firmly wedged between a rock and a hard place. He had no wish to run out of wind off the Somali coast and be forced to beach in that waterless, godforsaken hole. On the other hand, no longer able to guarantee a successful voyage north, it was he, not Ahmed, who faced financial ruin. Or, if he refused to set sail, possible death at Ahmed's cold-blooded hands. Still cursing silently, Abdel had dropped anchor as close as he dared to the short stone quay of the old harbour without tempting the now thoroughly bored police with an invitation to visit. Which had left him wavering between barely suppressed but growing outrage, and abject fear as he waited for the recently alerted Ahmed to come aboard. Doubtless, without any suggestion of compensation. Sullenly, Abdel contemplated the only course left open to him. Try to find a buyer here in Malindi for a few of the better female slaves, an action fraught with danger in itself, given the ubiquitous police presence, or dump the lot of them overboard and let the sharks clean up. But even to do that he'd have to put well out to sea again and try to claw his way east, sufficiently far away from the coast line to afford even less chance of making it back to a reasonable mooring. And without that, there would be unbridled danger until the north winds took up and he could head back home, due south.

"Aziz!"

The sharp, imperious call brought Abdel abruptly out of his reverie. Ahmed had managed to arrive without being spotted and was even now standing in the ship's waist, right leg still trailing over the port rail and left hand clutched firmly around a trailing line.

"So, I hear you've failed me, you useless son of a whore. You will not move from this stinking tub until I give you permission. Is that clearly understood?"

It was the contempt dripping from Ahmed's voice that proved the last straw. What had been a mere fantasy at the back of Abdel's mind hardened suddenly into a lethal decision. He, Abdel-Aziz, knew himself to be many things that, whether he acknowledged it or not, were generally rather less than flattering, but 'magnanimous' was not listed among them. By Allah, blessings be upon him, men had died for lesser insults and there was no way he was prepared to accept such a contemptuous dismissal in front of his crew. Turning slowly to face the source of his frustration, Abdel fixed Ahmed with the same basilisk stare that others had reason to regret, before spitting ostentatiously over the side in a bid to give himself time to slide a surreptitious hand towards the small handgun nestled against his thigh. A sudden and uneasy silence gripped the ship and it didn't take a genius to understand that something was about to blow. Unfortunately for Abdel, Ahmed was also one of those who got the picture. A lot sooner than most and with reactions to match. Abdel had barely begun to bring his now full hand up from within the folds of his loose-fitting outer robe when the flat crack of a rather more robust handgun rolled around the narrow deck and Abdel's left leg seemed to fold in upon itself as he followed it down to the dark, sea-stained planks. Desperate, he rolled to his right, trying to reposition his useless leg whilst bringing his own weapon to bear. But even before he'd stopped moving, Ahmed had covered the gap between them. And he was in no mood for reconciliation. His right foot stamped down hard on Abdel's gun hand, while his left lined up Abdel's now useless leg. The subsequent connection with the bloodied hole where the bullet had entered causing Abdel to scream involuntarily, before biting back the agony through clenched teeth. But he need not have bothered. A merciless hand grasped him by the beard, jerking his head backwards to expose his throat. Swift as thought, the razor-sharp knife, which had seemed almost to jump into Ahmed's hand as it replaced the still-smoking gun, was now drawn quickly and expertly across the jugular from left to right. And such was the power of the pulsating flow of arterial blood that it probably took Abdel less than thirty seconds to die. Slowly, Ahmed wiped the blade on Abdel's clothing, before straightening himself and turning towards the cowed crew.

"Raise the anchor, tie this dog to it then tip the lot overboard and if anyone else wants to get involved, I guarantee they'll join him."

For a brief moment, not a muscle moved amongst the crewmen. But no one doubted Ahmed would be as good as his word and none of them had the slightest wish to follow their captain into the water, alive or dead. Awkwardly and as one, they stumbled forward to do Ahmed's bidding, not knowing what would happen to them now they were leaderless. And acutely aware of the despairing moans filtering up from the illegal cargo chained below decks.

CHAPTER 54

Slowly, lazily, I rolled over, luxuriating in the warmth of the hollow we had fashioned out of the sand, well away from the little collection of African huts and half hidden behind a neighbouring stand of palms. It was a part of the beautiful shoreline that we had come to regard as virtually our own over the previous heady days and nights. Lying comfortably nose to nose, I had been gazing deep into Roz's eyes, and together we had been mapping out a glorious future, paying little if any attention to the recent past, or the complications that were bound to follow our eventual return to the real world. After all, if ever we thought about it, we knew anyway that we were bound irrevocably, awaiting only a priest to do the honours and thus were ready to sink or swim together, whatever the consequence. And happy for it to be so.

However, it wasn't just the predictable difficulty with the law that faced us; it was the far greater danger that lay 'somewhere out there', in the shape of one of the most threatening gangsters in the country. A million miles away from our happiness he might be, but even in the bliss of our wayward beachcomber existence, neither of us was so foolish as to imagine he would entirely give up the chase. We had caused too much trouble, knew too much, to be easily passed over (and to my great delight, I now realised I'd even cost at least one of them a considerable outpouring of effort, not to mention a substantial sum of money). Even today, when I think back over those wonderful, innocent moments, I know it wasn't just our surroundings that left us feeling utterly detached from reality – safe in our hideaway (although safety was exactly what those surroundings did give us most of the time).

No. It was more to do with that simple daily pleasure, the sheer joy of being together. There was an innocence, an excitement, a pure and simple enjoyment to every touch, every shared thought, and every mutual promise. And it took very little to leave us euphoric with excitement, every nerve thrumming, every precious moment together conspiring to shut out reality. I recall that only once in that fortnight did we properly consider the future, an exercise in anxiety as we thought first of our families and then of friends and how each might be reacting to the complete lack of any news. Should they be told? But I confess the only tangible effect of that brief foray into reality was simply to strengthen my determination to stay out of sight and carry on enjoying my lover's company to the full, prolonging that simple act by enticing her to continue absorbing the sybaritic beauty of the coastlands that stretched out all around us. Utterly naïve, but utterly right for the time.

★★★

Standing awkwardly, Ahmed warily observed the wrinkled old matriarch seated directly in front of him, surrounded by her sycophantic attendants, each of whom was clearly aware of his subtly changed status in the family hierarchy. It was easy enough to confirm the exasperating shift. A covert glance at the closed planes of their faces, and Ahmed knew beyond shadow of a doubt that his standing had been seriously weakened. A spoiled lothario, unused to any censure whatsoever, he seethed inwardly. '*You sneer now*', he thought vengefully, '*but one day every one of you bitches will pay with your life*'. He, Ahmed, who on any previous visit to the family firm needed only to lift a critical eyebrow to inspire a certain reassuring alarm, found himself apparently counting for little. His aunt, the power on the family throne, now sat silent. Controlled malice evident in every line of her body. And judging by the intensity of her imperious scowl, probably engaged in weighing up her preferred method for dispatching him. Permanently. Albeit not until after he'd provided a satisfactory and preferably believable explanation for her loss.

Ahmed was fully aware that he was in trouble on two counts. Abdullah, her favourite grandson, was missing, presumed dead, and right now he couldn't return even one dirham of her stake money, never mind show any profit on her investment. Capital supplied for the supposedly straightforward function of purchasing and exporting yet another lucrative cargo of good quality slaves. And Ahmed had every reason to be uneasy. Buhaysah had a very clearly defined sense of what was acceptable or not in her world and it didn't include failure. Moreover, money was her number one idol. Actually, it was his, too, but even with his agile brain, he could think of no suitable explanation on either count and he was only too aware that she was utterly ruthless, never having been known to give quarter or thought for anyone who had fallen within her definition of failure.

Well, now he had a choice. Say nothing and trust that somehow he could ride out the storm, even if that meant he might lose face permanently (which would also mean he would probably lose all hope of ever taking over the family business), or promise to produce Abdullah and at the same time get his cargo far enough north to find a buyer from whom he could obtain at least some return. Either action was fraught with difficulty, but right now the latter had the distinct merit of getting him out of his aunt's presence, a proximity that was beginning to unnerve him. And an action promised had the added advantage of postponing the inevitable day of reckoning. Perhaps even long enough to get him off the hook. Anyway, passivity wasn't in his nature and he remained, as ever, supremely confident of his own abilities. So, drawing himself to his full height and ostentatiously shaking out his white thobe[1], Ahmed motioned abruptly with his hand, silencing the women grouped around his aunt.

"Most illustrious Aunt, I understand why you are concerned for Abdullah. Nevertheless, if he is dead, God has willed it. If not, I will find him and, while I am doing that, I will sell the slaves and reimburse you with interest. That I can promise you." But even as he said it, they both knew it to be a lie.

CHAPTER 55

Israfel was entranced by Heaven's ever-changing, always refreshing beauty. Such was the ambiance, it was difficult not to break into a dance as he strode the crystal pavements leading him through the 'City of the Redeemed', stepping across a material that reminded him so strikingly of that more recent human invention, glass. As ever, he found himself stopping regularly, simply to greet his many friends, both Angelic and human. How often had he spent delightful hours in the company of great heroes from the humans' Bible, listening in wonder to their fascinating stories? Laughing uproariously over a thousand humorous incidents. Amazed and humbled by the degree of quite unmerited love the Father had shown to His special creatures all down the ages.

Love, that amazing proposition, central to Heaven's every activity. Certainly, he'd often read the Bible, known in Heaven as 'Father's love letters' (indeed, angels tended to prize and read them more than pretty well any of the intended recipients), but it was when the redeemed men and women brought personal reminiscences to bear that, for him at least, the chronicles took on their greatest significance. In the distance he noticed a long-standing acquaintance, Elijah (known to his own people as 'the prophet'), hurrying about some errand or other. Now there was a man with a purpose. Always on the go, even here in Heaven. It had been precisely such individuals, throughout Israfel's undergraduate years, who had done so much to successfully prepare not just him, but many of his colleagues for their initial Earth posting. And now here he was, a postgraduate back in Heaven for the first time since taking on his new project. A place he'd certainly missed since being assigned to Paul but, truth to tell, he had enjoyed every minute of the appointment to the hilt. Earth had so many new sights, sounds, experiences, even smells to offer. Not just the prized opportunity to look after a human, but the chance to hone his fighting skills where they really counted. Taking down fallen angels who had ignored the ground rules. As in desperation they frequently did (to his mild gratification). And now he had been called to a briefing with the Archangel Michael. Who would not be overwhelmed with the thought of meeting that mighty and renowned warrior in person? He, Israfel, had only ever seen him at a distance. Since he knew he hadn't messed up, it could only mean one thing. He, or his human charge, was being singled out for something special. And whichever way it went, he was going to be in the thick of it. Things didn't get any better.

Swiftly, Israfel picked up the pace. It wouldn't do to be late. Entering the garden where he'd been told Michael would be, he could see his boss kneeling, hands raised in worship, head cocked to one side, as though listening to something ethereal that Israfel could not hear. Stopping beneath a tree clothed in the full vigour of its green and gold beauty, Israfel let his gaze wander for a second or two to admire the iridescent blooms and dark, healthy leaves covering every inch of available space. There was just something about the place that instantly captured his spiritual and emotional attention. And with barely a pause he, too, began to worship the King of kings, rapidly becoming lost in wonder, love and praise. Carried away in ecstasy, he followed his Commander to his knees, rejoicing that he was counted worthy to take whatever task had been assigned, overwhelmed by a sense of well-being and gratitude. Such was his delight, that Israfel didn't remember how long he'd knelt there, until finally recalling he'd been summoned for a purpose. So, remaining discretely on one knee, he coughed politely and waited for Michael to turn and acknowledge him.

"Ah, Israfel, thank you for coming. You seem well." His Commander's firm but pleasant greeting, addressed to him as though they were of equal stature, quickly set Israfel at ease and it was brought home to him once again how privileged he was to be one of Heaven's elite warriors. "Israfel, we have much to discuss regarding your charge, Paul. Come, sit with me and I will sketch out for you something of his future. He is a chosen instrument of God's who has already suffered much, but who is set to suffer more. However, in due time, all these experiences will draw him towards God and this Kingdom. I can't overemphasise how important Paul is in the great scheme of things. He and others throughout Earth are being prepared for that period that humans call 'the end times'. The time when their Messiah, our sovereign Lord, will return in person to rule the Earth. So, your assignment is of the utmost significance and it's going to get infinitely more difficult and delicate as Paul's life progresses. I should also tell you that Satan has taken a direct interest in your protégé, as well as in the others involved in this immensely important task. Which means he might even manage to assign one of his more trusted demons to your particular case. At any rate, your main aim is to ensure Paul remains a free agent. Free to do and free to react how he will. But the aim also encompasses helping him with the mission I hope he will soon accept. Heaven has set great store by him and that's why, I will admit, I would normally assign a more experienced Guardian. However, your immediate superior has spoken highly of you and I know you've already shown yourself to be exceptionally astute. Moreover, and perhaps more importantly in this case, you've proved unusually good at reacting to the unique character of your somewhat feisty charge. Hence, I believe you're equal to the task. At any rate, this is your opportunity to shine. So, subject to your continuing to obtain good reports, I am happy to confirm you in post. That said, we can now get down to the details."

Thrilled, Israfel opened his mind to Michael, inviting him to speak directly into it. In Heaven's rarefied atmosphere, when it was appropriate to pass on precise instructions from God, neither had any need for words. Rather, it made sense to communicate directly at the subconscious level, where nothing would be lost in translation. So, continuing to listen intently, Israfel was both elated and saddened by certain aspects of the incoming information, which, amongst other things, outlined the more obviously difficult circumstances Paul was yet to face. Nevertheless, he was still able to glory in the likely outcome and in the fact that, if only fleetingly, he was being allowed the rare privilege of seeing into the future.

For Paul, there was to be much pain and sadness. For himself, there would be tricky and dangerous moments, but out of the totality of their shared experience would arise a mature, hopefully God-loving and always infinitely precious human being. At any rate, he was eventually going to be allowed to reveal exactly who it was that loved and cared for his charge, whatever the ultimate outcome. And, he noticed with a certain grim satisfaction, there appeared to be a rather tasty conclusion with regard to the on-going row he was having with Arcturus. "Right, Israfel." With the direct briefing over, Michael's spoken words cut through his deliberations. "I need hardly remind you that it is not normally for us to know the nature or timing of future events. Such matters are for God the Father alone and those to whom He chooses to reveal them. However, don't forget that with the privilege of revelation comes considerable responsibility. Father commands that these things be kept secret – especially from the ranks of our enemies. Any questions?"

Israfel shook his head. His briefing had been comprehensive and succinct. Moreover, he had been given carte blanche to run his own operation, the only caveat being he was to ensure he called on Heaven's resources if and when needed. He was even to be given the temporary acting rank of squadron leader, accompanied by the authority to call upon specific units of legionnaires as and when needed. It was this latter authorisation that gave him the real clue as to how important Paul was in the great scheme of things and the significance of his own role as Guardian.

CHAPTER 56

Precise times are of little import now, but I will never forget even the smallest unfolding detail of that day's events. Not the sights, nor the sounds, nor the smells. Nothing. Roz and I had risen early to take advantage of the coolness of the day. I could move much more easily now and had no difficulty keeping pace with her. No matter what she was doing, I wanted to be there. Never tiring in my longing to observe and be entranced by not only her singular beauty, but also her remarkable personality. In fact, every thought of her was a study in unreserved tenderness. That morning we quickly prepared our simple breakfast, packed some fruit and water into a shoulder bag and were well clear of the community before the first of our neighbours had shown their sleep-clogged faces. Walking always seemed to do me considerable good, so we had been pushing further and further each day and had, for the first time, decided to range well outside the domain inhabited by our friends, intending to head south towards Malindi for approximately five miles.

But first, we had to commandeer and paddle one of the local outrigger canoes across the creek, there to leave it until its owner no doubt saw it from afar. Not difficult and it wasn't extreme walking by anyone's standards, but to us it felt like a delightful little adventure and would, anyway, give us the opportunity to see something more of the coast that, like Roz, I now regarded as home. In any case, I had come to prize the solitude of the hushed, pristine white coral beaches. To delight in the almost relentless, gentle hissing of aquamarine breakers marching in solemn succession up the gently sloping sands, all set off by the salty warmth of the constant sea breeze. And, not least, the euphoria we derived from the closeness of intertwined fingers and the supreme awareness of each other's presence. As we trudged through the damp sand at the sea's edge, always seeking a firm footing and trying to ignore the lesser heat of early morning, we exulted in the calling of the spotted ground thrushes flittering in and out of the nearby bushes and revelled in the sheer splendour of our surroundings. Thrilled by the surpassing joy of being alive, together and in love.

Perhaps it was simply this beauty that touched Roz, but after we'd ambled our way through about a mile, kicking idly at the sand and searching for the less common cowries, she evidently decided the time and mood were ripe to share some very private thoughts about her memorable visit to Moiben church. I soon discovered that for some time the matter had not only weighed heavily on her mind, but closer analysis had persuaded her she needed to share the event, which she still failed to understand but, at the same time, couldn't deny. Why this should be, she had no idea, but urgent it remained and, for peace of mind, she felt compelled to open a discussion. And as I listened, I realised she was focusing on something entirely spiritual. Something in which, I must confess, I still had little or no interest, despite Adam's best efforts. Religion just wasn't my thing. But if Roz wanted to speak about her feelings, so be it. I would happily listen to her voice at any time, on any subject. I told myself, "*That's what love does*", but not for a moment did I think such issues could, or even would apply to me. Anyway, it seemed that what had really impressed itself on her was a very clear and unequivocal sense of peace. Someone or something had apparently imparted a quiet calm unlike anything she had ever experienced before. Added to which, inexplicably, she had been subjected to much the same manner of encounter on more than one occasion since. Impressions that, she insisted, she'd already tried to share with me but that, apparently, had fallen on deaf ears. No doubt ears distracted by pain (I told myself). Anyway, this experience (whatever it was) evidently included a definite sensation of something or someone standing very close and exuding a strangely comforting love towards her. Now that got my interest. Love (for her at least) was my territory, for sure. As far as I was concerned, there was only one person with any right to love her and that was me. Not that this was going to prevent her from rehearsing the whole experience right in front of me. And then came the bombshell. Even as she spoke, I could tell she was beginning to understand that something profoundly important lay behind it all. And despite myself, I was a little shaken.

"Paul, tell me. Have you ever talked to or thought about God?"

The question came out of left field and I had to confess I hadn't. And nor would I have welcomed any such discussion. Religion had simply never interested me and, to reiterate, never would. And in my less than humble opinion, given what I'd recently experienced, I could hardly be blamed. And yet, even as I complacently justified myself, the memory of an unforgettable fellow slave, my friend Adam, who had willingly laid down his life for me, jumped unbidden to my mind. He was perhaps the one solid enigma I couldn't get around. A strong, clear faith, accompanied by an enviable and frankly inexplicable peace, had coloured everything he did. Even choosing death to give me a chance of life was the product of this faith. And, if truth were told, I wasn't the only prisoner to have been struck by his attractive qualities. But enough of that. I was in no mood to concede the argument.

Which fazed Roz not one whit. "Since I was a kid, I haven't discussed the subject either. I haven't even given it much thought, with the exception of that occasion in Moiben. I don't know why, but a moment ago the whole subject of God just popped into my head. I certainly wasn't thinking about anything within a million miles of it, but I remember my parents did make me go to Sunday school. And my teacher certainly believed in God. I know she did, because she not only talked about her faith, it sort of shone out of her somehow and she was always kind to us, even the ones who didn't much like her and usually played her up. There was just something about her that was attractive. Attractive to all of us, actually. I once asked her about this and she said something about being friends with the Messiah, Jesus, even though you couldn't see Him. I didn't understand her answer and I didn't really believe her anyway, so that was as far as we got. But now I'm beginning to wonder. Do you think there could be a God, Paul? Suppose she was right and you can actually get to know Him? That would be something, wouldn't it, if you could be friends with God? The God who's supposed to have created the universe?"

I didn't respond, but that didn't stop her. She simply carried on, musing aloud.

"Whenever I've heard anyone talking about God, they always seem to end up with this Jesus. They call him the 'Son of God' and they say He loves us and offers forgiveness for the things we've done wrong. Apparently He wants to save us from Hell so we can be with Him in Heaven. Heaven? Hell? I don't know. Where did they get all that? Can any of it be true? I just don't know, but come to think of it, I'm pretty sure it would feel weird to have a friend you couldn't see." After a slight pause, Roz burbled on. "Actually, I suppose my brother did when he was small. He had a made-up friend. Maybe it isn't such a weird thing after all. And there's something else too, now I come to think of it. Until recently, I was convinced I hadn't done anything particularly wrong. But right now I'm not so sure. Maybe I'm not as good as I thought I was. Maybe I do need this forgiveness, although for what, well, I'm not sure. What do you think, Paul? Come on, speak to me. Do you think we need forgiveness? Do you suppose my old teacher could have been right and Jesus is for real? Then what? Where does that leave me? Where would it leave us? Paul, please, at least tell me what you think."

But even in the face of this earnest appeal I wasn't much help. Religion was the last thing I wanted to talk about right then, so all I managed to say was, "If He's so concerned about us, why wasn't He there when I needed help?" And then, warming to my theme, "Why didn't He do something about that slaving dhow? Plenty of people there who could have done with some help."

These unhelpful comments left Roz slightly confused and dismayed, because whilst she was obviously concerned and interested, all I'd managed to do was pour cold water over her ideas. She stopped talking at that point, but I could see she was still tantalised by her thoughts and for some minutes obviously continued to chew through the options. But even if I'd been inclined to humour her, all thought of this fled from my mind moments later, when our circumstances changed so rapidly, there was virtually no time to think. Almost no time to even react.

CHAPTER 57

Israfel was back and eager to get stuck in. First, he'd hooked up with Roz's newly assigned Guardian, Nadab. He remembered him as the angel who was on leave at the time, but who had distracted Arcturus for him when he'd had a run-in on the slave ship. He had immediately warmed to the junior angel, who he'd only recently learned had been appointed to look after Roz, so it was a pity their association as Guardians was only going to be short-lived. One of the distinct drawbacks to knowing something about the future. However, Nadab was excited and bursting to tell him about Roz's renewed interest in her experiences back in Moiben church when, amongst other things, the Spirit of God had calmed her and quietly spoken peace into her heart. Sensing her drift, he had apparently given her a little nudge or two and was now as certain as he could be that she was on the brink of committing herself to the King's cause.

But for now, what he presumed was Nadab's unauthorised interference with a human being was not Israfel's main concern. He had been de-briefed by the temporary Guardian before formally taking me back, only to discover that Roz and I were heading down a beach straight towards some of Ahmed's hired thugs. An armed and dangerous gang searching their way slowly north. Progress had been slow, because it involved stopping and closely examining every village they'd reached. Plus the use of a little unauthorised persuasion now and then, particularly when it involved young women. And that invariably ended in something of a bloodbath, as they were forced to cut off pursuit by incensed family members.

But the gang had their orders and these were not only to search carefully, but to do so without wasting too much time. The ginger-haired white boy was the prize. That was the important thing. And Ahmed had known he was unlikely to persuade the locals to talk, even if presented with generous bribes. The best he could do was employ a little common sense and start a search northwards from just a short distance north of Malindi itself. He was convinced that, if still alive, my physical state would, so far, have prevented me from venturing inland, needing time to heal sufficiently to allow easier movement. And he was equally certain that whilst I would be well hidden by friends, any hideout would, of necessity, be close to where a small boat could be brought ashore, as well as within easy reach of such medical help as might be available along the coast. Which necessitated a break in the reef. So it was his guess the boat would have beached near a small village, within an easy sail of Malindi. Probably that meant the first gap in the reef, or maybe just north of it. The winds close inshore and the chronic inability of lateen sails to tack crosswind would have seen to that. And gaps only occurred where there was an outflow of fresh water. As with a river.

So he had the makings of a plan, but probably little time if it was going to be successful. Consequently, straight after leaving his aunt, he had hired a new dhow and brought in one of his favourite captains and, with the southern monsoon winds abating by the day, ordered him to sail north with half the crew from the *Majid an-Najdi*, until he reached the first gap in the reef north of Malindi, the creek at Kipini. In the meantime, he'd had the remaining crew members driven overland to a point just south of the village of Mkondo with orders to start walking north, following the coast until they fetched up opposite his newly hired and pre-positioned dhow. Secretly, he remained certain I would be somewhere near Kipini – perhaps even Abdullah might be there – but it was best to be thorough. And now, unwittingly, the men coming up from the south were heading straight towards me and Roz as they ambled northwards. And at this late stage, constrained as he was, there was little Israfel could do about it.

Fatih was in the lead. His rifle slung carelessly at his side and paying little attention to his surroundings. His thoughts were still with the last village they'd checked. A particularly striking native girl had caught his eye and he'd wasted little time in the niceties. Some would call it rape. He just thought of it as his due for having had to waste his time with these people and now they were well north of the village and presumably beyond the likely range of any further hotheads. Having summarily shot the villagers who'd been foolish enough to mount an immediate pursuit virtually unarmed, none of them were expecting further trouble from any remaining firebrands. So it was with some astonishment that his attention was dragged back to the present upon catching sight of a white boy and a white girl strolling arm in arm along the beach towards him, apparently oblivious to anything but each other. A hissed command caught the attention of the others, dragging their eyes round to this unusual sight. It was young Ghazi, named as 'conqueror' by his doting mother, who was first to react. Fatih could only surmise that youthful energy meant he was less inclined to doze on his feet than the rest. At any rate, Ghazi, clearly alert, immediately blurted out, "Allah be praised, these must be the ones for whom we're searching."

At which point, we spotted them and, dropping the basket, which promptly scattered its meagre contents across the sand, started to run for the treeline. Fatih couldn't believe his luck. Ghazi must be right, judging by my rather obvious hair colour and the frantic way in which we had started running. Fear like that didn't originate in innocence. Not in his book, anyway. Swiftly issuing some terse commands, Fatih took off for the treeline himself, intent on angling his way in our direction, but out of sight, using the nearby trees and bushes as cover. Quickly, he directed all but two of his party to follow, indicating that they should spread themselves out in a line at right angles to the shore, that is, all except the last pair who were to continue along the beach, expressly to discourage us from retreating back the way we'd come. Once off the beach, the air was hot and still and the men rapidly started to sweat copiously as they brushed through the thick undergrowth, stepping carefully to avoid snakes and swatting warily at the dozens of enormous spiders sitting in their carpet-like webs, each net capable of covering a complete bush. Although that at least meant arachnophobes could clearly see where each of their feared enemies lay in wait. However, the brush was so dense they almost immediately lost sight of each other, although, by dint of much swearing and irritated whispering, they still managed to make steady, if somewhat erratic, progress.

Up ahead, Roz and I had dropped into a dense stand of bushes and were trying frantically to get control over our breathing, whilst at the same time burying ourselves ever deeper out of sight. The moment we had seen the dozen or so brutish-looking men coming our way and clutching guns, we'd known that whoever they were and whatever their intentions, they were trouble for us. Hiding in the depths of a stand of bushes, with scant time to assess our situation, we quickly realised this was far from a coincidence. It simply couldn't be. And if it wasn't, then they had to be from the slave ship and that meant we were in serious trouble if they found us. Which was not only deeply shocking but rocked us to the core. We'd been so confident of our concealment from the world in general that all these weeks on from my rescue, we'd almost come to believe ourselves immune. And now here was living proof that not only were we far from safe, but, careless in the extreme, we were probably the architects of our own downfall.

It took me a while to get my breath back and the pain of the violent exercise was reminding me of just how recently I'd been flat on my back. But it was Roz who really caught my eye. For some reason or other, she hardly seemed to be disturbed by the sudden change in circumstance. Not even vaguely. And no doubt about it, there was an unfamiliar radiance about her and an aura of tranquillity that, for my money, seemed totally misplaced. I can clearly remember almost breaking her arm in my anxiety to get over to her just how dire our circumstances had suddenly become.

CHAPTER 58

Israfel had little choice. Unlike me, he had instantly recognised the men for exactly who they were and what they were doing there. And right behind the advance he'd spotted an unruly horde of subordinate ogres, each of them slavering over its chosen human and all of them intent on inciting further mayhem. His orders prevented him from interfering directly with the armed heavies, so he couldn't stop them making an attack, but he could sort out the malicious creatures that were encouraging and urging them on from behind. Briefly, he debated taking them on alone but, thinking better of it, was about to call on his latest rank-related benefit and summon one of the elite Angelic squadrons, when a sudden banshee-like wailing, accompanied by a wall of shuddering sound assailed his ears, catching him unawares. Whatever the cause, it was clear something major had spooked the ghouls. They were scrabbling frantically backwards, away from their chosen prey as though their very lives depended upon it. Which, it turned out, they did. And even the two horrors that had managed to gain possession of a couple of gang members were trying hysterically to unhook their claws in a frantic bid to get away. But even as Israfel registered this, the two slavers who had been the subjects of possession pitched forward, themselves writhing and screeching in pain, before lapsing into a coma-like state, as though dead.

Surprised by the mayhem, Israfel followed the direction of the fiends' gaze and immediately understood the reason for their panic. A great and blinding light had appeared behind him. A pool of pure, dazzling brilliance extending from a door thrown open in Heaven was revealing a dimension normally closed off to both humans and demons. From it, an ethereal radiance was flooding the whole area where we crouched. And in that moment, as he took in the full import of the Heavenly features forever hidden from human eyes, Israfel heard the blare of massed trumpeters and a loud voice warning all of creation to 'make way for the King of kings'. Displaying the slick co-ordination for which they were famous, the elite Royal Guard paraded through the arched opening. Marching swiftly in close order formation, they began breaking off in a well-practiced honour guard manoeuvre, coming to attention in pairs at precise intervals along either side of the great highway that had suddenly materialised and now stretched from Heaven's door to an insignificant bush in the middle of an equally unimportant stand of coastal scrub. Clearly, there were remarkable events in progress. Although he'd never seen and certainly hadn't been involved in the like before, Israfel realised immediately that the stirring display by the incomparable Heavenly Host was simply a prelude to the imminent appearance of the King of kings, who always gave a personal welcome to new citizens of His Kingdom. Moreover, already striding between the guard pairs and radiating His own impossibly brilliant light (which even angels had difficulty facing), Israfel spotted the Son of God Himself. Swiftly, he unsheathed his weapon and dropped to one knee in a warrior's tribute to his Lord and Master, spreading his hands and dipping the tip of his sword to acknowledge the presence of Royalty.

A token swiftly and subconsciously aped for a few seconds by the evil spirits who, to their utter consternation, knew their game was well and truly up. They had no option but to kneel before the King of kings and vocally acknowledge His Lordship, but no entity not already redeemed or Angelic could find itself within sight of the full splendour of the risen, glorified Christ and hope to live, unless the sceptre of mercy was extended in its direction. A gesture that was never going to happen for these fallen angels. And even as they continued their frantic, ultimately doomed, but despairing retreat, the air began to dance and ring with the ethereal sound of a distant Angelic choir singing the praises of the eternal Prince of Peace.

Israfel was thrilled to his very core. Clearly, at least one of the humans, either Roz or Paul (both, he was hoping), must have responded to the gracious, mind-blowing invitation to life in all its fullness that God, through His Son, Jesus, extended to every human at some time in his or her life. And although Israfel didn't want to miss a single nuance of this thrilling ceremony, one he'd heard about, but never actually witnessed, he knew he wasn't thereby relieved of duty. Reluctantly turning his head back to the human scene being played out around him, he discovered that, released from the devilish pressure previously being used to drive them on, the crew had come to a grinding and indecisive halt, as though mesmerised. Yet without being able to see or even sense either the sacred scenario being played out ahead of them, or the rout taking place behind them. But then Israfel spotted the real problem.

Five young black men were slipping silently through the bush only yards behind the sailors, fully alert to the nearness of their presence but, like their prey, completely unaware of the spectacle ahead. They were armed with the powerful bows so beloved of the local residents and were clearly intent on nailing their quarry. Israfel had seen enough of men's dealings to know a massacre with no mercy was in the offing and, with a quick glance to ensure I wasn't in the line of fire, he moved to a vantage point from where he could alert the less experienced Nadab to developments. And seconds later, with barely sufficient time to reach his chosen location, events began to unfold rather more swiftly than anyone would have wished. A heightened momentum not even triggered by the slavers' demons. With nerves broken and despair writ large on every feature, the threat they posed had long since ended. In fact, a squad from the Second

Battalion of the Royal Guard had already been detached to clean up the mess left by the erstwhile demons, whose remains now constituted little more than blemishes on the spiritual landscape. So, even if that particular motley band of evil spirits had been spared and allowed to latch onto the villagers rather than the slavers, they would have been in no fit state to influence what was rapidly becoming a full-scale incident.

From the outset, it had been the men from the outraged village, fiercely determined young bloods intent on exacting a thorough revenge for their humiliation and the insults heaped on their extended families, who would prove the most adroit. Moreover, they needed no external driving force to stay focused. Just their burning sense of injustice. So, presented with the golden opportunity of an enemy who, for whatever reason, appeared momentarily off guard, they simply launched straight into their planned butchery. With almost military precision, the young men bent forward to notch long, sparsely fletched arrows to their gut-strung bows. Then quickly but silently, so as not to alert their victims, they drew the fearsome weapons back to full stretch before simultaneously letting fly. The five targets heard nothing, suspected nothing, saw nothing and consequently died in a haze of nothingness. It was as though each had suddenly sprouted an arrowhead from the middle of his throat and the clearest alarm any of them could manage was a low gurgle from a blood-filled oesophagus, each and every cry smothered before it was even birthed. Barely pausing, confident in their supreme ability at arms, the young men moved to their right, heading towards the beach, where they lined themselves up with the next batch selected to die. Unexpectedly, they found only three, but that scarcely altered the rhythm. The same deadly scenario was repeated and the three died just as quietly and efficiently as their compatriots. Then, still in the almost slow-motion ballet of their lethal hunting technique, the men drew together to orchestrate the next move.

They knew the numbers and they knew they were two short,

not counting the two moving down the beach. But even as they pondered the matter, Ghazi, one of the recently possessed duo who had fallen unconscious, started moving in the undergrowth as he regained awareness. It was to be his last activity, but the manner and fact of his death were noted. Fatih, with rather more sense, had managed to surface quietly. Which, given that he could see all five of his potential assassins from where he lay, meant he had some quick thinking to do. Slowly, inching his way forward, he started to move towards us, his intended victims. A sensible move, since it had the benefit of taking him away from the bowmen and towards the original quarry. Not that, under the present circumstances, he had much hope of capturing and holding us for Ahmed. But at least, if he could get near enough, we represented potential bargaining chips. And, right now, that was the most he could expect. As a flagrant rapist, he knew he could anticipate no mercy whatsoever. A swift death at best, but only if he was very fortunate.

He still had no idea why he had passed out, but, whatever the reason, he now felt distinctly lightheaded and disorientated. Empty, almost. Moreover, he was sweating with an intense sensation of anxious futility, whilst knowing that this unfamiliar sensation had little or nothing to do with the killers behind him, even though they were clearly intent on tracking and dispatching him. No, he had little fear of death, so this bewildering sense of dread merely added to the confusion of the moment. To the best of his knowledge, all he had been doing was lying on the plantation floor. Why, he didn't know. Nor, for the time being, could he begin to fathom the source of his growing and all-pervading sense of terror. And where were the rest of his men? Surely they couldn't all have been killed? But with that thought barely formed, he abruptly realised that if he didn't get to us quickly, he too would be dead or, possibly, unconscious again.

Fortunately for him, but unseen behind him, the avenging villagers had decided to move back and strip their first victims, intent on looting anything of value. And that distraction alone saved him. In fact, it took Fatih a good five minutes to reach us and neither of us saw him coming. But once on top of us, he had no compunction in jamming the end of his rifle into Roz's startled face, speculating that I would not risk anything that might lead to the girl's harm. Slowly and very carefully, keeping a particularly substantial and well-leafed bush between him and the spot where he had last seen his pursuers, Fatih then stood, forcing a bewildered Roz to rise with him. And it was this arrogant imposition on my darling that finally provoked me into action. I was already mentally kicking myself for failing to spot this armed maniac's arrival, and now this new and present threat to her was too much. In anguished desperation I remember tensing to make a grab for the gun, but Roz, bless her, must have read my mind, because she spoke suddenly, but very calmly. "Paul, don't do anything, I'm alright. Really. Just keep calm, for my sake."

Even now I can recall the extraordinary composure in her voice and it compelled me to lower my fists slowly and very carefully to my sides, although I kept a wary eye on this highly unwelcome intruder. What to do next? I couldn't think. Although the hostage, Roz already appeared somehow to have wrested the initiative from her captor and, strangely, it was to her we were both looking at that moment. In retrospect and given the circumstance of a loaded gun pointed straight at Roz's right temple, doing nothing was about all I could have done at the time, so it was probably a reasonable idea. Neither of us knew anything about the massacre that had already taken place a few hundred yards south of us, so we both remained certain that somewhere in front of us were upwards of a dozen armed and unquestionably dangerous men. This being the case, I reasoned, it was better to fake compliance for the time being and hope that, sooner or later, an opportunity would present itself to turn the tables somewhat. If only I had known. But then, how could I?

CHAPTER 59

Nadab wasn't paying attention to Israfel or any of the fast-moving human developments. He was concentrating on Roz and was already formulating plans to schmooze his boss concerning his part in the spine-tingling developments now taking place under his very nose. It wasn't every Guardian who could boast that his charge had become an honorary citizen of Heaven. Nevertheless, some thought was needed because, by specifically interfering in the secret and mysteriously divine aspects of a human life (while Roz had been walking on the beach), he was pretty certain that he'd still have to answer to his boss in some way or another. But surely from his own favourable perspective, what he had done could be trumpeted as a triumph, couldn't it? Surely he should be permitted one minor embellishment to his responsibilities? Which might be rational, he knew, but with a sigh he had to acknowledge to himself that it remained equally true that 'orders are orders', whatever the intention or outcome. And if this proved the case, it was hardly likely to be viewed as quite the brilliant coup he'd supposed. But for now, the rapidly accelerating spiritual development within Roz continued to attract his entire and undivided attention. In delight he had watched her move from animated chatter about God, to a quiet pondering of her nascent understanding. And then, to his intense joy, he had watched her make a sudden, decisive move towards belief, meeting a Heavenly response, which was already way ahead of her. Only to observe a moment later that both humans, suddenly alarmed, had been forced to run for cover.

Unfortunately, having let everything else pass him by for a

few seconds, Nadab wasn't entirely certain of the cause. At which precise moment, a somewhat exasperated Israfel had materialised at his side.

"Come on, Nadab, move! Anyone can see they're in real danger and so far you've done nothing, not even for Roz, never mind Paul. There's a bunch of very angry villagers over there executing the slavers on sight. They're high on bloodlust and it won't be long before they're in easy killing range of our two. And right now, they're clean out of ideas and momentum. They know they haven't accounted for all the slavers, but they're nervous and so they're likely to start milling about and will probably shoot on sight. Especially since they know they haven't got the leader. A man called Fatih, the one who instigated the rape of their mothers and sisters. Anytime now they'll spot him and he's close enough to Paul and Roz to place them in jeopardy. It's too late to divert the villagers and anyway, if you look, you'll see there's only one junior Guardian between the lot of them, so we can't expect much help there. We're going to have to hope nobody lets fly with an arrow until they've actually identified their target."

Israfel was just getting well into his 'senior and more experienced' stride when a clearly excited Nadab cut him off in mid-flow. "Israfel, look! Look at Roz, look at the way she's beginning to blaze. Only a couple of hours ago she wasn't sure about anything Heavenly. Since then she's obviously decided to respond to the Lord Jesus and invite Him into her life. And now look. The King has come to speak with her personally. Isn't that fantastic? Can you imagine it? She's going to be with us throughout eternity."

"True," replied Israfel, who was studiously trying to ignore the violation reported by Nadab, "but you need to understand that right now King Jesus is not only telling her Who it is whispering into her ear, but He's opening her eyes to our world, so brace up. Look, she's seen us. Superb! Pity we won't be at the party they'll be having in Heaven today." Even Israfel, his duties almost forgotten in the intensity and delight of the moment, continued to gaze entranced. Outwardly and to human sight, nothing unusual had happened. To all intents and purposes, Roz had simply stopped worrying about whether God existed or not and, in obedience to my shouted command and her natural instinct, had begun running for cover. And from that moment, as far as I was concerned, it was our tense and dangerous situation that needed to fully occupy every thought.

I distinctly remember feeling in that moment of recognition that we faced rather more pressing events than Roz's preoccupation with God and that any further discussion would have to wait for a more propitious time. Not only was I completely oblivious to the good that was happening, but I was also totally unaware that God Himself was watching developments with great sadness, as He contemplated the unnecessary waste of life for yet more humans. Which still left the very present danger we faced, compounded by the undetected killing spree. And unknown to us, the avenging villagers had caught the sound of Roz's voice and it was drawing them into an immediate and stealthy movement towards our hiding place. Intensely aware they had yet to account for three of the gang members, which almost certainly meant three guns intent on wreaking revenge, it was no wonder they remained extremely wary and on edge. But that in turn meant Roz, unprotected by the bush behind which Fatih remained concealed, turned out to be the first, vaguely human movement to catch their attention. And thus the first to which they could offer a reaction. So it was that I heard, rather than saw, the simultaneous flight of several arrows whispering through the air and, to my unspeakable horror, witnessed the love of my life suddenly, shockingly, sprout a pair of wicked looking shafts from her back. At which point, in total bewilderment and disbelief, she arched towards me, mouth twisting in pain and her eyes wide with terror. Even as she flopped onto my desperately out-flung arms, a great gout of blood spouted from her mouth, drenching me and preventing her from making even the smallest whisper of fear. How could I ever forget that terrible, appalling scene? Or forgive? In that instant, my heart was torn asunder and all that afterwards gave me hope of any kind in the midst of sudden, utter misery and the horror of irreplaceable loss was the recollection that in the last few seconds of my erstwhile partner's life, I clearly saw her terror fade. To be replaced by absolute, trusting and, to my mind, completely bewildering love for someone or something somewhere beyond us. Yes, I somehow knew beyond a doubt that her love for me remained and of that I stayed intensely aware, but, in her eyes, her gaze, there shone an acknowledgement of something beyond us both.

And by the time she had exhaled for the last time, several unbearably short seconds later, her expression had changed from fear into this unqualified and incomprehensible serenity. But of this I am completely certain: Roz, my utterly beautiful and selfless girlfriend, the young woman who had rescued me and given me hope where there had been none, the vibrant lady who had grown up to become the architect of all my most precious dreams and who, by her simple presence, was able to soothe away all doubts and fears, died completely free of anxiety that day. I saw it clearly etched in her dear face. Yet how or why this could be, I had no inkling. Nevertheless, for the sake of sanity and the defence of truth, I hold onto that memory as for dear life. At the time, all I could do in the extremity of my anguish was to bear her full weight, sliding gently to the ground with her, her head and hair turning wet with the sudden, uncontrollable tears of my broken heart. Even as I held her close, the persistent flow of bright red arterial blood created a starkly obscene counterpoint to the delicate brown of her suntanned arms. Its rapid, spreading stream darkening and caking her dusty khaki shirt. All thought of Fatih (I was to discover his name somewhat later and under rather different circumstances), the threat he posed and the results for which he was undoubtedly responsible fled from my mind, overtaken by the all-encompassing and unadulterated numbness of grief.

That morning I felt my heart as good as dead and its frigid detachment held me in thrall for uncounted time, until the anguish eventually morphed into an aching and permanent sense of loss. A loss that began in all too familiar a way, by gnawing at the edges of my sanity before seeping drop by foul drop into my heart, into my very psyche, where much of it remains to this day. For ages thereafter I walked in a profound and desperate silence. A silence of the soul. A darkness of the night. No matter the sound and fury around me, my shattered heart contemplated only its aching void. What little I can remember of that horrendous morning and the moments that immediately followed 'the incident' (I have never been able to call my love's death throes anything else) are stained and confused by the almost demented outpouring of my strident misery. Actually, had I but known it, shutting down emotionally to act like an uncaring and unfeeling marionette in the weeks that followed probably saved my sanity and thus my life. A life that, at the time, I would gladly have forfeited.

CHAPTER 60

And what of Nadab and Israfel in all of this? Unable to experience death in the human sense, Roz's untimely end simply couldn't and, indeed, didn't affect them in the same way and to such a depth as it had me. Something I was to learn much later. Neither they, nor any of their fellow Guardians viewed a human's passing as possessing quite the weight of misfortune that we tend to ascribe to untimely deaths, or any death at all, come to that. For them, it was whether or not the soul was prepared for transition from human to spiritual life that concerned them most deeply. And whether or not they had been remiss in their duties. Trouble was, they knew perfectly well that it was only when the human's mortal body had been discarded and it was too late to change anything that the essence of the person, the soul, discovered whether it was free to surge out into eternal life or sink into its counterpart: eternal loss.

But for those who had accepted the offer to join God's family during their lives and not only believe, but go on believing in Him throughout whatever time they had left, the relocation introduced them to an incredible, unspoiled and enjoyable future already prepared in every detail. Even down to a new, perfect and immortal body. And there was the rub: if they hadn't accepted God's freely proffered pardon before death, they remained Satan's property and he was content to simply bide his time until the Day of Judgement, then collect his own and take them down to join him in that ultimate Hell, the lake of fire specifically prepared for him and his associates. So, whilst their general approach to human existence remained deeply influenced by a profound sense of duty and care, a certain *laissez-faire* attitude to human life or death itself was hardly surprising. Because even as they watched the untimely release of this particular soul, they could also see and hear the scheduled approach of the angels who would escort the now immortal Roz into the King's throne room, there to be welcomed as the VIP she had so recently become. And as in every such case, they knew the celebrations would already be getting underway, with all Heaven rejoicing over the return home of another of the Redeemed.

Equally true, when it came to accounting for the events of the last few days, not a lot of this would cut much ice with Nadab's boss, because Nadab had sailed perilously close to one of the cardinal rules, which meant he faced the inevitable 'helmets on', one-way discussion that bosses tend to arrange when subordinates have crossed prohibited boundaries. Since the moment he had been created, it had been made clear to every angel slated for Guardian duties that the Lord Jesus Himself was the only one who could approach human beings to offer them the greatest gift of all time: the gift of eternal life as a member of God's family. Primarily because He was the only one appropriately qualified. Angels were simply not in this league. Since the dawn of time they had known they came into existence to be ministering spirits, expressly to serve humanity, particularly those humans who were destined to attain eternal life with God. Notwithstanding all of which, Nadab was particularly looking forward to his next meeting with Roz because, for the very first time, they would actually be able to talk face to face. Having said which, he could be certain he wouldn't get another Earth posting. Transgressing one of the cardinal rules laid down regarding humans had demonstrated he wasn't entirely reliable. Humans, that zenith of God's creation, were creatures of free will and this, above all else, had to be respected, even if it got them into hot water. That was their choice.

However, in this particular case, Nadab wasn't sure he particularly minded. In recent years within what humans called

Western Society, far too few angels had been able to enjoy the pleasure of observing 'their' human acknowledging God's supremacy, before the fleeting years drew life to an end. And after death it was, of course, too late to change things. Lifetime alternatives, either rejection of the Creator's offer, or simply deciding to go their own way, were decisions totally respected by God, not just for during their lifetimes but, more importantly, at the great Day of Judgement. The Day on which every action, every thought, every choice would be brought to light and every destiny fixed for eternity. Because that much anticipated, but still future day, would see the final dressing of all Redeemed humans in their new and glorious bodies. Arrayed in special 'robes of righteousness' provided by their King, they would be ready for immortal life in the renovated Heaven and Earth. Exactly the opposite to the future of those destined for certain other shores. As clearly shown in the humans' Book of books.

The moment Roz was hit and even before I'd managed to lower her to the ground, Fatih had taken off. The thought '*like a startled fawn*' ran bizarrely through my mind, but, actually, his movements were more those of a disconcerted snake. Sliding swiftly out of sight, he left only swaying bushes to close behind him and provide any indication that he'd ever been there, as his headlong rush took him diagonally away from the beach area. Actually, I didn't bother to note much more than the general direction in which he'd gone. I cared nothing for whether he lived or died. Indeed, if I'd given it any thought at all, I suppose I would have hoped he was caught and that whoever caught him would brutalise him in the same savage way in which my love had suffered. As far as I was concerned, Fatih's end could not come soon enough, and the more violent his death, the better. So wrapped up was I in the immediate task of cradling Roz's rapidly cooling body, that I barely even noticed the silent and subdued arrival of the hunters. They drifted in one by one like dark ghosts, checking to right and left as they came, but apparently content their business with the slavers was finished and there was no longer any fear of reprisal. It was only later that I discovered they'd already killed every last one of the remaining men, even the two who'd carried on along the beach. However, these African villagers were not in the same predatory class as those they had pursued and, faced with the enormity of what they'd done to Roz, they were clearly shocked and dismayed. Even as they arrived, they were beginning to question the validity of their actions, to squabble over exactly who was responsible for the lifeless body lying limply in my arms. They even tried to reassure me, saying over and over again, that they did not have a quarrel with either of us.

But nothing they could do or say would lessen my raging anger and sick despair, or the appalled sensations coursing through every vein and artery as I continued to clasp Roz, rocking backwards and forwards, moaning out her name, tearing at my hair and covering her dear face with tear-stained kisses. My heart lay broken and I can't say how long I sat forlorn on the unwelcoming ground, but I do remember that by the time I returned to any sort of rationality, the sun had long gone, leaving the deep shadows to embrace me in their temporary anonymity. The swift tropical chill also did its work, aided by the ice layering deep upon my soul. Quietly, these twin colds enveloped me in their unyielding grip, shutting me down long before our anxious friends from the 'home' village chanced upon us. When we failed to return they had at first decided we were making the most of a little privacy, but by the time they had eaten, the cooking fires had died slowly down and the silvery moon had risen to its zenith, they reluctantly concluded that something was wrong and it was time to start searching. Realising from the borrowed canoe that we must have gone south, the loping run of the young men had taken them at speed along the beach, so it wasn't long before they came upon two arrow-filled bodies still strewn grotesquely across the sand and realised that something had, indeed, gone terribly wrong. After that, it was but a matter of time before they discovered and spoke with the village hunters, who recounted all that had happened, interspersed with many and prolonged protestations of innocence. What our friends made of this at the time, I do not know. All I do know is that eventually I felt the tug of gentle, guiding hands, the murmur of hushed and stricken voices and the weight of Roz's body being tenderly lifted away. And with a flash of penetrating recollection I knew I had been here before. First, Matt, now Roz and a light dusting of me in between. Was I set to become the stuff of terrible legend?

Kindly, but firmly, I was persuaded to rise, turn north and follow the men bearing Roz on their shoulders. Miserable as I was, it was an awkward, stumbling journey, eyes blinded by tears and feet made leaden in my sick despair slipping clumsily in the soft sand, despite a sufficiency of light from the moon. Eventually we made it back to the creek where several canoes now lay alongside each other, drawn up like artists' charcoal sticks above the tidal mark, and I was glad when, safely on the northern shore, we were finally able to quit the soft sand of the beach and turn inland for the huts, there to oversee the tender placing, arranging and covering of Roz upon her own bed. Fortunately, most of the friends who had stayed behind appeared to be still asleep, so, for a time at least, I was spared their questions and sympathy, all of which I know I would have found overpowering.

Instead, with a whispered thanks and a "good night" to the equally tired young men, I moved to 'our' hut and sank down on the rough bed that had served the two of us so well for the last couple of weeks. But sleep would not come. Not that I expected it. Not until the horizon over the sea to the east was beginning to lighten could I even begin to reflect rationally upon the enormity of what had passed and, as I watched those first beginnings of a new dawn, a second storm of tears began to fall in earnest. At first, taking stock, my anguished spirit had almost failed as I recalled so much: my part in the awfulness of Matt's death, failing him in his hour of real need with my disastrous inability to act; the one failure having ultimately led to all the rest. The days of waiting and yearning for healing, which, mentally at least, had never really come. The arrival of Roz and her determined and loving support, despite her understandable fear of my father. My despairing attempt at suicide coupled with an embarrassingly futile effort to escape south for Mombasa as I fell into the hands of the terrifying megalomaniacs intent on their drug and slavery business. The nightmare of my imprisonment and bondage, beatings and solitary confinement. The dhow with its cargo of dejection and hopelessness, its stench and hunger, nausea, clamour and ever-present spectre of death and, later still, the incredible and totally bewildering midnight arrival on the ship's deck of my erstwhile saviour. Finally, the uproar of escape, gradual healing both of body and soul under Roz's ministry and above all, the astonishing encounter with a true and enduring love. The latter a privileged experience I could never again expect, or wish, to enjoy. And with that final reflection, the reality and desperation of my situation came roaring back to hit me right between the eyes. But this time, its attentions served only to harden my attitude and strengthen my resolve.

Sometime after the first shards of early dawn had appeared and started to wash the tops of the palms, I realised that no matter what else might happen, I was going to track down my tormentors and hound them without mercy. Beginning with Fatih. At the first opportunity, I would kill and kill again, mercilessly and without compunction. Why so implacable? Because I genuinely felt I had no future and every right to retribution. So with that settled, I determined that once again I would be long gone before the camp awoke. Gone before any policemen could arrive, as arrive they surely would. Only this time, I would travel alone. Alone as before, but this time free to determine my own fate. I was utterly resolved that never again would I succumb to captivity, or oppression. I had been there once and knew what it would take to ensure survival. I'd had enough and, from now on, I would be the hunter and they the prey. The first act of revenge would be directed straight at the man who had brought such dire and enduring consequences upon both of us. And with that I rose from the bed, conscious that there was little time to waste. Every minute spent sitting there was another minute of opportunity handed to the obscenity responsible for Roz's death, another minute that increased the likelihood of his melting into either the coastal bush, or a local township, where he could stay lost forever.

So, before that could happen, I had to find and take him. Only then could I obtain the answers to my questions and, at the same time, ensure by his lingering death some decline in the guilt and outrage festering in me. And whilst his death seemed of prime importance, he could also tell me who had sent him and, once that was determined, I could probably discover a way to unearth the perpetrator (probably my original purchaser, but perhaps the dhow captain?). Then it would be Giuseppe's turn and afterwards, the whole rotten horde of accomplices. Beyond which, their living or dying would be a matter of indifference to me and would probably be settled solely by how I felt at the time. Assuming I managed to remain undetected. And with that thought I began scrabbling together a bare minimum of food and water, plus some loops of bowstring that happened to be lying around. One piece of equipment I did make sure of, however, was the recently provided fishing spear, donated so I could feed the two of us on the exquisite local fish. Although an unfamiliar weapon, I had quickly acquired the knack of throwing and stabbing accurately, to such a degree that it hadn't been long before I was producing a satisfying variety to the menu. Now that skill might well stand me in good stead. Particularly as I had no other weapon and the last time I'd seen my quarry, he'd been armed with what looked like a fairly heavy calibre rifle.

CHAPTER 61

Israfel was embarrassed. He had watched with genuine concern as my attitude to life had taken a turn for the worse in the aftermath of Roz's death. Anxious and keeping careful guard that first night, he had brooded over me as I lay tossing feverishly on the bed, unable to sleep, every thought centred on revenge. Brooded, because he cared. Not that he had found my reactions unusual in a human. On the contrary, he had half expected this sort of outcome, but hadn't been prepared for the intensity of emotions involved, his own as well as mine. In particular, he was not prepared for the surge of almost human anger he had felt when Arcturus had stepped out of nowhere to gloat over me in his arrogant, condescending and slightly patronising manner. It was the carelessness of his approach, the deliberate and obvious disdain for any safeguard that had most irritated Israfel, almost causing him to forget his orders and strike out at the offensive monster. He knew, because he had been briefed, that over the coming years as my life progressed, I would make a number of near-fatal mistakes. But he also knew, even though it had not been overtly stated, that whilst he was there to protect and rescue me before I made any irrevocable blunders, he was also honour bound to allow me free rein wherever possible.

Which was all very well, but how was a Guardian supposed to know when he should or shouldn't intervene? Surely, allowing an evil spirit any form of influence over me was exactly the sort of occasion on which he should interfere? And yet here was Arcturus, blatantly moving in on me and with no riposte from Command HQ. Apparently, there was nothing he, Israfel, should do about it, except wait. Bide his time. Presumably, therefore, he'd already made the right decision in allowing me the freedom to choose and so (hopefully), to learn from any misjudgements. With a resigned shrug, Israfel rammed his sword back into its sheath and stepped away, signalling to Arcturus he would not be opposed. Which only produced a sneer from that devil's spawn and the gratuitous advice to Israfel to 'get stuffed'.

Actually, Arcturus couldn't believe his luck. From the moment I had lost Roz, I had become so engrossed in thoughts of revenge, so taken up with contemplation of reprisals through any unpleasant means I could devise, that I had unwittingly opened a pathway into my soul that was effectively extending an unrestricted invitation to infernal influence. And Arcturus was no slouch when it came to such things, sanctioned or not. All he needed was the merest sliver of opportunity to start drip-feeding his very particular and malevolent inspiration into any human foolish enough to expose himself to his malign power. Admittedly, he'd been advised by his commander not to push this one too far, since Lucifer had been personally warned off by the Lord of the Universe. But here was an opportunity being handed to him on a plate. I was sinking into such a deep and all-consuming hatred that I was gratuitously widening an already undefended channel into my very psyche. And if he, Arcturus, could manipulate matters in such a way as to pass the buck elsewhere, Josephus would hardly mind if Satan suffered as a direct result. But that depended upon ensuring any mayhem couldn't be laid directly at his own door. Of course, what Arcturus singularly failed to realise in all of this was that he himself was the intended 'cut out', should Josephus need a watertight defence. So, here was a human on Satan's 'problem' list, exposing himself voluntarily to any passing evil, all without realising it or, at least, without understanding the enormity of his behaviour. And Arcturus was perfectly placed to seize such a juicy opportunity and, by the same token, get back into the arch-fiend's favour. Actually, come to think of it, perhaps he could dish

Josephus as well while he was at it. Now that would be worthwhile. Even his immediate opponent, Israfel, seemed to have backed off for the time being. Again, Arcturus leered at his rival, but decided there was no point in continuing to flaunt his obvious advantage. Clearly, Israfel had received orders to relinquish the floor. For a brief moment, Arcturus wondered if he was being led into a trap, but then decided he was more than a match for any insolent angel. Particularly this one. Thus reassured, he stepped boldly forward and, to Israfel's enduring consternation, began to directly manipulate my psyche, insidiously suggesting in graphic detail how I might deal with my enemies.

★★★

Mind you, I was becoming all too used to this nefarious way of life. Quite prepared to slip quietly away before anyone stirred in the nearby huts, whilst knowing that, at the very least, I owed them a thorough explanation and an apology for dumping them in the police mire that was bound to follow. Nevertheless, I had few feelings of regret beyond the almost overwhelming feeling of nausea that was to become my constant companion in the coming days as I left a certain cold body behind. Albeit, to my subsequent shame, entrusting them with Roz and all the difficulties that would present gave me scant cause for concern at the time. I knew I had lost her forever and nothing I could do would bring her back. Now all that concerned me, beyond my own inner turmoil, was revenge and the swifter the sweeter. In fact, before the grey dawn had even begun to diffuse its silvery light, vengeance had become my consuming thought. So it was that the early shadows cast by the swaying palms found me seizing the opportunity to remain well hidden until I was clear of the settlement and able to risk a turn down to the beach, from where I headed back towards the scene of the previous day's debacle.

Leaving a canoe on the far side of the creek would give a rather obvious clue as to my intentions, but even I couldn't bring myself to cast it adrift, from where it would be pushed out to sea by the slow-flowing river. It represented a friend's livelihood, probably his entire wealth. So I wasted some time swimming across the river, only just making it in the end. However, the couple of hours' rest I'd managed to grab during the night buoyed me sufficiently and, travelling with just the spear and a light bag to weigh me down, I was able to move reasonably swiftly. Faster than I had the day before when, accompanied by Roz and devoid of care, we had together soaked up every tiny nuance of that brilliant and optimistic time, dawdling along our way. As my heart kept treacherously reminding me. But steeling myself, I hastened on to find the point from which our attacker had withdrawn so abruptly.

His trail was easy to follow. Clearly, he had little knowledge of how to move without leaving a marker on the scale of an elephant's highway and, with my knowledge of tracking, it was the easiest thing in the world to follow him. Naturally, the trail was cold, but I knew this would be the case and I also knew that unless he'd found an accomplice, or managed to steal a vehicle, it would only be a matter of hours before I caught up with him. Any extra weight I might have acquired while waiting for my leg to heal in those oh-so-far-off days was long since shed. Subsisting over the past few weeks on a healthy diet of fish, ugali[1] and love, I was now almost as fit as I'd ever been. So at an easy lope it didn't take long to cover the miles heading directly inland on a westerly track, following a trail that seldom deviated and from which I deduced he was making for the higher ground beyond the limits of coastal habitation. Within a couple of hours I had pulled away from the only available sources of water and, by the time the sun was fully overhead, I knew I would be getting close.

For some time, there had been little sound beyond the metronomic rhythm of my feet scuffing through the dust and the occasional plaintive bird calls up ahead, all subsumed by the sound of wind soughing through the low bushes. The palms were fewer now, spaced out and beginning to be replaced by the dense, thorny scrub of the inland wastes, thorns that continually tugged at my shirt and left long red welts on arms and legs. And of course, with the passing of the hours, the unremitting heat of the sun never ceased from striking down at me out of a clear, cobalt sky – albeit in my despondent anger and pain everything, even the sky, was coloured grey. Moreover, unrelieved by the friendly coolness of the coastal breeze and constantly drawing much-needed moisture from my sweat-soaked body, the heat was beginning to debilitate me. Although, frankly, I couldn't have cared less. Carefully husbanded, I had sufficient water for a couple of days and the closer I got to my quarry, the less I was concerned about anything else. Furthermore, having discovered where he had stopped for a few hours to rest in his frantic dash for shelter from the hunters he assumed were following him, I now knew for certain that I had him. So he was right after a fashion. He was being hunted, but even his original pursuers would not have been as implacably focused as I was. Nor as intent on draining him of every last vestige of information and dignity. I was fairly sure he had neither eaten nor drunk much, if anything, in the hours since we had parted. Having left the immediate boundaries of the coast, we had passed no potable water whatsoever and, after a careful search of his previous night's campsite, I had found neither trace of cooking fire, remains of food waste, nor even the pungent smell of human urine. All of which meant he, too, should be weakening rapidly and, with probably little or no water, would have to break cover and find human habitation or, at the very least, start quartering the terrain for traces of ground water before too long.

In fact, I more or less caught up with him just before the sun went down, fortuitously spotting him about a mile ahead, purely because he was reckless enough to crest a rise, allowing himself to be outlined for a moment against the sinking sun. With the position of my quarry now certain, I was able to pick up the pace, drawing in close with the intention of waylaying him as he settled early for what he no doubt thought would be a quiet and unobtrusive rest. Nevertheless, I was under no illusion that, given half a chance, he would kill me on sight and, since he still had his rifle, despite the obvious relaxation, I made sure to work my way carefully round until I could lurk unseen within easy spearing distance. It wasn't difficult, because for someone on the run, he was making an awful lot of noise and really wasn't taking even the basic precautions dictated by bush craft. On the other hand, if I wished to remain alive, I had to remain supremely cautious. This being the case, it took me a while to close to within about six feet of him, all the while using the crumbling wall of what appeared to be an old Arab house to stay hidden. Clearly, part of a ruined and ancient settlement. This protection, coupled with a large baobab[2] growing out of those same walls, the base of which he had chosen as a campsite, provided all the cover required. So, coming from directly behind the wide trunk it was a simple task to step over the wall and pounce. And I noted with a certain grim satisfaction that, although not designed for the job, such was the anger and fear with which I had driven the fishing spear, it had gone right through his thigh, pinning him firmly to the ground. Notwithstanding which, I still had to hurriedly kick away the rifle as he tried to scoop it up from its resting place beside the fire he had been busy kindling.

CHAPTER 62

When they finally discovered my early and unexpected departure, there was consternation in the camp. Some argued for me, assuming I probably wasn't very far away and simply wanting to be alone while I tried to come to terms with Roz's shocking death. These 'supporters' assumed they could expect me back within a few hours. However, the more astute amongst them were quick to realise I wasn't likely to be back anytime soon. Moreover, they felt they understood why. They knew I was keen to avoid the police, even if they didn't know the precise details, but they also recognised instinctively that, as Roz's lover and above all as a man, it was incumbent upon me to exact appropriate vengeance, whatever it might cost. So, given the problems to be expected in finding the culprit, I was unlikely to return in the near future. They only hoped I was after the slaver, the true cause of the troubles, and not the men from the next village down the coast to the south, some of whom they knew personally. In the meantime, it quickly dawned on all of them that they had a more pressing problem on their hands. A dead white girl, who clearly hadn't died naturally. Which, as far as the police were concerned, would, almost by definition, involve a local. So without me around to exonerate them, they could already guess who was likely to get the initial blame.

And then there was Bwana Lescal. Who was going to tell him that his only daughter had been murdered? Much more importantly, how were they going to tell him? There were no telephones available. And come to that, how were they going to report the matter to the local police in Malindi? Someone had to be volunteered for the job and so, reluctantly, but in the tried and trusted way of the people, the elders decided to convene a meeting at which they would settle the matter before anyone else got wind of the affair and took it upon themselves to notify the police. Jelani, the youngest adult male, was duly volunteered and, despite his protestations, was furnished with their convoluted but pooled explanation of events and ordered to start walking.

★★★

Fatih may well have lost his nerve when confronted by the double setback of a white girl's death and the realisation that he was next on the list for a flight of arrows, but, as I soon discovered, he was no pushover, not even when asked for his name. And when it came to providing information on his employers and the whereabouts of Giuseppe, amongst others, he proved almost impossible to crack. However, while he was still incapacitated by the pain of my spear thrust, I had quickly bound his elbows and wrists with some of the bowstring I'd brought along, before frisking him thoroughly to ensure he was now unarmed. Which brought to light the usual curved Arab dagger, plus a small but wicked-looking hook. The latter was of unusual design, being flattened on the inside curve into a razor-sharp blade, leaving the handle in line with the hook, so it could be easily concealed in the hood of his burnouse[1]. Undoubtedly carried as a useful 'mischief-maker', to which could be added the role of 'tormenter' when it came to hapless victims. And it wasn't long after this that I decided to put a halt to the endless stream of invective being directed my way, by loosening my spear from the ground and giving it a couple of judicious twists while still impaled in his leg. This did the trick, managing to both wrench a satisfyingly abject moan from between suddenly compressed lips and at the same time silencing any further invective. Which didn't prevent him from slipping me a murderous glare, a clear warning that I should not let him loose if I wanted to live. However, hoping to take advantage of the pain that was still washing through him, I immediately re-started the inquisition, but even after adding to the sum of his agony with a judicious pounding on his injured thigh, I still got nowhere. Which left me with something of a dilemma. I entertained no moral hesitation whatsoever over dispatching him, but, to do so, whilst no doubt providing an immediate degree of satisfaction, would simply squander the one chance I had of discovering something about the others responsible for my torment. And by the same token, indulging this need for retribution too early would put paid to any hope of extracting a fitting reprisal on the man I held directly responsible for my agony. I had no doubt at all that if those responsible found me first, or caught me at a disadvantage, I would not live to see the following sunset. I knew too much and had long since realised they would have to make certain I had no further opportunity to pass on information to the authorities. Which probably also meant they would be unable or unwilling to risk sending me north again, even as a slave. So death would be inevitable and if I knew anything about them, mine would not be an easy demise. Some thought was needed and as I wrestled with the problem, the ruined walls scattered around me reminded me of a story I had heard many years before.

The Arabs who first colonised and built the coastal settlements had been known to use their wells as refined instruments of torture. I remember being disturbed to learn that when they wanted to punish a particularly obstinate prisoner, or break their spirit prior to execution, they would tie them to a plank balanced over a well with their head projecting beyond the end of the plank. That way the prisoner could clearly see and imagine his ultimate fate at the bottom of the well. Of course, for maximum effectiveness this required something of a skilled balancing act and so they would offset the prisoner's weight with a heavy but cracked pitcher of water placed at the other end of the plank, thus initially achieving a balance in favour of the jar. However, a cracked pitcher leaks and grows inevitably lighter. Moreover, to refine the point, they would then sit around the well, telling the unfortunate captive how quickly the pitcher was leaking, or how long it was likely to be before his own weight would tip him sufficiently to send him hurtling into the depths to an often lingering, but otherwise certain, death. Of course, they didn't always tell the truth and with judicious refills, the torture could be made to last for days. It would indeed have been a hard nut who was not reduced to whimpering insanity within a few hours of this treatment.

And it now occurred to me that right there, in the old settlement, I was likely to find all that was needed to emulate those long-deceased tormentors. I was quite right. It didn't take long to find an old well and although it was partially blocked, it was still deep enough and, of most importance, it still had the majority of its original wall forming a workable lip. Thus the only other major ingredient required was a plank, or its equivalent, and, amongst all the debris scattered around, I found exactly what I needed. A cracked pitcher wasn't essential, because a pile of suitably weighted stones would do the trick equally well for my purposes and the nearby crumbling walls offered all the ammunition necessary. Thus, having gathered everything together and armed with Fatih's rifle, I yanked him to his feet and ordered him to start walking towards the well. Once we arrived I pushed him sharply in the back so that he fell more or less along the length of the plank and, in his debilitated state, it was easy to lash him down before he could mount an effective protest. Then all it needed was for me to manoeuvre the plank up onto the surrounding wall and gradually slide him out over the mouth of the well, all the while adding rocks for balance. How long it took him to realise my intentions, I don't know, nor did I really care. But it wasn't long before he started arguing the toss in a belligerent, loud-mouthed but increasingly apprehensive way. At first, he didn't believe me when I described exactly what I was about, but it didn't take long to convince him. Simply kicking off one or two stones left him feeling a distinct sway whenever he moved and I hardly had to mention that it would only take the removal of one more weight to seal his fate. After that, he went very quiet. I left him in the dark for an hour or two while I lit a small, carefully concealed fire and heated the meagre rations I'd brought. Then I went back to question him and quench my thirst, making sure I did the latter within his sight. Still no co-operation.

So, with the promise that there would be no drink that night, I bade him farewell, removed sufficient weight to ensure the plank would tilt if he so much as breathed too deeply and took myself off to find a suitable place to bed down for a few hours of sleep. I must have been tired, because the next thing I knew the rising sun was piercing my eyelids and bringing in the consciousness of a new day. And with that, I remembered Fatih. Leaping up, I discovered to my satisfaction that he hadn't attempted suicide during the night, so I had him all to myself for as long as I wished. A matter that gave me no small satisfaction, as I was certain he would crack before the day was out. Actually, looking back, I realise that during that day I wildly overstepped the norms of civilisation, not to mention humanity. But at the time I simply didn't care and in the end the pantomime produced the results for which I was searching.

"Fatih, do you want some water?" His tongue, swollen and dust-dry was barely able to move in a mouth that must have tasted like the proverbial sumo wrestler's jockstrap, ensuring he was totally unable to enunciate any words. Just nod his head wearily and with considerable difficulty, joint outcome of how tightly he was secured and how stiff he had obviously become during the long, cold night. Which meant he was exactly as I wanted him.

"OK, you can have a little." Deliberately, I rationed him to just enough to enable speech. Then I set the bottle down within his field of view. "Now, let's hear what you've got to say. We'll start with who sent you to look for us?" I gave him the benefit of an expectant and, I hoped, almost kindly look designed to encourage him into giving me what I wanted, but I strongly suspected he wouldn't crack that easily. In fact, I fully anticipated the whole exercise would take most of the day and not a little persuasion on my part. But I was ready for that. Although I had remained emotionally numb over the previous thirty-six hours or so, there remained one overriding mood. Suppressed rage. I seethed with it and was ready to embrace anything that might assuage the anguish. Which is why, utterly exasperated, I eventually lost count of the number of times I questioned him on the same subject.

However, at this early stage I did at least hold my temper, until it was clear I wasn't going to get through to him. He'd obviously decided I was less of a threat than those he was protecting. That is, right up until I produced the fishing spear with its wicked spread of three long, barbed spikes. The same tips that had already torn a considerable chunk out of his leg. That's the advantage of barbs. They don't come out easily. Not without ripping open the flesh they've pierced, as well as removing it in large chunks. So I began by merely scraping the barbs over the skin of his wounded thigh, making a less than subtle point. The action opened up the damaged veins again and also produced some curious sounds from Fatih. But not the words for which I was waiting. So, unbinding one of the prongs from the spear's haft, I began to experiment with its sharp tip on his back and sides, discovering how easily it could be slid into human muscle and tissue. Which, whilst not inspiring him to talk, produced some noteworthy if restricted reactions, as he tried desperately to shrink away from the probing steel, without tipping himself down the well. And that was when I remembered how I'd once been threatened myself with the 'death by a thousand cuts'.

Silkily, almost gently, I dropped down until my face was in line with Fatih's. "Hello, Fatih. I have no doubt you remember that well-known expression, 'death by a thousand cuts'? Yes, I can

301

see from your face that you do. Well, since you don't seem willing to co-operate, I'm going to have to use that hook of yours. It's a very interesting shape and should provide a fascinating variation on the lacerations the average knife produces. But I think you know that. Anyway, don't worry, you won't die from this. I just want you to experience more pain than you ever knew was possible. I've got plenty of time and no one knows you're here, so don't expect any help. Oh, and I have a feeling it would be particularly interesting to watch you die at the bottom of the well if you don't give me what I want. Of course, you could give me the names I want right now and then maybe none of this would have to happen." I must admit, Fatih had courage. He flinched often and he moaned continually, but even after I'd started to slice into him with the hook, opening his flesh piece by piece and letting in the ubiquitous flies that had arrived en masse, he still managed to hold his tongue.

Until I found what might be termed his Achilles heel. Some while before reaching the hook between his legs, I had mildly put it to him that he was in danger of losing his manhood. Even so, there must have remained some hope that I might, after all, let him live. Some assumption borne out of the sheer indifference inherent in the cruelty and violence being perpetrated with such chilling gentleness that finally persuaded him to talk. There is, after all, something about a man who neither loses his temper nor raises his voice while unhurriedly reaching towards a pitiless goal that is intensely intimidating. Anger, even basic cruelty, can be stoically endured. Unhurried, cold-blooded and seemingly disinterested purpose allied to merciless brutality is another matter altogether. And I should know, having been well taught by the very man whose name was first revealed. Prince Ahmed. The Arab who had bought me for slavery. Ah, the frisson that gave me. Here was someone I could truly hate. Furthermore, he was rather like Fatih, who clearly did not deserve to live. A man who warranted anything and everything coming his way. Someone who really could begin to pay for the young life so unjustly snuffed out. And not just as an inadequate restitution for myself, but as revenge for all those other countless souls who had suffered at his hands without any means of redress. Slowly, I withdrew the hook from between his legs. Finally allowing the proverbial dam of information to break.

Almost perversely, as if, coupled with a desire to stop the pain, he really believed the claim that I might let him live. If only he would give me the information I craved. Out poured a torrent of the most damning evidence. Names, dates, actions, even addresses. It was as if Fatih finally needed to purge himself, to seek a sort of spurious absolution by giving me everything I'd asked for. It was all there and I had difficulty keeping up with it. But amongst the dross, were the names and places that I really needed to commit to memory in order to complete my revenge, or 'crusade' as I now preferred to see it. And perhaps, as a possible by-product, to put a definite spoke in the wheel of the vile trade that was going on under the very noses of the Kenyan police and the society they claimed to protect. Yet in all of this, I neither realised, nor even cared, that I was slowly but surely travelling beyond the very pale that I considered slavers and drug dealers alone inhabited. Simply by emulating their malevolent and heartless indifference to helpless individuals. Folk they exploited without mercy. Just as I was doing even if, at the time, I felt able to justify my actions by pointing to Fatih's own activities. But that was a discovery for later times. Right now I waited under the shade of a nearby baobab until the sun had passed its zenith, had delivered its deadly heat and had begun to slide down the great bowl of a still steely blue sky. Then, with Fatih believing he was about to be set free (as if), I slowly removed one balancing stone after another, until the board ceased swaying and tipped decisively towards the well's maw. With a final hideous and despairing wail, Fatih slid headfirst into the gaping hole, to land with a sickening thud about twenty feet below. A fall that didn't kill him, because

I could still hear the occasional moan. So I let the stones finish the job and, by sundown, had filled the well almost to its lip. Confident that no one would ever find the body, I proceeded systematically to clear the area of all trace of human activity. Which included carefully scraping up the patches of blood-soaked dust and filtering them down through the stones, there to lie hidden and, presumably, beyond even the reach of wild animals. Once satisfied with the results, I retrieved the spear and bound the missing barb back into place. Then, before leaving, I collected Fatih's weapons, including his rifle. Which meant I'd not only obliterated all trace of him, as was my intention, but had found some use for his existence. Unfortunately, I hadn't reckoned on the quite extraordinary sea change that was to overtake me mere weeks later, the direct result of a guilty conscience.

CHAPTER 63

Ahmed was concerned. Not for himself or his remaining businesses. No. He had those gripped firmly and, as ever, most were running like well-oiled machines. True, continuing to finance them was an altogether different matter, but this remained something to be considered later. Much later. For now his more primitive cravings were insisting on immediate attention and, with a new female slave immediately to hand, there was every reason to allow the less pressing problems to take care of themselves. Unfortunately, however, that failed to address the inconvenience of a certain Fatih. Fatih had been gone for over a week and should by now have reported back, but there had been no word. Instead, he had begun to receive some disturbing second-hand rumours and whispers about a massacre further up the coast. All bound up with reports of a white girl's death. Which, given Fatih's orders and intended quarry, almost certainly meant his men were involved and might well have achieved the aim. Ordinarily, getting word of them through the gossip mongers would not have bothered him, as Fatih was more than capable of looking after himself. Moreover, if things went wrong, Fatih would never reveal anything of his commission or its source, no matter what pressures were put on him. Or would he? Unfortunately, Ahmed was beginning to sense that something was amiss.

Nevertheless, if it wasn't for his aunt's persistence and unremitting irritation over Abdullah, he would long since have turned his full attention to his slaves and certain other, equally demanding, matters. It wasn't as if he still retained any particular interest in the white boy. Bad things happened in business. Annoyances from which you recovered; moved on; put down to experience. Of course, if the boy showed up he would take considerable satisfaction in destroying him slowly and painfully. But there was still his aunt to appease and she would be far from happy that, yet again, the outcome of a promise had been delayed, no matter what the reason. Ahmed sighed and made a mental note to send one of his men to look into the problem of Fatih and get some answers. Tomorrow. Flicking his finger idly at a passing fly, he resumed his study of the human form. That of the girl appealingly naked and defenceless in front of him. His tongue flickered across his thin lips. His aunt would definitely have to wait. For the moment this slave was of far more interest.

★★★

Nearly 600 miles northwest of Mombasa, the Uasin Gishu's District Commissioner was having a bad day. It was a regrettable part of his diverse job and one that he sincerely hated, but also one he simply couldn't avoid. Whenever the police discovered the body of a 'white' who had died in violent or suspicious circumstances, it was required of the local Commissioner to be the conveyer of the bad news. Consequently and in this case, it was he who had to break it to the 'nearest and dearest'. His was the universally dreaded, sudden knock at the door, often in the 'wee small hours', but always at a singularly inappropriate time. In this case, it was for the Lescal family, although at least the hour was halfway civilised. Nevertheless, this assignment had to be up there with the worst. A young, intelligent and evidently innocent white girl with a bright future in front of her, murdered by 'person or persons' unknown. And now not only did she lack a future but, he rather suspected, so did her family. All it took was a terse telegraph from his counterpart in Malindi, setting out the bare facts, and a family's world imploded. Moreover, for now there was precious little in the way of additional evidence. Just sufficient information to destroy a family, but not enough to help them in any way. And here he was, standing awkwardly in front of them, unhappily aware of his role in bringing such dire news.

As kindly as he could he had delivered the appalling facts and now, following the shock of his pronouncement, he waited within a tension that was palpable. It was as though their world had ground to a halt. Two taut, grey, tear-streaked faces, two violated spirits and only the sound of ragged breathing to confirm their continued survival. Yet not very far below the surface a storm was brewing and soon, he knew, it was likely to erupt in a maddened outpouring of grief. In his many years as a policeman, he had seen it so often; the initial, shocked response to whatever awful intelligence had been imparted; the struggle for breath in a suddenly alien and uncertain world; even the ability to speak rendered near impossible for the moment.

Warily, he watched and waited. He hadn't known Ted and Vera Lescal long, but what he did know of them and their young son, he liked and respected and would have given anything not to be the bearer of such sad news. They seemed a quiet, hard-working couple who largely kept themselves to themselves. Just the four of them, only they were three now. Three in an altogether different sense than had been the case, when their daughter had left for the coast. New to the area, not long arrived from Malindi, they'd settled in quickly enough and were proving to be more than capable of overcoming whatever misfortune had robbed them of their previous life. But something had been tugging at the furthest recesses of his mind. And now he had it. A suddenly remembered fact about the girl, Rosalind. Something of a beauty, she had become mixed up with that young man Paul Moncton, the one who had apparently killed a couple of Askaris some months back. No trace of him or of his body had ever been found and he was now widely assumed to be dead. Perhaps somewhere out in the bush. Perhaps eaten by wild animals, as happened on occasion. He made a mental note to dig out the reports he knew were filed somewhere in the general office. A long, keening cry from Vera pulled him rudely back to the present. Perched on the sofa, to which she had involuntarily sunk on hearing the news, she was holding her body in tight-wrapped arms, rocking slowly back and forth, utterly isolated in her misery. His heart went out to her, just as her husband, Ted, his own eyes streaming with fresh tears, reached out to gather her into his arms, as though by this simple act he could eradicate reality and transport them back to a time that predated such anguish.

Gulping, she finally managed to mouth, "Are you sure?" Her eyes pleading with him to be wrong.

"I'm sorry, Mrs Lescal. I am sure of it. The District Commissioner wouldn't have telegraphed me if he wasn't absolutely certain. I'm afraid I don't have many details yet, but I understand she was killed by archers. Which would point to someone from the coastal tribes. Her death was reported by some of the locals who had befriended her. As soon as I know any more, I promise you will be the first to be informed." As a response, a reassurance, he knew it was totally inadequate. But it was all he could think of for now. He simply didn't know any more. And already in his mind, he was beginning to wonder about Rosalind's relationship with the Moncton boy, and what exactly she had been doing down at the coast alone and apparently living with natives. It was unusual, to say the least, for a young white girl to be on her own, so far from home. And asking for trouble, in his opinion. But then, what did he know? Long divorced and with no children of his own (his love for the job had been largely responsible for the current state of affairs), he suddenly felt inadequate and supremely unqualified to judge what was right and wrong when it came to young girls and their headstrong ambitions.

CHAPTER 64

For Israfel, embarrassment had turned to deep unease. He had watched me first torture and then casually jettison Fatih, before interring his still living body under the layers of rock with which I had choked the defunct old well. However, it was not what I had done that was the nub of the problem. Israfel well knew that humans seemed almost naturally inclined to kill each other and, given the right circumstances, would do it quite often and with little compunction. Moreover, he was well aware that Fatih had effectively brought this calamity on himself and would have been just as summarily dispatched had any one of a half-dozen associates, or victims, from his past caught up with him while he was vulnerable.

No, the killing was not what disturbed him. Rather, it was the rapidly hardening attitude that was impelling, almost overwhelming me. Admittedly an attitude driven by anguish over Roz. But a distorted mind-set nevertheless and not altered for the good. In particular, it was the palpable lack of emotional response to anything I was doing that concerned Israfel. He knew that, given true remorse, even a Stalin or a Pol Pot – for all their slaughtered millions – could still seek and, if genuinely remorseful, obtain forgiveness from the Son of God who had loved them enough to embrace death on their behalf. But he was equally aware of the danger that a human soul could grow too callous to care, too sure of itself to ever want, or ever think of accepting forgiveness. Leaving the human in question (me, in this case) faced with eternal condemnation, come the final Judgement Day. Not necessarily because of murder, or some equally reprehensible crime, but simply because, in general, the human psyche prefers to go its own way, without being bothered by God. And God, being entirely reasonable, always honours such desires (and ensures his Guardians do, too). The inevitable and effective result being self-conviction and an immutable sentence that has the human in question joining the horde of demons. And as far as he was concerned, that was an inconceivable end for his charge. It wasn't that I didn't deserve such a fate. I did, just like all humans. However, I had not only been assigned a rising star for a Guardian, but one who had been promoted specifically for the job. So, as far as he, Israfel, was concerned, it simply couldn't end with a whimper. In any case, he had been given specific insights into my likely future, which meant Heaven had more than a passing interest in the outcome. And it was a future that needed him to use his specialist knowledge and Angelic powers wisely. Which also meant that, pretty soon, he had to come up with a strategy that would turn matters around, without violating the principle of free choice. Favoured or not, I still had to be left entirely unhampered, able to make my own, unfettered decisions.

And right then I was facing a dilemma, feeling duty-bound to tell the Lescals what had happened, who had been responsible and why. However, I was equally adamant that I wasn't going to present any opportunity whatsoever to the police, who would no doubt arrest me on sight. At least not before I had caught up with certain adversaries and exacted suitable vengeance. Problem was, that still left a dilemma. Should I first visit Malcolm and Jill Joubert, who had been so good to Roz, to sound them out, perhaps even enlist their help and practical, common-sense guidance? Or should I just telephone Roz's parents out of the blue? Not to put too fine a point on it, such an impromptu call could prove less than helpful, and might even end in a shouting match, or one of the parties breaking down mid-conversation. In any case, this was a discussion that, to say the least, I was dreading. More practically, from what Roz had told me, the Jouberts could be relied upon to hold their own council until I was once again beyond the reach of the law. Which, to my mind, settled the matter.

Having erased all sign of Fatih, I had retraced my steps to the coast, but, with the urgency of pursuit now gone and my meagre rations long since consumed, it took me a couple of days fighting slowly ebbing strength and escalating thirst before I finally reached 'our' settlement. But I made it and, to the intense satisfaction of my hosts, I was able to reassure them that Roz had been suitably avenged. Moreover, I avoided compromising their position by consciously withholding the 'how and where'. Just assuring them they were no longer obligated, as kith and kin (which they had come to consider themselves), to exact their own revenge. A night's sleep in my old hut with its almost unbearable memories and I was ready to set out again. But not before the villagers had revealed to me that they'd had to inform the police about Roz, with the inevitable result that a number of Askaris and their officers had spent the previous day crawling all over their huts, questioning everyone, even the youngest toto and taking the usual reams of notes and photographs. Necessary, but an action that had done little to endear them. Eventually, towards evening, they'd left, taking poor Roz with them and, by great good fortune, I hadn't reappeared until the following day.

So now I could rest assured official wheels were turning and Ted and Vera would have been informed, which meant, in turn, that I was glad for them in a way and relieved for myself, even though it did nothing to let me off the family hook. They would still want to talk to me, especially when they heard that I'd been with Roz when she was killed. As they surely would, although our friends had withheld all but the barest details from the police. Enough to trigger the dispatch of another patrol along the coast to collect a number of corpses, in what was fast becoming the stuff of police nightmares.

Fortunately, the Jeep started at the third attempt. It had seen little use since Roz had arrived at the coast, but the hot weather had kept the battery in reasonable order. And now it was going to be needed as never before. I had no other means of transport, and I was going to have to move quickly. It didn't take a genius to realise that Fatih's failure to report back would, sooner or later, alert those in control of the slaving and drugs partnership. 'Sooner' being rather more likely than 'later', given the caution inherent in those notoriously jittery trades.

CHAPTER 65

So it was that, early the next day, I set out with little likelihood of ultimate success, but an utter determination to see through this, now full-fledged, one-man mission to destroy Ahmed, Giuseppe and any associate who might chance to get in the way. A sober assessment of my predicament would have seen me switching off the engine and dismounting the vehicle there and then. But I was in no mood for such defeatism (realism?). The police had lost track of me. I had a gun. I probably still enjoyed an element of surprise and, above all, I harboured a burning sense of injustice, which was feeding an insane desire to kill or be killed. The final outcome being largely a matter of indifference, as I'd either wreak havoc and destroy the perpetrators of the foul trade that had created my personal Hell of the past few months or, after what I hoped would still be a suitably ferocious and successful act of revenge on my part, those same activities would end my own miserable existence. And of course, trapped in my private Hell, unreachable in the profound torment that drove me and utterly lost in the misery that comes with deep grief, I cared not one whit for how the world might perceive my proposed behaviour.

However, like everyone else who drove the coastal road and was thus beholden to the ubiquitous chain ferries and poor roads, I had no option but to endure the several hours it took to reach Mombasa, even at the sometimes reckless speeds I employed. And nor did it help to have to circumvent some irritating hold-ups behind endless processions of old and rickety African buses. Which meant that, by the time I arrived, the sun was already drawing close to the western horizon. Still, the monotonous hours had produced a bonus, in that they had allowed me time not just to think, but also to cool down, metaphorically speaking. To edge towards rationality and start to map out a halfway sane strategy for dealing with the problem, in so far as I could determine. Anyway, by the time I crossed from the mainland onto Mombasa Island, I had decided to waste no further time in procrastination, but go straight to the Jouberts, tell them the whole story and throw myself on their mercy. With that decided, I quickly navigated my way across the island, finally merging into the lane that led to their long, low house with its wrap-around veranda and comfortable sofas shrewdly placed to avoid the direct sun. Fortunately, they were both in, so I didn't have to tell my story twice. They greeted me warily enough, almost as though anticipating more bad news, but, for all that, their hospitality was impeccable. Anyway, who could have blamed them had it not been so? I wasn't going to be anyone's flavour of the month. So, whilst my arrival drew some heartfelt tears from Jill, her husband Malcolm, of whom I'd heard so much, welcomed me civilly enough. Moreover, between the two of them, I was soon ensconced on one of the sofas with a chilled beer in one hand and a welcome plate of hurriedly prepared food in the other.

It wasn't easy. It was never going to be. But in the end, I convinced them that whilst I was entirely to blame when it came to the two of us dropping out of sight, I was far from being the villain of the piece. I wasn't even close to being the architect of the terrible calamity that had overtaken us. Moreover, I was able to explain, at some length, the relationship Roz and I had developed since she'd rescued me. Something I was determined to confirm, because not only did I feel absolutely beholden to Roz, not only did I remain utterly in love with her, but she needed to be decisively vindicated in her friends' eyes. I had to admit that we had become so completely engrossed in each other, that I had done little more than encourage a fleeting contemplation of family and friends, only realising too late just how much this must have hurt all concerned. With some degree of shame I now admitted essentially preventing Roz from making any outside contacts, despite her protests. So in this respect, but in this respect alone, any fall from grace was entirely my fault. Which involved me in a number of profuse apologies, coupled with a heartfelt acknowledgement of guilt that went some way towards mollifying their reaction. After all, not only had the two sitting in front of me been more or less forced to accept an esoteric responsibility for Roz, they'd then had to acknowledge to their friends, the Lescals, that they'd lost all contact with their charge and didn't have a clue as to where she might be, search though they had. I marked with a certain grim humour that there was no one quite like our native friends for clamming up once they had undertaken to keep a secret.

But I also discovered that because my action, or lack of it, had instigated a particularly diligent, if ultimately unsuccessful search, the undertaking had produced an encouraging effect on Malcolm's injuries. Within a couple of weeks or so of Roz going missing, Malcolm had dragged himself back onto his feet and, despite what must have been some pretty intense pain, had managed to get the raw wound in his side and the flayed muscles of his back working in approximate harmony again. Even managing to return to some semblance of fitness, although he was by no means the Malcolm of old. Nevertheless, as he listened to my explanation, I could see his eyes beginning to light up and his mind to revolve around my proposals. He, too, had every reason to loathe the same people. Both for what they had done to him and for what they had done to Roz. In fact, once I'd covered most of what had happened in the days since I'd first been captured, I could see I had made a good and useful ally. It was clear that I'd been right to start with the Jouberts. Malcolm even offered to call the Lescals and fill them in on the latest details, but for all my appreciation of his gesture, I knew I had to make that call myself.

Just two days later I'd put the Lescals completely in the

picture, having decided to confide fully in them. Consequently, and despite their heartache, they had agreed to keep my whereabouts secret. For his part, Malcolm was as ready as he was ever likely to be, given the lack of sufficient time to heal properly from his bullet wound; Jill's repeated protests had finally been silenced and I was recovering physically, if not emotionally, from the events of the past few days. Thus it seemed appropriate to put our hastily sketched plans into action.

Very early on the Wednesday morning, long before there was even a hint of light in the eastern sky, Malcolm and I sneaked out into the cold night air. Making sure we didn't wake Jill, we rolled out his old Jeep and made our way swiftly back to Mombasa. Only this time we drove directly to the square outside the old harbour, where we intended to park up before pursuing the hunt on Shank's pony. The time for pussyfooting around was over and we were each armed with a knife and a Colt 45, the rifle having been left behind as of little use in the close confines of the streets and homes we intended to visit. Always provided Fatih had stuck to the truth, the intelligence I had gained from him would be invaluable, so we were first going to call on two of Ahmed's principle collaborators, both of whom were, by all accounts, to be found in the harbour area. Which meant the time for testing the validity of Fatih's material had finally arrived. Not only that, but also the time for assessing the rationality of my somewhat unorthodox methods for extracting that information. Albeit we were rather too late to do anything about it if he'd been lying, just to stop the pain. And there lay the problem. If he had, we could be frustrated before we'd even begun. A point not worth dwelling upon.

CHAPTER 66

The first address proved to be a small, dingy-looking terraced house in a dark and smelly alley just off the old harbour entrance. No sound or light emanated from it and although it appeared unoccupied, we nevertheless jemmied a ground-floor window shutter as quietly as possible, discovering it just to the left of a solid-looking entrance door. Carefully done or not, the sound of the latch bursting in the predawn silence sounded to us like the proverbial thunder clap, but, making sure we hadn't been seen, we climbed swiftly inside. Nothing. Just a couple of empty rooms and not a trace of any previous owner. It was as though, before leaving, someone had been determined to clean every last suggestion of human activity from memory. But perversely, that in itself gave us some small hope. Any normally vacated house would surely contain some hint of its former occupant? It was only if a resident needed to wipe away all trace of himself, to vanish into thin air without fear of pursuit, that it would be so thoroughly cleansed. And surely, only someone whose activities wouldn't bear the light of day would be interested in doing that? So we began to hope that this first address wasn't the start of a complete fiasco, from which there could be little hope of recovery. Rather, we decided to look upon it as an indication that Fatih hadn't actually sold me down the river. More likely, what it did do was indicate the preternatural wariness inevitable within the feral world of the criminals we were after. A hasty look around the remaining room confirmed our first impressions, and we got out as quickly and quietly as possible. Strike one.

The next address was only a few hundred yards away but, in

the labyrinthine streets of the old Arab quarter, it seemed more like half a mile by the time we arrived. Once again we were presented with a run-down fleapit, but this time we were immediately sure it was occupied. The hint of a dimly flickering light behind one of the ground-floor shutters gave the game away, deftly backed up by the stench of something indefinable wafting under the front door. We hadn't expected anyone to be up and about at this time of the morning, so we were particularly wary as we approached, taking care not to disturb a stray dog loitering nearby. However, with the occupant obviously awake, clandestine entry was out of the question so, after a quick debate, we took the bull by the horns, approached the door openly and simply knocked quietly.

Interestingly, from behind the door came abrupt, scuffling sounds, as though someone was attempting to hide evidence (or that's how it seemed to our suspicious minds), but then all noise ceased for a moment or so. An interval during which we were sorely tempted to try kicking our way straight through the door, until the clatter of bolts being dragged back came as something of a relief. The door opened a mere crack, but behind it we could clearly detect the outline of a short, hooded figure. The figure issued a single, terse demand for identity in Arabic and it was clear there was little likelihood of exchanging pleasantries. Fortunately, I speak the language fairly fluently and, although unable to provide a satisfactory answer to the specific demand, I took a guess that his was the name Fatih had provided and the enunciation of it was just sufficient to hold him, while we threw our combined weight against the door, catching him by surprise and knocking him smartly backwards.

No longer obstructed, we pressed in swiftly before closing and bolting the door behind us. Once in, we could see the room was clear except for our man. The problem was he had regained his feet as swiftly as he had been felled and was now brandishing a rather fearsome curved knife and heading straight towards me.

Fortunately, Malcolm is a big man and it quickly became clear why my choice of companion had been a wise one. Stepping between me and my oncoming assailant, arms swinging in a fair imitation of a haymaker on the loose, one of Malcolm's big fists brought the man to a sudden halt, pitching him his full length along the ground. This time, we took no chances and with Malcolm hovering in the background bemoaning the pain in his hand, never mind his side, I swiftly turned the stunned man over and secured his hands behind his back with the tape we had wisely brought. Then it was a simple matter to sit him upright, prop his back against the nearby wall, bring the lamp closer and take stock. We seemed to have bagged ourselves a middle-aged, reasonably athletic-looking man with the kind of strong, aquiline features that would have marked him out in virtually any social gathering. So far, so good. The fact that he had been prepared to attack told us nothing. We could hardly have expected any other response, given the circumstances of an early morning and definitely unexpected visit. However, something in his demeanour as he began to come round told me we might be onto something here. I had always hoped, indeed assumed, Fatih had included some useful names, not just those of mere 'rank and file' criminals. Simply because he couldn't know how much I already knew, he was far more likely to have mentioned the bigger fish, because he'd still been hoping to get out alive.

Which meant we were now firmly into my type of territory and knowing Malcolm would not approve of what I was about to do, I suggested he keep watch whilst I used my superior command of the language to embark on an interrogation. Fortunately, he readily agreed, although I'm convinced to this day he had a pretty clear idea of what was likely to happen. Wanting nothing to do with what he considered to be distinctly uncivilised behaviour, Malcolm had stepped smartly outside to ensure we remained undisturbed.

"So, Kareef, for that is your name, is it not? You are perhaps wondering why we are here and why you find yourself restrained and, believe me, in some real danger of your life. Ah, I see you don't believe me. Well, let me tell you a story. There's a well-known Arab business man operating around here. His name is Prince Ahmed. As I'm sure you know, he runs not just the local slave trade, but drugs and ivory, too, and he often deals with a man from upcountry named Giuseppe. Giuseppe supplies Ahmed with all these things. Now, I have no doubt you know exactly who I am talking about and, for my part, I have neither the time nor the patience to wait while you decide whether or not to tell me where these men are right now, and how well they are guarded. I was given your name by Fatih, whom you also know. He was happy to tell me where I could find you and how you fitted into the picture. Unfortunately, however, Fatih is no longer with us. He took too long to understand that I meant what I said. As a result he died in a great deal of pain. Now, I also know you are one of Ahmed's enforcers, so please don't waste my time denying it. Fact is, you do things for him that can't be entrusted to anyone else. I know, for instance, that if Ahmed wants a slave taught a 'final' lesson, you're the one he turns to. A useful ally, Kareef, aren't you? One who always makes sure the other slaves get the message, never mind the one you've been sent to kill. So, there it is. I don't really care what happens to you, but I might allow you to live if you tell me now – and quickly – what I want to know about Ahmed and Giuseppe. Oh, and by the way, please don't think that I will be any easier on you than Ahmed would if you fail to give the right answer." I sat back, watching Kareef closely, expecting that, if anything, he would be harder to persuade than Fatih. However, my recent experience in breaking Fatih had been a useful and informative exercise. I no longer had any qualms about what was likely to happen, or even how I would go about it. Which made everything relatively easy.

So when, as expected, from underneath his hood Kareef contented himself with glaring defiantly, daring me to do anything about it, I was more than prepared. With a sigh (purely for Kareef's benefit), I leaned forward, pulled down the lobe of his left ear and sliced it off, figuring that immediate drastic action would have a more salutary effect on him than continuing threats. Moreover, I found I had begun to enjoy inflicting pain. Which, when I thought about it, was rather odd, really, but I put it down to becoming inured to suffering through months of my own intense pain. At any rate, with a hiss of pure malice undoubtedly laced with agony, Kareef jerked his head back against the wall, barely able to believe that a white boy could have the effrontery to do such a thing to him. Feigning indifference, I tossed the segment of human tissue onto the recently lit fire, which was beginning to spark into fierce life in the centre of the room, and stared off into space.

"Kareef, believe me, I'm not playing games here. You will talk in the end and, for your own sake, I suggest you make it sooner rather than later. Next time I will remove something of rather more value to you and I'll do it with the help of the fire over there. So, I'll ask you again, where are Ahmed and Giuseppe right now?" I already knew how terrified of Ahmed his men were, so it didn't surprise me that, at this stage, Kareef preferred to take his chance antagonising me, rather than the boss he knew to be a coldly calculating killer. However, by the same token, I possessed a number of advantages over Ahmed. For a start, I was the one present, the one meting out judgement and then again, I was the one with the now nicely blazing fire, the razor-sharp hook and the insensitive conscience, both the latter bequeathed to me by Fatih. Unfortunately for him, Kareef hesitated for a second time, showing no sign he intended to play ball.

So, once again, sighing ostentatiously, I leant forward and gripped his foot, which, by virtue of his sitting position, was severely hampered in its movement and couldn't be easily snatched away. Simultaneously, I pulled one of the more substantial and now nicely blazing sticks from the fire, brought it close to the sole of his foot and steadied myself, in order to press it firmly down, with every intention of searing through to the bone if necessary. However, and fortunately for us both, Kareef was beginning to get the picture and to accept that I had few qualms about implementing any threat I might make.

"OK, OK! I knew where Ahmed was a week ago, but Giuseppe is upcountry, and I can't tell you when he might return. That is all I know."

"Well, Kareef, you speak with much conviction, but, actually, I don't believe you. Either you can't or you won't tell me. Which is it? Whichever way it is, unless you come up with something rather more convincing as an answer, I'm going to burn your feet until you are permanently crippled."

As I spoke, I scraped the still-flaming brand across the thick skin on the bottom of his foot and watched him shrink back in agony as a row of blisters formed almost instantaneously. Seeing the glow begin to die down, I put the wood back into the fire and let it rekindle, making sure Kareef was aware of the process.

"Next time, I'll be sticking this to both feet, not brushing over them, and by the time I've finished, you'll be crippled for life. Do I make myself clear?" Kareef nodded. "OK then, let's try again." Slowly, hesitantly, Kareef began to spit out the details of where I could find Ahmed that day and, perhaps more importantly, the number of guards involved and the guidelines by which they operated. Only if I knew how to circumvent them could I hope to get near enough to Ahmed to finish him off, as I fully intended. By the time Kareef paused for breath, having once again denied knowing anything of Giuseppe's whereabouts, I was sure he was telling the truth and that I now had all I could expect to learn. Satisfied, I grabbed him quickly by the hair, jerked his head back and ran Fatih's hook across his throat. It took all my strength to hold him tightly until he stopped jerking and the blood had stopped spurting, the product hissing as it sprayed across the fire. Then, with the life drained out of him, I removed the tape from his wrists, pulled him away from the wall and placed his own knife back in his hand, wrapping the fingers tightly in place. Then, standing back and already appalled by what I had just done, I threw the hook into the fire before beginning to tremble deep down and uncontrollably. Somewhere in my conscience I had caught a glimpse of what I had become and I didn't like it one little bit. I was no longer a safe person to be around, because brutalised cruelty wasn't really my line and yet it was clear this was the way I was developing. Only after several minutes of violent shaking was I able to regain control and gather sufficient strength to call Malcolm in to give him the news of Ahmed's whereabouts. As to the rest, I lied easily, telling him that Kareef had broken free, forcing me to kill him before he got the better of me and escaped. Whether or not Malcolm believed this, his face gave little away, merely accepting that at least we now knew Ahmed was still on the island and, as far as I was concerned, could probably be approached by a determined assassin.

CHAPTER 67

In his warped and prejudiced way, the malevolent devil Arcturus really couldn't have been more satisfied by the latest turn of events. To all intents and purposes, he had the field to himself and was once again acting as the main opponent of a specific human being. More than that – a human on Lucifer's 'hot list'. Me. But much better as far as he was concerned, there had been little hint of reprisal from the normally ever-vigilant Heavenly host. Not even when he'd taken a chance and crossed what had been cited as Heaven's 'line in the sand'. The one he'd been specifically warned about. He'd not even admitted to himself how apprehensive he'd been to start with, especially when he'd incited me to kill, knowing I might well die first. However, with Israfel apparently missing from the scene, Arcturus had finally convinced himself that the only reasonable explanation lay in said angel having been forced to acknowledge he'd met his match. Although this would also have had to mean Heaven downgrading its interest in me, a fairly unlikely possibility. But then Arcturus was no chess player.

Most importantly, as far as he was concerned, there had been no sign of a Guardian for days now and with those infuriating angels apparently well out of the way, everything seemed to be on course to achieve his own venomous aim. All accomplished with only one slight glitch – one that had admittedly caused him a smidgeon of momentary doubt – the awkward but tiresome detail that I actually had recognised and now appeared to loathe what I was fast becoming. Nevertheless – and here was the clincher – as far as he was concerned, I continued to respond well to the monstrous advice being dripped unobtrusively into my subconscious ear. Satisfying proof of which, as far as Arcturus was concerned, was the bloody and totally unnecessary death of Kareef. And so, placing it within Hell's warped context, all that had to be done was to keep the venom trickling into my co-operative mind until, in due course, he would reap certain rewards.

Actually, to Arcturus, the raw, violent and bloody death of any human was like pornography to the sex obsessed. So every time he had a moment to reflect, his mind would inevitably direct its gleeful thoughts back to my contretemps with Kareef. Before turning, with some pleasure, to ponder the likely course of future events (conveniently overlooking the slight embarrassment of my momentary foreboding). His daydream climaxing in a mouth-watering, vicarious thrill that ran through every fibre of his being. And at the very least, he thought, this latest venture had to be good for several more gory deaths. The more brutal, the better. Moreover, if it all went to plan and I was also killed, he could then present Hell's hierarchy with a *fait accompli*, which, in its consequences, should far outweigh the disgrace of his past failings. And then perhaps it might really be time to bring Josephus to account. To drop him well and truly into the proverbial, with just a hint in the right quarters about how Josephus had been rather too swift to consign two particularly useful senior devils to Abbadon (they having submitted a joint report showing Josephus for the incompetent he really was. Only to have him intercept and dispose of this analysis). Brilliant. Could there be a more effective, a more suitable demon to take over than himself? After all, looked at from his own, obviously unbiased view, it was clear that his overall game plan would present a model of excellence. Why, the Directing Staff at Demon Command School might even consider using his tactics and ideas at their abortion of a college, citing them as an example of how experts achieved their goals. He could already see himself as their idol. But then, as always, miserable reality set in and he knew, deep down in what passed for a heart, this would never happen. Only those at the very top of the hierarchical tree were deemed worthy of having any notice taken of their schemes and a fiend like him, even one with proven warrior status, was currently as low on the scale of satanic merit as it was possible to get and it was hardly likely that matters would improve, or that he would aspire to any greater heights (or was it 'depths'?) given the commuted death sentence still hanging over him. Still –even an excrescence could dream.

★★★

If at that point I'd had the least inkling of what was going on in the spiritual realm far beyond sight or comprehension, I still wouldn't have considered turning aside from the path upon which I was resolved. As far as I was concerned, every last one of the men connected with my loss deserved to die and I fully intended to be their nemesis, even if it really did turn out to be the last thing I ever did. With Kareef in the bag and some concrete information on Ahmed's whereabouts and strength of personal protection, I felt there was little point in pursuing any other informants at this stage. Consequently, I suggested to Malcolm we return home, prepare to weather the inevitable storm from Jill and put together a game plan for executing the elusive Ahmed. Before he had time to discover what had happened to yet another of his henchmen and reassess his security – in which case, I might lose him entirely.

Jill was the relatively easy bit. Working out how I could get through the comprehensive security ring surrounding Ahmed and get close enough to have any real hope of killing him was a problem of a completely different order. But, having discovered his location, we were at least able to drive unobtrusively past the address before returning to consider the problem at length. By evening we had a plan, but I was certain what was intended had to be done alone. Especially as I wasn't prepared to risk Malcolm's life again. After all, I could hardly forget he'd put it on the line when he thought I was in Ahmed's other address. Moreover, unlike my darling Roz, I was in no mood to risk going against the, by now, implacable Jill. Plus Malcolm had a pressing private matter to take care of regarding a certain Superintendent Terence Foley. So it was that with a slight heaviness of step, but a determination beyond my years, I began to prepare for what would prove something of a turning point in my odyssey. There was no doubt confrontation had to be engineered that night, because if it wasn't, it would probably never happen. I wouldn't get another chance once Ahmed had any inkling of the way the wind was blowing, so intervention would have to be swift and conclusive. Hurriedly I prepared the one weapon Malcolm possessed that would withstand a soaking. His elderly spear gun, after I'd adjusted the trigger mechanism, one of Jill's knitting needles furnishing the essential tool.

★★★

Given the tight confines of suburban Mombasa, it was never going to take very long to arrive outside Ahmed's exclusive residence on the eastern edge of the island. The opulent building's longest, low-lying flank faced out to sea and was thus exposed to the best of any on-shore breeze. My problem was the whole complex was surrounded by a high wire fence, complete with arc lights that blazed outwards across a deliberately cleared strip of ground. No doubt to provide a free field of fire to the guards. Which did not bode well for any land entry, although I had no doubt I could quickly put paid to the lights, even if crossing the barbed wire was likely to prove rather more of a hurdle. So our earlier and unobtrusive reconnoitring of this obstacle to progress now proved its worth. Having obtained the requisite information, I had bought some heavy-duty, insulated wire clippers and it didn't take long to trace the power line from a nearby distribution point to where it approached the compound, deep though it was buried. And it was then that I began to really understand how much I had come to rely on my well-built friend. As I contemplated what lay ahead, Malcolm's absence, his huge and bluff company, suddenly seemed rather important to my peace of mind. However, it remained but the work of minutes to uncover the main house cable (as Ahmed was about to discover, if you want real security in Africa, always oversee the plans and their implementation yourself) and with a heartfelt prayer that there was no immediately available generator to take over, I plunged the compound into sudden but instantly animated darkness.

It was like stirring a hornet's nest, but there was little time to linger to contemplate, or even appreciate, the results. So hefting my only serious weapon, the already cocked spear gun, I hurried down to the sea's edge as quickly and quietly as possible, trying to keep low, with real fear wrenching at my guts. Wading rapidly into the gentle swell, I tried hard to put the rather too fresh thoughts of sharks and their ilk out of my mind. Then, steeling myself, I swam out for about a hundred yards until certain I was well clear of the barbed-wire fencing that marched steadily seaward on ever longer posts. An obstacle specifically designed to deter unwanted guests from joining the owners in what they considered to be their well-deserved privacy. At last able to turn back and careful to avoid any splashes, I drifted towards the private, but deserted beach, that now lay exposed in front of me. At least I could rest assured there would be no fixed obstacles underwater from this point, because their presence would pose owners and guests alike unnecessary danger.

CHAPTER 68

There's one genuine problem with phosphorescence. Well, if you're trying to stay under the radar, that is. Even if the little critters aren't in the mood to flash while you're moving through their liquid home, they can certainly wake up when you surface and they realise you're leaving their natural habitat. As your body streams with the last vestiges of salt water heading south, on a 'good' night you can look for all the world like the proverbial 'pillar of fire'. And this was one of those 'good' nights. Hoping against hope that any guards on the beach side of the building weren't under the impression they were being visited by one of Africa's countless ghouls or, worse still, an unwanted intruder, I dashed up the beach towards a shadowed corner of the house, where I could just make out a couple of shuttered windows. Fortunately, in the blacker shadows just below the roof, this European-style house signalled conformity with its contemporaries by revealing evidence of the gap that was so often found along the top of such walls. A breach designed to encourage the passage of cooling air, but one that was usually just wide enough to allow a relatively slim body to roll through without hindrance.

With my ragged breathing back under control, there were few other noises to be heard at my end of the house, but I was aware of quite a lot of distant movement. Someone, somewhere, had begun thinking sufficiently clearly to organise the handing out of lighted candles, with order being gradually restored and rooms checked for intruders. Consequently, there remained little time if I was to reach Ahmed before his bodyguards got back to their designated posts. So, assuming he would be in bed by this time of night and perhaps even distracted by some companion or other, I made my way stealthily past the preoccupied guards, until reaching the far end of the house, away from the brightly lit rooms I'd noted prior to cutting the power. In essence, the more discreet end, where I fondly hoped I would find Ahmed's lair.

I was not disappointed. Arriving in front of a heavy, carved door set into a wall that ran the whole width of the house (it had to be the owner's), I could just catch the occasional burst of muffled laughter. But no candlelight flickered from under the door so, with any luck, Ahmed had not yet been alerted to what was going on. Actually, I hoped the guards were too afraid to bother him after he'd retired, particularly if it was only to tell him bad news. Hopefully, that would be his (and their) undoing. However, expecting the door to be locked from the inside, I had already decided that boldness was the only feasible way to gain entry. So, stepping forward with my heart lurching unsteadily, I knocked forcefully on his rather substantial door and, with my hand cupped in front of my mouth to mute the sound, called urgently for audience in Arabic. Which produced exactly the reaction for which I had hoped. An impatient demand to know why he was being disturbed 'at this time of night'. A second, equally muffled call preceded the impatient clicking of a key and the sound of a heavy bolt being drawn back. Seconds later the door was jerked open and in the darkness I could just discern the outline of a surprisingly lean body. Nervous anyway and frightened by the speed of his appearance, I whipped the harpoon up, aiming for somewhere just above the centre of the figure and loosed the only spear I had, knowing the needle-sharp, weighted and barbed missile would do its work. Although I must confess even then, at the far recesses of my mind, I was still hoping it wouldn't act too quickly. Until I caught the explosive exhalation of breath, followed immediately by a distinctly female shriek of shocked pain.

Unnerved by what I immediately realised was a fatal mistake

(probably fatal for both of us, actually), I dropped the weapon, turned and fled, bouncing off walls, slamming into doors and generally creating mayhem with individual pieces of furniture, acting for all the world as though pursued by the hounds of Hell. Beyond blind panic, I don't remember much of that exit, except that as I scrambled back up the wall, several poorly aimed bullets drilled chips off the plaster around me and some rather better aimed shots passed altogether too close for comfort as I sprinted for the safety of the sea. There to begin a dialogue with myself on what exactly I was supposed to be doing. And that, surely, didn't include indiscriminate killing? Or simply antagonising a very dangerous enemy, if he should ever get even a hint of who was involved.

It didn't take me long to retrace my footsteps and get back to Malcolm and Jill, but although I arrived well before dawn, both were already up and neither was in the mood to hear any excuses concerning the failure of my latest bout of organised mayhem. It turned out that far from obtaining satisfaction over Jill's harassment, Malcolm had been read the riot act by Superintendent Foley, who was now certain the Jouberts knew more than they were prepared to divulge. Someone, somewhere, had clearly spilled the beans, or been forced to confess as to who it was using (abusing?) their hospitality. Which meant that henceforth, *Kwetu* was off limits to me. Whether I liked it or not. And I was very clearly back on the run, because the police were in no mood to listen to anyone regarding my innocence or otherwise. Particularly now I had stupidly added to the sum of my offences, without gaining anything.

★★★

Ahmed was incensed. Not only had his personal security been blatantly breached, but one of his favoured slaves was probably

331

beyond use. And it has to be said that, whilst he wasn't overly bothered about the girl, he was very concerned over the inevitable loss of face. Calling first for his chief of personal protection, he informed him in considerable depth and at extremely high volume of his fury concerning the incident. Added to which, as of that moment, the man was out of a job. Then he started yelling for the man the staff feared most, next to himself. His resident 'fixer'. A weasel of a man, with the dry and dusty manner of an undertaker, but one whom you misjudged at your peril. A quiet word in his ear and the departing chief never made it past the back door. Instead, like so many others, he disappeared swiftly into an anonymous lime pit, kept specifically for such purposes. Then and only then did Ahmed summon his personal physician who, knowing the financial value attached to this particular slave, set about the task of trying to resuscitate and repair her with an alacrity not commonly observed in his performances. Had I known of his success that night, I might not have been quite so circumspect over making myself visible to the police during the succeeding months. But hindsight is a wonderful thing. For now, Ahmed contented himself with terrifying the staff and ordering a thorough search for the culprit. A positive result to be with him by sun-up, latest. And, with those same staff fully aware of their former chief's fate, the intensity and enthusiasm of their hunt couldn't be faulted. Which was why, having finally discovered who was involved, they caught up with the Jouberts late that afternoon. How they did, I do not know to this day. All I do know is what I read in the following day's papers. Two whites murdered, reasons unknown, but with evidence of underworld involvement. And, of course, in my misery I knew exactly who was responsible. And thus, by implication, whose fault it was. Mine. I remember beginning to shake as I read through the article, and then to weep. To weep for the friends I had endangered and now lost, to weep for vanished innocence, to weep for what I had obviously become and, above all, to weep for the unbearable presence of a dark, drear and growing void in my life. An injury from whose wound I felt I was unlikely to recover. A void that was at once ethereal yet solid, dead yet growing. An awful, bitter, but inescapable burden. A reservoir of despair that flourished for want of love, for want of Roz. Yet how unutterably relieved I was that she was not there to witness what I had begun to regard as my ultimate degradation. For, in those days of vengeance, this was exactly how I viewed the reasonable assumption that I'd killed a slave (albeit inadvertently), a woman who had no doubt been through much the same anguish as I had endured and who was definitely a sister in adversity.

The overwhelming storm of anguish that now swept over me was long overdue and the flow of tears deeply cathartic in its own inimical way, laying me low for most of that day, but purging my perceptions and steeling my determination to get even. This, when I would have been better occupied throwing in the towel, striving for liberation through confession to the police, not continuing to search out yet more ways to even the score.

CHAPTER 69

It wasn't every day that Heaven involved itself quite so directly in the affairs of individuals. Certainly not to the extent that destinies were changed or events carefully re-fashioned by specific angels. If there was one thing humans were expected to do, it was get on and live useful lives – lives that combined their God-given intelligence with their most precious possession; free will. Mostly, the end results were reasonable, but sometimes a particular human would foul up so comprehensively that it took nothing short of a miracle to straighten things out (which, of course, agitated everyone on Earth). Nevertheless, once the decision had been taken to intervene, skilled angels would be commissioned to manoeuvre events discreetly and unobtrusively. Aware that, eventually, the affected humans would conclude that the resultant, if somewhat baffling outcome of their bungling was simply down to good fortune. This being how it tended to look from the human perspective. And today was one of those days.

Which meant Michael himself was called upon not only to plan, but to lead a 'clean-up' exercise. And in this case, he was going to have to boost his forces with a battalion of the elite Praetorian Guard. Problem was, in more recent centuries, any direct involvement by Michael had always managed to trigger uproar in Hell. Well, that was after the various satanic spies deployed for the sole purpose of covering divine operations had woken up to what was actually going on. In truth, given any halfway intelligent undercover agency, significant intervention from Heaven should have been easy to spot and even simpler to anticipate. It was straightforward – although Arcturus was not about to admit anything — his 'loose cannon' act had comprehensively breached protocol, causing alarm bells to ring in both kingdoms.

For days now, I had been heading in a decidedly unethical direction or, more specifically, rushing headfirst towards a criminal and totally unscrupulous finale, probably one that was going to end in my own abrupt termination. A state of affairs over which Israfel was fully (and painfully) aware. More importantly, as far as he was concerned, was that he'd been effortlessly outflanked and comprehensively beaten to the draw on practically every development in my recent sorry progress. And it didn't help that he'd also been forced to endure Arcturus' arrogant boasting. 'Arcturus the Great' (as he had begun to style himself) was busy regaling any passing putrescence with the story that he alone was responsible for the comprehensive humiliation of of one of Heaven's 'chosen'. An achievement, moreover, that had been accomplished in direct conflict with a rising star of the Angelic pantheon. An outcome clearly fashioned by his own unique powers, combined with a dazzling intellect, etc. etc.

True, Israfel had really only failed to anticipate my latest debacle. But, fortunately, the Archangel Michael himself was on the case, due not only to his concern for me, but a fatherly disquiet over Israfel. And I have to admit, it couldn't have been easy for either of them. One moment I was lost and spinning into a world of desperate sadness, the next bent on retribution; malevolent, implacable and driven by a misdirected purpose. Never mind every step on this route was followed by a precipitous fall back into gut-wrenching guilt and the pit of despair. Nor was this helped by Ahmed, who had directed his thugs to go after anyone connected with me. Quite sure that striking at friends, or family, would hurt, although at this stage, it was never going to stop me. But the distressing thing was, he couldn't be certain of this until after the Jouberts had paid with their lives. Something that not only caused me deep anguish, but for which I blamed myself entirely. Although I could, and did, post my suspicions anonymously to the local police station, I was left to strengthen my wavering resolve alone. With the Jouberts gone, and the Lescals understandably unsympathetic, I had nowhere to go, no one to turn to for help.

I hadn't known it at the time, but in the supernatural world there had been a lot riding on my reaction to these setbacks. My tribulations were being viewed as fitting opportunities to test and strengthen the boundaries of my character. All because I had been singled out for a particular destiny, as I was eventually to discover. Just like every other human, I had been prepared with suitable gifts and abilities before birth to fulfil my specific calling, but this calling remained contingent upon my willingness to assume the role. An entirely voluntary commitment. Yet here I was, once again setting off on a downward spiral, following the dangerous track of violent retaliation. So far having failed to grow into anything remotely resembling a genuinely compassionate or sympathetic individual capable of fulfilling his true destiny.

★★★

That morning there was a distinct buzz circulating Heaven's lower halls. The very atmosphere seemed to have caught the excitement, spurring the gorgeous and abundant birdlife into thrilling and extraordinary refrains that trailed upon the ear like warm honey. And all because Michael, that prince amongst angels, had been seen virtually dancing as he entered one of Heaven's vast amphitheatres, accompanied by a number of officers from the more prestigious of the Praetorian Guard regiments. Warriors rendered conspicuous by their efforts to look suitably stern. Battle-hardened angels every one, but individuals whom every inhabitant held in considerable awe and most longed to emulate. Never mind the thrill of actually being close to the most famous and perhaps the most beloved soldier of them all. Rumour was following upon rumour and the mansions, halls and galleries of Heaven had begun to seethe with a tangible exhilaration. Such was the perceived nature of the extraordinary occurrence that some were actually speculating this might be the start of what humans referred to as 'the end times' and if the gossip was half as informed as it purported to be, then they were all in for a period of considerable delight and satisfaction. Stern they might be, but even these warriors were spellbound as they waited, certain it would not be long before they learned the true nature of Michael's news and their assignment.

CHAPTER 70

As for the Archangel himself, he was still endeavouring, albeit unsuccessfully, to suppress his excitement and act with a little decorum as he swept into the hall ahead of his Guards. To those seasoned veterans it was obvious the Captain of the Lord's Host was privy to something stupendous, something breath-taking. Perhaps some battle plan guaranteed to overcome their arch-enemy or some far-reaching strategy to prepare Earth for its next phase. Often, they were the first to catch rumours about events in the Heavens, but clearly not this time. By reputation, Michael was calmness personified and no one could remember seeing him in this mood. Renowned throughout all time for his serene and unflappable demeanour, Michael was a warrior who had seldom put a foot wrong in his all-important role. But today things were different and calling them to order, eyes still sparkling with suppressed laughter, Michael let his gaze wander around the officers now crowded around him. Benefitting each individual in turn with the full wattage of his radiant smile.

Composing himself finally, Michael raised his hands to encompass each and every one of the Guards pressed around him, before beginning to address them; "Dear friends, fellow warriors, like me you take great pride in loyal service to the King of kings." Not a few backs stiffened in delight at this. "Today we find ourselves in momentous times and I know I can rely on your support. As you will all remember – how could any of us forget? – we've fought together on countless operations and served the Lord God against the enemy since Satan was first demoted from his position of 'first amongst equals' and thrown out of Heaven.

Now I know all of you, like me, have looked forward to the Great Day of Judgement, promised from the moment Satan fell from power. That Day when humans and demons alike are to be judged for what they have or haven't done and, for our part, we are then to submit ourselves to the authority of the redeemed humans. That Day, when we'll all discover just how merciful the Son of God is towards those who, throughout their lives, have gone on believing in His name and accepted His offer of eternal life. Just as important, that is also the Day when Satan and his misbegotten whelps will finally have to face the full measure of their defeat. Well, today I can confirm that particular Day has come a giant step closer. The exact timing has yet to be divulged – it is for our Father alone to know – but His Son Jesus has commanded us to begin final preparations amongst the human race for that great event.

"As you know, He intends one day to return to their world to take up His long-promised role as the Supreme Sovereign of the planet. But that doesn't mean we are relieved of the restraint there's always been on sparing fallen angels whom we don't defeat or kill in actual combat. For the time being, whether we find them here in Heaven or out on Earth, God still intends to leave sufficient of them around to provide the human race with clear alternatives. So, human free will is to remain sacrosanct and whether their choices are good or bad, it's entirely up to them. That said, we can rejoice unreservedly because the time when the Son of God will return in person to govern His world with justice and with peace is getting closer. Be excited with me because, at last, we can begin to prepare for that time when, at the Name of Jesus, every knee in Heaven and on Earth and under the Earth will have to bow and every tongue confess that Jesus Christ is Lord, to the Glory of God the Father."

For a moment there was stunned silence whilst the enormity of what Michael was saying sunk in, to be swiftly replaced by a great roar of approval as a look of sheer rapture spread across every face in the serried ranks around their leader. Taking their cue from the senior Guard, each one of them snapped to attention, drew himself to his full, impressive height, unsheathed his great sword, brought the flashing hilt to his lips in the time-honoured salutation and dropped to one knee, lowering the tip of the sword to the glittering, glass-like paving in front of him as, together, they paid homage to their Lord and King. Praise rolled from their lips as a surge of anticipation rippled through the ranks, each contemplating the campaigns that lay before them, the myriad opportunities to support and prepare the human race, the privileged position they held as elite troops, with the exhilarating possibility of occasionally mixing it with the very worst of the satanic hoard. With a number of old scores yet to be settled, the very thought of what lay ahead had them practically salivating.

"Anyway, before you all get too caught up in trying to work out who pulls the best detachments, or how you get nominated for the more important operations, let's get some of the basics straight. Where's this all leading? Well, first and foremost, as I've already said, you are not being given 'carte blanche' to eradicate the enemy. Not yet, at any rate. So just forget the list of names you particularly want to encounter." Even though this had already been mentioned, a general groan accompanied Michael's reiteration of the point and some wry smiles were exchanged. No doubt about it, every one of them had at some time or other in the preceding eons enjoyed the thought of what they would like to do to certain demons, should they be presented with the opportunity to trap or kill them. Which brought them to the Commander's final revelation and, although of little surprise, it didn't particularly please them. "In fact, there is coming a time during which some of those monsters whom we've already dispatched to Abbadon are going to be allowed out again to hound the human race. But, as you know from your reading of the humans' Bible, whilst this amnesty will not last long, you will nevertheless need to remain particularly alert."

Michael knew they were professionals, so he pressed straight on into the usual deployment details and it didn't take them long to get down to some serious and specialised analysis of the situation. There was a lot to do and it was quickly evident that all Heaven was going to be placed on alert with them. A total war footing, no less. Which meant every angel would be involved one way or another. Even Heaven's human citizens would have a role to play. This was a whole new ball game and it was going to affect all creation, whether those living on Earth liked it or not. Moreover, such would be the scale of conscription, they could see they weren't going to be fighting in their usual units, but were going to have to share themselves out amongst the less experienced squadrons, as the best way to provide quality leadership throughout the force.

"And so the legions are being told, even as we speak, the names of their new squadron commanders, and that means I want you to get out there now and start introducing yourselves. You'll find the list of postings on Daily Orders at the back of the hall."

Slightly subdued by the practicalities, it was only now that they began to grasp the full impact of what Michael had been saying. Here was the realisation of so many dreams. Hopes they'd nurtured since time immemorial for the human race to be given over to peace and justice, and the expectation that Heaven and Earth would finally be brought together in genuine unity. So, greatly encouraged, they turned smartly to the right, saluted, fell out and massed around their Operation Orders. After which a stream of Guards could be seen heading out to the four corners of Heaven, each wondering what shape his new command was likely to be in, each ready to get stuck in. Leaving Michael to return to the particular problem represented by Israfel and yours truly.

CHAPTER 71

As the days fled by, the continued absence of Roz meant the great aching void of grief in my heart had simply darkened and deepened. Now, frozen in anguish, but strangely warmed by hatred, I would still have left town in a hurry if I'd had the slightest inkling of what was about to happen. Angry I might have been. Stupid I'm not. Well, that's my opinion anyway. I'd made it safely back into Mombasa after the disastrous foray into Ahmed's bolthole and was hunkered down with only misery for company in a shabby hovel that passed as a hotel in the black quarter of town. Trying to decide what to do next. I had no option with the room, because although my white skin stuck out like a sore thumb, I could at least guarantee freedom from police interference. And anything (so I thought) was better than exposure to the inevitable questions that would follow if I turned up without a verifiable address and without luggage in one of the more normal haunts for 'whites'. The Mombasa Club had its attractions, not least cold beer, but to book in I'd have to show some form of identity and that would be my downfall.

It was late, and I'd finally overcome my inhibitions sufficiently to lie down on what passed for a bunk in the sticky heat and thriving bug life of the stifling room I'd been allocated, when I heard what sounded like a fierce altercation starting up immediately below me. Either they were close or the walls were even thinner than I'd thought. Anyway, it wasn't long before the sound of heavy footsteps on the stairway drew rapidly closer and, pretty soon, I could make out individual voices, although what I heard made my blood run cold. It wasn't so much the words as the voice. A voice I'd have known anywhere. A voice whose owner I'd hoped never to encounter again. My old friend, the maniac with the sjambok. Panicked by the suddenness of it all and certain I had to get out, or be taken captive again, I turned and stepped rapidly over to the tiny opening in the wall doing time as a window. However, given that it wasn't even large enough to allow satisfactory passage to the incoming dust-laden air, I knew before it began that any attempt to exit that way was doomed. Which left only one option. To stand and fight. Frantically, I cast around the darkened room, looking for the one thing I'd retained that might do as a makeshift weapon. Jill's knitting needle; first pressed into service on the spear gun and since kept purely because I'd forgotten to return it. But necessity is, as they say, the mother of invention and armed only with this needle, I stepped back to the door just in time to get slammed to the floor as it burst in on me, hammered down by my erstwhile gaoler. A man who, in my frank opinion, was little short of a freak.

The blow practically knocked me cold and I hit the floor pinned down by the rough-hewn planks, while my assailant remained balanced atop the slab of a door, clearly enjoying my despairing groans as I fought for breath. Starved of oxygen, a condition that delivered an almost surreal confusion as I slipped in and out of consciousness, the last thing I remembered seeing was the almost luminous features of that smirking fiend leering down at me. The next thing of which I became aware was gasping for air as someone lifted the door away. But there was to be no respite. I was jerked unceremoniously to my feet by my worst nightmare, a creature so confident of his dominance that he didn't even bother to check me over. And that was his mistake. I think it was the despair I felt at being once again in this maniac's grip that strengthened my resolve. At any rate, realising I had only one chance, I deliberately relaxed into his arms, falling against him and causing him to shift his grip so he could employ both hands to hold me up. In doing so, he released my right arm and, thus freed, I was able to bring my right hand up in a swinging arc over my left shoulder holding the needle as far down the shaft as I could. To my intense satisfaction I felt, rather than heard, the point meet with some faint initial resistance before, with a decisive shove, I became aware that it was sinking through an almost liquid medium, which, it soon became obvious, was his eye. The scream had barely got started in his throat when it cut off into a strange gurgling sound as he began his last slide towards the floor, the end of the needle now slithering almost of its own volition deeper and deeper along the path taken by the optical nerve on its journey to the brain. Here it became firmly wedged before starting to interfere with even his basic thought processes. And by the time it was dragged out of my now redundant hand, his passing was almost unremarked and certainly unlamented. Except by his somewhat smaller associate, who took off as though all the hounds of Hell were after him, which, if I'd had my way, they would have been. By the time the landlord arrived from the downstairs bar to advise me in no uncertain terms what he thought of the goings-on in his 'high-class' establishment, I was well on the way to leaving. Picking up my few possessions hadn't exactly taken long, and stepping smartly around the somewhat unsightly form now spread-eagled on the floor and across the comprehensively demolished door, I made a dash for the narrow stairs, intent on leaving that apology for an inn well before anyone else with my demise in mind could catch up with me. Moreover, I didn't slow until I'd put what I believed to have been sufficient distance between the proprietor and myself to guarantee he wouldn't come in search of me. At least, not before daybreak.

But that left me with a more immediate problem. Where to find a place in which to hole up and, more crucially, what to do about the whole sorry mess? As far as I could tell in my frenzied state, nowhere was safe anymore. If Ahmed had been that keen on finding me, the resultant death of his very own mutant was going to make him even more determined to exact revenge. Clearly, I was firmly attached to the horns of a dilemma. There were only three choices: the police; run forever; or turn and face him down. The former was out. I couldn't run forever and if it was to be taking the fight to Ahmed, then reason dictated I needed things to be closer to my own terms, which meant I would have to reach him before he found me again. Pounding the streets that night, too frightened to stay in one place, I eventually reached the conclusion that the only rational course was, indeed, to face him down by striking first. All through the rest of that night I mulled over the matter until, eventually, early indecision hardened into utter determination. Determination to take on the fight wherever it might lead. Ahmed was the one posing the immediate threat and, since I'd failed to annihilate him, it would be only a matter of time before his thugs once again traced me. And neither they, nor any conceivable course of events dictated by Ahmed bore thinking about. But where and how to start? I had to assume that, by now, Ahmed knew about his thug's demise and would have had the common sense to ensure he was himself beyond harm's reach. After all, he had the means to pursue his aim from the shadows and, given what I'd already done (though with entirely the wrong result), he would undoubtedly be motivated to make sure he wasn't caught out again. And then straight out of left field, the spectre of Giuseppe stepped firmly into play.

CHAPTER 72

"Right, Israfel. Can't say I'm particularly happy with your recent efforts, or perhaps I should say lack of them. Paul's gone completely off the rails, admittedly not helped by that excrescence, Arcturus, whispering in his ear. However, since I admit you were sensible enough to return and acknowledge your failure, I've sweet-talked the boss. Which means you'll be pleased to know we're going to give you one more chance. Don't blow it this time. And whilst you're not being pulled off the job, I have no choice but to recommend you for some refresher training. Unfortunately, however, that's going to have to wait. We've got an unusual situation developing and I need you back on Earth to salvage something from the Paul affair."

Tamar, recently appointed as Israfel's immediate superior, eased himself away from the base of the exquisitely coloured and scented fig tree he'd been leaning against and eyed Israfel speculatively. As a senior commander, he knew far more than this recent promotee. His own briefing on the matter had been detailed and comprehensive. The orders were clear. Specially selected Guardians, Israfel amongst them, would shortly be given specific directives and guidelines. Selected, because they were about to be entrusted with an utterly vital role in the world's 'coming of age'. God had meticulously prepared the strategy, having brought to birth a number of specially equipped babies shortly after what humans called their 'Second World War' And now had come the announcement that it was time to start involving these young men and women who were to play their parts in the last chapter of human history.

The time known by Christians as 'the age of grace', a period of time that had so far lasted around 2,000 years, was destined to end in some pretty spectacular fireworks. Sensationally, the events Heaven's citizens found themselves discussing were precisely those foretold as forming the prelude to the final battle of Armageddon. The time when the whole human race would become involved in what was to be both a spiritual battle and a physical battle (whether they liked it or not). A war to end all wars. Together, the combined phases were expected to be a fairly protracted affair, lasting over a period of several decades. But now it seemed, the gun had been fired for the 'off'. The last and decisive confrontation between Heaven and Hell. And the angels already knew who would win. So now was the time for those designated humans to be offered their roles as ambassadors to the King of kings, assuming they really did want to engage with their destinies. And it was the Guardian angels who were to make themselves visible and known to their charges as a timely encouragement. Thereafter, assuming the right response, each Guardian would go on to befriend and prepare their human for his or her specific task. There was only one problem as far as Tamar was concerned. Was Israfel up to the challenge? He wasn't entirely sure, but there was nothing for it except to get on and brief him. Only time would tell.

Israfel was excited, as well he might be. Until only recently, he'd fully expected to be summarily dismissed from his post with a flea in his ear. Now here he was, not only reprieved, but chosen to pull off an elite Guardianship during the very time when some of the most thrilling and prophesied events in all human history were about to unfold. Invigorated and inspired, he felt that, at the very least, this called for a dramatic entry back onto the case. Which, to his immense satisfaction, had the quite distinct merit of catching Arcturus fairly and squarely on the hop. A pleasant change, he thought, given recent events. However, there was work to do, plans to be devised and results to be hoped for or, if necessary, engineered. All to ensure I not only survived, but would respond to God's overtures. Israfel was beside himself with delight as he realised just how free he was to influence me. An independence no other Guardians had been granted for as long as could be remembered. So, having checked Arcturus wasn't about to do anything foolish, Israfel gave careful eye to his surroundings. He saw immediately that quite a few things had changed since he'd last been on Earth. Particularly in the matter of demons. There were definitely a lot more of them in evidence. Apparently, they'd caught an inkling of what was about to happen, but since they couldn't be sure (and Israfel knew none of Heaven's plans had leaked), they were obviously trying to overplay rather than underplay their hand. Nonchalantly, Israfel sheathed his sword, stepped towards where I was still pacing in circles and, with a pointed stare in Arcturus' general direction, let it be known in no uncertain terms that he was back on the job and not about to be taken by surprise again.

Which did little for Arcturus. He knew he'd humiliated this particular angel and he knew that after losing out over a human charge, they seldom got reappointed. Which wasn't too much of a problem since he'd wanted to have a go at this Guardian ever since the 'dhow incident'. However, that didn't alter the question or the surprise. What was he doing back here? And why had this particular angel not only returned to Guardian duties, but even been assigned to the same human? Something unusual had to be going on, although he'd been unable to get any useful intelligence out of his disaster of a headquarters for some time. True, he'd become acutely aware that there were far more demons mixing it with humans than was customary, but that in itself was neither extraordinary, nor grounds for any particular alarm. He'd often detected fluctuations in the resources assigned both to Earth and to the battlefields of Heaven and, given the hellish incompetence he was used to, the present increase offered little surprise. But that said, why were these morons so disinclined to speak to him about what they were doing here? Why were the recent arrivals so obviously alarmed, yet without any real (or apparent) awareness of a changed situation? From where he stood, they seemed to be panicking around in ever-decreasing circles, getting nowhere. Not for the first time, he felt his own anxiety begin to mount alongside a conviction that, whatever the circumstances, he could do rather better than the current hierarchy. If only he was given half a chance. But the situation remained a puzzle and Arcturus didn't like puzzles. They had a nasty habit of getting you eradicated. But for now there were more important things to think about. How to take down this annoying angel for a start. Without risking a one-on-one challenge, which might prove fatal to him. Whereupon he realised, not for the first time, that he must be losing his nerve. And it would be tantamount to signing his own death warrant if he were to show any obvious weakness in front of this particular warrior.

At which point he caught Israfel looking pointedly in his direction. And being reasonably confident he only had to wait and I'd do something stupid enough to let him back into my psyche, Arcturus took pleasure in simply ignoring the glare.

CHAPTER 73

As soon as I saw Giuseppe I knew, beyond any doubt, that this was one of those splendidly fortuitous chances, and Ahmed could wait. I had to get the slaver, had to use this unique opportunity to exact revenge for many if not most of the woes of the past months. The sight of him had immediately forced the enormity of my loss to the fore. An emotion never far away, but one that scythed like a dagger through my heart, leaving that treacherous friend, bigoted motivation, to quickly excuse the murderous thoughts now bubbling to the surface. At the same time, assuring me I was also duty bound to avenge the suffering of the many. In fact, merely doing what anyone else in my position would do. Moreover, Giuseppe clearly hadn't clocked me. Probably didn't even realise I was alive, let alone in his immediate neighbourhood. Unless, of course, he'd been talking to Ahmed recently.

In the same instance, I also realised you just didn't get two such opportunities with a man like Giuseppe. Occasions when he was without the immediate protection of his bodyguards, or cronies. So, it had to be now or never – the real problem being, how to strike the first, decisive blow. I had no weapons and I certainly wasn't strong enough to prevail over him in any sort of fist fight. All I had was the element of surprise and the only way to keep that was to stay firmly back out of sight while I dreamed up some sort of realistic plan. In a hurry. As justification, I told myself I owed it not only to me, but also to Roz, to Malcolm and to Jill. Each of them. And with that thought supplanting all else, the genie finally came fully out of the bottle and a homicidal rage began to burn within me, leaving me to cast about in earnest for some way of terminating Giuseppe with prejudice and, hopefully, bringing about the downfall of his slaving organisation. A shift in mind-set that didn't go unnoticed in certain quarters. Hanging back a hundred paces or so, and eyeing each other warily, both Israfel and Arcturus had sensed my mood swing at almost the same time. The one with deep concern, knowing what was likely to happen; the other with all the fiendish delight that only a genuinely psychotic reprobate can enjoy. And that led to an immediate altercation between the two of them, because there was no way Israfel was going to allow Arcturus to influence me further, or drop any more poisonous thoughts into my mind. Nor was he disposed to back away from what was now an inevitable fight.

With the predictable result that both lunged for their main weapon at the same time, each fully conscious of what had happened on the previous occasion they'd come to blows. But even as he advanced, angling for an early thrust into the heart that would finish the matter, Arcturus felt the first scintilla of fear course through his veins. His only real mistake being to let it show in his eyes, because at once an exultant Israfel fell back, dropping his shield arm, feigning clumsiness and enticing Arcturus to follow. Beguiled, but also made reckless by gathering apprehension, Arcturus followed like an amateur, rather than the battle-hardened swordsman of innumerable confrontations with Heaven's warriors. And even as he pressed forward, he realised he had already opened himself to a fatal riposte. Skilled gladiators though they both were, each confident in their ability and each respectful of the other's dexterity, already one of them knew he had the edge. Ever light on his feet, Israfel continued to back-pedal, adding to his opponent's concern by dropping to one knee and feinting to his left, across the front of his shield, whose coruscating light was let loose without warning, causing an already half-mesmerised Arcturus to slightly overcompensate for the parry. Enough to give a skilled swordsman like Israfel the one opening he needed to finish the dual. And strike he did, but to Arcturus' consternation, only deep enough to disable his sword arm, before realigning the blade as fast as lightning, leaving Arcturus to stare down its glittering length, the point held unwaveringly just short of the bridge of his nose.

"So, Arcturus, defeated again. Not as good as you thought really, are you? You know full well I could obliterate you right now and that would ensure your immediate passage into Abbadon's custody. In fact, nothing would give me greater pleasure, but I'm going to spare you for the moment. I have a little job for you, which you will perform, whether you like it or not. And be under no illusion. Any hesitation from you, and Josephus will be advised of what you are planning with regard to his demise. Yes, we do know. Unlike you, we have the ability to read minds and, where necessary, we use that gift. I suspect Josephus would take great satisfaction in putting you to the sword, loathsome creature that you are. That is, shortly before he dispatched you to the place reserved for you and your ilk. A fate Josephus has already promised you, I hear. Yes, we also keep a close watch on Hell's activities. In fact, one way and another, we know everything there is to know about you. Whatever you do now, you're in it up to your eyeballs. Not only are you in trouble with your boss, but you've been tried and found guilty of treachery in Heaven, too. Abbadon's care is almost too good for you. So listen carefully unless you want to join him right now. And be assured, if I have to repeat myself, you certainly will." With which, Israfel began to outline the exact role Arcturus was to play in the immediate future.

★★★

Still pacing along the street behind where I supposed Giuseppe to be, I was beginning to get a little frantic. Forced to stay well back, it was a good five minutes since I'd last had clear sight of him, although having realised he was heading for Ahmed's shore-based hideaway, I'd been able to relax a little, believing I could anticipate the general direction. My difficulty was I could think of no possible scenario in which I would come off best. I simply didn't have the weaponry (a knitting needle would be about as useful as a snowball in Hell for this scenario). That is, until I rounded the corner at the next street junction and found myself facing an elderly gentleman being threatened at knifepoint by a much younger male who was not only weaving a fine-bladed flick knife back and forth in front of the old man's terrified eyes but, more importantly, was standing with his back to me.

It wasn't that I saw in this scenario a possible solution to my own problem, it was simply that I responded involuntarily, much as anyone might. Neither pausing to gather myself, nor even to consider the matter, I charged straight into the young assailant's back, knocking him to the ground before he had time to react. The knife skittered close to a nearby drain, but before I could gather myself, the youth had regained his feet and scarpered round the corner, as if on some powerful drug. Weakly, I picked up the knife with no intention other than to hand it to the old man, only to have him thank me profusely before himself taking off at high speed around the corner. Bemused, I stood in the middle of the pavement, a long-bladed and vicious-looking knife balanced in my hand while passers-by, oblivious to what had actually happened, looked somewhat askance as they hurried past, obviously under the erroneous impression that I was the one bent on robbery. Rather than stay there, an object of curiosity and concern to all, I hurriedly folded the blade and slipped the flick knife into my pocket, ready to resume my pursuit of Giuseppe.

I suppose I must have travelled several hundred yards before it dawned on me that I now possessed the very sort of weapon I had been hankering after. A razor-edged knife, easily concealed in the sleeve of my sweat-stained shirt. And round the far corner, nodding sagely, Israfel metamorphosed quietly from an old man back to an invisible angel in the prime of life. Leaving Arcturus to fret and fume with irritation, as he abandoned the persona of a young hooligan, to resume existence as a somewhat older, but now distinctly humiliated ruffian in his own right.

With my immediate difficulty sorted, I started to run, desperate to catch up with Giuseppe before he disappeared or reached the sanctuary of Ahmed's lair. It never occurred to me to be concerned over killing in broad daylight, or plain sight. That it might not be the smartest thing to do simply didn't enter my head. I was utterly intent on reaching my prey and couldn't have cared less about the aftermath. A mood that didn't alter one whit as, once again, I found myself drawing close to Giuseppe. Slowing immediately, I tried to bring my somewhat ragged breathing under control, but for some reason or other it wouldn't submit. Even in my confused state of mind, I knew that approaching someone from behind with feet slapping the pavement and breath heaving in and out in great grasps was likely to draw attention, never mind alert a weasel like Giuseppe. Fortuitously, albeit fairly slowly, my breathing came back under control, although, as I drew ever closer, my heart rate certainly didn't. However, it probably wouldn't have mattered what the circumstances were. I would defy any man who had once fallen victim to Giuseppe to approach him with equanimity, particularly when bent on mayhem. And there I was, yards from his exposed back, holding a concealed knife with intent. At which instant, he turned and looked straight at me, almost as though some sixth sense had warned him he was being stalked. I suppose I could, indeed I should, have retreated there and then, but something foolish within me wouldn't let me do this simple thing. As a result, I kept on walking, straight towards him, with what can only be described as a silly smile beginning to play on my lips.

"Hello, Giuseppe. Recognise me?" I'll give him his due. He didn't hesitate for a second. With one long stride he lunged towards me, left hand reaching for my throat, the other diving into his unbuttoned jacket. Which even I knew meant only one thing. He had a concealed weapon. Probably a pistol. Made suddenly swift by terror, I pressed the knife's catch and blessed all the powers that be that I'd been holding the knife the right way round. The blade flashed up at the same time as I swung my free arm forward, lunging desperately towards his gun hand. And even as I did so, the gun slid out from under his jacket, but the knife tip snagged him just below and to the side of the middle knuckle and since he didn't stop (couldn't stop!), the continued movement drove the blade straight through his hand.

Which did absolutely nothing to halt his headlong advance or palpable aggression. Caught up in the terror of the moment, I almost failed to register his hand releasing my throat, but out of the corner of my eye I did notice him beginning to juggle the weapon from the injured to his newly freed hand, obviously still intent on putting a bullet into my exposed chest. Sheer unadulterated fear made me desperate and lent me the strength to push the barrel to one side, whilst at the same time pulling back frantically on the knife as I sought to drag it out from between the bones of his right hand. The knife must have cleared his hand at about the same time as the gun went off, because within an instant of the blast, I felt the blade driving up between his ribs. A fact that a number of witnesses later assumed and affirmed to be self-defence. A fortuitous assumption I would do nothing to dismiss. All I could be sure of at the time, and am since able to remember clearly, is that the bullet somehow missed me, whilst Giuseppe deflated like a burst balloon. And even though I'd started the whole thing and had the advantage of surprise, the intense shock over yet another killing at such close range held me frozen in its grip, just long enough to be dragged to the ground by his weight, the knife having refused to come out of his chest. I doubt I spent more than a few seconds in this compromising attitude, but by the time I came to my senses and turned to run away, an excited crowd was already gathering. Which served merely to hasten my departure. A retreat made with the same sort of alacrity I'd observed in the young hooligan of recent acquaintance.

CHAPTER 74

Eventually, heaving lungs and leaden feet forced me to a stumbling halt. Still drawing great gulps of disagreeably warm air, I looked around, trying to get a bearing on where blind panic had led me. The crowds had thinned to a mere handful of disinterested traders sitting indolently in the tiny booths that lined the pavements, and from where they sold the ubiquitous African carvings made exclusively for tourists. Giving silent thanks, I realised I'd ended up not all that far from the Muslim Institute. An area I'd come to know reasonably well. So, with breath slowing by the second and the heated silence of a Mombasa noonday wrapping itself close around me, like a familiar blanket, my thought processes slackened to a more rational pace and I began to consider how best to lie low until the initial hue and cry had died down. To my mind, there was absolutely no doubt my exploits had either already reached the ear of the police, or they would quite soon and it wouldn't take long to get a description and put two and two together, undoubtedly making four in this case. There weren't many white boys with ginger hair in this neck of the woods and even fewer who were wanted for questioning. I had to get under cover, or risk everything, because there was no way I was giving up on my plan to destroy Ahmed. Giuseppe had been an unexpected bonus, but the real object of my hate was still out there. Still running his filthy empire.

So, with a last look around to make sure I wasn't being followed, I started angling for the back of the Institute, knowing its estate spilt out into one of the dense mangrove forests that flourished in the inter-tidal range lining the island's many creeks.

However, to get there I decided to follow what I hoped would be not only a reasonably direct, but also a prudently discreet route. Huge land crabs, poisonous sea snakes and who knows what else infested the swampy undergrowth, but it offered a haven in which a determined, or desperate, man could hide.

Fortunately, the tide was out and I was able to push deep into the marsh, stumbling over grotesquely tangled roots, struggling against the grip of a slimy combination of mud and sand, all the while trying to avoid an unholy mix of spiders, mud skippers, monitors, sea snakes and crustaceans various. Every step further into the mangroves virtually guaranteed an escalation in the buzzing, rasping and rattling going on around me as branches swayed and innumerable denizens of the quagmire swirled, hopped and swam frantically out of my way. Trying hard not to cut myself on the various molluscs clinging to the lower branches, I finally managed to reach the tideline, at which juncture I had no option but to turn my efforts upwards, climbing the most substantial mangrove I could find. Which inevitably meant slipping and sliding on the seaweed and limpet-draped limbs, until I was well above the obvious tideline. I knew I couldn't stay long, because sheltered from the sea breeze as the creek was, the heat was already oppressive and with no potable water available, my now well-developed thirst was unlikely to be quenched. However, I had to have time to think. To get the latent panic under control. To manufacture a plan that would get me out of my predicament. Difficult, without knowing anyone on the island, but not impossible. Somewhere there surely had to be a place I could hide more permanently, where I could avoid coming to the attention of law enforcement agencies. The problem was, where?

And this was precisely the opportunity for which Israfel had been waiting. Trapped, with little chance of doing anything beyond pondering my somewhat hopeless predicament and having to cling on tightly to prevent an untimely fall out of the thinning foliage of my chosen mangrove, preoccupation had rendered me defenceless. Moreover, like a number of the other Guardians around the world, Israfel had been specifically cleared by Michael to take advantage of just such a moment as this. Not to interfere directly, but to make himself known. But as Israfel had long since appreciated, I was highly unlikely to pay much attention until I had exhausted all other possibilities. Essentially, by reaching the end of my tether. Albeit, from my point of view, I felt nowhere near that. Unfortunately, however, no sooner had I found a sufficiently sturdy branch, dispatched the inevitable bugs and settled down with a reasonable likelihood of remaining in place, than my annoying conscience began to clamour for a hearing. And by clamour, I mean there was absolutely no chance of giving thought to anything else. This insistent demand soon resolved itself into a number of unanswerable questions: "*Just exactly what do you think you're doing?*" and "*Who do you think you are, acting as judge and jury?*" All tied up with going around shamelessly bent on killing whoever got in my way and, during all of this, being the immediate cause of catastrophe for the very people for whom I cared.

To my intense surprise and consternation, I actually began to burn with shame. For the first time in a long while I was thoroughly embarrassed, and it seemed there was nothing I could do to call a halt to this 'parade' of past crimes. Entirely involuntarily, scenes from preceding days began scrolling across my mind's eye, only to expand into what looked like just about everything I'd ever done wrong. Which meant I was soon persuaded that large chunks of my life had been an unmitigated disaster. All of this without as much as a 'by your leave'. Indeed, the completely uncalled for exercise in futility (as I supposed it to be) continued centre stage for what seemed an age, but was probably less than the time it takes to record. Leaving me both nonplussed and, at the same time, profoundly mortified. Guilty, even. A perplexity of mind I'd not experienced before and a state of affairs that didn't sit well with either my raging anger, or implacable resolve to go on killing. But the real shocker was that along with the display had come an insistent, eerie whisper, repeating over and over again; "Remember Roz? Remember Adam? Remember when you were in your cell, at the end of your tether? Remember the shark that missed you by just enough? Well, I was there all along." Now I knew I was losing it. Who on earth was 'I'?

★★★

Arcturus was having a bad day. Not only had he been shamed (panicked?) into a completely uncalled for metamorphous into human shape by his Angelic opponent's threats, but now he was being forced, through this freshly inspired Guardian's insolence, to stand back and watch a mortal (surely, one of his own) going through the very process all demons were programmed to fiercely oppose with every trick in their dark natures. There being a very good reason for such an arrangement. Profound self-examination by a human was rare, but when individuals actually got down to it, the result was too often a change of character or, at the very worst, a change of allegiance. In fact, it was one of the gravest of the infamous 'risk situations' demons had to face, when an individual could so easily slip out of control and go over to the Enemy. And if that happened, Arcturus could see what he considered to be his carefully nuanced plan for deposing Josephus going straight out of the proverbial 'window' and his suspended sentence coming straight back in. Too awful to contemplate.

So, following the incident in the street, he'd already gone out on a limb by swiftly calling in on HQ in an effort to ingratiate himself with one of Satan's many personal aides. The intention being to drop Josephus in the proverbial, ahead of time, through a subtle word about the reasons (and even likelihood) of failure over the matter of Paul, and the role played by his irritating boss. Also, with any luck, to arrange some support for when things got out of hand, as he now felt they were bound to do. But to his astonishment, he'd discovered Satan already knew about the Moncton case and was actually prepared to release some of his own personal protection squad to assist. But never mind the reason because now, with a little luck, he could still see his devious scheming coming to impressive fruition and wouldn't that be one in the eye for Josephus. And his peers. Although right now, back in the field and sensing that if he didn't get involved fairly soon, something would go irretrievably wrong, Arcturus had started edging towards me. At the same time easing his sword from its scabbard, just in case there was any sudden attack. Despite a weather eye on Israfel, one never knew when or where an assault might materialise. But for now there seemed to be only the one preoccupied angel.

Which Israfel undoubtedly was. In fact, he was entirely focused on what was running through my mind. Which meant he, too, was nervous. But for very different reasons. As far as Israfel was concerned, I was about to get as open to 'matters spiritual' as I was ever likely to be, and thus the moment could hardly be more propitious from his point of view. All that was left to be done was determine the most auspicious moment for materialising beside me, and do it in a way that wouldn't cause me to fall headlong off my perch in fright. Since he'd already been whispering in my ear, he assumed that I was at least alert to the possibility of there being someone else around. Actually, had he but realised it, there was no way on this Earth I was going to avoid practically wetting myself if another being appeared right alongside me in my tree, being under the reasonable impression, no, knowing, I was alone.

CHAPTER 75

Even a novice, be he angel or demon, should have seen the next move coming, never mind an old hand like Arcturus. But uncharacteristically, he completely missed it. Too busy trying to slip in under Israfel's guard, he managed to blunder straight into the troop of elite legionnaires that had just been mobilised to assist Israfel. Materialising right alongside him, each one immediately donned a grateful smile on realising exactly who they'd got surrounded. Furious, Arcturus slammed his massive bulk into the angel nearest to his only escape route and fast footed it away, pirouetting like a pro to avoid several flashing blades intent on skewering him like a kebab or, worse still, separating him from his head. Surprisingly, they all missed. Nonetheless, satisfied that the immediate area around the mangrove swamp was now secure and with the excitement of the unexpected engagement quickly over, discipline reasserted itself and they spread swiftly out to ensure an all-round point defence.

Grateful, Israfel turned back, to continue with the process of making himself known to me and, to give him his due, even he felt the least he could do was materialise in a position from which he could be usefully employed catching me, if it came to that. Hence his sudden appearance about three feet below and to my right, which, as you might imagine, still managed to raise my heartbeat well above safe levels. For at least the succeeding five minutes! Although, by great good fortune, I already had my left leg and foot firmly wrapped around the trunk. This being the sole reason I didn't immediately pitch headlong into the mud below.

What's more, the apparition spoke! "Paul, don't be afraid, I'm here in peace. Believe it or not, I've been looking out for you. In fact, I'm your Guardian angel and my name is Israfel."

Which (apart from being a pretty naff opening gambit) was about as effective at slowing my racing heart as a lukewarm snowflake might have been in cooling Hell. Although, what I didn't know was that my galloping heart was, indeed, having an effect on Hell. A desperate Arcturus was even then trying frantically to mobilise the promised help, which, for reasons best known to themselves, had been extremely slow in getting out of Hell and into East Africa. The phrase 'don't you know there's a war on?' did occur to Arcturus, but he'd commanded too many of Hell's Squadrons to bother wasting time, or sarcasm, on the horde now beginning to muster almost casually in front of him. Even the officer in charge wouldn't have recognised the sarcasm, never mind the troops. Instead, he busied himself with cursing them roundly and driving them straight towards the angels he'd just evaded, whilst guaranteeing them an early plunge into Purgatory if they didn't achieve what he wanted. Namely, a distraction in the Angelic ranks, so he could get in close to either completely blindside or, at the very least, confuse me, before it was too late (in his biased view).

And in point of fact, he did have a modicum of success, despite their poor showing. Elite legionnaires the Angelic squad certainly were, but even they could be prone to complacency. They'd seen off the only opposition, hadn't they? No one else around, was there? And they weren't used to demons being able to organise anything, so when what looked like a complete regiment of satanic fighters suddenly exploded around them, it was enough to disconcert even those seasoned warriors. Almost, but not quite. Which meant that, although the arriving mob failed to carry the day, Arcturus was able to take advantage of the general mayhem by sneaking in under the radar, while everyone else was preoccupied. Fortunately for their Commander's peace of mind, the angels took very little time to regroup and even less to sort out a counter-attack, which, when it materialised, at least managed to ensure that honours were even by the time the two sides drew apart to take stock. Actually, there were quite a few casualties on both sides, not that the demise, or wounding of any of his troops meant anything to Arcturus. He was just infuriated that even Satan's own specially selected legionnaires had failed to carry the day, despite holding the advantage of surprise. Admittedly, they were better than those with whom he was normally burdened, but that cut little ice, because he could still feel the dread of his commuted sentence curling around him. Nevertheless, he had managed to get close enough to hit me with a degree of mind control, with the sole purpose of persuading me to reject outright any overtures from the Guardian even then introducing himself.

Fortunately for all concerned, it wasn't long before Arcturus was compelled, by force of arms, to retire to a safer distance – thus releasing me from his malign manipulation, which I neither understood, nor recognised as such. I simply assumed I was (to put it mildly) confused, rattled even, and that there was really nothing more to it. But it wasn't that simple. Certainly, the overt influence telling me to ignore what I could plainly see had gone, but, even with a lot of blinking on my part, there yet remained a rather tall, muscular young man positioned just below and to my right, apparently still performing the mildly disturbing trick of standing in mid-air without the benefit of any obvious attachments. Moreover, and to my intense confusion, he persisted in looking straight into my eyes, whilst exhibiting a noticeable relish for the act. Not only that, but he started speaking again.

"There's quite a lot I have to tell you. However, first, you need to understand that although I look more or less like you right now, the fact is I'm very different and I'm not normally visible to human eyes. I'm an angel [*No. Really?*], I'm already immortal and

I live in other dimensions. What's more, I have a number of powers you humans don't possess. One reason I'm able to stand here in mid-air, for instance. But, I can see you need a bit more convincing and I don't blame you. Fact is, we angels do exist and we're active in your world, even if very few people believe in us. You don't know it, but, for this last couple of years I've been your Guardian. Now, I realise you won't find anything I have to say particularly easy to accept, but I would be extremely grateful if you could do me a favour and suspend your disbelief long enough to hear me out. After all, what have you got to lose? Right now, short of leaving this tree – and please note, the tide is coming in – you're rather stuck with me. So, if you'll do this one thing, I promise that when I'm done, I'll leave you completely free to make up your own mind on whether or not I'm to be trusted. And if you do decide to trust me, then you can consider what, if anything, you want to do about it. On the other hand, if you don't like what you hear and genuinely don't want me around, then I'll disappear back to my own world, get myself relieved of duty and leave you to get on with life."

"*Fat chance!*" I thought.

"So, let's cover some of the events that have been going on around you over these last few months. When I'm done, whether you choose to believe me, or not, and whatever action you decide to take, it will be of your own volition. OK? Right, where to start?" And so began a lesson on the contrasting physics of Earth and Heaven, the place that, as he put it, "is considered by your philosophers to be 'up there', 'out there' or 'beyond understanding'".

"When I leave Heaven to act as your Guardian, I simply limit myself to a dimension just one beyond your ability to comprehend. From there I not only see all that is going on in your world but, if and when I get approval, I'm able to directly affect activities around you. For instance, do you remember when you went to commit suicide? How you were torn by thorns in your mad dash to your secret place, convinced that somehow, in doing so, you would be able to make amends to Matt? How you placed that urine-spattered rifle barrel in your mouth by the waterhole, found a stick to activate the trigger and were then frustrated by a slip-up around the trigger guard, before being cut short by a command to stop? That was me. So when I show myself to you, as I am doing right now, all it means is I have simply stepped into a dimension you understand. But now for the difficult bit. There's a Supreme Being who not only created all of this, but who keeps the whole thing ticking over. You've heard Him referred to as 'Almighty God'. He not only cares about His universe, but He's particularly concerned for every single human being. Every single one. And that, of course, includes you."

Well, up to that point, I was with this being, this 'talking angel'. I have to admit that, despite myself, I had not only been more or less convinced (how else, other than if he was telling the truth, could he have known such intimate details regarding my suicide attempt?), but I'd also been spellbound. In truth, since first Matt's, and then Roz's death, I'd been aching for something, someone, to distract me and take the edge off the deep and abiding guilt, coupled with pain that was eating my soul. True, Roz had been a brief and wonderful respite. For a few giddy weeks she had been the solace, the source of healing I so desperately needed. Then just as suddenly she was gone. Perhaps it was because of her death, perhaps because of his reference to a caring God, but all at once I was overwhelmed by a powerful sense of revulsion, a burgeoning disgust against this being, whoever He might be, welling up from somewhere in my innermost core. All combined with a clear, bewildering but unprovoked resolve to reject everything I was being told. Where it came from, I had no idea. The only thing I did know was that I was listening along quite happily until, suddenly, I found myself hit by an overpowering feeling of nausea, as if something unclean had invaded my conscience. Which was weird because, from the first moment of his manifestation, I had somehow known, deep down, that the being revealing himself in front of me was fundamentally good and, as far as I could tell, nothing had changed. So why the unexpected revulsion?

CHAPTER 76

By then Arcturus, the author and perpetrator of that bewildering and untimely emotion, was getting desperate. He knew exactly what would happen if he lost me to the Enemy, and it didn't matter which way he looked at it, the result wasn't going to be pretty. So, frantic to get within range and start countering whatever ideas Israfel was putting in my head, he had been forced to let caution go to the winds and accept the risks inherent in metamorphosis. His problem was that, when Israfel had assumed human form, although he'd made himself vulnerable through loss of supernatural status, he had also been forced to abandon the advantage possessed by all such beings – that of extrasensory perception. So since everything was now operating purely on human terms, Arcturus was unable to hear or even guess at what Israfel was saying. Until and unless he followed Israfel into the same configuration and then positioned himself within human audio range. Accordingly, he needed to quickly field some diversion or other, if he was to stand any hope of distracting the squad of angels looking for him. He knew full well they were determined to take him down, or at the very least make sure he stayed out of the reckoning.

Besides, being forced to adopt human form would make him vulnerable and thus easy prey. So he needed allies. And quickly, if he was to save the day and avoid the torment of an early meeting with Abbadon. But his troops, most of whom had already adopted human form (they always got such a kick out it), were all out of voice range – and 'out of range' spelt trouble. It had been a long time since he'd been obliged to direct troops by yelling at them, but he could think of no other way to acquire their immediate attention. Other than by abandoning his strategic location long enough to reach their assembly point, which would, inevitably, expose him to unwanted attention. Frustrated, he nevertheless accepted that if he abandoned 'Plan A' and managed to get the troops back into the supernatural realm, he couldn't thereby guarantee they'd catch, or even recognise any subliminal message anyway. That was the trouble if you were a demon. The other side had long since commandeered the pick of the telepathic frequencies and with a force of angels nearby, the place would be alive with extrasensory traffic. So there was nothing for it, but to resort to the kind of histrionics he'd long considered beneath his dignity. Ignoring, for the moment, that any call would be tantamount to shining a beacon onto his exact position. His bellow, when it came, temporarily achieved the aim and, with their attention caught, Arcturus signed his troops back into battle with urgent chopping motions of his hands.

Hoping for the best, he turned back to the task in hand. And so absorbed did he become as he once again crept carefully under the mangroves towards Israfel, that he entirely failed to keep a check on his 'six o'clock', or developments back on the battle line. Until it was far too late. The first point at which he recognised the stupidity of this tactic was when his fate was effectively sealed by the arrival of a great silver chain dropping its loops and coils around his neck, arms and legs. What's more, he had no sooner felt its cold embrace than, disconcertingly, the chain started acting like a living entity. Draped around his extremities, this apparently living chain began to rearrange itself, drawing ever tighter, each link shrinking in upon itself, until he was held securely but comfortably in what felt like a friendly, almost discreet embrace. But one that also prevented him escaping into any other dimension. Not that he didn't immediately attempt resistance. From which point, all comparison with moderation ceased, because the more he struggled, the tighter the chain drew and nothing would persuade it to loosen. Which meant the constricting pressure around his chest soon began to leave him in despair of life itself. Supernatural or otherwise. Finally, when he'd stopped twisting and turning long enough to consider his position, he found he was not only held fast, but surrounded by the very angels he'd been trying to avoid. All of them regarding him with contempt, tempered by amused satisfaction. Which did absolutely nothing for his ego. Snarling, Arcturus tried one last despairing twist to loosen a hand sufficiently to grasp at a dagger dangling from his sword belt, but the result was inevitable. The chain simply pulled itself even tighter. Defeated, he had to content himself with spitting a stream of imprecations at the angel captain, although that gesture of defiance achieved little, as a strange sort of cover was immediately thrown over him from behind. A shroud that had the double effect of reducing his vision, much as a pair of dark sunglasses might, and silencing him, thus foiling any further hope of interfering. Neutralised, Arcturus could only rage impotently, although, had he but known it, the act was almost a kindness as the angels knew what was coming in the form of annihilating light. Seething though he might be, he'd heard of these living chains that the angels sometimes used, albeit, never having seen one, he could only guess as to its abilities. Nor had he ever been subjected to one of these humiliating masks. The devious gadgets the angels sometimes used were spoken of with awe and loathing, although not often from experience. At any rate, no one was ever known to have escaped once confined and he assumed it was now only a matter of time before he was filleted. But even as he considered this, he found himself thrust unceremoniously forward in the general direction of Israfel. At least, this was what he supposed, as he could now distinctly hear if not clearly see all that was passing between the boy and the Guardian.

★ ★ ★

"I'm sorry. What were you saying?" I couldn't grasp why, but for a moment I felt as though I was surfacing from a bad dream. One moment I'd been fascinated by the sight and sound of a young man floating effortlessly in front of me. The next, revolted. And now here I was seemingly my own man again. At any rate, the revulsion and queasiness had left and I was immediately able to concentrate on this rather appealing figment of my imagination. Only, when I thought about it, there didn't seem to be much of the 'figment' about him. Moreover, I had to admit, he knew more than he should do about my attempt at suicide. And how could he possibly know? I'd only talked to Roz about it and she hadn't had the opportunity to pass anything on, even if she'd wanted to. So, clearly, I was faced with all the makings of a first-class dilemma.

At which point the apparition said, "Right. I'm going to leave you now, as you clearly have enough information to be getting on with. However, I won't be far away and I'd be rather grateful if you could give everything currently surging through your mind some careful thought." Why was it that, far from being reassuring, his words and immediate departure actually meant I became even more agitated than before? I just knew he'd looked into my somewhat messy and embarrassing mind and had seen everything. Which did absolutely nothing for my composure. And not very much for my rather precarious balance, either.

Surprisingly enough, given what had just occurred, the ensuing silence found me revisiting the rather chaotic and depressing thoughts that had been filling my mind immediately before the apparition had appeared. But what to make of his claims? I really didn't know. However, what remained uppermost in my mind was a parade of my more obnoxious ideas, pretentious attitudes and regrettable actions. Leaving me less than ecstatic, as they once more marched across the landscape of my mind, clamouring for review. And the sum of their parts was unnerving, consigning me to that trio of monsters, namely: shame, embarrassment and, quite frankly, utter dismay at what my life had become. Slowly, the ever-widening range of thoughts began to crystallise into a totally unfamiliar and, to me at least, singularly alien concept of wickedness. Or sin. Where did that word come from? And then I remembered. Roz and our discussion immediately prior to her death. Which startled me, to say the least. Because I also remembered, somewhat inconveniently, the context within which she had been exploring her thoughts. And her exact appearance, her serenity, peace almost, in the moment of death. And then there was Adam. Plus all those times when hope had appeared out of nowhere, even when I was banged up in solitary. It was all rather confusing. Until, underneath it all, at the very back of my mind, there emerged the kernel of an insistent thought. *Absolution.* Some sort of 'get out' clause. Resilient I might be, but the parade of unattractive events that now populated my thoughts was starting to convince me even I might need some sort of pardon. Essentially, some form of decontamination that would sanitise me from the overpowering sense of guilt that was eating into my psyche. Some relief from the creature that had stared back at me while looking deep into what I suppose you might call my 'soul'. Believe me, self-examination really isn't all it's cracked up to be, even if you are recommended to undertake it by the local 'trick cyclist'. Start the process and demoralisation can follow all too easily. One minute you're nodding along in agreement, quite happy to wander about in the past; the next you discover you're concentrating purely on the bad bits. Infinitely too aware of your 'secret' self and, inevitably, finding yourself cast in a far from perfect light.

Coupled with which, I now found myself recalling something of what Adam had said about the God he believed in, or was it the Jewish Messiah, the one they called Jesus? At any rate, someone – presumably Jesus – had apparently taken the bad things I'd done (my sin?) and paid the penalty that I should be paying. Because this God, who was evidently good, expected us, His creatures, to build our lives around Him, on pain of being found guilty when judged, if we hadn't. In fact, I was beginning to recollect with rather too much clarity exactly what Adam had been telling me, even if I hadn't been ready to accept it. He'd actually asserted that this Jesus had put himself in harm's way, accepting death voluntarily on a Roman cross, so anyone who acknowledged this sacrifice as being offered on their behalf could benefit in life as well as in death. Well, that hardly made sense. As far as I could remember, it had all taken place around 2,000 years ago. So how could it possibly apply to me? And yet – And yet –.

Could there really be any truth in it? Adam had said it was definitely true, because it was too good not to be. And he was certainly clear about the matter. Since the moment he'd decided to respond to this strange invitation and actually asked this Jesus person to meet him, he'd apparently been astounded by the life changes he'd experienced. But what he remembered first and foremost, was the way he'd been made to feel completely clean, inside and out, the moment he'd accepted this one-way offer. Apparently the guilt he'd often felt and the shame regarding some of his less savoury habits all went at the same time. Taken clean away, by all accounts. A result that made him particularly glad when it came to remembering the way he'd sometimes treated his long-suffering foster parents, amongst many others. Moreover, as the months had passed, he'd discovered certain other aspects had also been cleaned up. Not that he'd experienced amnesia exactly, but unless he deliberately revisited bygone affairs, or made a particular effort to recall them, they no longer bothered him in quite the same way as before. He somehow knew he'd been forgiven, discovering he'd also acquired a new friend who, at some subliminal level, had promised never to leave him, no matter what happened. Which was weird, but he claimed it had changed his whole outlook for the better and given him purpose. Particularly after he'd been taken captive.

CHAPTER 77

As far as Israfel was concerned, this was definitely one of his better days. In fact, things seldom came any better. He'd carried out his orders to the letter, made himself known to me, pointed out that if I was at all interested, I'd have to take the next step myself and imparted just sufficient of the bare facts for me to make a decision. Which apparently meant expressing regret for the bad things I'd done (he'd stressed I was actually required to mean it) and inviting Jesus to take over where I'd singularly failed. Job done, he'd stepped away for now, back into more familiar dimensions. But not without checking to make sure Arcturus was firmly secured, with his minions out of the picture. That scabrous bunch had departed the fix the moment they'd seen Arcturus captured. Which had come as no surprise to the angel team, although it didn't stop them keeping a weather eye out for further violence. So now Israfel could content himself with watching from the side-lines, knowing I was protected, temporarily at least, from further attack.

★★★

As for me, things weren't quite that good. In fact, I was well on the way to feeling thoroughly miserable. I think the enormity of what I'd gone through and done was really beginning to bite. I'd been here before, of course, but this time it all seemed rather different. The problem was, on this occasion it looked like I had to make a choice. I could either carry on as before and try to work my own way out of this mess, or I could grasp at the lifeline

I was evidently being offered. Well, that is if I actually believed what I was rapidly beginning to consider a figment of my overwrought imagination. And, had I but known it, this was exactly why Israfel had withdrawn. I had to work out my own salvation (although I certainly wouldn't have called it that), in pretty much the same way as any other human. It was one thing to have an apparition standing in front of you claiming he knew all about you and offering a 'get out of gaol free' card. It was quite another to balance on a precarious branch in a mangrove swamp, endure the stultifying heat of a windless coastal day and examine your own belief system whilst unconstrained by said alien. I don't know how long I struggled with this dilemma, but I do recall finally deciding to at least give his suggestion a go. In any case, it fitted with something that had been bothering me for some time. Sometime after listening to Roz on the beach, watching her serenity in the face of death and returning again to the hard evidence of Adam's clear conviction, I'd drifted towards a readiness to investigate their claims for myself. And clearly, this not only presented an obvious opportunity, but the angel had delivered a rational explanation for my friends' confidence. Besides, no one else would know if it all turned out to be a mistake. So I promised myself, if nothing came of it, I would simply forget the whole issue and get on my way, not quite rejoicing, but at least content that I'd given it my best shot. It was as woolly, but as resolute as that. The only problem being, I hadn't yet met the One who really cared about me and knew nothing about His determination to rescue me, and issue an invitation to become a fully paid-up member of His kingdom.

★★★

Israfel was beginning to realise that, actually, his day could get a whole lot better. He'd been concentrating on watching and evaluating my thought processes, trying to guess the likely outcome (even he wasn't privy to the exact timeline concerning my future) and had noted with considerable satisfaction that I was at last getting around to making some sort of a decision. Influenced, he noticed, not so much by his recent appearance, as by the sum of my experiences with other humans. A little snippet to be borne in mind for the future. Slightly crestfallen, he was just considering his next move, when a stentorian voice like the sound of some immense waterfall announced from immediately behind him. "Angels! Behold, your King!" And with that, all thought of my dilemma passed from his mind as he snapped to attention, wheeled around and started looking for the source of the commotion. Which, given the awe-inducing glare of intense white light that had suddenly burst around him, wasn't difficult. And Israfel knew there was only one source of such a light and thus it could only mean one thing. The imminent arrival of the Son of God and, since he stood directly in the path of the radiance, the Supreme Commander was obviously coming his way and from no great distance, either. Electrified, he hastily genuflected, snatching at his sword in an effort to pay the proper respects.

And as he did so, a rich, compassionate yet gentle voice reverberated in his ear; "Rise, Israfel, and come with me. We are here to welcome your charge into our Kingdom."

Hardly daring to believe that he was actually being invited by Royalty to witness first-hand an act of redemption that would set all Heaven rejoicing, Israfel rose quickly to his feet, hurriedly sheathed his sword and swung in behind Jesus, adjusting deftly to the measured pace of the Praetorian Guard. Proudly, he looked at me, his ward, still balanced in the tree, just beyond the King, who was now almost dancing as he hastened forward with outstretched arms, as if to both support and encourage my first hesitant steps of faith. Truly, this was love on display, and by now the penetrating, mysterious light was even spilling into Earth's sphere, bathing me in a pure, if unearthly, radiance. It was no wonder the King of Kings was always trying to communicate the power of love to his children, Israfel thought. It was the coinage of the Realm, the one supreme, irresistible and enduring force in the universe. No other emotion was powerful enough to overcome it, as disconcerted citizens of Hell were forever discovering for themselves. Swiftly now, the King leaned forward to wrap His arms around me and to whisper in my ear. Words that I can never repeat, although Israfel was also privileged to be within earshot. Tears of joy spilled from us both as we listened. King Jesus welcomed me home as only He could. Pouring overwhelming love into me, a destitute and arid soul positioned awkwardly in front of the King of kings.

I didn't fully appreciate it at the time, but my earnest prayer (despite myself, that's what my first tentative enquiry had become) was fully answered. To my astonishment I knew, intuitively, that Jesus was there. I heard subliminally, but saw no one and couldn't have articulated, or described what was happening. But at an instinctive level I recognised, suddenly and beyond any shadow of a doubt, that not only was the past forgiven, but I had been cleaned up and welcomed into my rightful inheritance. So real was the feeling that, for a moment, I truly felt as though I had come home. I felt safe. And, at the same time, something within me wanted to prostrate myself and acknowledge my insignificance, my utter inadequacy before this Jesus, the very one Adam had described. Only the precariousness of my location prevented the gesture.

CHAPTER 78

I'll give him his due. Israfel at least had the decency to back off for a few minutes while I attempted to sort myself out. It wasn't easy. I was by turns trembling, euphoric, excited and painfully aware of the fragility of my perch. Still clinging to the tree like a limpet, I was using a body that was convinced it had been subjected to at least a million volts. But strange as it might seem, that wasn't what was uppermost on my mind. What was concentrating my thoughts were the changes I noticed taking place within the secret me, the soul.

Deep down, I knew I was undergoing the most profound, the most overwhelming transformation of character, although none of it was against my will. It wasn't easy to put into words, but it seemed as if somehow I had metamorphosed from a chrysalis into a butterfly and I was loving it. I didn't know how, but judging from a new lightness of spirit, freedom from guilt and conviction that things had definitely altered for the better, I had to admit something of the utmost significance had just happened. Exactly as Adam had predicted, way back on the dhow. His assertion that when I was genuinely ready to acknowledge God's existence, when I actually wanted the rescue package on offer, and when I was prepared to prove it by asking forgiveness for my past misdemeanours and invite Jesus into my life, He would respond. And He had. Uncanny but, given Adam's character, somehow unsurprising. He had laid it all out for me. Nevertheless, I will admit, I really hadn't believed him. Until, that is, the last episode with Roz, the memory of her Moiben encounter and a number of other recollections had me pinned down and wavering, like a rat in a trap. Forced up against reality. And now God had responded and, for the time being, that was enough.

Which brought me right back to the immediate and the company of a rather persistent angel. Angel? Yes, suddenly I found I did believe in such beings. "You'll probably be surprised to know that for some reason or other, I trust you now."

"Don't worry, I know. I've been watching you and listening in on your thoughts," came the nonchalant reply.

Oh, great. Not only capable of parking himself in mid-air but able to read thoughts as well. This was something I was obviously going to have to get used to – although even as I began to think it through, I realised he must always have been able to read my mind, whether I had been aware of it or not. And suddenly, I was beetroot with shame.

Israfel laughed. "Forget it. I've been around long enough not to pay much attention to your less wholesome thoughts and, before you get there, very few of your actions embarrass me either. Besides, the Son of God has forgiven you everything that lies in your past. He's taken the guilt and shame associated with your sin, for that's the name God uses to identify human wickedness, and accepted it as his own. He's able to do this because, like I told you, He paid the penalty that justice demands for every immoral act, or thought, ever committed. Remember what you did to Fatih? Even that's been forgiven by God, although human laws must still run their course. Jesus has cleaned you up and He promises your crimes will never be mentioned again, unless you choose to revisit them. Your sin was dealt with at the Cross and that really is the bottom line. Metaphorically, Jesus took the place of every human who's ever lived because, since Adam and Eve were created, not one of you could prove your innocence before God's Supreme Court of Justice. And there's a long story behind the whys and wherefores associated with that, which I'll tell you one day, when you're ready. Anyway, that death on that Cross was the most important event that's ever happened in your world. It was the turning point to all human history. God, who is both judge and jury, having found you humans guilty, is also the one who went on to pay the due penalty. That way his sense of justice, his integrity, is satisfied. Which means the consequence for all human sin has been taken by Jesus, the Son of God, after he'd shown the world by living as a man on Earth that it is possible to live a completely innocent human life. All every other individual has to do is accept this. Difficult, I know, because pride gets in the way. But it's the same for any and every human who's ever lived.

"Get over yourself, accept Him and He is able to give you a place in His eternal Kingdom. Understand that God is what is called 'holy'. In other words, He is pure beyond anything you can understand and so nothing unholy, or sinful is able to live with Him in Heaven. But He created you humans to enjoy Heaven with Him and, because of His love, that intention has never changed. Which meant He had to find a way to vindicate you lot. Something He did 2,000 years ago in Israel. And just now I had the privilege of watching as He approached you with this free gift. But understand this. When you accepted, He also gave you two other important gifts. First, faith in Him, to help you really get into this new phase of life. Secondly, His Spirit, known as the 'Holy Spirit'. The person who is prepared to draw alongside and remain with you, to help throughout the rest of your life. Which benefits me too, I might add, since I now get the advantage of the Spirit's direct insight and wisdom in your affairs. Anyway, you're one of His people now, unless you choose to walk away, because you haven't and never will lose your ability to make a free choice. And you should also know that eons ago God prepared a special place for you in Heaven. A place that is dazzling beyond your imagination. And it's all yours if you'll go on believing in His Son. You're now the beneficiary of everything Heaven has to offer and believe me, I'm already looking forward to enjoying it with you. Together, we'll worship God and I'll have the privilege of acting as your servant for eternity."

"Anyway, now that you've accepted Him, I'm free to tell you a little bit about what's going to happen here on Earth and why Heaven is particularly interested in you. You don't know it yet, but along with a number of others from every nation on Earth, you were specially chosen and uniquely equipped for life even before you were born. The intention being to prepare you for an extraordinary and, believe me, momentous task. Congratulations, my friend. I can now reveal something of your part in all of this. So, we'd better make you a little more comfortable. This could take a while."

Trust me, I needed no further invitation. I was already heartily sick of hanging around in the swaying top of a mangrove and Mombasa's oppressive heat was really getting to me. Between that, a raging thirst and the ever-present but indefinable smell of something rotting nearby, the situation was becoming unbearable. Israfel even suggested that if I trusted him, no one on the shore would see me. Not wishing to look a gift horse in the mouth, I took him at his word, climbed down and made my way carefully back out of the swamp, looking for a rather more salubrious spot upon which to settle. Following his recommendation was obviously worthwhile, because almost immediately I discovered the perfect spot under the shade of an ancient cashew nut tree. Slumping down, I admit that, initially, I watched the locals with some concern, but, after a while, it was clear they were not only ignoring the two of us, they really didn't seem to know we were there. I could have sworn there was some sort of mass-induced blindness at play, but an enquiring look at Israfel elicited nothing. So I relaxed, accepted a cool lemonade with quite the most delicate hint of citrus I've ever tasted (where did that come from?) and began to listen, astonishment growing by the minute.

"It will take you a while to come to terms with what's just happened. Especially to understand it," Israfel began. "But when you've had time to think these events through, you'll be amazed at how right it will all feel. So, before we go any further, I'm going to show you something that you'll find disturbing. However, I'm only doing so because you need to be absolutely certain that none of this is a stunt. In the past you had no defence against what I'm about to show you, but, as of now, you have the Holy Spirit living within you, and he is more powerful than all your enemies put together. So all you have to do is remain calm and keep your wits about you."

With that, he turned to his right and gestured towards the shoreline, although I couldn't see anything there at first. Until it hit me like a bolt from the blue. Standing mere feet away, but only visible from certain perspectives, stood what looked like a tight square of armed Roman soldiers. Only they weren't. They were angels, radiating a muted (for my benefit, I later realised) but impossibly white light and, what's more, their clothes looked vaguely familiar (I'd read about Roman soldiers at school). Gawping, I perceived that there was something about them that was both alien, yet strangely familiar. And then it struck me. I'd seen the spitting image years before in a children's book containing illustrations on how angels were thought to look. No wings, just rather human but at the same time extra-terrestrial. And the artist had obviously met some, because the likeness was uncannily accurate. But it was what they were guarding that really caught me by surprise. The moment I had spotted these warrior angels, I had felt a wave of empathy beaming towards me and knew instinctively they were utterly trustworthy. However, in the same split second I noticed a warped and ugly something that stood upright, but tightly bound, between them and became aware of a seething tide of hatred, rage and bile. Resentment and fury such as I could never have imagined, let alone withstand, blazed out from every plane of the contorted body, the blackened face, the flame-red eyes that stared straight at me, as if intent on shocking me into submission. And I knew beyond a doubt that given half a chance, the captive in front of me would as readily and easily swat me out of existence as I would a poisonous spider. But even as I looked, I felt rising within me a totally unfamiliar wave of righteous power and anger, pushing back against the malevolence (for I could think of no other term that would do the thing justice), and then words jumped unbidden to my mouth (although even as I spoke, I realised I could zip my lip if I so wished). "I command you, in the name of Jesus of Nazareth, tell me your name."

"Arcturus, Your Majesty," came the subdued response, the fanatical aggression quenched in an instant.

"Well, Arcturus, I have decided to let your commander, Josephus, deal with you. Word is reaching him even now that you are plotting his downfall and I know he will be less than generous. Indeed, he is quite within his rights to rescind the commutation on your recent death sentence, but do not think you have got off lightly, because I will see you at the great Day of Judgement." Even as the words streamed from my mouth, I knew they were not mine, but had to be from the aforementioned Holy Spirit. Secondly, I could see what Israfel had said was true. The one who was now obviously linked to me had, with just a word, deflated this malevolence like a pricked balloon. A balloon that had begun to tremble as though in the grip of a high fever.

"So, Paul, you've now seen a scion of the Enemy's force. Satanic scum. A fallen angel (you humans tend to call them devils or evil spirits) who, like all his fellows wants, above all else, to ruin human lives, dragging them down to his own despicable level. And believe me, he and they will stop at nothing. Not that humans need any provocation to sin – you're all perfectly capable of creating mayhem on your own and then you tend to blame anyone or anything, rather than yourselves. And to be frank, you've been just as bad as the rest. The things you've done aren't all down to Satan's minions. Certainly, they'll try to whisper in your ear that you should kill, take drugs, rape, steal or just be unpleasant to your nearest and dearest. You name it, they want you to do it, and this one's been behind much of the mayhem you've had to endure over the last few months. So now you know they actually exist and you're aware of just how effective they can be, I must warn you to be on your guard – although as I've already said, you won't be on your own and certainly in these early days while you're learning more about God and His power, I'll ensure that none of them gets anywhere near you. Deal?"

"Deal." I was beginning to enjoy this. A soothed conscience, my very own Guardian angel and now a promise to keep me out of trouble. Sounded pretty good to me.

CHAPTER 79

In the meantime, as soon as they heard their Lord's decree, the angels holding Arcturus ordered the living chain to release him, whilst they removed the covering that had prevented him from being blinded by the light of holiness radiating from the Lord and now (to a considerably lesser extent) emanating from me. Giving him a smack on the back of the head with the flat of a sword, they bid him get upon his sorry way, accompanied by suitably ribald comments as to what he could expect when Josephus caught up with him. Arcturus didn't have the nerve to respond, or the weapons, although he'd normally have given as good as he got. It was simple. A frantic and very real fear of God, Abbadon, the bottomless pit and his date with the latter had caught up with him and was even now pressing hard on his mind.

There was no time for anything but fevered thoughts on how to lose himself behind impenetrable cover somewhere. Anywhere. To vanish, preferably forever, and certainly before any of Hell's hordes could catch up with him. He was under no illusion. If caught, he could expect no mercy whatsoever. But scheme as he might, he understood with a dreadful sense of despair and foreboding that he'd been given an order, and there was no force in Hell capable of putting off his inevitable demise. And Josephus was not credited with a fearsome reputation for nothing. But then, nor had Arcturus got where he was without some ability to duck and dive. Which, when he coupled it with what he'd heard passing between Israfel and me while the angels held him, could surely deliver the definitive bargaining chip he felt was required? Genius, he thought. In fact, the further he explored the matter, the more he realised what a gem of information he held. Never mind rumour, never mind orders, he actually knew why Heaven was humming and furthermore, he had heard some specifics straight from the horse's mouth, so to speak. Which was worth a bit in anyone's currency.

★★★

"Well, Paul, we need to think about your future. For a start, there's the matter of your police file to clear up. Nothing to worry about regarding the crimes they only think you've committed, because the charges won't stick. However, if you want to get the best out of your new life, you're going to have to begin by turning yourself in voluntarily. I'm certain it won't be long before you come to the same conclusion, because you have to be honest and own up to the whole story if you want to live with yourself. Although God is the final arbiter on guilt and he's forgiven you, you still have to submit yourself to the proper human authorities, pay the price for breaking human rules, and attempt to make amends if and when you've harmed someone's family or property. But also remember this. You aren't where you are because of what you've done, good or bad. Rather, you've been saved to do good works in the future. Of course, the police won't believe you at first, but if you stop running, that in itself will give them pause for thought. True, they'll need a little persuading and they'll be particularly interested in the part you played regarding Fatih, Kareef and that poor slave girl, although I doubt if Ahmed will ever say anything about her. He's too vulnerable to the law himself. But that said, there's no way you can, or should, avoid trouble regarding the first two, so you're going to be spending some time in gaol on their account, although it isn't likely to be a long stint, as the law is going to be inclined towards leniency, given what's happened to you, not to mention your friends, the Jouberts. Moreover, you hold the key to blowing the local slave trade wide open. They're also going to be interested in Roz and her part in all of this. Yes, I know, you're still hurting and grieving over her, but she's fine. Actually, I can assure you she's in excellent spirits. Enjoying all her new friends and bowled over by the gift of a brand-new, immortal body. But what she's really looking forward to is the time when you and she can be reunited – although not as lovers, I hasten to add. In Heaven men and women neither marry, nor are given in marriage. You'll find that being close friends and sharing happy memories is all you'll need, and the Lord Jesus will supply you with everything else you could possibly want."

"But back to our theme. First, the police. Tell them everything you know, and be prepared to act as their undercover agent, because that's what they're going to expect of you. It won't be easy bringing down the slavers and, from time to time, your life will be in danger, but you will not be on your own and the end result will be rewarding – freedom for so many. You can't, you mustn't leave your fellow slaves in the lurch, especially since you alone hold the key to any future they might have in human terms. So first, settle your account with the human authorities and this time you'll find your incarceration is a useful time in which to prepare yourself, because what God has just done for you is only the beginning, not the end, of your life's journey. A couple of years from now, you'll be ready to set out with me on the expedition of a lifetime. A mission on which you'll achieve your true destiny, provided you go on believing and trusting in Jesus. You and the others who have been selected to make up an elite band of evangelists will be starting at more or less the same time."

"Individually, you're to be prepared for an utterly essential task. And, by the way, when I talk about 'evangelists', I simply mean people who are prepared to tell others about the one true God and his offer of eternal life. And in your case, we'll want you to relocate to your motherland, Britain. There you'll reveal some fascinating information to any who will listen. Most won't, of course, but what you'll have to say will concern the coming Day of Judgement. You'll be warning Britain that what the Bible says on this subject is true in every respect, even if most of them are too busy to listen. Or too sceptical. However, there are some who will listen and those who do and who act on what they hear will be spared much of what's to come. Soon a vast war is due to break out in the Middle East and it's going to involve a great deal of hardship for a lot of people. But don't worry, these things will not harm you personally."

"Anyway, I think that's enough for now. There's much for you to learn, much more for you to absorb, so right now I'll leave you to get on with it. While you remain here, you'll stay concealed, so don't worry about being spotted. And don't be afraid, even when you go to the police. You have but to ask and help will be available, although I won't necessarily manifest myself to you again. In general, it's not a good idea and anyway, it depends entirely upon my orders. More importantly, the Holy Spirit is now your principal guide and teacher. You'll get to recognise his voice and when you do, listen carefully. So, finally, let me give you God's endorsement." At which point he raised an instantly glittering hand, palm towards me, and declared, "The blessing of God the Father, God the Son and God the Holy Spirit rest upon you now and in the future." Which left me with a great peace and a mental note to enquire about this mystery. "We're going to have a great time together, you and I, and this time I'll make sure you get enough food in prison."

I watched him fade from view and could have sworn he was laughing as he went, but he left me with a distinct feeling of euphoria. For the first time in a very long time I felt 'good to go'.

Unfortunately, it didn't take long for the immediate impact to fade and I soon found myself relegating the experience to illusion, or an overwrought imagination. However, what refused to go away was Israfel's advice to confess everything to the police.

Which only encouraged me to start justifying myself. Most of it wasn't my fault anyway – some, maybe – but surely it was really all down to 'them'. And in any case, what the police don't know about, the police won't worry about. Right? Right.

To my lasting shame, it took me less than an hour to return to my old way of thinking. Less than an hour to convince myself that my judgement remained superior. Which left just the one problem. Unless I could be sure of clearing my name apropos the Eldoret Askaris and perhaps, for good measure, appraising them of my prime candidate for the Jouberts' killer, there seemed little point in breaking cover. Only one need seemed paramount – stay ahead of Ahmed even if, for now, he could have no idea where I was. Thus reassured, I began to walk slowly back towards the town centre, mind in neutral, thumb in etc. etc., until the quiet *snick* of several rifle bolts being rammed home shocked me into the present. Confused, I glanced up to discover not only several Askaris glaring at me over the ends of raised rifles (*not again, surely?*) but a stocky white figure, clearly in command, eying me speculatively.

"Well, young Moncton – I'm assuming that's who you are – it's good to meet you at last. Happy chance, perhaps, but let me make myself clear. I am Superintendent Foley and I have a certain reputation around here for getting exactly what I want and, right now, what I want is you. So, on your knees and get your hands in the air. Make it quick and I might not have you shot. And make no mistake. Any wrong move will be your last. These men are well aware that you killed a couple of their compatriots, and they're only too keen to repay you in kind."

Even with my heart apparently on strike, I had begun casting around frantically for a way out, struck by the thought that I should have followed Israfel's advice after all. Fortunately, it didn't take me long to spot the one slim opportunity left. All of which was noted by one of Hell's numerous underlings watching intently from the shadows (did it ever stop?). And with real pleasure, Josephus would confirm to Satan that he had just the right demon to assign to the case. Assuming death hadn't already intervened.

NOTES

CHAPTER 1
1. Donga – Dry river bed.

CHAPTER 3
1. Giriama (or Mijikenda) – One of a group of nine Bantu peoples, living along the East African coast (between Mombasa and Malindi).

CHAPTER 4
1. Syce – One who looks after horses.
2. Mzee – Term of respect for an old man.
3. "Ndiyo, bwana" – "Yes, sir."

CHAPTER 5
1. "Huko, bwana, huko" – "Over there, sir, over there."
2. Bundu – Any uncultivated or untamed land.

CHAPTER 10
1. Marram grass – A tough native grass that can withstand dry conditions.

CHAPTER 11
1. "Haraka, haraka. Watu mpega kifungua." – "Come quickly. Someone's broken the lock."
2. Askaris – Used either to describe local Kenyan soldiers or, as in this case, policemen serving in the Colonial Police Force.

CHAPTER 13

1. Murram – In Africa, laterite soils were and are used to build roads – known colloquially as murram in East Africa. Virtually all of East Africa's roads, other than those in towns, were so constructed at the time.

CHAPTER 15

1. Kanzu – A long, usually white garment worn by African men, particularly those in catering or service.
2. Betel – Betel, or the areca nut, is the seed of the areca palm, which grows in parts of East Africa. It is commonly referred to as betel nut, and is a frequently used minor drug often chewed wrapped in betel leaves.

CHAPTER 16

1. Jalabiyas – Arabic Islamic clothing for men, usually long, white coverings roughly equivalent to the East African kanzu.

CHAPTER 17

1. Sjambok – A heavy whip, usually made of rhinocerous or hippopotamus hide.

CHAPTER 18

1. The fallen angel described in the Bible as king over evil spirits dispatched to 'the bottomless pit'. In Hebrew he is called Abaddon, and in Greek, Apollyon.

CHAPTER 20

1. Gharry – Car.

CHAPTER 21

1. Summuni – Half a Kenyan shilling (twenty shillings to the British £ at the time).

2. "Jambo, abari yako?" – A standard Swahili greeting: "Hello, how are you?"

3. Kikoi – The ubiquitous and usually only garment worn by men in the hot coastal belt.

CHAPTER 33

1. Kwetu – literal translation – Us.

CHAPTER 37

1. Totos – Children (toto – child).

2. Posho – A form of porridge made from maize.

CHAPTER 40

1. "Kuwa Kimya" – "Be silent."

CHAPTER 54

1. Thobe – An ankle-length garment, usually with long sleeves, similar to a robe.

CHAPTER 61

1. Ugali – Thick, cooked maize grain, known more commonly as posho.

2. Baobab – Particularly ugly water-filled tree found in dry areas (known as the upside-down tree, because that's what it looks like!)

CHAPTER 62

1. Burnouse – A long, loose-hooded cloak worn by Arabs.